WHEN SOUNDS COLLIDE

a novel

M. DAY HAMPTON

RIVER GROVE
BOOKS

What follows is a fictional story inspired by the many unknown people and untold stories at the edges of historical records. Tread softly, for you will be deep in the author's imagination.

Published by River Grove Books
Austin, TX
www.rivergrovebooks.com

Distributed by River Grove Books

Design and composition by Greenleaf Book Group
Cover design by Greenleaf Book Group
Cover images used under license from ©Adobe Stock/Maxim Khytra;
©Adobe Stock/Distinctive Images; ©Adobe Stock/Nick Starichenko;
©Adobe Stock/AnnaStills; ©Adobe Stock/miloje
Interior images used under permission from Sheri Marshall; Darwin Andoe;
Melanie Gruenig; Daniel Gonzales

Publisher's Cataloging-in-Publication data is available.

Print ISBN: 978-1-63299-923-8

eBook ISBN: 978-1-63299-924-5

First Edition

To David Martin Thibaut and Ronnie Custis.
Thank you for teaching me the power of friendship
and the grace of unconditional love.

ACKNOWLEDGMENTS

I have not said it enough, but without Jennifer, I don't know where I would be today—certainly not an author. Thank you for understanding my silence and blank stares while I subsisted in the *zone,* mentally writing and rewriting and wondering if it was any good, if it mattered, or if I'd ever finish.

To begin writing a book, only a spark is needed. You never quite know where it may stem. My moment of inspiration was a kind statement from a friend, a reminder of the power of encouragement in the creative process. 147,000 words followed, but this was not accomplished alone. Editor and friend Mary Kole from Good Story Company is simply amazing. Thank you for navigating through my labyrinth of ideas and words, offering encouragement at every bump, and seeing in me what I failed to see in myself.

To my mother, Audrey, who once told me I could be anything I wanted to be.

To my solidly professional team at Greenleaf Book Group: HaJ and Leah Pierre, thank you for your pledge of encouragement and guidance. Maxine Marshall and Claudia Volkman, both of you are remarkable. Thank you to Jenny Cribb and Matt MacMillan for their support with my website and marketing efforts. A special thanks to Laurie MacQueen for her design mind and artistic talent.

Finally, to my readers, I am grateful for each one of you and for those I have yet to meet.

PART I

1875
NORTH CAROLINA

F ar from town, Custis lived inside a poem. The sky was still waking with a cool wash of morning as birds flitted from tree to tree. He knew the area the deer liked to graze at sunrise, the place where squirrels stashed their cache hidden away from greedy magpies. He understood where the foxes liked to hunt and the burrows where the rabbits chose to hide. He followed the brown path, a trail beaten down smooth by those who wore tattered shoes or no shoes at all.

Warm fingers of sunlight warmed the back of his shoulders.

Custis walked a little faster.

He coddled a box under his arm. He should have left even earlier.

The mercantile would have been open for barely a quarter hour, the store full of morning regulars trying to avoid the sweltering balminess of the coming day, with Mrs. Herman most likely garnering every penny possible. That, or she was deciphering a large black ledger to see whose account needed to be cut off.

The scent of shaded maples gave way to the treeless smell of a town hurried with commerce. There was no more prose of nature. He separated the aroma of fresh bread from the bakery against the spicy cologne from the barbershop and the earthy odor of passing horses as their carriages avoided indecisive pedestrians.

Custis could smell the sweat from his hat brim each time he removed it, yielding to people he did not know on the boardwalk. They'd acknowledge others with greetings, but never him. Maybe because he was only ten years old, but probably not. It was a reminder of his station in life. That, and the occasional glimpse of his reflection in the storefront glass, the same reflection the world saw.

The box under his arm was bound with string, tied in a bow. Custis prioritized the carton, adjusted it as needed, and kept it level. A cobbled alleyway led to the back door of the mercantile. Custis sat on the wooden steps, untied the lid, and examined the contents. Twelve fresh, perfect eggs nestled in clean, soft straw. He replaced the lid, stood up, and rang the bell. He held the container with both hands and waited.

Custis didn't much like Mrs. Herman. She reminded him of a banty rooster, strutting when there was no need and pecking others for no reason. Her protruding front tooth looked like a beak. She had terrible breath, wore too-tight clothes, and was selectively unkind.

Custis heard her footsteps. He felt the wicked intention in her stride vibrating through the floorboards. He swiftly removed his cap. The screen door screeched open.

"You're late, boy. My customers already come and gone."

Custis was right on time. He made sure of it. But he said nothing. This was her way of pecking, a haggling tactic, minus any charity.

"Ugh. Let me have them."

Custis gingerly held out the box.

Mrs. Herman pulled it out of his hands and unintentionally touched his finger. She glared at Custis, pushing him a step backward with her eyes. Her lips curled and exposed her crooked tooth. "Don't you touch me, boy."

Her voice was piercing. Custis wanted to bolt, but he needed the sale. He stood immobile and diverted his eyes. The banty rooster turned and strutted back into the store, her head leading the way for her sickled tail-feathered rump.

Custis waited. His hands trembled. Ten cents was worth the confrontation. He'd take it home and place it in the hidden kitchen jar. He liked the sound of the dime dropping onto the other coins. Sometimes two nickels with their clunkier jingle sounded as if he had more money.

The screen door flung open again.

"Two of those eggs were broken, cracked right in half. I'm not paying you full price."

Custis wanted to hate Mrs. Herman but knew the road to hell would just get wider. Usually, she paid just under a penny apiece, so he'd maybe leave with eight cents for the whole perfect dozen this time. She dropped a nickel into his hand and returned the empty box.

Custis looked at the nickel. He kept his eyes downward. Maybe going to hell wouldn't be all that bad. He couldn't tell his mother; she would be so disheartened. They depended on every penny. He had forgotten to remove the box lid, displaying the twelve perfect eggs in front of Mrs. Herman. But Custis needed to do what he was supposed to do. *Don't argue. Turn the other cheek.* Custis opened the lid on the box and saw that Mrs. Herman had even taken the straw.

He was running out of cheeks.

"I am sorry, Mrs. Herman. Now, here, I can't take your money. You take this nickel back, and I'll take my eggs. I don't want to sell you broken ones, ma'am. Your store is too nice to have damaged merchandise." Custis held out the coin. "I'll be back tomorrow morning with a new fresh dozen plus one for free for your trouble. Why, I can sell this broken dozen right now, down the street. Mr. Bill got new whelps without a momma. He can use those eggs for all those little pups."

Mrs. Herman cocked her head.

"Now, don't feel obliged, ma'am. I need to be fair squared up with you, fair being fair. Mr. Bill will pay me a penny apiece, including the broken ones. He's gonna break them anyway."

Custis thought he heard a cluck.

Mrs. Herman blinked her beady eyes as her head tilted slightly. "You just keep your nickel, and I'll keep the eggs."

"I insist, Mrs. Herman. Let me do the right thing, or my momma will be madder than I want to know. I'll bring you a new box tomorrow."

Mrs. Herman huffed, scratched around in her apron pockets, and retrieved a handful of coins. Her crooked fingers picked out another nickel and a penny. "Here, I got customers waiting. You just take this, and don't you dare bring me any more broken eggs. You hear me?"

"Yes, ma'am, I sure do."

Custis reached out for the money, careful to hold his hand out flat and taut. He watched Mrs. Herman's craggy-skinned fingers release the coins. She jerked around and flounced back into her roost. "And don't you forget my thirteenth tomorrow."

The door slammed closed. Custis put eleven cents into his pants pocket. He thought about the thirteenth egg. It really wouldn't be free. Mrs. Herman had paid for it today. And as far as the pups went, he didn't feel bad either. He didn't even know a Mr. Bill.

Custis was small for his age but was unaware of this fact. He had no friends and was not allowed to go to school. As he walked down the boardwalk, he glanced at his reflection in the cluster of small-paned windows and imagined he had the globular vision of a dragonfly. His eyes no longer saw the whole boy but, instead, segregated images that didn't quite fit together. His clothing was threadbare, limp, and nearly colorless. Dark hair protruded from beneath his baker-boy cap, which was too tight for his head. His cheeks always looked as if he had been running, a persistent tinge of pink under his tawny skin. He tried to keep his face barren of emotion. He received fewer accusations and reproaches that way.

Custis paused at the open door of the haberdashery and breathed in the scent of mingled leather and cigars. It was a place he was not permitted to enter. A small sign tacked to the siding announced *No Coloreds*. The shopkeeper busied himself, pulling down an assortment of hats from behind a refined wooden counter. Each cover was presented to a man who looked like a banker, or lawyer, or some other soul of value. The client petted their brims with care and admired his reflection in a small, round, mirrored stand.

A set of leather-bound books sat marshaled on a shelf nearest the door. Their spines, new and unblemished, stood sentry. Gold lettering too small to read embellished each one. Custis squinted, leaning forward, but was careful not to breach the doorway. With only one more step, he would be able to see what words these magnificent books might hold. Where could their stories take him? What life could he have within their pages? Would they offer him refuge, purpose, astuteness, or maybe even fortune and happiness? There, within his reach, separated by an invisible barrier so strong no man dare break it, was a better world waiting.

"Get back, now, go on," the shopkeeper said.

Custis jerked his head and looked at the men. "Pardon, sir . . . sirs." He shouldn't have been so close. He stepped away.

"Just a minute, now," the banker, or lawyer, or other soul of value said. "Maybe, with those eyes, he *can* read."

"Go on, skedaddle!"

Custis gave a quick nod and stepped to the edge of the sidewalk. He closed his eyes hard. *Windows to my soul. They can't see inside of me now. Run fast.* Custis turned and ran. He ran until exhaustion replaced the things he could not have or what he could not be.

Custis reached the other end of town, the part that had a different type of bustle. The part of town where men wearing sweat-stained shirts and tattered, buttoned-up trousers would come to buy or barter for hardware and seed supplies. They'd frequent the wheelwright, ironworks, smith shops, and taverns. Some would visit Miss Sylvia's Café but always seemed to be hungry when they left.

The dirt streets were dry and dusty, filled with horse manure and splattered with spit and tobacco. It was better to avoid the alleyways on this side of town. The ones next to the taverns were the worst. They smelled of piss and filth. Empty, broken crates lined the walls of the buildings and offered hiding places for drunken men, feral cats, and hungry dogs. Except for the sky, all colors had been consumed, layer by layer.

Three young boys huddled around the front of the stable yard. Custis had seen them before. Neighborhood boys—Lucius, son of the livery owner, and brothers Bradford and Emmert McReynolds, a family of local chicken farmers. Had the McReynolds boys not been so encrusted with dirt, their hair would have been coppery red rather than looking like foul straw hanging limp. The three of them always seemed to be getting into trouble. Town people called them delinquents.

The boys stood underneath a large, colorful poster nailed high on the livery door. The fresh hues stood out against the backdrop of dust and drab. Bradford pointed at the lettering, touching the bottom as he attempted to pronounce the word. He got a little closer, but it didn't seem to help.

Emmert laughed. "You don't know what it says. You're just as stupid as Lucius."

"That's a giant hog! The mother of all swine."

"That's one of them dinosaurs. That's plain to see," Lucius said as he flipped his unkempt hair away from his eyes. "Look at the size of it!"

Now all three fingered the poster, arms stretching upward and muttering back and forth about what they thought the letters meant.

As Custis walked closer, he saw the image of an enormous hippopotamus in the center of the poster. Two small children perched on saddles atop its back. They should have been holding on for dear life, but instead they appeared to be having fun. Beautiful script writing surrounded the beast in shades of yellows and greens, while images of red-and-white-striped circus tents bordered the edges.

It was as if the colors were mesmerizing to all who stood nearby, magically taking away boundaries and dissipating distance. Custis wriggled his way closer to the poster to see the printing. He had never been to a circus but had read about them many times. Now he could see one in real life. His excitement surpassed all thoughts. "It's a hippopotamus. It's a circus coming to town."

The startled trio quickly turned.

Custis was lost in the poster. His mind could have belonged to a poet, a teacher, an author, or a scientist, but his heart was only ten years old. Colors and sounds and smells swirled inside his head. He saw the ringmaster in a black top hat and red tailcoat. He heard an elephant trumpet as people clapped and rose to their feet. He didn't notice the gaping reaction of the delinquents.

"See, right here. That says *Gigantic Railroad Circus. September 11th. Afternoon and night.*" Custis took another step, brushed past Bradford, and nearly touched the poster with his finger. "And right there, that says *Also, Daring and Dangerous Equestrian Act.* That means lots of special horses and riders."

Custis didn't see it coming. A fist rammed into his midsection. The blow knocked all the air from his lungs. Custis doubled forward and fell to the ground. How could he have been so careless? He had been too close, maybe inadvertently touching the boys. But worst of all, now they knew he could read.

"You some smartass or something? You think you're better than us? Seems you forgot your place."

"Yeah, just because he's a mongrel crossbreed colored don't make him have brains. He's just like all the rest of them. He can't read. He's just making that shit up."

Another kick to his legs, another to his back. The strikes came so rapidly.

"Go for his eyes, take out his eyes. Then we'll see how good he can read."

Custis curled his arms around his midsection. He needed air, but his lungs wouldn't expand. *I can't be blind, I'd rather die, but Momma won't know what happened to me. She'd be all alone.* If he lost his eyes, they had no money, no means to pay for a doctor. How could he read without eyes? It was his job to take care of his momma when she got old—she had told him so many times. And someday he was going to be a famous scientist. And without eyes, he'd be helpless. He had to break free. *Imagine working the problem. Process the calculation—one step at a time.*

He needed to protect his stomach and take the kicks to his legs instead. He rolled like a pill bug into a ball and filled his lungs with air. Another breath—and then he could run. Lucius was fat, too big and slow to keep up. Bradford was a coward and would do nothing without orders from his brother. Emmert was the leader, the threat. *Separate the numbers—reduce the equation.*

Custis took one more hard kick to his hip, then sucked in enough air to fill him with one last chance to flee. He felt his body spring upward. Custis kicked with all the power he could muster. He imagined every nerve cell in his body interacting into a coagulating force strong enough to break free. Like dynamite, it would be a massive explosion of sound and light. Muscles synchronized and charged. A solid kick to Emmert's groin. The blow lifted Emmert off the ground.

Where are the sparks? Where's the noise?

Custis turned and ran, not knowing whether the strike was enough or if the boys were directly behind him. He heard nothing and wondered if the knock in the head had cost his hearing. Custis ran for his life. He ran from hatred, he ran from intolerance, he ran from demons, he ran from ignorance. He even ran from God.

Custis coursed the railroad tracks. The steel rails were comforting. In perfect order, a constant, a never-changing value. Strong, loyal, permanent. Exactly fifty-six-and-a-half inches wide. His run slowed to a jog, now long, comfortable strides. Each scrappy shoe sole hit each timber-sleeper seamlessly. Repetitive. Solid. Enduring.

The tracks worked in perfect unison, entreating the boy into a faultless, metrical world. Someday he'd follow his rails to their end. But today, like yesterday and the day before, the rails of steel would lead him home. They would take him past the last of the city limits, through the final cluster of unkempt shacks, into the shaded woods, back to the only refuge he had ever known.

The rails wound through the woods with a steadfast creek at its side. Shade from the pines and maples gave Custis fleeting respite from the hot afternoon sun. The dappled sunlight made him dizzy, or maybe that was the kick to his head. Now and then, a sound would come from behind. He'd pause, turn, and anxiously look back down the long, receding track.

He followed a footpath into the woods, stopping short of entering the door of a cabin. He dusted off his clothing with his cap. The indention of the cap brim circled his head. Clean from his eyebrows up, he wiped his face with his sleeve and tucked in his shirt.

WHEN SOUNDS COLLIDE   13

The screen door screeched as he pulled it open. The one-room cabin walls were filled with makeshift shelves full of books, magazines, and newspapers. Every nook was filled with old worn volumes and boxes labeled alphabetically, all neatly stacked and organized.

He hung his cap on the hook. "Momma?"

Custis's mother stood in the kitchen. She wiped her hands dry on a dishrag. "Child, you know better to enter this house without bringing in fresh water. And it looks like you need some cleanin' up."

Custis had one job this morning, and that was to sell the eggs and get straight back home. Custis turned his head away and picked up the wooden bucket next to the open door. He wouldn't tell her about the fight. She'd be mad, but then her anger would turn to disappointment, then into fear.

"Where you been, son? You know I needed help with gettin' back this sewing."

Custis perked up. She must not have noticed any bruising or blood—no swelling on his face. Maybe she wouldn't notice the goose egg on the back of his head. Most of the blows had been low, and his clothing mercifully covered his injuries. "Sorry, Momma. I just got busy with selling the eggs. I'll go get the water."

Selling the eggs. His mind snapped to. *She's gonna ask.* He didn't have the box or string. He'd dropped it during the fight. She'd notice for sure. *How will I explain it away?*

"Don't you forget to put that dime in the jar, son."

She didn't ask to see the money. Maybe later he'd surprise her with the extra penny.

"You go get your chores done, and then after supper you can finish readin' to me."

He felt her watching as he walked out the door.

"Where my egg box, son? I know something happened today. You gonna tell me?"

Custis stopped. *She knows.* A long, anticipatory pause. His voice would be the first to reveal unwished emotion. He had put himself in danger, and now he had brought it home. He wanted to keep fear as far away from his mother as he could, but he would not choose to lie.

"No, Momma."

"I didn't figure you would. You old enough now you gotta learn to take care of yourself. You been stickin' your nose where it don't belong? You know what's right and what's wrong. You know what the rules are."

Custis nodded. "I know, Momma."

"I got you one of them science books today from Mrs. Cramer. She say they don't need it, and she's tired of it just collecting dust."

Custis felt as if all bad things had magically disappeared. He loved to read novels, manuals, poetry, newspapers, and even accounting ledgers. Science was his favorite. He had an innate curiosity of how and why things worked. As a celebrated scientist, he could move far away and buy his mother a brick house, tall and wide, surrounded by stone fences and roses of every color. No longer would she clean other people's homes or wash their laundry. She would be able to go to church on both Sundays and Wednesdays and stay as long as she liked. They could eat until they were full and never worry about tomorrow.

Custis carried the bucket down a dry, grass-lined path. The creek provided fresh water for most of the year. The coolness felt good on his hands. As he washed his face, the calmness around him was alluring. He sat on the bank and removed his shoes, tattered and way too small. He meticulously aligned them, side by side, as one would do with a brand-new pair. His feet were dirty from the day. A blister had popped and was tender to the touch. He immersed his bare feet to the smooth rock bottom. How could something so simple feel so good?

Custis wrapped his arms around his knees, his feet still submerged. The lack of ripples farther out enticed him deeper. *Smooth runs the water where the brook is deep.* It never failed to surprise him that Shakespeare seemed to know a little bit about everything.

Custis crowded his feet back into his shoes, wincing at the discomfort. He pulled the bucket out of the creek. Water spilled out and splashed down to the ground. Droplets spattered on the top of his shoes, turning dust into a reminder of the day. He paused and tried to clean his shoes off on the back leg of his too-short pants. A swishing came from the woods. He turned quickly toward the noise. He listened, motionless, then heard a distant snap. His body tensed, waiting to evaluate the next noise. There was nothing.

The once simplistic sounds of a bird flitting on the dry-leafed forest floor or a squirrel springing from branch to bough no longer evoked a sense of prose. Fear was taking over. Custis started humming and pretended he wasn't scared.

x x x

Custis stayed outdoors, near the front door, for as long as he could before his mother would sense his vigilant behavior. He couldn't bring himself to tell her about the circus poster. The guilt inside twisted and whorled. He couldn't undo his horrible mistake. He'd have to be clever and attentive when going back into town to sell more eggs. He'd find a new route and never return to the harsher side of town.

There, on the porch, he heard no more mysterious sounds and forced his thoughts back to the evening routine. Custis read aloud to his mother every night. Usually, the stories involved mathematics, some sort of science, or chemistry. It didn't matter the subject. She'd bring papers and books home and habitually fall asleep while Custis read aloud to her. After Custis had finished with the discarded newspapers, he'd tear out interesting articles he wanted to remember. He placed the cut-outs into various boxes, based on the subject, and neatly stored them on a shelf. Then he'd wad up the remaining paper, putting it between the interior wall studs. "It's insulation, Momma," he'd explain. "The wads work by slowing the conductive heat."

His mother cleaned houses on the other end of the tracks and rescued books from her clients when discarded as clutter. But the finest books always came from Mrs. Cramer who graciously claimed they were just collecting dust.

Mrs. Cramer was old. She loved children, having none of her own. She had taught school for most of her life and never stopped, even after marriage. She took on Custis as her particular secret project, considering him "an unwelcomed but unique child of God." Every summer while her husband was abroad on business, she hired Custis's mother, although her house never really needed cleaning at all.

"You be careful with this book, son. Mrs. Cramer sneaked this out of Mr. Cramer's library just for you. She could get into real trouble if anyone was to find out. You know that. She called you 'remarkable.'"

Custis and his mother would traverse through jungles with Robinson Crusoe, ride the ocean searching for Moby Dick, or visit the dark streets of London in carriages pulled by beautiful black steeds. Those particular storybooks, some leather-bound, Custis handled as if they were delicate treasures. Careful to never fully open and stretch the spines or turn pages with unwashed hands, he faithfully returned the books to Mrs. Cramer with nary a mark.

Custis was forbidden to acknowledge his reading skills to anyone other than his mother and Mrs. Cramer. Not even to Pastor Jacobson, although he probably suspected.

"Some people just ain't as smart as you," his mother would say. "They won't take kindly to it. There be no boasting in this household whatsoever."

Of all her rules, this one was most often reiterated. But now, the delinquents knew he could read.

Custis pulled the lantern in closer.

"Son, maybe tonight you can read me one of them poem books, you know the one about going down the open road where everything is so beautiful and free." After his mother had fallen asleep, Custis switched books and was on chapter two of *The Last of the Mohicans*. A thud came from outside. Chickens squawked. Custis closed the book and quickly stood up as his mother was startled awake. The lamplight barely lit the room.

"Something got in," she said as she flung off the blanket.

"Wait, Momma." He imagined the boys, all standing shoulder to shoulder. They were waiting in the darkness, just on the other side of the door. Custis had brought home something ugly and dangerous his mother would now encounter. It was all his fault. He looked at her face.

"Something got in the coop. It probably that mean ol' badger again."

Of course, a fox, or badger, or weasel. Maybe a pinecone or limb strike to the top of the coop. Custis had allowed illusory images back into his head. The boys would not have traveled this deep into the woods. At night the forest was too dangerous, even for White boys. Custis took the lantern and picked up the ironwood fire poker before going out. His mother followed. The light took away some of the darkness.

"I don't see anything, Momma."

"It's in there. Mark my words."

Custis shouted, "Get out of here!"

Just in case, he preferred to scare away any intruders rather than trigger a confrontation with a badger, fox, or even bear. The chickens settled, and all was quiet except for the occasional rescinding cluck. Custis checked the wire fence perimeter. All was good. A light breeze had come up. He could feel the warmth of the night as he held out the lantern toward the edge of the woods.

"Must have just been the wind, Momma."

"No. Something out here. First thing in the morning, we need to figure out a better fence. Bring more rock up from the creek."

Both of them quietly walked back inside. Momma lay down on her bed. "You better turn out the light, son. Save the oil. And don't forget to say your prayers, thank God for all that he has given us."

"I will. Just one more chapter. It's at the good part."

"Even thank God for Mrs. Herman. There be a reason for every-thing, son. Did she try and cheat you again?"

"No, Momma, she didn't cheat me." Custis refilled the lantern with oil and read six more chapters. His eyes were weary, but his mind was still restless. He closed his eyelids and felt their soothing coolness as he placed his forehead on the table. Never again would he be so careless.

It seemed like only moments passed before the chickens stirred again. Custis jarred awake. His mother was still sleeping in her bed. He waited and listened, but there was nothing. He turned off the lan-tern and lay down on his cot. A faint beam of moonlight shone down through the window. His books surrounded him. He was with his friends again.

A thud came from outside. Custis jumped to his feet. He stood motionless, trying to evaluate the sound. Quietly, he walked to the door and listened. Warm outside air seeped through the board joints bringing with it the sound of chickens fussing. *I can't lose more chickens.* With only his drawers on, he unbolted the door and stepped from the porch onto the soft, dry grass. The lantern seemed extra bright now, and that was good—a couple of nervous clucks, a couple more steps toward the chicken house.

"You! Varmint! Get out of here!"

The wind had picked up. Leaves rustled above, some falling down-ward and then gently flittering away, consumed by the darkness.

Two beady eyes reflected in the lamplight, just inside the fence. Custis stepped into the run and watched the young fox scurry under the wire and escape into the woods. Custis lowered the lamp. A fox, under normal conditions, was a reviled intruder, but tonight Custis had never been so thankful. He picked up a couple of large rocks and placed them on the bottom of the wire. It would do for tonight, but tomorrow he'd fix it properly.

Custis checked on the chickens inside the coop. Maybe an egg or two had fallen victim, but everyone was safe. George, Carver, Washington, Mildred, Francis, Helen, and Harriet—all hens except for Helen, the rooster. Custis gently picked up Francis. "It's all right. He's gone now." He kissed her head, set her back on the roost, and latched the door. Custis held the lantern up, rechecked the run, and stepped out onto the grass.

"Hey, varmint." The voice came from behind him.

Custis whirled around and saw the three figures standing before him. *The delinquents.* Custis couldn't move his body. Even his mind stopped processing.

A fourth and more prominent figure, a bull of a man, appeared from out of the darkness. A chain hung down from his hand. "I hear you been kickin' people in the balls," he said while exposing his overrun teeth in what must have been a grin. "Nobody does that to my brothers, especially not the likes of you."

Lucius held a rope, Emmert a knife.

"Guess what we're gonna do?" the bull-man said.

Custis wanted to scream. He wanted his neighbors to hear his cry in the night and come to his rescue. But his scream would wake his mother, and she'd have to watch him die. She would be a witness. They would have to kill her too.

Custis was just out of arm's reach; just a mere thirty inches away, and his life would be over. Thirty inches. Two and a half feet, and that would make a small head start. His mind worked in a calculated fury. *Four directions—no, six directions.* North, south, east, west, up, down. But now, a neoteric seventh direction. Custis bolted sideways. He threw the lantern at the closest delinquent.

Custis was fast and wiry. He was ahead by twenty feet. He'd run and lead them deep into the woods. He knew the area, but now they knew where he lived. The boys would be lost in the darkness, and Custis could easily circle around. He'd get his mother and take her to safety, to the church, where he'd tell Pastor Jacobson. He slowed down and feigned an antagonizing laugh, hoping they would give chase. It seemed to work. The boys were loud, sounding full of hate, and gave a clumsy chase.

The woods in this part of the county were fickle. At times the forest was full of promise and fresh new life. It offered safe passage and gave hidden sanctuary to those in need. It provided food, subsistence, and trade. It kindly gave refuge from the summer's scorching heat and cleansed the creeks to offer a cool drink.

But at night, its darkness ruled with callousness. Beneath the thick canopy, the forest floor grew intense and twisted, without configuration. Trails could be missed easily, and markers could disappear. Broken branches reached out with dangerous intentions, and gnarly roots could easily break leg bones. Custis's gait was usually long and practiced. But now he ran on the balls of his bare feet across the uneven ground.

Custis heard one of the boys fall. A thud and broken branches. The others were still following. Custis felt pain in his feet. Excruciating pain. Branches and briars tore at his bare chest and arms. The tentacles of the forest floor wrenched tightly around his legs. He felt as if he were wrapped in wire cutting into his skin. Custis fell. A hand wrapped tightly around his ankle. The bull-man's grip had the strength of a gator, squeezing his foot with a force enough to twist his entire body. Custis kicked with his other foot, landing it hard in an indiscernible face. He broke free and ran again.

Custis had the lead back. The boys were out of sight. Maybe they were circling around and were heading back to his house. His mother was alone, and there'd be no one to protect her. He slowed and tried to regulate his breathing. Briars pulled at his drawers, a branch nearly ripping them off. Another fall; his head collided with a tree. He had to get to the church, get help, get to his mother. Custis crawled on his hands, deep in forest duff. He sank to his knees, breathed, and pulled himself up alongside a boulder.

A clearing lay just ahead. Custis could hear water, a creek maybe, where he could drink and rest and regain his awareness. The darkness had stolen his bearings, and fear had distorted his certainty. He waited and listened. Maybe the delinquents were lost as well, but he couldn't be sure. He breathed through his mouth, trying to quiet his gasps.

Custis folded his hands in front of his mouth and closed his eyes. Tears came down his face. The fault was all his. He should have never read from the poster. His plan to circle back and take his mother to safety had failed. He placed his hands tightly over his opened mouth, squeezed his eyes shut, and cried as quietly as he could.

Not a sound came from the woods. The pain from his injuries over-powered the analgesic effects of adrenaline.

Custis stood and instantly fell back down. In the darkness, he felt his leg. His hands shook uncontrollably. He reached down farther and felt his ankle; it was distorted and swollen. He hobbled to the creek and placed his bare and bleeding feet under the cool water.

The half-moon was behind a screen of clouds, but the wind would expose its light soon. His silhouette might give him away. He crouched as low as he could and drank from the stream. He couldn't walk. He didn't have time to make a crutch. Behind him, over the forest horizon, he saw light. A dome of faint glow and a twist of flickering smoke rose in the distance.

A muddled voice came from within the woods. Custis immediately dropped his body flat to the ground. He needed to get as low as he could. *Don't move and give away your position.* It sounded like Emmert. Custis's eyes skipped back and forth. He heard nothing. *Hallucinations.* It was a sign of head injury; he was sure of it. Maybe it was Pastor Jacobson.

Maybe his mother had discovered he was missing and gathered help from neighbors. Another voice. Now it sounded like the pastor.

Custis held his breath and listened. Should he stand and scream for help? If he didn't, and it was the pastor, he'd be left behind. Custis started to raise his head.

"I saw him, right over there!"

Lucius's voice.

Custis plunged his head and dug deeper into the damp dirt between the river rock. The left side of his face was deep in the mud. Whether he would be discovered was now up to the moon.

The voices came closer.

A shoe stepped within inches of Custis's face. "I sure don't see him."

"I swear . . . you idiot. You can't do nothin' right."

"You think he could just disappear? Disappear into thin air?"

"He was right here. I swear I saw him."

"Shit. You always seein' things. You're a scared little pissant."

Custis couldn't hold his breath for much longer. With his eyes closed, he heard one brother drinking from the creek. He listened to his guzzle, then droplets falling and hitting the surface of the water. After his drink, the boys would leave, unsuccessful in their hunt. Custis was nearly in the clear and would triumph, one more time.

"Well, well, well. Looky here, boys."

The bull-man stood back up. He stepped on Custis's foot and dug his boot into Custis's broken ankle. Custis felt the vibration of breaking bones. The pain was unbearable. Excruciating agony so intense his body convulsed. Something wicked was inside, immobilizing all voluntary movement while pulling nerve fibers from torn muscles through shards of splintered bone. He strained to scream, wrenched to breathe, and tried to fight. But this was his punishment for reading, his penalty for defying the rules. *Please, God, don't let them get my mother.*

The boys pulled Custis from the creek edge, up on the bank, and kicked him ruthlessly. Custis's limp body jarred with each blow.

Custis rolled back down the embankment and landed face-first in the creek. Hands tightened around his neck. He felt his body being turned over. *Funny,* Custis thought, *the water feels so good, like being baptized. I praise and thank You with my whole being that I am baptized into the body of Christ and born into the family of God.*

Lucius abruptly stood up. "Oh, shit, I think he's dead. He's not moving. Quick, cover him up with rocks."

Custis wanted it to be over. *Please protect my mother; she has done nothing but serve You. It's all my fault.*

"That's enough, run!"

The pain was gone now. His body was shutting down. Soon he would leave this world into which he had unwittingly come. *Save my mother.* Now, he was ready to be with God.

Custis was unable to open his eyes. He couldn't move or breathe. His chest was heavy, weighted down. He concentrated on his eyes. One scarcely opened. At first, he saw only blackness. It was still nighttime. He could see the sky glowing just beyond the tree line, but now it had turned to flame. It was a massive fire.

Please, Jesus, don't let me go to hell. I didn't mean to betray my momma. I'm so sorry. I pray the Lord my soul to keep. If I should die before I wake, I pray to God my soul to take.

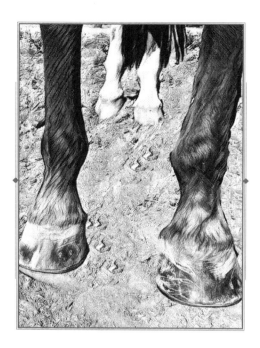

ustis heard trickling water and felt nothing but heaviness. No pain, no sorrow, no happiness. His body was numb. He strained to move, but nothing happened. He saw complete blackness. *They're gone. They took my eyes like they'd told me. I must be blind now.*

Out of one ear, he heard humming, soft singing above the sound of trickling water. Custis saw a fleck of light. That meant he still had one eye. Custis saw a murky image through a small slit aperture. Everything faded away. He concentrated on making the slit open again. He saw an image in the distance—a horse. *The horse must be singing. I made it to heaven. I caused all this, and God still let me in. He forgave me.* Custis was sure he was crying, but he couldn't feel his tears nor hear his wail. *God forgave me, Momma. Momma?*

Darkness.

The sound of trickling water returned. A song. A girl's soft, angelic hum. A horse's sigh. Muted light. A fuzzy encirclement of a meadow. A girl was in the field. He could tell by her long hair and lavender clothes. The colors blended, transforming into a vast meadow of purple lupine.

Then darkness again.

A horse's shod hooves. The sound of chomping on grass. Custis tried to focus on the blurred image. A squeal accompanied by an angry stomp. The horse bolted sideways, then stood firm-legged. Another squeal and snort. Two small black riding boots. The end of brown leather reins touching the ground, next to the shoes.

"Stardust, don't be afraid. It's just a pile of rock. What's the matter with you?" It sounded like a young girl, but her speech was raspy and sounded forced.

Custis wanted to reach up, feel his head, but he couldn't move. There was something wrong with his eardrums. He tried to talk but nothing came out.

The black boots came back into focus. Another snort, the sound of a hoof hitting and scraping at the ground, was nearby. He felt the vibration. Both stopped, seeming to deliberate. Something twitched out in front of him, coming from beneath the rocks. It was a finger. Custis could wiggle his finger. He wanted to lift his hand and beg for help. But his hand wouldn't budge. *Wait until she is closer.* His fingers were now on her boot, and he tapped as hard as he could.

He heard the girl gasping. The hooves left the ground. He could hear a deep, throaty, grating roar as horses do when scared. *She's still here.* The black leather boots came closer. *She's right in front of me.* He felt a change in the heaviness of his body. The girl was moving river rock, digging for something. *She's digging for me.*

x x x

Sarah sank to her knees. She used both hands to lift the last of the heavy stones.

The small body was almost unrecognizable as a human. Sarah breathed in hard. Her swift and exact movements wiped away some of the mud and blood from the engorged face. She pulled an arm from beneath the body and held its slackened hand. It was the same size as her own.

Sarah stood and looked upward toward the morning sun, then back down to the body. She breathed in deeply and turned toward the horse. "Stardust, come here, Stardust." The horse nickered and took a forward step.

She removed her summer hat and recklessly pulled her lavender blouse over her head, nearly taking her white camisole with it. She gently covered the body with the blouse and leaned down to the face, her hands just barely away.

"I will be back for you. I'm getting help." She softly laid her straw hat over the disfigured face. "I promise."

This part of the creek was nearly three miles from the ranch house. She rode hard and direct, coming to a sliding stop in front of the stables. The horse was lathered with sweat and snorting for air. Sarah jumped to the ground. Her long light-amber hair was windblown and tangled. Her father quickly came from inside the barn. He dropped a bucket from his hand and frantically ran toward the commotion.

"Father! Father! Help! Help me! Father!" The words were unversed, the tone and exigency almost foreign. No longer was her voice hushed and hidden away.

Her father stretched both arms out to his side as if trying to ease a runaway stallion. "Sarah. What's wrong, Sarah?"

Her voice was cracked and airy. She struggled to get the words out. "Father, help. We need the buggy." She clutched her throat as she ran toward him. "It's a boy. I think he might die."

Her father stood, open-mouthed. She hadn't spoken a word to him for three years. He must be confused. He looked so terrified. There wasn't time to explain.

"Father! Do you hear me! The wagon." Sarah broke free from his arms and ran into the stables, her father stirring himself and following.

"Sarah, what is going on? You're speaking—what boy?"

"He's down at the creek, in section seven." She tried to clear her throat. "Where it turns flat on this side of the woods."

"What happened to your clothes, Sarah? Are you all right?"

Sarah pulled Billy out of his stall. He was the biggest horse and usually reserved for the buckboard. "Had to cover him up. There wasn't much left of him. He's hurt bad, Father."

"Listen to me," he said as he grabbed Billy's lead. "I'll go get him, but I'll need a faster horse. The wagon won't make it over the ridge."

"I'm going too. I know exactly where he is."

"No, you stay here."

Sarah pulled a saddle from the rack. Her long hair flipped from her face as she hurried to a stall. She glared at her father. "I'm going."

A voice came from behind. "Mr. Tennison? You all right? Let me help you." He looked at Sarah. "Miss Sarah."

"Give us a hand getting these saddles on, Buster. Everything is going to be fine. Sarah found somebody who needs help. I need you to get James and Robert and stay right up here at the house until I get back. Sarah's horse is pretty worn out. Make sure she gets wiped down and watered."

"Yes, sir. We won't leave sight of the house."

x x x

Sarah and her father pulled the two horses to a stop just short of the creek. Sarah was on the ground first. The lavender blouse and hat were just as she had left them.

Her father lifted the hat. "Dear Lord. He's bad, Sarah, awful bad."

Sarah started to cry. "We can't leave him out here."

Sarah's father touched the boy's chest with his open hand. "He's barely breathing. The ride back will kill him." Her father gave her a look she hated. She'd seen it before, a prelude to giving up.

Sarah stared downward, fixated on her father's hands—big, bulky, and weathered and moving with experienced precision. The kind of hands that could easily cause harm but only bore gentleness. The same hands Sarah had watched softly close her mother's eyes for the last time.

"We can't take him. He'll die." Sarah's father stood and stepped back away from the body.

He shook his head as he stared downward.

Sarah broke her stare away from the boy. Her father was saying things she didn't want to hear. It was happening again. She wanted to cover her ears with her hands, scream for help. The unanswered questions were returning, creeping in like an invasive vine and strangling out life. Sarah tightened her lips and wiped her tears away with her arm.

"I'll have to carry him back myself, keep him still as much as I can."

Sarah dropped her head and burst out crying. She imagined the strength he would need. She had never loved her father more.

"Sarah, listen to me. You need to ride as fast as you can and go collect Doc Lyman. Don't tell him about the boy. Just get him to the house, now! You understand me?"

Sarah nodded.

"Don't go back to the house. Cut through the south end, right there." He pointed outward. "It'll be faster. Now go!"

Sarah's father quickly removed the saddle and bridle from his horse and let it fall to the ground. He picked up the limp body and pulled it close into his chest. The boy whimpered and mumbled for his momma. He looked so diminished in her father's arms.

"I got him, Sarah. You go."

Sarah straightened the reins and broke a run toward town without saying another word.

The boy seemed to lean his head hard into the man's chest as if to gather comfort. "It will be all right now, son. I got you. Everything will be just fine. I promise. And one thing you gotta know is that us Tennisons don't break promises."

After a mile or so, the ground turned to rolling meadows and then into flat, plowed fields. Doc Lyman and Sarah were just ahead. They had brought the wagon and supplies across the pastures, where the ground was smooth, and stopped at the edge of the ridge. The wagon bed was lined and padded in blankets. Doc Lyman helped lay Custis on his back, placing his arms and legs as straight as he could.

"He's still alive, but I'm not sure how," Doc Lyman said. "I thought it was you, Martin. I thought something terrible had happened to you. Sarah told me just to get here fast. I thought it was you." His voice sounded off, as if he needed to cry.

Sarah repeated the words in her head. Three years of pent-up emotions had been about her mother's death. She had never imagined the possibility of losing her father too. She watched him move with precision. She wanted to say she was sorry. She wanted to take back the quiet war she had raged against him. He had tried so hard to fix what was broken inside of her. But for Sarah, it was easier to hide in her world of silence.

Her father's voice was stern. "You and Sarah get in with him. I'll take the reins. Sarah, tie your horse to the back of the wagon."

Without hesitation, all three silently took their positions. Doc Lyman did what he could with what he had. Each time the wagon jostled back and forth, Sarah's father looked backward. He watched Sarah as she watched the boy. Doc shook his head each time he wiped away blood or mud.

"Sarah, come on up here with me. We'll get him home, and then you can help."

Sarah did not break her stare at the boy. "No. I'm staying here."

Sarah rubbed her throat, winced at the dryness, and stretched out her neck. Three years of one-sided, quiet conversations with only her animals was suddenly over. As she wiped her eyes, she felt the grittiness of dust and dried mud on her face. Sarah reached for one of the canteens next to the doctor. She imagined the cool water already wetting her throat, took off the lid, and raised the canteen toward her lips. She looked at her father and paused. He was wet with sweat and caked in dirt. It must have been grueling to carry the boy so far and for so long. Without taking a drink, Sarah returned the lid and placed the canteen next to her father on the buckboard seat. He must have noticed the movement. He looked at Sarah, smiled reassuringly, and took the canteen.

The Tennison estate consisted of 1,032 acres of land located in the top portion of the county. On the Piedmont Plateau, low rolling hills and scattered woods created a paradise between the fall line and the westward edge of the Appalachian Mountains. Clay soils supported crop fields and pastureland for cattle grazing. Two narrow rivers crossed through, one bordering the north end and the other straight down the middle, fed by various swift-flowing streams and trifling rills.

Sarah looked up from the buckboard. Only a couple hundred yards more. The stately white house looked like it perched itself on a slight rise backdropped by three large barns keeping it company. Most of it had changed since her mother died, still beautiful but lacking completeness. Once a farmstead thriving with experimental crops and cattle managed by her mother, the ranch now felt like a well-maintained ghost town. She remembered her mother's laughter and could still feel her gentle hands braiding her hair. Her face and arms always seemed tanned from the sun and her eyes always bright with excitement. Sarah remembered how she smelled of lavender and rosewater and how she played fetch with the dogs. She'd remember the little things about her mother on purpose, careful to never let the memories fade away.

Sarah's father slapped the reins. "We're at the alfalfa fields. It'll be smoother now."

The jostling subsided until the wheels crossed over an abandoned irrigation check. Doc grabbed the side of the buckboard while keeping his other hand on the boy.

Sarah looked out across the field at the easternmost barn tucked safely in the lee of the hills. Pink dots from the climbing rosebush her mother had planted partially covered the west side of the building. Sarah pretended to see her mother's Hereford, Ayrshire, and Galloway cattle peppering the faraway hillocks. But there were none.

For the last few years, Sarah's father had allowed the ranch to wane into a gentleman's farm. He mostly raised quarter horses for pleasure and thoroughbreds for auction. He took care of the financial side but mainly tended his railroad transportation investments. Sarah could not understand the distraction, as if he was intentionally forgetting. Sarah wanted her mother, and the ranch was her last connection. She ran away each time her father mentioned the death. After a while he stopped trying. Sometimes, she hated herself for being so angry.

From the attic window, far above the rest of the house, Sarah expected to see Mary looking out at the pastures. She'd see them coming across the field toward the house—a buckboard and a riderless horse—and know something was wrong. She imagined Mary quickly turning and running down the three flights of spiraling stairs.

Mary had been employed since long before Sarah was born. Her room was up in the garret, the attic corner. It was one of Sarah's favorite places, a sanctuary of sorts. It was there she and Mary could see for miles.

They'd dream of traveling to faraway lands and meeting people from different countries. They'd watch incoming storms and the cattle grazing in green pastures, and they had a bird's-eye view of approaching visitors down the long extended graveled lane. Mary cooked, cleaned, did the laundry, tended the vegetable garden, and even offered her opinion on nearly everything. But mainly, Sarah knew Mary loved her. Mary had told her many times about how she had witnessed her birth, watched her first steps, and patched up her scraped knees along the way.

Sarah jumped from the back of the wagon as it neared the side kitchen door. Doc Lyman hopped down, landing with a solid thud and an accompanied grunt. "Martin, grab the other side of the blanket, and we'll sling him inside. Sarah, get my bag and supplies."

"Be careful, just be easy," Sarah said.

Two of the ranch hands, Robert and James, ran from the barn and met the wagon with urgency.

"We got him, Doc Lyman," James said as he reached out for the blanket. "Big Red came back to the barn, Mr. Tennison."

"Have Buster go get the saddle later then. It's down at section seven, at the creek."

Martin pulled on one side and rolled the edge in his hands. He glanced up at Sarah. "Go inside and get Mary. Tell her to clear the table. Now!"

A woman's voice interrupted. "Mary already knows. Lord Jesus, I seen all the commotion from upstairs." Mary covered her mouth with one hand and reached out with the other as she stepped onto the porch. "What happened, Mr. Tennison?"

"Take Sarah and clear off the table. She'll tell you all about it."

Sarah ran toward Mary. "It's bad."

Mary stared at Sarah. "You talking! Miss Sarah!" Mary wrapped her arms around Sarah and kissed the top of her head. "It'd be all right now. Your daddy get everything just right." They turned together and rushed to the house. "Lord Jesus, thank you."

Robert circled back to the front of the wagon and grabbed the reins.

Mary and Sarah were still clearing the table, throwing things on the counter, items landing on the floor, as they brought the sling inside. Martin's white shirt and tweed vest were wet with sweat, the front covered in dark blood, mud, and dirt. His face was red from the heat, layered with crusted dust except in the places wiped away with his shirt sleeve. His black hair, damp with sweat, partially hung down to his eyes.

Mary filled the pots on the stove with fresh water. Sarah brought in more supplies. She stacked the clean linens and fetched anything else she thought might be helpful.

Sarah watched as Doc Lyman manipulated his fingers over most of the boy's body. The hardest part was over—he had survived the ride to the ranch. It could only get better now.

"I don't know where to start. I can't see because of the dirt and mud. He's so swollen now. Maybe that's why he's still alive—the cool water and mud kept the swelling down before you found him."

Mary wrung out a wet cloth and gently patted his face. "I'll get him all cleaned up, Doctor Lyman. Then you can have a clear look at him. Sarah, hand me another fresh pot."

Martin sat in the corner, his head in his hands.

Mary finished and covered the boy's lower half with a clean white sheet. She looked down, closer, touching his chest, maybe feeling for his heart. "You know this boy is Black, Mr. Tennison."

The room was still.

"I wasn't real sure." He looked up and made eye contact with Doc Lyman. "That's why I didn't have Sarah tell you. I didn't want talk in town if it got out. My fear is someone tried to kill him."

Sarah stared at her father. He had known from the beginning while at the creek, trying to protect a soul he did not know. She wondered if that was what he tried to do three years ago when her mother was failing. She blinked and looked away. She needed to get upstairs, hide deep inside her mother's wardrobe, and be consoled by the clothing and darkness.

Dr. Lyman placed his hand on the boy's head. "He can't be more than nine or ten. Probably same age as Sarah."

Sarah tried to hide her teary eyes from Mary.

"Come, Miss Sarah, let's get more water, bring in more wood for the stove."

Sarah felt Mary's hand take hers. She wanted to pretend it was her mother.

Martin approached the table. Doc Lyman took off his glasses and rubbed his eyes with the back of his hand. Sarah stopped in the kitchen and listened.

"This isn't good. You can't do this. You can't leave him here," Doc Lyman said. "He's too badly hurt. He's gonna lose his sight."

"I know, Doc. But he got Sarah to talk again. She hasn't said a word in three years. Look at him. He's a little boy. A human being."

"He has one broken leg, two broken arms . . . probably defended himself from something just awful. Even if he did survive, it'd take months, maybe years. He couldn't even relieve himself with those two broken arms. If he lives, he'll most likely have some sort of brain injury. Who's going to take care of him?"

Sarah turned and watched the two men stand over the boy.

Doc Lyman put his glasses back on. "It's not like you picked up some random Black boy to work on the ranch. Someone did this to him. This boy will never be right. They meant to kill him. It will ruin you, Martin, ruin you if this gets out."

"Something happened out there. He got Sarah to speak. Three years, Doc. And now, because of this boy, she called me 'Father' again." Martin's lips tightened. "I felt something when he was in my arms." Sarah could tell by his voice that tears were to follow. "Doc, I swear I felt angels. I was so exhausted from carrying him; my legs buckled. I tripped and fell and when I picked him up again, he felt weightless. And my legs felt so strong."

Sarah turned, walked outdoors, and gathered wood from the shed. With each log nestled into the crook of her arm, she sensed the graduating heaviness. The weight of two more made her back arch backward in counterbalance. *How much would a boy weigh, anyhow?*

As Sarah walked back into the kitchen she thought of her father's words. *Angels, he felt angels. Why is this happening?*

She heard the doctor's low voice.

"He'll be a burden, and he will be your Achilles' heel. He's gonna die anyway."

Sarah stood silently in the doorway. The armful of firewood crashed to the floor. Doc Lyman had given up so easily. Her fingers turned into fists. He was the doctor, the only one that could help. She felt her father looking at her.

She stomped toward Doc Lyman. "You let my mother die! You let my mother die!" Sarah screamed. "You said she'd be all right. You both did. You lied to me!"

Martin tried to wrap his arms around his daughter. Sarah broke away and struck the doctor's chest with her fists. Martin pulled her away and held on tightly.

"You let my mother die. You let her die, and now you're letting him die too. I hate you! I hate you!" Sarah tried to twist free. The sensation of being restrained and comforted conflicted with her uncontrollable urge to flee. She cried out in despairing surrender, finally slipping deeply into her father's chest.

Martin eased his grip and gently wrapped his arms around his little girl. He stroked her hair and kissed the top of her head as she buried her face into his bloodstained shirt.

Doc Lyman looked down. His voice was soft and genuine as if coming straight from his heart. "I would have just as soon died myself to let your mother live."

Sarah suddenly remembered the sound of her mother's voice. It was clear and kind, and moved with a soft spirit cadence, just like Doc Lyman's. How could she have forgotten her voice? Sarah had strived to memorize everything about her mother. It had to be with remarkable clarity to last the rest of her life. But those memories had left Sarah, just like her own voice.

"I loved her, Sarah. I promise you. There was nothing we could do. Sarah. Sarah, listen to me. I loved her too. I'm so sorry." Doc Lyman slowly lowered himself to his knees and faced Sarah directly. He cleared his throat and strengthened his lips with a strained smile. He nodded as if making a promise he would never break. "I will do everything I can to help this boy. But he's bad, Sarah. I need your help."

Sarah cried into her father's chest.

"Please, Sarah, will you help me?"

Sarah wiped tears from her face. She nodded and took a second for her voice to catch up. "I never go to that part of the ranch, but Stardust took me. I was picking wildflowers for Momma when he touched my shoe."

Sarah rubbed her throat and sniffed her tears away. "I told him I would take care of him. I promised him."

"We're all gonna take care of him now, Sarah. I can't say that he'll live, but I give you my word I will do everything I know how to do."

х х х

The room was silent now. Doc Lyman warily pulled up a stool, sat next to the table, and looked at his pocket watch. Mary regularly swapped out the cool cloths filled with ice chips. Abrasions and cuts were cleaned and sutured; bones were set and splinted. The bedding was changed out and cleaned again.

"Right now, I'm worried about his brain swelling. I can't get to his eyes to see his pupils. He's going to get worse before any improvement. We need to keep his airway open as much as we can. If we get past that, then infection. It will take a long time to heal." Doc Lyman leaned his head against the wall. "We won't know until he wakes."

Sarah cleared her throat. "When will that be?"

"I don't quite know." Doc Lyman paused. "Sometimes it's better this way—time to let the body repair itself. We need to keep him hydrated. Keep him on his side to let his mouth drain out best it can. Let gravity help us out a bit. We'll have to turn him from side to side so the blood won't pool. If he regains consciousness, I can keep him halfway sedated with a tincture of opium, but that will be only temporary. I can administer ether. Sometimes brain injuries can do strange things to a person. Hard to determine."

"Like what?" Martin asked.

Doc Lyman inhaled and closed his eyes for a moment. "Brain injuries are entirely unpredictable. A person can die straightaway from a simple punch to the nose, while others might miraculously survive a horribly traumatic injury. Some people barely recover and end up with paralysis or catatonia. We have asylums all over this country full of mere shells of people. Some say death is the easy way out.

"There was a strange case several years back. Phineas Gage got a forty-three-inch iron tamping rod blown through his head while working on the railroad. The rod entered under his cheek and exited through the top of his skull. He got up, got into a cart himself, and was taken to the town doctor. Survived for several years. But they said his behavior and personality changed drastically. He became fitful and irreverent. Mean, very mean. The reports said he previously never had such behavior. He died twelve years after the accident. His skull and rod are kept at Harvard University Medical School. Saw them with my own eyes."

Sarah listened with intensity. She locked eyes with Doc Lyman, and he abruptly paused.

Martin cleared his throat. "If he lives, does that mean he's going to be dangerous?"

"We're only touching the surface of an unexplored realm of the human body. We just don't know, Martin. We just don't know."

Sarah had fallen asleep on the floor next to her father's feet. Mary washed up the last of the pots and some dishes from earlier in the day.

"Who do you think could have done this? He's just a child," Martin whispered.

"There are ugly people on this earth," Doc Lyman said. "Before Sarah came and got me, I heard there was a house-burning in the colored part of town. Maybe that had something to do with it."

"I didn't see any burn marks, but that doesn't mean much, I suppose. Who knows?"

The room was silent except for Mary opening and closing an occasional cupboard. The two men sat next to the table and waited.

"I've had a feral daughter for three years now. I promised her mother I'd raise her myself. There would be no boarding schools, and she'd stay right here with me." Martin looked down and shook his head. "Fine job I've done, haven't I?"

"You did the best you could. I haven't had time to examine her, but I suspect her raspy voice is a little uncomfortable. It will go away in time. I can give her some throat serum in the interim."

Martin nodded his head.

"Go get some sleep, Martin. I'll sit right here next to him till morning."

Martin picked up his daughter. He looked toward Mary and whispered, "You go get some sleep now too." He carried Sarah upstairs and put her to bed.

x x x

Morning came quickly. Martin walked into the kitchen, got his own coffee, and sat back down in the corner chair. The boy was still unconscious. "How's he doing, Doc?"

"Completely silent all night. So motionless, I thought he must have passed on. Sarah still asleep?"

"Pretty tense day yesterday. About what she said—she didn't mean it, Doc. She's just a kid with big feelings. If there's anyone to blame, it should fall on me. I should have paid closer attention, tried harder."

Doc Lyman slowly shook his head. "No, Martin. We all did what we could, what needed to be done. Heather wouldn't leave the ranch. The surgery in Boston would have just prolonged her pain. And she knew that."

Mary helped redress the bandages and change the bedding. She gently touched the top of the boy's head. "Mr. Tennison, this child needs a bed. I want him to have my room. I can sleep in the barn."

"You will do no such thing. He needs to be down here next to the water and supplies. He needs an around-the-clock watch. We'll clean out the pantry, put a soft bed in there for him. All of us can keep an eye on him then."

Martin looked at Doc. "We'll set you up in a room right at the top of the stairs so you can be comfortable, in case of late nights when you don't want to ride back into town."

"Speaking of that, I need to go into the office, get some more supplies. I'll leave word at the hospital that I'll be gone for a couple of days, at least until we really know what we're dealing with. I'd like to watch the boy as much as I can without causing suspicion."

The carriage house was in sight of the primary residence. The two men silently worked together and pulled Doc's rig out of the barn. Doc Lyman climbed up on the seat and gathered the reins.

"Listen, Doc. I understand if you don't come back. Not gonna hold it against you. I know this could ruin not only me, but anyone associated with it. I don't want you to be harmed. I've been searching my brain for common sense all night, but no matter what I come up with, it gets down to one thing—that little boy in there deserves a chance like all the rest of us. Just, if you would, tell me how to take care of him."

"My first reaction was to let him go. I was scared, Martin, scared for you and me both. I thought about riding away, turning my back. But I can't do that." The doctor paused as if gathering the strength to continue. "What Sarah said in there hit me pretty hard. These last three years, she's thought I let her mother die. I loved your wife. I did all I could, Martin. I helped bring Sarah into this world. I was the first person to touch her on this entire earth. I placed her in her mother's arms and introduced the two of them. I remember the look on Heather's face when I did. I still see her eyes to this day." He looked up at Martin. "Sarah reminded me of what is important and what's not and, among other things, to do my job. I guess it's the Hippocrates issue as well. By doing nothing, looking the other way? Is that not causing the first harm?"

Martin patted the horse, straightened the forelock, and let go of the reins.

"I still see her eyes too, Doc. I see them when I lie down at night, when I look at Sarah. I see them when a new calf or litter of pups is born. I can still hear her laughter when I watch a new filly bouncing out in the pasture. I see her every spring and fall.

"Yesterday Sarah seemed to transform right before my eyes into the likeness of her mother. They have the same eyes, the same wild hair, and the same idiosyncratic mannerisms. They share the same heart and boundless mind. She was so smart. Heather refined crop production, lines of selective breeding, plant genetics, deliberated with the country's top agronomists, and then mucked out horse manure with a two-year-old at her side. She loved new life. She'd get so mad at me for shooting an ol' coyote up to no good. I wish I could take it all back and never kill another thing." Martin stepped away from the buggy. "This is what she'd do. It's what I'm gonna do."

As Martin watched Doc Lyman's buggy leave the ranch, Buster walked up next to him, followed by James and Robert. Buster had been the barn manager for the last couple of years. He was a quiet man and used his tall stature to his advantage. After the war, he came up from Georgia, where he had been enslaved since childhood. "You let us know, Mr. Tennison, what you need us to do."

Robert took off his hat and held it in his hands. His skin was dark and weathered. He was the oldest of the ranch hands, walked with a limp, and worked harder than two men put together.

"That boy gonna be all right, Mr. Tennison?"

"I don't know." Martin looked at the men. "I want you all to stay close by. No farther than the bunkhouse. No one says a thing. I'll let you know how the boy is doing."

Buster stepped closer to Martin and stared down the lane. "No one gonna say a thing."

"We can take turns keeping a watch out," James said.

"I'd appreciate that." Martin sighed deeply. "This cannot get out. Some folks seem to crave any excuse to rile. Before you know it, it's too late. They'll try to ruin us."

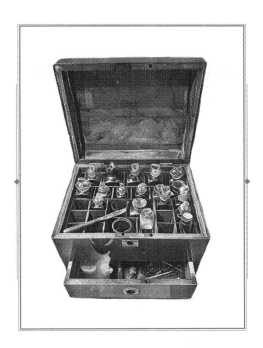

Doc Lyman placed the last medical supply box in his buggy. Glass bottles clinked together as he arranged the boxes and adjusted the crates with a covered blanket. A man on horseback rushed down the street, sliding to a halt behind the buggy.

"You Dr. Lyman?"

"Yes."

The man was out of breath. "Sheriff Abbott told me to come and get you. He needs your help with a possible crime scene. House burned down over in colored town."

"I heard some talk about a fire."

"Seems a body didn't make it. Might be an accident, or we might have us a murder."

"I'll follow you." His intuition told him this would be the rest of the story connected to the boy. Doc Lyman pulled himself up into the buggy and looked over at the covered supplies. He should have packed the bottles more securely. "Let's take it easy. No reason to rush if everyone's dead."

The man on horseback led the doctor through town, down a dirt road, into the woods, past the last huddle of wooden cabins, to a small clearing.

Slight puffs of smoke were still rising from the charred remains of a leveled house. Nearby trees, singed black at their base, offered high outstretched limbs of scorched branches overhead. The surrounding ground was burned. All color and texture were now reduced to powdery black and gray ash.

On the perimeter of the woods, several men stood solemnly. Their clothing and faces were dirty with soot. Doc Lyman recognized Pastor Jacobson but not the others. Sheriff Abbott was bent over, examining something in the burn scar. It was the only thing of any height that remained.

There was an odor in the air, a putridly sick stench that could consume all oxygen out of a person's lungs. Doc Lyman covered his mouth and nose with his handkerchief and warily approached the sheriff.

"Thanks for coming out. Looks like an adult."

Doc Lyman bent over and used his handkerchief to move the body. The leg fell off. The sheriff stepped back and closed his lips together, hard, before filling Doc Lyman in with the particulars.

"Pastor Jacobson over there said he and the closest neighbors got here first. Everything was already burning hard. Best they could do was stop it from spreading into the woods."

Doc Lyman stood up. He discarded the handkerchief to the ground. "Any others?"

"Well, Doc, that's where I need your help. Looks like whoever this is got out of the house but didn't get very far. Everything else inside burned too hot and fast. There's nothing left except an iron skillet."

Both men stepped away from the body and slowly walked toward a small pile of burned debris on the downhill side of the clearing.

"The pastor there said Miss Loraine lived here with her boy. Kind of kept to herself. She was nice and all. Never missed a Sunday, but also was always working somewhere else."

"What about the boy? How old is he?" Doc Lyman asked.

"The boy, about ten, named Custis—real odd, so to speak. Didn't go to their negro school. Guess the other children picked on him." Sheriff Abbott paused, kicked what remained of an oil lamp, then continued. "If the boy's alive, no one here will be able to take him. Nobody can afford another mouth to feed. Nothing left for him, by all accounts. I got my men searching nearby, in the woods, just in case he did get out. Maybe it was him that did this. Started the fire and killed his own mother."

Doc Lyman looked at the burned lantern. The glass chimney, broken into pieces, lay nearby. He pointed at the debris pile, distorted wire border, and burned-out posts. "Looks like a chicken coop, or what used to be."

"Most likely. But see how it burned? Slower and not as hot. Looks like it started here, near the coop, and then burned the dry grass right up to the house."

Both men walked back toward the body.

"Just look at that, Doc, as hot as a steel inferno." The sheriff looked upward into the nearby trees. "Look at how high the flames got. I checked for oil or a kerosene accelerant but couldn't find any sign of residue except right there at that broken lamp." He looked back down at the ashes. "This should have been a little ol' cabin. What made it burn like this? Maybe the boy is in there and we just can't see any remains."

"Maybe so. That would make sense. I'll have to do an autopsy to determine if that body is female."

"No offense, now, Doc, but we ain't doing no autopsy unless we have a real reason to do so."

Dr. Lyman slowly nodded his head. "It looks like you got it all figured out, then, Sheriff."

"Well, I'll wait here a little longer. Wait for the boys to come back. See if they found anything in the woods. No use you stickin' around."

Sheriff Abbott walked Doc Lyman back to his rig. "Thanks, Doc. I just needed you to see this firsthand before anything got to it. I appreciate you comin' out." The sheriff adjusted his hat, looked at the covered boxes in the buggy. "Doc, where you going to with all this stuff?"

Dr. Lyman diverted his eyes back to his horse. "Couple towns up in Davidson County." He cleared his throat. "Running short on supplies and need a doctor. Set up two small surgeries and the yearly clinic over there. I'll probably be gone for a week or two."

"A week or two around here is a long time to be without a good doctor."

Doc Lyman smiled. "There will be a doctor at the hospital, but I sent for help from over in Charlotte, anyway. Got a young new doctor coming here to help out at the office for the first part of the week. Named John Clay. His daddy is a doctor too. A surgeon in the war. Maybe he'll stay on. We got enough business, that's for sure."

"Sure do, Doc, sure do. You take care, and thanks for helping out here. Pastor Jacobson said he'd see to it the body gets buried. I told him to wait until tomorrow just in case something comes up and we need another look."

Sheriff Abbott pulled up the corner of the blanket. He paused and looked at Doc Lyman as if he had more questions. Doc held his breath, waiting for accusations. But Doc's lies had added up—his mind was only playing games now. They looked at each other for a few seconds. Sheriff Abbott let go of the blanket but held the stare. The kind of stare that probably knew the difference between the truth and a lie.

"We gotta do what we gotta do. I have an investigation, and you got sick people." Sheriff Abbott stepped away from the buggy. "I really can't tell if this burning was a heathen act or just plain accident. Don't get me wrong, but in a way, I think it'd be better if word got out that the boy died right there with his momma. Ain't no easy life left here for him, is there, Doc?"

Doc Lyman turned his face toward the horse. He fiddled with the reins and caught himself fidgeting in his seat. The sheriff's words were odd, not something he would normally say. But it wasn't that exactly; it's what the sheriff chose not to say. "No one here seems to be able to take care of him. You're right, Sheriff. No good would befall the boy or this place."

"Listen, when the men get back from the woods empty-handed, then the investigation is closed, unless a witness decides to come forward and I can prove otherwise."

Doc Lyman wanted to breathe in reprieve without giving notice. Years of doctoring had taught him to never overexcite, to always remain calm no matter the circumstances. That was his job. "You're a good man, Sheriff."

"I suppose."

Doc Lyman tipped his hat, made a quick click with his tongue, and slapped the reins on the horse's rump. The glass bottles jostled as the buggy rocked from side to side. Doc felt uneasy inside. Life had suddenly turned fragile. On occasion, he had been one of the few physicians to lend services to the Black community. But now, the task of fixing broken bones and dispensing medicinal remedies seemed elementary compared to navigating through what might lie ahead. This was something deeper, more sinister. Someone had tried to murder this child.

x x x

The sounds of the day had hushed, the sun leaving behind the sky for the moon. The kitchen windows were lit by candle flame, the library alight with oil lamps. Framed land maps, schematics of track and train, and various legal documents infiltrated shelves of multiple books, volume collections, and ledgers. Doc Lyman sipped from a snifter of brandy.

"Odd."

"What do you mean, Doc?"

"I've never drank liquor. I've fought in a war, held a man's living heart in my hands, buried so many people I've forgotten their names, but this small child is what it took for me to fall apart."

"I think as we get older, we feel more deeply."

Doc Lyman told Martin about the burn site, the missing boy, and the conversation with the sheriff. Martin listened without saying a word until Doc was finished.

"I need to tell Mary and Sarah too," Martin said. "I just need to find the right time for Sarah."

"I don't think there will be a right time."

"Someone left that boy for dead. Buried him like an animal so the vultures couldn't get to him."

"No. They buried him so no one could find him. If the same people who did this find out he's still alive, they'll come for him."

Martin leaned back into his chair. "I'm not going to let that happen, Doc." He rubbed his face. "Sarah kissed me good night. First time since her mother died. If that boy lives, he'll be safe with us, right here on the ranch."

Martin found Sarah sitting at Custis's bedside about an hour before sunrise. The pantry had been cleaned out and restocked with medical supplies. In the middle of the room, Custis lay on his side in a small child's bed just large enough to support his body.

Sarah wiped sputum from his mouth, then rested her forehead on the edge of the bed. She whispered into her hands. "There's no good reason to take him. He's hurt so bad; he's had enough. Momma, I know you're an angel now, so you know I'm still pretty mad at God. But you tell God to make him better. And thank you for this food, or whatever else I'm supposed to say."

Martin stepped back out into the hallway and leaned against the wall. He closed his eyes and breathed in, priming the strength to face his daughter. "I don't think I've seen that bed since you were a little girl."

But Martin knew it wasn't true. It had been up in the loft along with the other things belonging to his wife. Occasionally late at night, when he couldn't sleep, he'd walk the squeaky floorboards in the attic, shuffle boxes and surround himself with things he refused to abandon, sometimes until the early morning hours.

"Mary and I brought it down. It fits just right in here."

Martin softly touched the headboard. Heather had sat next to the same bed every night and read aloud to Sarah. Martin slowly ran his fingers across the iron railing as if searching for something residual. It was all in the past now, but it somehow managed to still feel so raw.

"Dr. Lyman is going to give you a break now. I want to speak with you and Mary, together, outside."

All three walked to the back porch. The morning was fresh, and the air was still cool.

"I think we know where he came from. His name might be Custis. His momma died in a house fire over on the other side of the railroad tracks. He has no one else."

"He got us, Mr. Tennison," Mary interjected.

"It's a difficult situation. People cannot know he is here. If anyone finds out, we could be in jeopardy. And talk of me allowing a colored boy to live in my house and taking care of him will rile up half the county."

"Ain't nobody gonna find out," Mary continued. "As far as anybody is concerned, that boy is my nephew, and I come to have to take care of him, Mr. Tennison, just like my own. Now you know my boys—I ain't heard from them since the war. I been saving my money every month, been stowing it away."

"Mary, you don't have to worry about that, please. We don't know if he's even going to live." Martin looked at Sarah. "Honey, you need to stay inside. Buster will make sure all the chores are done."

"Are they going to try and burn us out too?"

"The sheriff doesn't know what happened exactly. It looks like it was an accident."

"An accident? What happened to Custis then? An accident?"

"The sheriff doesn't know about Custis. As far as he's concerned, Custis died along with his mother. That's why we could be in jeopardy if word got out. Someone wanted him dead. Whoever caused the fire went after Custis. Maybe he witnessed the whole thing. We don't know for sure, but we need to be careful."

"What did they do with his mother's body?"

"Dr. Lyman said the neighborhood church out there will take care of her."

Sarah stared at her father.

Mary reached out to her. "I can go and make sure everything is done proper."

"You can't," Martin said. "We can't get involved or have any connection, or people will find out."

"No. She'll be all alone." Sarah turned, left the porch, and walked straight to the stable.

Martin looked as if he needed to follow. "Where are you going?"

"It don't matter, Mr. Tennison. This is what she does—gone most of the day and into the night sometimes. But she always comes back to us."

"I've tried to tell her what happened to me, but I just can't do it, Mary. There are no words."

"I know, Mr. Tennison. Everybody know."

Martin followed Sarah into the barn. She was saddling her horse.

"You won't stop me, Father. I'll leave in the middle of the night if you try."

"I know you will. I'm not going to stop you." Martin reached for the bridle and bit and handed it to Sarah. "Stay off the roads and away of town."

Sarah paused. "I don't want her to be buried all alone." She turned her head and stood motionless in front of her father.

Martin knew this was the moment. His insides trembled. Words that he had practiced for three years were nowhere to be found. He told his mind to let his mouth find the words that had been waiting in his heart.

"I didn't leave your mother, Sarah. I went back after everyone was gone."

"You left me there. I needed you."

Martin stepped closer to his daughter. "After she died, I held her hand for two days, waiting for the funeral. I wanted to stay right there with her so she wouldn't be afraid. I waited there and watched them put her in the casket, and I never let go of her hand. They wanted to close the lid, but I wouldn't let them. I wanted to crawl in there and stay with her forever. Of all the things, the hardest was thinking about that casket closing for eternity, knowing I would never be able to see or touch her again. I was terrified I'd forget what she looked like. I fell apart, Sarah. I had no capacity or strength left to take care of my own daughter. I just couldn't bear to watch her be put in the ground."

Sarah stood rigid, her eyes fixed and welling.

"But I went back after everyone left. I stayed there and slept next to her grave. Doc was the one; he was finally able to pull me away and brought me home to you. He told me that my anguish was a testament to the profound love I had for your mother. He also said I would fail my wife if I was not taking care of our little girl. But it was too late. You wanted nothing to do with me anymore. You were so hurt."

"You wouldn't let me into her room," Sarah blurted out. "I couldn't say goodbye."

"I didn't want you to see her withering. She had been so strong and healthy, but then she just couldn't fight it anymore. She asked me to let her go. She was in such excruciating pain. That's not what I wanted you to remember about your mother. I told my beautiful wife to go, that it was time to leave us. Cancer is a *greedful* bastard. It just keeps on taking and taking and taking until there is nothing left. I thought I was protecting you.

"Mary told me you never said a word to anyone at the cemetery, that you didn't even cry. You were so brave. I've been trying to tell you what happened to me, why I failed you so miserably. I never wanted you to have a memory of your father unable to function as a husband or father, or even as a human being. I could not fathom a world without her, so I hid inside myself. I was trying to shield you, but it was I who needed the protection too. You are the reason I am still on this earth. I love you with everything I've got."

Sarah wiped her tears away. "I remember what she looks like, Daddy. We'll never forget. I can still hear her voice too, her laughter when she was trying to teach you to dance."

Martin palmed the tears from his face and breathed in. A slow smile broke into a soft laugh. "I was such a blundering idiot."

Sarah fell into her father's open arms.

x x x

Sarah stood among the pine, safely concealed by ferns and redbud brush. She watched the burial from a distance. Black men, probably wearing the only set of clothes they had, lowered the blanket-wrapped corpse into a grave near the churchyard. The pastor read from a book held out in front of him. She squinted and adjusted her head as if trying to listen. She barely heard a word, a slight nod to the cadence as though she had memorized the passage by heart. Soon, everyone walked away except for a man who shoveled dirt back into the grave.

The man finished and patted the dirt with the back of the shovel, removed his hat, and bowed his head. When all was clear, Sarah walked to the unmarked grave and placed a sprig of wild winterberry holly at the foot of the mound. "No need to worry. I've got him now."

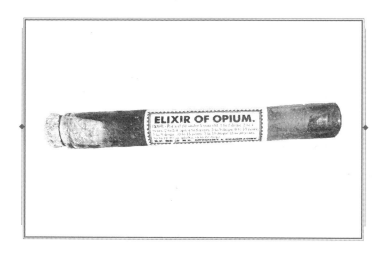

ver the next several days, Custis fell in and out of consciousness. Doc Lyman managed to get water and small amounts of
broth into Custis's mouth three or four times a day. He could
see his teeth—he had bitten his tongue. It would heal without sutures.
At times, Custis wept for his mother. At other times, he screamed.

"Momma, go. Pastor Jacobson. Go. Run now."

Doc Lyman didn't leave his side. "It's probably the opium. It takes
the pain away, but I'm afraid it leaves delirium in its place."

The facial swelling finally began to recede. Doc Lyman eased up on
the dosage, and Custis became more and more conscious.

"Come on, time for you to wake up now. Come on."

Custis barely opened his eyes.

Doc Lyman leaned into the side of the bed. He gently placed his hand on top of Custis's forehead. "It's all right, boy. You're safe here. Nothing else is going to happen. I'm a doctor, and we're taking care of you."

Custis passed out again. Doc Lyman stood up straight and called out to the others. Martin walked into the room, followed by Sarah and Mary. Doc Lyman kept his hand on Custis's forehead and fumbled with his stethoscope with the other.

"He came to. He came to and looked right at me." Doc Lyman lightly touched Custis's face and slightly pushed open his eyelid.

"Did he say anything to you, Doc? Does he have brain damage?" Martin asked.

"I can't tell. He has broken blood vessels all through the sclera, but look at the color of his iris. I've never seen such green eyes."

Doc Lyman pushed open the other eyelid. "Both pupils are reacting. That's an excellent sign. We need to keep him stimulated. Keep his brain working. Sarah, maybe you can read to him."

Sarah quickly left the room without saying a word.

Martin placed his hand on Custis's shoulder. "Will that help, Doc? Reading to him?"

"Not sure . . . certainly won't hurt. But it's good for Sarah. It'll help heal her voice."

Sarah came back into the room, carrying several books. "I know exactly what book I'll start with, the one any boy would love." She looked up at her father and grinned. "*Little Women.*"

Doc Lyman looked at Martin, smiled, and nodded. He placed his hand on Sarah's head and patted her incessantly fussy hair.

x x x

Sarah read aloud to Custis until his medication wore off. She'd come in closer and try to soothe him by telling him about the ranch and the horses. The only thing that seemed to help was opium. Doc administered another dose.

"Rest now," Sarah told him. "No more pain for a while. It's going away right now."

Sarah read to him throughout the day. Sometimes her voice gave out, and Doc Lyman would take over. When the evening came and all was quiet, Mary sat in the kitchen and listened to the stories. She'd cry at moments, giggle softly at other parts. Mary couldn't read but instead delivered long narrations about her boys. Most of the time, he slept while she reminisced.

Martin watched Sarah from the kitchen as she read aloud to Custis.

"Sure is nice, ain't it, Mr. Tennison?" Mary whispered. "I mean, hearing her voice again."

Martin slowly smiled. "Her soul's returning. I've enjoyed listening to your stories and Doc's yarns and fairy tales, but I love hearing Sarah's voice. She reads with the articulation of a great storyteller. Her mother read to her—every night. I was always too busy. Locked up in my library, working." He breathed in deeply, closing his eyes for a moment. "I wish I could do it all over again. So many things would be different."

"You was working hard, Mr. Tennison. You supported this family, this ranch. You the one that keep everything going. Now, don't you go get all melancholy, Mr. Tennison. Why, Miz Tennison would be so proud of you right now, and just look at Sarah. Readin' up a storm, just like her momma did."

"Yes. Just like her momma did. She always told me that Sarah needed to hear me even though she wouldn't understand the words yet. Even before she was born. Said the baby needed to hear her father's voice. It would give her a sense of wholeness, and she'd have a place with me where she'd know it was always safe. Maybe Heather had a premonition."

Martin returned to his library and finished up some work. After rummaging through a new pile of correspondence and tidying up the desk, he leaned back in the chair, tapping his fingers on the armrest.

Martin abruptly stood up, removed two books from the shelf, and walked into the kitchen.

"Mary? Sarah?" He looked around and softly called out again. No one answered. Martin put one book, *Around the World in Eighty Days*, on the kitchen table and kept the other under his arm. He heard Custis stir.

Martin sat down next to the bed and pulled up the blanket to cover Custis's deeply bruised chest. It was barely rising. Martin took in a sympathetic breath as he watched Custis labor for air.

Martin scooted the chair in closer. He opened his book and began reading. His voice was soft with inflection. Custis turned his head, as if he were really listening. Martin saw Sarah standing in the doorway. She tilted her head and looked at her father. His voice fluctuated with each new detail. He held out one arm and motioned Sarah to sit next to him. She leaned in under his arm and listened to her father's enchanting tale of railroad engineering.

x x x

Colors blurred, a phantasmagoria of reds, figures circled, voices distorted. Excruciating pain ravaged his body. He sensed heat, a thermal burning of all his cells. His muscles felt as if they all had been pulled from beneath his skin. Exposed viscera, jiggling, beating, panting as their bright colors drained away. He was the cadaver he had read about, the one supine, exposed, in the center of the theatre. The doctors had taken his brain, held it high for others to see.

The hallucinations eased each day. He took water and broth more readily and stayed conscious a little longer. Each time, Doc Lyman barraged him with questions.

"What's your name?"

"Custis."

"Where are you from?"

"The woods."

"Where do you live?"

"The woods."

"Do you know where you are?"

"Hell. Am I in hell?"

Sarah jumped in. "No, you're not in hell, Custis. You're going to be just fine. You're on the Tennison Estate, and we're here with you, taking care of you."

Custis wanted to shake his head, but it hurt way too much. *Who is this girl? I've heard her before. Purple. She was purple. The angel, so I can't be in hell.*

Doc Lyman broke back in. "What's the last thing you remember, Custis?"

"A hippopotamus. Then I was walking on the rails."

Doc Lyman breathed in deeply. "Definitely hallucinogenic."

"Do you know what happened to you?"

"I don't believe I can remember."

"It's all right, Custis. You're gonna be fine."

"What happened?" Custis tried to lift at his arms. "What happened to me?"

Doc Lyman spoke softly. "Your arms are broken. We don't know exactly what happened. Sarah found you, and we brought you here to the ranch."

Each morning he was asked the same prodding questions. Custis gave the same answers.

The mornings were the worst for everyone. Custis could not recall any events or information. He couldn't remember who the doctor was or why Mary was always fussing about. The darkness pulled him down into a spiraling cauldron where sickness brewed in his stomach. He wanted to reach up and hold his eyes open with his hands, but someone had taken his arms. His eyes could barely open, but only for brief seconds, to let in distorted light and images.

"Where am I?"

"You on the Tennison Estate," Mary answered. "You here with Mr. Tennison and Miss Sarah and Doc Lyman. We all takin' real good care of you."

"Who are you, and where's my momma?"

"Well, she couldn't take care of you right now, so she wanted us to watch over you for a little while. Is that all right?"

Custis tried to get up, but the pain was unbearable. He fought passing out.

Mary held him down as Sarah called out for help. "He passed out again, Doctor Lyman. He was trying to get out of bed and go home."

"Let's let him sleep for a little while." Doc Lyman motioned for them to meet in the kitchen.

"I think the best thing we can do is keep him still to let his bones heal properly. That won't happen when he's trying to get to his mother. We need to tell him, then focus on keeping his brain stimulated. We've passed the safe threshold of continuing with heavy sedation. We don't need addiction or psychotic episodes to add to our problems."

"Doc, I'll tell him," Martin said. "Mary, I want you to be there with me, just in case I can't find the right words."

"Mr. Tennison, as sad as this is, it would be my honor to stand right there behind you."

"No, Mary. You're going to be standing right next to me."

Martin took Sarah's hand.

"I want you here with him too Sarah. You're a part of this, more so than anyone else."

Sarah felt her father's hand tighten. She was about to hear the words she never wanted to listen to again. She filtered through flashes of the past, upstairs, her mother dying, the look on everyone's face, everyone crying. She remembered her father on his knees, in front of her. *She's gone, Sarah, she's gone to heaven.*

"We have to tell him, honey."

"Father."

Martin waited for her thoughts, but tears came instead. Sarah reached out and took his other hand. She looked downward. "Now I know how you felt when you had to tell me." She began to cry. "I'm so sorry, Father. I didn't mean to be so unkind to you. I didn't mean it. I didn't mean it." Sarah looked over at Mary. "Please forgive me, Mary, I just didn't know what to do."

Martin grabbed Sarah and hugged her closely. He must have known the words were coming straight from a little ten-year-old girl's heart. "It's all right. It's all right."

Mary rushed over and stroked Sarah's hair with her hand while wiping away her own tears with her other hand. "I know, Miss Sarah. No need for apologizing. You was just so sad."

Doc Lyman blinked hard, then wiped his nose. "Let's go tell him."

Martin began letting go of Sarah, but she held on even tighter. He tried to smile as he enfolded back into her. He wrapped one arm underneath Sarah's legs and lifted her onto his lap. "It's all right, we can stay right here, just like this, until we're all ready."

White people with sad faces stood next to his bed. He could see more light. The definition of figures and colors was easily discernible. They were so close. He wanted his momma, not these White people. What were they about to do? Fear surpassed his pain. He wanted to run but couldn't move. A man, a stethoscope around his neck—he must be a doctor, a White doctor who was about to touch him. Custis tried to push backward. He turned his head away—it was the only thing that could move. A tall man and a little girl stood on the opposite side. Custis studied the wall behind them. It looked like the haberdashery. Lots of bottles, goods, and packaging, all stacked neatly on bright, clean shelves. He was in a store for only White people.

"I'm not supposed to be in here. Why are you keeping me here? Why do you have me tied down?"

"Custis, I'm Doctor Lyman. You got hurt really bad and broke your leg and arms. I know you must be all mixed up, but we're trying to help you."

Custis knew he was breathing deeply—he was fighting for air, but his lungs were not cooperating.

"I need to get home. My momma is alone. She'll be worried. I can't be in here, sir."

Mary squeezed in from behind his head and touched his forehead. "Yes, you can. You gonna stay right here with me—Mary. This been my home since way before you was born."

Mary's home? So many provisions. She must be the richest Black woman in the world. Why is she allowed to be so rich? Custis was in a different country, a place on the other side of the world. The kind he had read about, the kind with strange trees and animals.

"Am I somewhere else? Where did you bring me? I want to go home."

Mary leaned in closer. "You still right here, in North Carolina."

Doc Lyman whispered, "He has no short-term memory; that's predictable right now."

Martin held on to Sarah's hand. "Custis, we want you to know you are safe and welcome here. You are about the strongest boy I have ever seen. You are amazingly fierce."

Why is this White man inside Mary's house? "I need to go home."

Martin leaned in. "Custis, there was a bad fire. Your momma didn't make it."

Every muscle left in Custis's body seemed to fight the words entering his head. His rigid body pushed hard, down into the mattress, as if backing away with no other direction to flee. His face grimaced as his eyes turned fixed and glassy.

Sarah stepped in closer. "I'm sorry, Custis. You're gonna be up in no time. Doctor Lyman here is the best doctor on this side of the Mississippi. Maybe the other side too, but I've never been there."

Their words abruptly transformed and moved in blocks like the setts and cobblestones in town where he wasn't supposed to go. Voices turned choppy, with conflicting pitches and unbalanced cadence. They kept talking, but he could no longer decipher their secret language. He wanted to shake his head, but the throbbing pain thwarted any movement. *She died. Is that what they said?*

Nothing moved. The motionless people stood over his paralyzed body. The world had stopped turning. Custis was stuck midpoint between the minute and hour hands of a clock. Even the sounds were frozen, not even the ticking of time.

"Fire?"

Doc Lyman nodded his head. "Yes. They tried to put it out, but it was just too much."

"Is that how I got hurt? Did I burn to death?"

"No, Custis. We don't know what happened to you. And you are very much alive."

"Is my momma dead? Is that what you said?"

"She died. They couldn't save her."

Custis never wanted to cry so gravely in all his life. But it would show weakness and embolden others to harm him even more. He closed his eyes, trying to squeeze images out of his mind. But it was too much, and he cried out with abandon.

Custis felt Sarah touch his fingers. He tried to move his arm. It was heavy and wouldn't bend away. Her fingers were warm and soft and white. Now he would be beaten. He'd seen it before. He didn't mean to touch her. He tried to roll himself off the bed, but more white hands held him down.

Voices swirled and slowly began to gather in proper order. Sarah was even closer now. Her eyes looked like the sky in the summertime. She was so close he could see her dark lashes.

"When you get better, we can ride horses together. Your momma wants you to be happy again."

"Do you know her?"

"No. But I know how it feels to lose a momma."

"I don't know if I told her goodbye."

x x x

Doc Lyman had reduced the tincture of opium as much as he could and only administered it at night. Mornings were the worst. Sleep was the only thing that took reality away, if only for a little while— the time to steal just a few more minutes of, where memory doesn't live. Loud, clanging voices circulating—all betraying the last bit of darkness just before sunrise. Custis fidgeted in his bed and finally said, "I gotta pee."

Custis watched Mary bring a pot to the bedside. She began to pull the sheet away from his waist. *Wait, how has this been happening? She's probably already been looking. But now it's different. I'm wide awake. She's going to be touching me where she shouldn't be touching.* Custis pushed his splinted arms downward, keeping the sheet tight to the mattress.

"Can't we get the doctor this time?"

"You ain't got anything I hadn't seen before. I raised three young boys all by myself. So you are sadly mistaken if you think we gonna bother the good doctor just so you can pee. You listen to me now. Who you think been taking care of you so far? You in no position to negotiate. This ain't no time to be shy. You can either let me help you pee in this pot, or you can just lie there in the stink of your own piss all day long until your butt turn beet red, then Mr. Tennison most likely gonna throw you out. I ain't changing no more nappies or sheets now. It all up to you."

Custis sighed hard and grunted. His lips tightened. He jerked his head to the side, away from Mary, and lifted his splinted arms.

"Now that's what I thought. We gonna be doing this for quite some time. Might as well get used to it."

✗ ✗ ✗

Custis tried not to cry in front of anyone. But after darkness came, when he was all alone, silent tears came unfettered. Being scared is the mind falsely rigging the body. It doesn't have all the facts, so it makes up its own. Custis knew how to trick it to leave him alone. But this time was different.

The fear was so big it could fill the body of a full-grown man. The railroad tracks had been taken away. He had no way out, no passage to safety. He'd have to live in the woods all by himself. He cried for his momma. He cried to be in his own home, and sometimes he cried to die. Custis was alone, helpless, trapped inside a broken body, unable to move.

Sometimes Sarah would fall asleep in the pantry chair. She'd wake in the darkness and find Custis staring at the ceiling.

Sarah leaned on the edge of the bed and rested her head. "I know how you must feel. Empty, like everything inside of you is gone."

"Sarah. That's a nice name. Soft. It feels good to say aloud. Sarah."

"I was named after my mother. Heather Sarah Tennison. But people called her Heather, and I guess so they wouldn't get us mixed up, they called me Sarah."

"My momma's name was Miss Loraine."

Sarah pulled her chair closer. "My mother died too. I loved her more than anything I can ever remember loving. She had cancer. I prayed hard that Doc Lyman could save her with his medicine. I don't know why doctors just can't reach inside and pull it all out. Then I prayed straight to God to save her for me, a favor just between God and me. But he didn't. She died real bad."

Custis tilted his head toward Sarah. *How can someone grow up without a mother?*

"I know she went to heaven, though. She told me she could hear the angels. Said she was going to be stopping at those pearly gates. She wasn't going in, and she'd tell God she was waiting for her daughter. Her beautiful daughter." Sarah smiled. "She always said I was beautiful. But I'm not so beautiful, really."

"I think you're the prettiest girl my eyes have ever seen."

Sarah's voice abruptly changed. "You have brain damage."

Neither said a word, and then Custis giggled.

Sarah scooted in closer and looked closely at his face. "Where'd you get those eyes, anyway? I've never seen anyone like you with green eyes before."

Custis shrugged his shoulders.

"Just think about it, Custis. My momma and your momma are up there right now, probably telling each other all about the both of us." Sarah paused. "It's gonna take a long time to stop missing her. People are gonna say, 'Oh, she'll always be with us,' 'She's in our heart,' 'Time will make things all better.' I swear if one more person says, 'Time heals,' I'm going to bust them right in the mouth. Don't believe any of it. Don't be a damned fool." Sarah continued, "'God only takes the best.' 'They'll always be with us.'" Her voice turned serious. "No, they're not! She's dead, and she's never coming back. It will never be the same. I'm still trying to get used to it."

Custis could feel his eyes watering. He couldn't move his arms but no longer wanted to wipe the tears away, to hide his sorrow from this girl in front of him.

Sarah reached up and patted his eyes with cotton. "Men have tears in them too," she whispered. "It's all right to cry. You lost your momma, and there's nothing more painful for your heart to have to go through. Ever. There'll be days where you want to die too. Nobody understands.

It's the most breath-thieving sorrow on the face of this earth. My heart went with my mother, and it's never coming back. You just have to live with it. You need to try and lose yourself in something else far, far away. That's what I do. I go far, far away."

Sarah was quiet for a moment before her smile returned. "You know what we should do, Custis? We could raise herdbook shorthorn cattle. My momma was just beginning to develop the breed before she died. I know where all her plans are, up in the attic. Maybe while your legs heal, I can read them to you since you can't go far, far away just yet."

After Sarah left the room, Custis thought about far, far away. He couldn't move; his body was wrapped in splints and gauze. He thought about his books, the stories that could take him there, and Sarah. He had never had a real-life friend before—just his momma and forest animals.

x x x

Custis became more aware each day. He drank extra water and took on soup. He seemed to never forget to close his eyelids and softly say, "Thank you for this food."

Doc Lyman returned to his home but still came by just about every other day. Martin moved Custis up to Doc's reserved room at the top of the staircase. Sarah checked on him during the night and sometimes found him staring at the ceiling.

"You awake, Custis?"

His whispered voice came from the darkness. "Yes."

They'd talk for hours, usually about the ranch, horses, and dogs.

"We had chickens. I named the chicks when they hatched, but they were all yellow fuzz. I didn't know if they were boys or girls until they got older. I never had a dog before."

"My mother once told me that a person shouldn't go through life without owning a dog. Then one day she came home madder than all get-out, carrying a beat-up hound she took away from nasty ol' Mr. Teeter. She said he was the exception to the rule."

Together, Custis and Sarah planned on creating a new breed of working dog, but the shorthorn would have to come first. Then Sarah read stories aloud by candlelight, always whispery, making sure not to wake her father.

Custis didn't care what book it was if Sarah was the one reading it to him. He had never listened to someone else's voice so much. It had always been his own. When Sarah read aloud, he closed his eyes, and everything else went away. Her voice lulled him. It became his medication, easing him into another world.

Sometimes it would be Sarah who fell asleep. Custis would remain still and quietly wait until she awakened again.

"What happened to her?"

"What happened to who?"

"My momma. I mean, after she died in the fire?"

Sarah closed the book and looked at Custis. "I went to her funeral. It was so pretty—there at the church in the woods. Everyone was dressed up. All the men wore those big, tall black hats that are worn only on special occasions or by the president. And the women all wore long, flowing dresses and big, floppy bonnets. So many people there—why, I lost count, near a hundred. Surrounded by flowers of every color you could imagine. The air was full of sweet honeysuckle and jasmine. I can still smell it. The pastor said wonderful words all about her. But especially how much she loved her son. Yes. She sure must have been a wonderful woman to have such a ceremony and all."

"What about the coffin? Did you see it?"

"Did I see it? Of course. I think it must have been a special coffin."

"Was it made from loblolly pine?"

"Oh, better than that. It was covered with so many flowers I could barely even see it."

"I don't ever want to go back, Sarah. You know what you said about going far, far away? Well, that's what I want to do too. Go far, far away."

"You're with us now. You don't ever have to go back unless you want to."

Custis was quiet. His mind was grabbing on to old memories and new. "You found me in a creek." It wasn't a question so much as it was his mind mixing old memories with new. "Am I a Water-Baby in the Other-End-of-Nowhere?"

"What are you talking about?"

"It's a story by Charles Kingsley, and *you are not to believe a word of it, even if it is true.*"

"Do I need to get Doc Lyman back here to see if you're going crazy?" Sarah continued reading her book. "The lawyer rose to his feet. Free from su . . . super . . . superflu—"

"Superfluous. Is it spelled s-u-p-e-r-f-l-u-o-u-s? It's an adjective," Custis interjected, seemingly without a thought.

Sarah closed the book. "You can spell? You can read?"

"No. No. Not very well."

Martin came into the room.

"Father, he can read and spell."

Martin's eyes focused on Custis. "You can read? You go to school?"

"I'm sorry . . . I'm sorry. I don't read. I mean, I don't go to school, Mr. Tennison."

"Custis, it's all right if you read. It just surprised us, that's all."

"I'm not supposed to say anything. I'm sorry, Mr. Tennison."

"Did your mother tell you that?"

Custis nodded. He could hear Momma's voice and feel her disappointment. Custis still could not recall what had happened to him. Fragments were missing. It wasn't supposed to be this way. He could remember his house, his books, his pet chickens. He even remembered mean ol' Mrs. Herman. Why had his brain misplaced or omitted certain events?

Martin stood next to the frightened boy. "It sounds like your mother loved you deeply. I'm sure that she was only trying to safeguard you from people that believe differently. As long as you are here, with us, on this ranch, it's all right if you know how to read. No one here will hurt you. I'm so happy you know how. I've been trying to teach Mary, but she's just so stubborn. Maybe you can help me teach her, and then maybe we can get her to study up on some new recipes for us. Sarah's mother used to bake the best cherry cobbler. No one could follow that recipe like Sarah's mother."

Sarah stood next to her father. "Yeah, or maybe you can read for yourself instead of having me do it, story after story."

"No, Sarah, I love to hear you read."

"She's just being ornery with you."

"No, I'm not! It about killed my throat. And all this time, he could have been reading to his own self."

Martin smiled. "I think it's wonderful, Custis. You can come into my library and choose any book you want when you're able. Would you like that?"

"Yes, sir." Custis suddenly imagined thousands of books, hundreds of shelves, librarians, and clerks. Their photographs were still in his head. Granite stairs leading up to big mahogany double doors. He could read forever now. He wanted to tell his momma. "You have a library?"

"Yes, just down the hall."

"Your own library? In this house?"

"Yes."

"But how does a whole library fit in your house?"

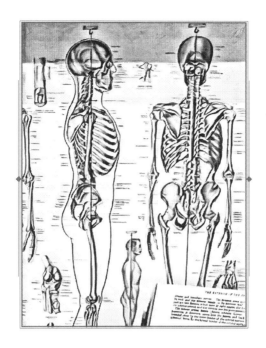

8

Mary had pushed Custis's bed next to the large bedroom window. He watched Mary hang out clothes and work in the garden. She'd check on him regularly, and he'd talk about tilling the dirt and adding ash from hardwoods. Custis explained why potassium, nitrogen, and phosphorus were necessary for her vegetables and flower gardens. He explained why dark clothes dried differently from lighter clothes. It felt good to be able to think again. But sometimes, frustration took over when he could only recall conclusions, not the foundations.

"Turn the page, please."

"How'd you learn how to read if you never went to school?" Mary asked.

"I don't really know." He recalled Mrs. Cramer but kept it to himself. "I'm still not used to . . . to people knowing."

Mary stopped what she was doing and bent down to speak. "Now, listen. Mr. Tennison is a good man, and he wants you to be happy. Believe me, I understand why sometimes you gotta hide things. But no more. Not as long as you here on the ranch."

Custis nodded. But it just didn't make sense. His mother loved him and would never lie. And Mrs. Cramer. She could have been arrested and thrown away in jail. But now, everything was different. The ranch was either a magical place or a kingdom in a faraway land with its own rules and laws.

"And why you won't shut up until Mr. Tennison or Doctor Lyman walk in?"

"I'm not supposed to look at them. It's disrespectful." He looked away. "When people see my eyes, they laugh at me. They ask questions I don't know about."

Mary hugged the boy in front of her. "No. Not no more. It's disrespectful to hide your eyes when they talking to you. You understand? In this house, we respect with kindness. And as long as you right here on this land, you can be you. Just you. You can read, and you can talk, and you can share whatever you want to share. But if you ever be bad-mannered on purpose-like, Mary going to have your little ass. You hear me? And you don't even have to read that, 'cause I'm telling you right now all about it. No disrespecting."

Custis nodded.

"And let me say this about those eyes. They are a gift from God. That beautiful green tell us that change is coming. God blended all his colors together and decided you'd be the one."

The one to what? Custis remembered seeing colors, red and white stripes, and a voice calling him names. *A circus tent poster.* He tried to recall where he had seen it. It was hanging on a fence or nailed to a door. Somewhere.

"Primary colors. They're the source of all other colors. Is that what you mean? Yellow and blue make green."

Mary shook her head.

"Sometimes, I don't know what in God's name you talkin' about. I mean, change is bound to happen to us. You the one sure to do it. That's why you gotta get better. You have lots of work to do for this world."

✗ ✗ ✗

Over the next few weeks, the swelling in Custis's face receded enough to see that his nose was severely misshapen. His eyes were clearing. Cuts were mending, and sutures were removed. Doc Lyman examined Custis's pupils.

"Your vision looks fine, reactive, but your nose is broken, Custis. You're still breathing through your mouth. I need to fix it for you. It's going to hurt," Doc Lyman said. "I'm going to have to possibly break it again to get it right."

Custis felt his chin tremble and heard his jagged exhaled breath. "My momma died, and nothing can ever hurt that much again."

"It will hurt for only a few seconds, but you need to lie still."

"Are you going to hit me in the face to break my nose again?"

"No, Custis, not at all. I'm going to gently pull upward with a probe, just for a few seconds. And as soon as I let go, it will stop hurting. Martin, you need to hold his shoulders, and Sarah, you get his legs. Hold down at his knees."

Sarah carefully lay across Custis. "It'll be all right. Just a few seconds."

Martin stood directly over Custis's head and face. He positioned his hands on the front of Custis's shoulders and waited.

Custis felt his body being held down. Rocks, and more rocks were keeping him underwater. He couldn't breathe. He opened his mouth and felt water oozing in. He looked directly upward. Martin was sweating and closed his eyes.

Doc Lyman inserted a wooden probe up the left nostril and lifted it upward. Custis's body shook and went rigid. His screams turned to a growl, seething through clenched teeth. His head pushed back into the pillow, trying to escape from the pain. As the doctor raised the probe, Custis sensed air enter his nostril. He felt the vibration of clicks and pops, alignments being made. Warm blood drizzled out.

Martin suddenly looked pale and crumpled to the floor.

Doc Lyman pulled the probe out. "All right. That looks good. It's all over now." He patted Custis's shoulder. "You have the courage of three grown men."

Custis took a deep breath, looked down to the floor, and then at Sarah. "What's your father doing on the floor?"

Doc Lyman helped Martin to his feet. "He'll be all right. He just got a little lightheaded."

Doc Lyman packed Custis's nose with tiny strips of wet cloth so tightly, it felt as if the material had entered his brain. "This will keep everything in place. I'll remove it in four or five days." Doc Lyman finished the examination. "Well, everything else looks good. Is there anything that still bothers you, Custis?"

"Well, I was just wondering if only my radius bones are broken and not my ulna, too. I was thinking that if we shorten the splints to my elbows, I can turn pages." Custis stopped and glanced at Doc Lyman. "And Mary won't have to help me pee."

Doc Lyman smiled. "How do you know about radius and ulna bones?"

"I heard you talking." Custis deflected his eyes. "I read about them. Sarah showed me a book about human anatomy while she read a book about equine structure."

"Let's see what we can do."

Doc Lyman fashioned new splints and checked his upper arm. "Do you know what these bones are called?"

"That's the humerus. Not funny, but that's what the bone is called, h-u-m-e-r-u-s. It's surrounded by the deltoideus, brachii, and radialis muscles."

"Let's look at that ankle. So, you like Shakespeare, I hear." Doc Lyman unwrapped his leg. "Quite the writer, Shakespeare."

Custis nodded. "Sometimes I have to read his words twice to get them in order in my head. Do you think the ligaments are torn, or is it a lateral or medial malleolus break?"

Doc Lyman stopped and looked over his glasses at Custis.

"I read about them too."

"What else do you know, Custis?"

"What do you mean?"

"What else do you like reading about?"

"I read stories. But I like to read about math and chemistry the best. I like the way things move. Atoms. They're free and can go anywhere. All matter is made up of atoms, constantly moving. Your eyes can't see them, but they're there. Someday I'm going to be a scientist. I hope I can still be a scientist with brain damage and all. Sometimes I don't feel any different than before."

"You don't seem to have any brain damage, Custis. Have you gone to school?"

Custis lowered his head. "No. No schools for me, just for others."

"Do you have any other family? I mean, besides your mother?"

"No."

"What about your daddy?"

"Momma never told me."

"All right, Custis. You're doing real fine. Pretty soon we'll get you walking around. In the meantime, start trying to lift your legs and build up your muscle strength."

"I already started, Doctor Lyman."

Doc Lyman walked downstairs and found Martin in the library.

"Sorry, Doc. His scream just went right through me."

"You've been dealing with a lot. Just take it easy for a while. Sarah's voice is progressing. She's going to be just fine."

"I couldn't be happier about that, Doc. It's so good to hear her again. But her voice is only the symptom, not the cause. I was able to finally tell her what happened to me when Heather died. I made a horrible mistake by keeping it from her."

"You're doing fine, Martin. You had to fix yourself first. Otherwise, you can't take care of anyone else."

Martin nodded.

"Custis is doing remarkably well too. He's putting on some weight." Doc Lyman sat down on the couch. "He is very smart, Martin. He's what we call a polymath. Knows a lot about—just about everything."

"You mean a genius?"

"Well, yes. He could be a wonderful doctor if he had the right schooling. Said he wants to be a scientist."

"That's not going to happen, I'm afraid. No schools here for him."

"There are schools in the North that will accept him. Colleges . . . I mean eventually."

"I can't bring myself to send him away to boarding school up North after what he's been through. He'd feel abandoned all over again."

"You know, there's no prerequisite of schooling for universities. It's an entrance examination and sometimes just an interview if you have the right connections. I can help get all the books he'll need. There's Wilson Place College for Negros in Ohio, but they are limited. Mostly law and teaching—some science, but limited."

Martin rubbed his face and held on to where his beard might be if he had one. "He's that smart?"

"Yes. He's exceptional."

"He's Sarah's age. Another six or seven years of schooling, and then he'd be old enough to fit in at that level?"

"Even at that, maybe sooner. But give it some thought. It will be a major commitment for you, a life-changing decision for him. Leave him here to wither away or send him north.

"You can't hide him forever, Martin. He needs to go to school. He has a purpose here on this earth. Look what he's already done for you and Sarah."

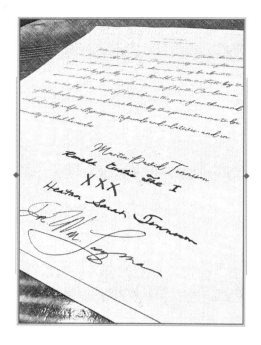

2

Before sunrise, when the household was still asleep, Custis made his way down the stairs as quietly as he could. He gripped the banister with one hand and his crutch in the other. At the kitchen table, he sat in the darkness, waiting for Mary. On cold mornings, he'd start the fire in the stove. The soft moving glow and the pop of the kindling served as her warning so she wouldn't startle.

She made breakfast and watched Custis eat. "You eat just like my boys. Everything in sight."

Just as the sun began to rise, Martin walked in and asked for a cup of coffee.

"Mr. Tennison, I'm so sorry. I got to talkin' with this child, and time just went away from me."

"It's all right, Mary. I'm a little early this morning."

"Custis, what do you think about going to school someday? I mean, not right now, but someday when you get a little older?"

"You mean a university?"

"Yes, Sarah will be going to school right here in Carolina." Martin leaned against the kitchen sink. "There are schools in the North. In Ohio. I've been reading about it. Wilson Place College. You will be welcomed in a few years. You can study your science. Doc said you could be a great physician someday."

Custis was silent. *Wilson Place College. A real school? In the North?* Custis recalled seeing college photographs that showed men, Black men, wearing dark suits and white ties, stiffly sitting in front of shelves plumped full of thick, leather-bound books. Stoic faces and scholarly eyes staring off into the distance, solving great mathematical theories, laws of physics, and medical quandaries. *And in the North.* A place his mother had spoken about.

Martin set his cup on the table and crossed his arms in front. "Wilson Place is a fine school. You'll be old enough in a few years."

"Well, I've been thinking."

"Yes?"

"You always thinking and talking," Mary butted in.

"I'll need a necktie. Everyone that goes to college wears a tie."

"You can have one of my ties."

"I'll still need something else. I don't have three names. You have to have a tie, and you gotta have three names."

"All right, then. If you had a chance to pick your own name, what would it be?"

Sarah walked into the kitchen, sleep still in her eyes and her hair uncombed. "I like Custis Fenimore Cooper." She plopped down at the table.

"My daddy's name was Cornelius," Mary said.

"Custis Cooper Cornelius. My tongue gets messed up." He leaned back in his chair. It was an important decision. If he was going to add to his name, he'd do it in honor of his mother. He remembered her words. *You may be smart, son, but I be wise. And there a big difference. You may know all your ciphers and words, but I know the ways of this world.* "Ronald." It was a name he had once read in a book, an Old Norse name that meant being a wise ruler.

"Ronald? Who on this earth is named Ronald?" Sarah asked.

"Well, Ronald Custis. I'm gonna be the first famous Ronald. A famous scientist. Ronald Custis."

"That's only two names."

"Ronald Custis the First. There, four rightly surnames. But I'll have to have proper papers to make it official."

"Well, that's it then, Custis. Everyone, meet in the library at noon. Doc Lyman will be here by then too."

Everyone went their separate ways and started their day except for Custis. He wrote down his new name, looked at it, and placed the paper into his pocket. *Why didn't Momma give me more names?* Miss Loraine and Custis. That's all he had, just words now.

Just before noon, they all gathered in the library. Martin had changed into a coat and tie. Doc Lyman was already in his. Mary had put on a fresh dress. Sarah was in her boots and riding britches but managed to wear a new straw hat.

Martin handed Custis a black necktie. "Here, put your tie on."

Mary helped with the tie, then patted his chest. "You look just like my Chester on Sunday morning."

Martin stood behind his desk. "All right, everyone, come to order now. Stand right here in front. Custis, you stand right here and raise your right hand."

Custis stood tall. It was the first time he had ever worn a necktie. It looked just like the ones sold in town.

Martin held an official-looking piece of paper. "It has recently come to my attention that one 'Custis,' known to be an eleven-year-old male, born on August 26, 1865, is without a proper name. So, whomsoever it is about to concern, I hereby officially name you Ronald Custis the First, by the power entrusted to me by the people in the state of North Carolina on this 30th day in the month of November in the year of 1876, and is now known by this present name to be used exclusively and for all purposes, to friends and relatives, and in the community in which he resides." Martin sat down at his desk, placed the document before him, and signed the bottom.

"Mr. Custis, you need to sign right here, stating all the information contained in this document is in accordance with facts or truths to your knowledge."

Mary had tears in her eyes.

Doc Lyman shook Custis's hand.

Sarah grunted. "I am not calling you Ronald."

Custis signed the certificate along with Sarah, Mary, and Doc Lyman as the witnesses. Martin hallmarked the document with three inked stamps. "It's official."

Custis held the certificate in his hands. That small piece of paper had the capacity to transform the world—just like his books and railroad tracks.

10

Some say that Carolina in the spring is God's way of using every tint of green the human eye can possibly visualize. A kaleidoscope of emerald, hues unnamed, tossed down with abandon, then faultlessly settling into perfect place. Eastertime slipped in easily among all things newborn. Buds swelled, others in whole leaf, and new growth abounded as mountain air carried the fragrances of daffodil, magnolia, and hyacinth. Spring rains fell from woolen gray skies, only later to be resolved into summer's sultry evenings.

Pasture grass, deep and tender, surrounded the estate. After almost a year, Custis no longer used a crutch. His limp was waning but always managed to return when he was tired. When he couldn't sleep at night, Custis snuck outside into the barn. He made his rounds, checking the status of newly hatched chicks and a newborn colt he had named Thunder.

The stable was outfitted with stalls for at least eighteen horses—nine stalls on either side, meticulously clean and organized. The horses were mainly working quarter horses, six feisty thoroughbreds, and three Tennessee Walkers standing at seventeen hands. Custis walked down the dimly lit hall accompanied by Hatchet, the barn cat. Horses alternately nickered, maybe saying good morning but most likely prodding for a treat, each one getting a handful of oats, a pat on its head, and a rub on the cheek. This was his poem now, a new life and animals to care for.

Custis had made friends with the chickens, watched the dog have puppies, learned to stay clear of the thoroughbreds, and helped design a furrow irrigation system for the lower pasture. But most of all, he liked when Sarah rode her horse. He'd walk along beside Stardust with Sarah riding bareback. Occasionally, he'd grab the lead rope and hold on just so he could be closer. They'd be gone for hours, exploring the four corners of the estate where soft rolling hills touched the bottom of the sky.

"Custis, you're being stupid. You can ride up here with me. We could travel so much faster."

"I like to walk."

"I know what's going on. It doesn't matter out here. No one is here except you and me."

"It's just not right, Sarah. Your daddy gave me these shoes to walk, that's what he meant by it, and that's exactly what I'm gonna do."

"My daddy bought you those shoes because you didn't have any."

"There's nothing to hold on to up there, Sarah, except you. I'm not allowed to touch White people."

"They said you can't learn to read or write or go to school, and you're doing that."

"You don't know what it's like."

Sarah was quiet. She lightly pulled on Stardust's reins until the horse slowed. Sarah looked down at Custis. "Who made up those rules anyway?"

Custis didn't answer.

"I've heard what they say—the kids at school, the people in town. I see how they treat coloreds. They broke Buster's leg once. Father had to go get him from jail. The sheriff said he didn't do anything wrong but had to put him in jail for his own protection. If you don't want to ride up here with me, it's all right. But I'm gonna ask Father if you can have your own horse. You can't walk fast enough."

"I've never ridden a horse before."

He could never quite tell Sarah he was afraid. Sarah was so perfect. She knew how to do everything. Someday he would too ... just not right now.

They crossed over a set of train tracks. Sarah stopped Stardust. They straddled the rails. Sarah looked down the lines each way. The overhanging trees transformed into lush green tunnels, a waning passageway consuming the steel. Sarah leg-nudged Stardust and reined her down between the rails.

"Where do you think they go, Sarah?"

"This way, all the way to New York City. Sometimes Father goes for work. When he comes back, he always says he's so happy to get home, where the air is clean and where the nights are asleep like they're supposed to be."

"Is that where far, far away is?"

"No. My far, far away is different. It's a place where there are no other people unless you permit them to be there. It's a place where sometimes I want to stay forever. I see my mother there. She talks to me and tells me things I need to know. Things about life. We laugh all the time. She tells me the best stories about when she was a little girl and about me when I was small. And I tell her things about me, too. She already knows all about them, but I think she just likes to listen. We walk together. She's not sick anymore. She's the prettiest woman I've ever seen. I tell her I want to stay, but she always says my father needs me. So I always go back home."

"You must look just like her, Sarah."

Custis looked down at the sleeper timbers. Out of habit, he began to count them silently. Each one perfectly placed, measured, leveled, and set. He imagined being inside a passenger train. Was it smooth, or did it lug along like Stardust's gait? Was it as loud inside the car as outside? Was the sound muffled, or was the train so fast that it outran the sound? How fast would something have to travel to outrun its own sound?

The tracks wandered through the trees and traversed onto an elevated berm. The ground below on either side looked soft with flowing grass. Marshy in places, plugs of cattails and sedge dotted the bottom of the berm below.

Sarah looked out into the distance. "Have you ever seen the ocean? The waves?"

"No. Not with my eyes. I've read about it. Sir Isaac Newton. Gravity creates the tides, and wind makes the waves. Can you imagine that? The moon, way up there, has enough power to control the ocean, way down here."

A quiet stillness surrounded them.

"I could stand before the ocean for about a million years. Once you see the ocean, you'll never forget it. The sound, the smells. Mist on your face. Every time I go back, the waves are still there, welcoming me. They'll never disappear. You just know the sea with all her glory will be there, waiting."

"That's called faith."

"My mother is like that. I mean, the thoughts in my head. She never goes away. She comes to me, always—over and over and over again, just like the waves. No matter what I do, she's always there, waiting, forgiving, washing everything away. That's her promise, just like the waves. She's my gravity."

"Someday, I'm gonna find the rails that take us both there, to the ocean. We'll both go far, far away."

Stardust shuddered as if trying to dislodge a pesky fly from her back. Custis grabbed the lead and reached up to brace Sarah. She laughed at her unplanned near-tumble and patted Stardust on her neck. Custis abruptly retracted his arm and placed it behind his back.

"I thought you were going to fall!"

"She was just shaking off the dust."

"No, she was shaking *you* off!"

"She loves me. Maybe she's allergic to you. Are you afraid of horses or something?"

"No."

"You are too. How can you be afraid when you help James all the time with the grooming and long ropes?"

"There's a difference between working them and riding them."

"Stardust isn't like the others. I've had her since she was a little filly. Father gave her to me when Momma died. He was the one that named her Stardust. Dust from heaven, where Momma lives. He was trying to make me feel better, but I was so mean to him."

"We better get back. We'll stop at the river and give her a drink."

As Custis walked, balancing himself on the rail, Stardust abruptly stopped. Her hoof was lodged between the rail and a loose iron spike.

Sarah jumped down and held on to the reins. She looked down and tried to get the horse to move. "Her hoof is caught. Help me push her back."

Custis stood in front and pushed on Stardust's head. "Back up, girl, easy, go on."

Stardust moved her body, but her front leg stayed extended. The horse stiffened.

"Can you pull out the spike, Cus? I can't get her to budge."

Custis bent down next to the horse. The spike was loose but wouldn't come out. "No, it's in there. Shove her. It's the only way."

"She's too scared now. She's gonna twist her leg. Her leg's gonna break. We need to keep her calm."

Custis looked at the hoof again. "It looks like it's her shoe that's stuck, not her hoof. We need to take the shoe off."

"I don't think we can. We don't have any tools."

Custis had watched the farrier work many times. *It shouldn't be difficult.* He gripped the fetlock and pushed back on the horse's knee. Custis rested his left hand on the steel rail, then grabbed it with both hands. He felt vibration.

Custis sensed panic swelling inside. He wanted it to be only his imagination, but his brain said otherwise. He was too experienced with the tracks. His focus narrowed. He tried to hide his emotion, but that was only a temporary solution. If he allowed his fear to take over now, he'd become weak, and he would fail. He didn't want to tell Sarah. She'd be terrified. "Hold on to her."

The track was still clear.

Custis slid down the berm and grabbed two rocks, one flat and the other round. He scrambled back up and looked down the track each way. He hammered one rock into the other against the front of the trapped shoe. Stardust threw her head back and pulled at the reins. She would break her leg for sure. Custis hit again and again. The sound of the rocks striking together—he'd heard it before. In the creek—darkness, pain, rocks being tossed on top of his body.

A low rumbling sounded from the distance. Sarah stood up straight. She looked down the line, then back down at Custis. "It's coming, a train, hurry. Hurry."

Custis wanted to look up, but he'd lose his concentration. Another blow, then another. The train emerged from the distance. Its horn boomed in blasts of three, the sound coming closer and closer. Custis beat at the front of the horseshoe as he screamed at Sarah.

"Get off the tracks! Sarah, get back!"

Stardust jerked back. Now the horn was one solid, continuous blare. He could no longer hear his own voice. The horse attempted to rear. Custis looked up. Sarah was frozen. He rushed at Sarah and pushed her backward, down the berm. He turned and grabbed the reins.

The train moved with thundering vibrations. Sarah screamed, but the train had won. She stood up, all alone. The freight train continued with its speed—clanking, clanking, clanking.

The last car, followed by the caboose, passed. Sarah was still screaming. She crawled up the embankment on her hands and knees, slipping on the grass but regaining herself each time.

"No! Please, God, no!" Sarah cried out as she pulled on clumps of grass. "This isn't supposed to happen!" Sarah reached the top, stood up, and sprang across the tracks. Stardust was far out in the meadow, nervously prancing at the tree line.

Custis was on his back in the deep grass. Sarah erupted in tears and slid down the berm. She fell on top of him, sobbing and hugging his neck. "You're my best friend. I thought you were dead. I was all alone again. You're my best friend."

Custis felt Sarah's weight on top of him. It was real. He would be safe—they were all alone. The tall grasses would conceal the contact anyway. He felt the horror of the train leaving his body as Sarah cried. He hugged back and felt her tangled hair against him. "You're my best friend too." Custis had never seen her cry before. *She must be so scared.* So was he. "We better get back home."

"Let's get to the river first and get washed up. We can't let Father know what happened. He'd be so afraid."

x x x

The riverbank, full of bending greenery, gave way to a rocky beach where the river ran shallow. White, lacy threads of water weaving between smooth, round rock led farther out to the deeper side. Sarah bent down, cupped her hands, and drank. She washed Stardust's front legs in the cool water. "Look, Custis, her shoe is gone. She pulled right out of it. Thank you for saving her." Sarah's straw hat fell forward, landing on the water's surface.

"My hat!"

"I'll get it." Custis stepped into the creek. The ripples pushed it out farther, with Custis following. The hat weaved and bobbed, floating with the current. Custis jumped from rock to rock, hopscotching down the stream, trying not to fall, his arms out for balance as he quickly surveyed the next best route. Custis slipped. He landed on his butt in shin-deep water.

Sarah laughed hysterically.

Custis slapped the surface with his hands. The creek was cold, he was drenched, and his butt hurt. But there was nothing he liked more than when Sarah laughed. It was the kind of laugh that was genuine, the type that caused her head to go back and close her eyes. The kind that made him laugh right along with her.

Custis stood, refocused, and jumped after the hat. It gained speed and entered deeper water. He was up to his knees, then his waist.

"Do you know how to swim? Custis!"

Custis lost his balance. He fell neck-deep and screamed out for help. His head dipped under the surface, bobbing up then down again, his arms flailing about, slapping the water. "Hellllppp! Sarah, help me!"

Sarah sprang to the river's edge, running over slippery rock, her eyes fixed on Custis. The water deepened and was over the top of her riding boots. She stumbled and slipped. Sarah reached out to him, then dove into the water. Her head surfaced, arms stretched out as far as she could. "Custis, grab my hand, grab my hand!"

Custis stood to his feet, the water now up to his chest. He was laughing so hard he might fall again. "Of course I know how to swim!"

Sarah stopped, her neck just above the surface. "You're an ass!" She turned back to the shore. After a few strokes, she was able to stand up. "A damned idiot ass!"

Still laughing, Custis swam down toward the hat. The river turned deep, and he effortlessly glided with the current. "I got it. I got it. Wait for me!"

Sarah grabbed Stardust's reins and pulled herself up. Her wet clothing looked cumbersome as she threw her leg over Stardust as a stream of water arched over the horse's back. She looked at Custis. He was hastily trying to get back to shore. "Serves you right! Find your own damn way home." She turned her horse and rode away.

By the time Custis reached shore, he had been taken downriver by the current a good distance. His muscles were exhausted, and it almost felt easier to be in the water. He lay on his back, catching his breath. He closed his eyes and let the sun warm his skin.

A voice came from the distance. Custis knew Sarah wouldn't leave him. He smiled, rolled to his stomach, and rose to his knees. Three men were walking directly at him. No, not men. Three boys: Lucius, Emmert, and Bradford.

11

Custis's world went quiet. It had gone back to the circus poster, reading aloud, the attack, and running away. He remembered that shadowy night, the wind through the cracks of the door, conveying the wickedness to come. He recalled everything. The chickens. The lantern. Running in the darkness. He remembered the pain. He remembered the look on Lucius's face, his hands around his neck, squeezing out the last breath of air. He remembered the heaviness, the rocks enshrouding his body.

This time they would kill him. He could no longer run away. But strangely, Custis felt a calmness come over him. Maybe it was angels lingering. Perhaps it was the devil, a monster laughing and lying in wait. He had read about this type of reaction. He was no longer using the ancient part of his brain. The tunnel vision was gone. Custis triangulated his thoughts.

He had survived death once and tasted a whisper of what life could be. His education was waiting. This life was more than what he ever had. Dreams were going to come true. He had come so far. Thoughts of Sarah burst through his mind. She was on her way home and would be safe. She loved him. She had nearly said so. They were best friends. No one would ever be allowed to take that away. Certainly not these heathens—the heathens responsible for his momma's death. Custis felt the oxygen filling his lungs, strength reaching deep into his muscles. He would stand and fight. Now, he would be both angel and monster. Custis rose to his feet and kept his arms at his side. Each hand clutched a river rock.

The delinquents were thirty feet away. Lucius dropped his fishing pole. Bradford stopped dead. Emmert looked stunned and nervously laughed. "He's alive! Must have nine lives after all."

Emmert removed the creel from around his waist, dropped it to the ground, and walked forward. Custis didn't move. The other two followed and tightened the gap between them.

"You ain't gonna run this time? You just gonna stand there and let us kill you?"

"He so scared, he can't move."

They stopped fifteen feet away.

Custis was quiet as he evaluated each boy. His mind factored in position, weight, motion, behavior, energy, and force. "I'm not going to run anymore."

Custis slowly bent his elbows, raised his hands, and held the rocks out in front of him. Their wetness shimmered in the sunlight. His hypnotic green eyes studied each boy. He imagined the rocks becoming an extension of his arms.

"I am going to smash these into one of your heads, crack open your skull until I can see your greasy brains splattering out. It may be a blow to your frontal lobe, but it is pretty hard, that part of the skull. Maybe to your temporal, right above your ear where the bone is soft, you know, like a softshell crawdad. It will only take one second—just one blink. If you look at me just right, I can slam it into your face, breaking your eye sockets, smashing shards of broken bone from your nose right up into your brain. I just need one of you. Just one. Then I can die. Just one, then you can kill me. Bradford? Will it be you? All I need is just one shot. Lucius?"

Emmert pushed the others away. "Spread out."

Bradford picked up a large rock. Custis evaluated its mass. Too heavy to throw. Lucius grabbed several smaller stones. They would hurt if hurled but not turn deadly. Emmert was the main nemesis. Custis chose him.

Custis glared at Emmert and envisioned brain matter oozing from his shattered skull. Emmert still held his fishing pole. He gripped it and took one slow step forward—his eyes fixed, his hands tight.

Custis evaluated the pole. *Six feet, made from cottonwood rather than hardwoods of maple, hickory, or ironwood. If it's old, it will snap with the first blow. If fresh, it will bend and warp.* Emmert changed his grip and held the pole like a medieval lance.

"I'm gonna ram this right through your gut and watch you die slowly."

Next would be the charge. *The pole will reach first. Need to deflect. My hands must hold the rock. Step off the track as the train approaches. Turn and let it bypass. Redirect.* Custis felt a rumbling in the ground.

The sound of four hooves colliding with earth. *Dig-ah-dig, dig-ah-dig, dig-ah-dig.*

A horse and rider burst between the two, knocking the pole from Emmert's grip. Just as suddenly, the horse turned and hit Emmert dead center. A hollow thud, then an airless grunt. Emmert's body was tossed backward and landed flat on the ground. The horse spun around. Its flank knocked into Lucius with force to fling him five feet away. The bridled neck hooked around Bradford, wrenching him inward into the spiral, then bashing him to the ground. Hooves lifted high and came crashing down on his legs. Bradford screamed out. The horse reared and whinnied as Emmert charged. A rear hoof landed on Emmert's face. Blood and teeth splattered outward.

An arm reached down and grabbed Custis's shoulder. Sarah pulled him tight against the horse and began to lift and drag him away. He couldn't get on. His legs slipped.

Sarah screamed, "Get on, get on," but there was nothing to grab.

The horse circled tightly, stepping on Lucius as he tried to crawl away. Sarah pulled Custis's arm as he made one last attempt. Custis jumped and clutched Sarah's waist. She leaned back in the opposite direction, trying not to fall. He swung his leg over the horse's rump and pulled himself up. His arms were around Sarah's waist, his chest tightly against her back. They were in a fight for their lives, and he wasn't about to let go.

She kicked the horse, turned the reins, and yelled, "Go, go!"

Stardust took off with the speed of a warhorse. Custis didn't let go of Sarah until they reached the barn. Sarah took Stardust into the stall. Custis followed with a bucket of water.

"I remember everything, Sarah. When I saw them coming at me again, everything came back. They tried to kill me. They're the ones that buried me in the creek. They came to my house. Chased me into the woods. I wanted them to follow me to get them away from my house. They killed my mother. I should have warned her. She died because of me. I should have never left her alone." The guilt was crippling, far worse than any injury he had ever bore.

"*They* killed her, not you. We have to think about what we need to do now. We just have to think." Sarah quickly curried Stardust as Custis held the bucket out with both hands.

Stardust drank with vigor. Custis's forehead rested on her forelock. She had acted more magnificently than any horse he had ever seen or read about.

Custis closed his eyes. "Thank you, girl. You are so brave." Tears pooled in his eyes. He squeezed his eyes closed and cried.

"We have to tell Father. There's no other way. It's only going to get worse. They might know who I am."

Custis backed up to the wall and slid to the ground. He was surprised at the weakness of his leg muscles. He had felt brave at the river, but now his hands trembled. His primal sense of hypervigilance now had turned to weariness—an equal but opposite reaction.

Sarah sat down next to him as Stardust moved in closer, as if to offer protection. "I'll stay right here with you. And when you're ready, we'll go tell Father together."

Custis wept easily and leaned into Sarah. "I should have told my mother. It's because of me that she died. I need to leave the ranch before something happens to you. They'll burn this place down too."

"You're not going anywhere. Father will protect us."

"It's not safe here anymore."

Sarah placed her head on Custis's shoulder. She let him cry. "Please don't go away. I hope you stay and live here a long, long time because my heart really likes you."

"You're my best friend and all of me really likes you."

By the time Sarah and Custis entered the house, it was early evening. They found Sarah's father in his library.

"I was wondering when you'd come in." He looked at their clothing, both disheveled. Martin closed the book and uncrossed his legs. "What's wrong?"

"Father, we know who did it."

"Did what?"

Custis broke in. "I remember who buried me. They must have started the fire, too. They killed my mother. I should never have run away."

Martin stood up, called out for Mary, and took both children into his arms. "Are you two all right?" His voice was shaking.

"They tried to kill him again, Father. They were down at the river near the pond."

Mary came into the room. Custis boldly spoke up. "Sarah stopped them. She and Stardust. Then we rode as fast as we could back here."

"Who are they? Who are you talking about?"

"Emmett and Bradford McReynolds and Lucius."

Mary shook her head. "Those three are hoodlums—nothing but trouble, Mr. Tennison. Just because they attend church on Sundays, school on some days, they up to no good on most days. Lucius's daddy owns the livery. He's a hateful man too. I hear all about them. I know the good Lord says there'll be no judging, but he also says there'll be no hatin' or killin' or stealin', and they all been doing that, and that's all up higher on the list than just plain judgin'."

"Do you know the boys, Sarah? Did they recognize you?"

"I've seen them before. They trespass down the river. I'm not sure if they know me, exactly."

"Where are the boys now?"

"We left them at the pond."

Martin looked directly at his daughter. "Did you hit them?"

"Just as hard as I could."

Martin's eyes widened.

"I don't think they're dead, but they're hurt pretty good. Stardust kicked one in the face."

Martin walked behind his desk and took his hat from the hook. "Where at the pond?"

"This side, near the river's east bend. Right near the ironwood grove," Sarah said.

"Mary, will you help get these two cleaned up? Get some food in them. Then I need to hear everything that happened when I get back."

"Where are you going?" Sarah asked.

"I need to ride out and make sure they're not dead or dying. You, miss, stay put!"

"But you can't go by yourself. What if something happens to you?"

"Nothing is going to happen to me. Sarah, you stay home." He pointed at Custis. "You too, hear me?"

"I will. I didn't mean to cause all this."

Martin sounded mad. "You didn't, Custis. I've heard about them before this." Martin's movements were quick as he put on his hat and removed a holstered revolver from his desk. "I've dealt with one of their fathers in town. Unexpected wagon repair. I didn't much care for him then. Appears he's handed down his meanness to his son. Mary, lock the doors after I leave. I'll tell Buster and the men to stay close."

✗ ✗ ✗

Long after Sarah had fallen asleep, Custis slipped out of his room, sat on the staircase in the darkness, and waited. Martin returned well into the night. Custis heard the squeak of the back door and quietly walked toward the kitchen. The light was dim. Mary was asleep at the table. From the darkness, Custis watched Martin wake Mary.

"Where are the children?" Martin asked.

"I made them go to bed, Mr. Tennison. You find those boys?"

"No, but I found where they had been. There was a good amount of blood. It looked like a wagon had been there, too. Obviously all of them got out."

Martin placed Sarah's hat on the table. It was crushed and covered in dry mud. "I found this."

Mary touched the ragged brim. "It's ruined."

"I don't want you going into town for anything until we figure some things out. In fact, no one will leave the ranch. Sarah and Custis will stay within yelling distance until I say so. Everyone in town knows who lives and works out here. Last time, they would have strung up Buster had it not been for the sheriff. And Sarah's been in town with me too many times for those three boys not to know who she is. This is not going to end well. We're far too outnumbered."

"I'll try to keep the children busy. They must be so scared."

"They got shook up pretty good. Go to bed and get some sleep, Mary. I may need your help in the morning."

Custis turned and went up the staircase as quietly as he could. He closed himself in his room and pulled a blanket from his bed. He lay in the corner, covered himself tightly, and enfolded his arms around his knees.

12

Before the ranch awoke, Martin slipped outside and stowed away a loaded shotgun and rifle in the horse barn. The revolver concealed in the back of his waistband was cumbersome. He dawdled with the front fencing, managed various repairs, and cleaned out stalls—work generally completed by the hired hands. Frequently looking outward, Martin meandered in the front pastures, loitered with the horses, and busied himself chopping wood. In the evening he sat by the front window inside the house, his foot nervously tapping. He had six souls to protect—three on the inside the house and three on the outside.

The following day, hours before sunrise, Martin watched Custis sneak out of the house and slip into the barn. Martin remained in the dark, in front of the window, waiting for daylight with a rifle across his lap.

Custis had made himself a bed in the hay. Hatchet was safely tucked in and seemed offended by Martin's early morning intrusion. Martin left the boy alone and busied himself elsewhere until Custis woke up on his own.

"You sleep out here all the time?"

"Mostly. Am I in trouble?"

"No, but for a while, I want you to stay in the house. I need to know where you are. You like staying out here better than inside?"

"I like talking to the animals, making sure they're all right. I read to them and make them fall asleep. I like waking up when it's dark and hearing the horses whispering to one another. I like the smell of alfalfa and oat hay. It makes me happy."

"Sometimes, when I can't figure things out, when my mind won't rest, I come out here too. I check on the horses, brush them down whether they need it or not. Just touching them makes me feel genuine. I suppose through their instinct, they understand. They communicate back to me. They give me the peace to clear my head. A long time ago, every now and then I'd find Sarah's momma out here, all by herself. That's when I knew she was unsettled or that I was in trouble for doing or not doing something."

Custis listened quietly and nodded his head. "Out here, I can think of other things I can do. Things to make and build."

"Yes, a good distraction." Martin's voice was calm and reassuring. "You know, we may hear from those boys, maybe others. Grown men can do strange things when their mind is broke. Usually, things like this come to a head, then folks go back to their own life. We have lots of people looking after us. We can call for the sheriff if need be. And Mary. Why, she's like a mountain lion when someone gets her riled up.

Pity the fool that takes her on. I'm not going to let anything happen to you."

"I can go away, Mr. Tennison. It's me they're after. Sarah didn't mean to hurt anyone. She was trying to save me."

"We don't want you to go away, Custis. You're a part of our family now. The Tennisons stick together and take care of one another. That's exactly what Sarah did. We will get through this and come out just fine, but only if we stay together."

Hatchet wrapped himself around Custis's legs.

"See, even Hatchet wants you to stay. Maybe you could be a veterinarian someday."

"Yes, sir. But I am going to be a scientist."

"Yes, you are. You know, Sarah's mom once experimented with alfalfa seeds. She also had her own demonstration fields, right here on the ranch. She was working on a new breed of cattle, too. I guess she also was a scientist."

"I read about a new type of dog from Scotland. That's way on the other side of the world but in a higher latitude than us. It's black and white and herds in the sheep all by themselves. Faster than the sheepherders can. We could start a breed of our own to bring in all the cattle and horses."

Yes, a distraction. Maybe more relevance to keep him from running away. Martin smiled and let Custis ramble.

"And I was thinking about the old gristmill. If we could take the wheel, move it here near the stables, and use it horizontally, we could tie the thoroughbreds to it and walk them mechanically. But then we'd need a water raceway to create the energy to turn it. So then I thought, to eliminate the water, we could make a steel tower with radiating arms off a central pivot point. At the end of each arm component, a short rope would connect to the horse's halter. It would take two horses to balance out opposite sides and turn on its own horsepower. We could design it so the horses would have to walk in a circular alley. Not be able to turn around on their own. That way, they could walk themselves. We could call it the 'therapeutic walker.'"

"Maybe you're going to be an inventor of great triumphs."

"No. I already have my tie. I want to go to college and be a scientist. I think about it all the time."

"You will make a fine scientist. Get on into the house, clean up, and before you save all humankind, get some breakfast." Martin watched Custis jog toward the house. He cupped his mouth and yelled, "Then we'll work on that therapeutic walker."

x x x

Martin watched a horse and buggy coming up the lane. He stood at the open barn door, the shotgun at his side. Buster was across the lane replacing damaged boards in the horse runs. Martin whistled at him and motioned with his head. *Only one buggy, not even stirring up the dust.* As the rig approached the barnyard, Martin was relieved to see Doc Lyman and waved Buster off. He placed the shotgun back inside the barn and met Doc with a handshake. "Can you stay for supper?"

"Of course I can. It's Friday. You think I'd miss out on Mary's beans and cornbread?"

"What brings you out, Doc?"

"I had to call on three young boys. Live over on the other side of town."

Martin was quiet. The boys must be alive. Alive enough to identify Sarah and Custis.

"The boys were pretty bad. The worst one had his front teeth knocked out, broken nose, a concussion. Out of the other two, one has a broken leg, the other has busted ribs. They said a girl on a horse would've liked to have killed them all. Said she was with a boy, a Black boy with green eyes. They said the girl was Sarah."

Martin lowered his head. "It's true. Those were the boys that hurt Custis last year. Sarah and Custis were out riding and ran into them at the river three days ago. They were going to kill him for sure this time. Sarah did what she had to do to stop it."

"Sarah and Custis all right?"

"You know Sarah—she's tough on the outside but so tender on the inside. Custis is all right, still kind of shaken. Found him sleeping in the barn this morning. Guess he's been doing it for a while."

"Talk is that people are real upset. Lucius is Thomas Ewald's kid. He's getting that part of town all riled up."

"We'll send for the sheriff, but he's going to be outnumbered. Half the town might turn into a wild mob. This isn't the first time the Ewalds have been tangled up in something like this. You can't stop such hatred."

"Martin, I'm afraid the sheriff is already involved. He showed up at my office. Asked what I knew. I didn't lie to him. I said you may need help out here. He's just one man. Seems like he'd be on the right side of the fence, though."

Buster rushed up to Doc Lyman's rig. "We got a rider coming up fast, Mr. Tennison. Real fast."

Martin moved with precision, grabbed the shotgun, and tossed it to Buster. "Doc, get inside the barn," he ordered as he pulled the revolver from his waistband and held it down at his side.

Buster released the safety and stood next to Martin. "Mr. Tennison, I swear that looks like James's boy, riding like the dickens."

The rider dismounted before the horse was fully stopped.

Buster relaxed his stance and stepped toward the rider. "Charlie, what the blessed heck is wrong with you?"

Charlie's face was moist with sweat. He leaned forward and breathed in as best he could. "There's talk in town. Everyone all upset and gathering around. Talk of a lynching of a colored boy. They're coming out here, Mr. Tennison."

Martin returned the revolver to his waist. "How many?"

"I don't know for sure. All I know is that I had to get out here and tell you."

"It's all right, Charlie. I appreciate you rushing out. We'll have to handle what comes to us. Get that horse in the barn and water him down."

Doc Lyman uncovered a shotgun from inside his rig, broke it open, and rested it in the crook of his arm. He walked over to Charlie, handed him the gun along with a fistful of shells, and walked back over to Martin. "You know, you could send Custis and Mary away. Send Sarah up to her aunt in Virginia, just for a while, till everything passes."

"According to Charlie, they're coming today. If we can get through to tomorrow, I'll do just that. I never wanted to teach my children to run. It goes against my grain, but I can't be sure I can protect her against what might show up."

"I can help out. I'll take her to the train station first thing in the morning for the early leave. It's too late for today."

"It'll be like trapping a wild animal. She's not gonna want any part of it. Is it Custis they want, or is it really us they're after?"

"I don't think they even know, Martin. Ewald has half of a brain to begin with. Combine that with his cohorts, and there's no brain at all between them."

"In the morning I'll send Custis with Buster and Mary to Virginia as well. Custis can't ride the train with Sarah, and I don't want him going by himself to a place he doesn't know. Not even his old church would be safe. They'd burn it down for sure and lynch anyone who got in their way. I'll send enough cash with them to give to Sarah's aunt. She's got quite the spread. Buster will know what to do there. Hopefully, in time this will all blow over. I'd appreciate you tagging along tomorrow morning. I don't want to take a chance of running into the mob halfway to the train station. The ranch will be unprotected, but I'd rather protect my family."

Custis crouched down inside the house, next to the open front window. He leaned against the wall and rested his arms on his knees. Martin and Doc Lyman walked up the front porch stairs and stood at the open door. Sarah was yelling from upstairs. Doors were slammed, drawers sounded like they had been thrown across the room, and loud but muffled voices continued in the background.

"What was it you said, Martin? Trapping a wild animal?"

Martin barely nodded.

"Good description."

Martin rested his hand on the back of a rocking chair. He gently rubbed the wood. "I made these chairs for Heather. Our first anniversary. She used to rock Sarah in them for hours. The only thing that seemed to keep Sarah from crying sometimes." He smiled. "Better have a seat, Doc. This may take awhile."

"Life sure is strange. You go along thinking how everything is going so gradually. Then it busts out in all directions."

A cloud of dust bloomed on the horizon down the long drive. Both men stood.

"It looks like several," Martin said. "Couple buckboards and five or six horses."

Custis jumped to his feet as Sarah bounded down the staircase and out to the porch.

"Father? Who's coming, Father? Are they here?"

Custis stood beside Sarah, and both of them looked at the trail of dust beyond the front gate. Custis felt the wickedness in the air—the kind of specter that touched his skin with silent whispers. There was no twirling pattern skyward produced by heat or flame. Unlike smoke, it was lingering, suffocating, moving like an amoeba consuming all oxygen.

"Sarah," Martin said firmly. "Get upstairs and change your clothes. Get on the frilliest dress you have. Mary! Help Sarah get upstairs and get her out of those britches. And do something with her hair. Now!"

Mary looked at the dust cloud. She grabbed Sarah's arm, and both rushed back into the house.

Custis stepped between Martin and Doc and rushed down the steps. He broke out into a run straight toward the ranch gate. He'd end it there, give himself up. They wanted him, not Sarah. They only lynched coloreds, and they wouldn't stop until they did.

Martin yelled, "Custis, get in the house, now!"

Custis stopped and turned toward Martin. "They're here because of me. They want me."

"Custis! Stop right now and get back up here." Martin rushed down the steps and grabbed Custis's arm. "I will handle what comes next."

Custis was surprised at Martin's grip. This must be what fathers did. There was no hatred in his grasp, no domination, no maltreatment. It was controlled fear, tangible evidence that Martin cared, loved, and wanted to protect him.

"No matter what happens, you stay inside until I call for you. Do you understand?"

"Yes, sir, I understand, but I'm not leaving you. I can fight too."

"We may have to resort to that, but let's try my plan first. Will you trust me?"

"I'm not too scared, Mr. Tennison."

"I know you're not, but I am, a little. You let me try to deal with these folks first. I know you and Doc have my back. Please step inside the house and tell Mary and Sarah to stay inside until I say so. That is your job."

"Yes, sir."

Custis returned to the house and stood just inside the door. Doc Lyman met Martin at the bottom of the porch stairs.

"Doc? Not sure how this is gonna play out, but I'm saying my prayers right now." Martin removed the revolver from his waistband and handed it to Doc. "Don't let them come inside. Don't let them take Custis, no matter what they do to me."

Doc Lyman took the revolver without question. He examined the gun. "1873 Colt Peacemaker. That oughta do it." He opened the cylinder, spun it around, then placed the gun in his front waistband. He took off his hat and removed a small derringer. "Got this one, too. It probably won't kill them. Just piss 'em off." He put his hat back on and concealed the small gun in his hand. "These must be the people I was telling you about. The ugly ones that walk amongst us." Doc returned to the porch and stood directly in front of the door.

Martin walked out to the water trough, never looking away from the oncoming wagons. The procession entered under the ranch arbor. The mules pulling the buckboards seemed old and slow. The teams stopped short of the trough by about fifteen yards. Two men sat in the front of each buckboard, with two or three more men in the back, two women, and two young boys. Some of them held rifles. Another had a double-barreled shotgun. Both boys were in bandages, one with white gauze over most of his head and jaw. The other had bruising, some abrasions, and his leg in a splint.

Martin leaned against the water pump. He placed one hand in his front pants pocket.

"Gentlemen, ladies," Martin said, sounding kind.

"My boy almost got killed. He got a broken leg, busted in half."

"My boy here got his teeth knocked out," said a woman in the back.

"Looks like some pretty serious injuries." Martin squinted and rubbed his jaw. "And by the likes of the size of your boys, they look like they put up a pretty good fight."

"My son is hurt real bad. Had to leave him home with his mother. Broken ribs, and can't ride," said the man driving the wagon.

Custis stood behind Doc Lyman.

"Are they going to kill him?"

"I don't think so, Custis," Doc whispered. "Just look at them. Rather than coming alone, the men brought their wives and children. Probably not prepared for a deadly shoot-out after all. Look at those old wagons and sad mules. Not much of a getaway plan going on there. Perhaps they want a payoff or maybe just have bloated egos?"

Custis wondered how Doc arrived at his hypothesis. Academically, Custis was brilliant. But when it came to people, he had experience of only *friend or foe*, minus the *friend*. In his short life he had been isolated from an entire social sphere. As an only child forbidden to attend school or play with other children, his mother had been his only friend. Custis watched carefully. He wanted to be like Doc—to be able to easily interpret silent communications.

Martin nodded. "Looks like they were tangling with a bear. Your boys got some muscle on them, too. I'd hate to see what the bear looks like now. Yes, sir, you must be really proud." Martin placed his hands on his hips. "I don't understand why you're here, though. You need the doctor? By a stroke of luck, he's here and just fixin' to have some supper."

"Doc already been out. We're here because you're hiding that colored boy that caused all this."

"Boy?" Martin looked briefly toward the house. "The only boy here is Mary's nephew. Martin called out to Mary. "Mary! You got your nephew handy?"

Mary stepped from the kitchen door with her arm around Custis.

"This boy lives here with Mary. We're not hiding anyone. He lives here with Mary and James and Robert and Buster, who work here on the ranch. As a matter of fact, they're some of the most hardworking people I've had on my payroll. Buster over there, best farrier around."

The group looked toward Buster. He was standing next to the frame of the barn doorway with his right arm out of view.

"Your daughter hurt our boys. It cost us labor. He can't work for months now. And now we still owe Doc Lyman for fixin' them."

"My daughter?" Martin tilted his head. "My daughter did this? To these two, I mean three, big, strapping young men?" Martin called back toward the house. "Sarah! Sarah! Get down here right now, right this minute."

Sarah stepped from the kitchen and walked past Custis. Custis's mouth fell open. She was wearing a dress—a pink lacy dress. The color of delicate flower petals, the hue matched her clean pink cheeks and lips. Her hair was neatly combed down. It hung in soft ringlets, bouncing with each step. A loose pink bow tied up a lock of her hair. This girl was an imposter.

"Yes, Daddy?" Sarah walked out and stood behind her father.

Martin turned halfway around and took Sarah by the arm. "Don't be afraid, honey; these folks won't hurt you."

Sarah put her arm around his waist and burrowed her head into his chest. She leaned on one foot, taking an inch or two off her height.

The men all stared at the little girl standing next to her father.

Martin kissed the top of Sarah's head. "Where did this all occur again?"

"Down at the river's east bend," one of the men said.

"Oh, yes, on my property. We've had trouble with trespassers there. Squatters. Probably going to have to fence it someday." Martin paused, but started right back up. "Now, let me understand this. What you're telling me is that you think my little girl here took on your three big sons?"

One of the men on horseback fidgeted in his saddle. "You got another daughter?"

"No, just this one."

"I expected her to be ... older. And bigger," said the rider as he returned the rifle to the leather scabbard. He snickered, then looked toward the wagons. "That green-eyed colored boy can't weigh more than a sack of feed. He's barely scrapin' sixty pounds." He pulled the reins, turned his horse, and moved away from the others.

Lucius's father looked at his son. "This is the one that beat you up?"

Lucius's mouth, jaw, and head were wrapped in bandages. He probably wanted to nod and tell everyone about the beast of a horse Sarah had ridden. But the only thing he could manage was to look away.

Two more riders rode hard up the lane. It was Sheriff Abbott and a deputy. Both dismounted next to Martin. Sarah took their horses by the reins and led them to the water trough.

The sheriff looked curiously at Sarah, up and down, then faced the group. "This is where everything stops. No more. Your boys have done enough damage. I've got a dead body in the ground near over a year now."

A man's voice from the wagon shouted, "No need to lose any sleep over a dead colored, Sheriff."

Sheriff Abbott squared off, planting his feet firmly. "All I gotta do is find a little piece of evidence, and I can prove who did it. Me and my deputies are just waiting for one more little foul-up. And I promise you, personally promise all of you, a step out of line is all I need."

Sheriff Abbott nodded his head at the women. "Ma'am." He looked back at the men. "Funny thing about going to jail for a while . . . men lose their livelihood, their businesses go under—years of hard work gone, just like that. Pretty soon, someone new is sleeping with your wife and raising your kids. Someone else is living your life for you. And remember, Mr. Ewald, a fifteen-year-old boy can be hanged just as easy as a full-grown man." The sheriff looked at a man in the back of the wagon. "But you know all about that, don't you, Mr. McReynolds?"

Sheriff Abbott reached into his vest pocket and pulled out an envelope. "I have an affidavit with an arrest warrant declaration. All it needs is a signature. You understand, Ewald? This is over." He placed the envelope back into his pocket. "Now, I don't exactly know what happened to your boys, but what I think you have, right here, is obviously a case of mistaken identity. It'd be easy to prove in a public court of law that this little girl did not cause all this damage to three grown boys. You best find out what really happened before you get a town all riled up with conjecture."

McReynolds tilted his head like a confused old hound.

"Con ... jec ... ture. Bullshit," Sheriff Abbott said sarcastically, attempting to hide the fact that McReynolds didn't understand the word conjecture.

Ewald glared at the sheriff, then focused on Martin. He chewed on his wad of tobacco and spat without breaking his stare. Dark drool came out of the corner of his mouth and seeped down the creases of his unshaven chin. He slapped the reins on the mules and turned the wagon. The others followed.

Sheriff Abbott watched until they were halfway down the lane. Martin walked up to his side. "Did those boys burn down the house?"

"Don't know for sure—for a court of law to convict them anyway, but had they not been there in the first place, probably wouldn't have occurred." Sheriff Abbott adjusted his hat. "I got the rumblings of what was going on in town the last couple of days. Then Doc told me all about what happened that night, how you found the boy. I figured they'd be coming out here." Sheriff Abbott continued to watch the wagons. "I can't get any judge in this county or state to prosecute cases like this. Not when it's negroes who need their help."

Martin nodded. "I appreciate your help and where you stand. Not many others like you, Sheriff. I'm just trying to do the right thing."

Sheriff Abbott looked at Martin. "Nothing seems to change overnight." He handed Martin the envelope. "Can you give this to Doc? It's his stipend from the county."

"I will, Sheriff, I certainly will."

Martin watched the sheriff and his deputy ride away. He turned and strode past his pink-laced daughter, still standing at the trough. "You, young lady, have got to stop beating up boys." Martin stepped onto the porch and handed Doc the envelope.

Custis kept focused on the sheriff riding down the lane. It looked like more riders were at the gate entrance with the sheriff, maybe fifteen or twenty.

"Mr. Tennison, I think they're coming back."

Martin and Doc quickly turned. "Here we go again, Martin."

"Everyone, just stay put."

The riders did not appear to be in a hurry. All were on warmbloods and rode two abreast. As they approached the house, Martin and Doc looked confused. Martin stepped off the porch as the riders stopped just short of the tie post. All were armed with scabbard rifles and shotguns.

Martin nodded once. "Tate. Matthew." Another quick nod to the others. "Smitty. Good to see you."

The rider he called Tate crossed his arms on his saddle horn. "We heard about a lynching. Figured you could use our help, but it looks like it's been handled."

"I appreciate that. For now, we're all right."

"We passed the Ewalds and McReynolds. They acted like we weren't even there. Like we were ghosts. I think just seeing us ride by put the fear of God in them."

Some of the men chuckled. "He shit his pants."

A man from the back circled to the front. "Some of us don't care about coloreds one way or the other. Some of us think they need to stay in their place. But you're a good man, Tennison, so we all figured there must be more to the story. You always treated my family good, treated us fair on the horse sales, too. Can't imagine you doing nothing wrong enough to deserve this."

Another voice from the back. "Doc, we heard you was out here too."

Doc Lyman stepped forward. "Yes. How's Jenny doing now?"

"Real good, Doc. Better than ever, thanks to you."

"That's good to hear, Gus, real good. Give the kids my love."

Tate looked around at the men and then back at Martin. "Nobody here wants to see harm come to any of your family. We just wanted you to know that."

"You'd do the same for us," came from a voice in the back.

"Well," said Tate, "we'll let you alone, be on our way."

The riders turned their horses and loped down the lane.

Martin turned toward his family. He looked pale. "OK, everyone in the house, now."

Mary pulled Sarah and Custis inside. Doc followed and closed the door as Martin sat down on the bottom step. He leaned forward and rested his head in his hands.

A quietness overcame the house except for the brazen sound of a kitchen chair scooting across the floor and a high-pitched, almost musical tinkling of a coffee cup onto its saucer. Custis stayed near the door and watched Martin through the glass. A man, brave and courageous but brought to his knees when no one was looking. Human behavior was so incomprehensibly divided. What made people so different? Custis didn't know how to fix what was in front of him. There was nothing to add, subtract, or multiply.

13

C ustis fought for sleep. The illusory sound of horses' hooves and clattery wagons had shattered his rest throughout the night. He visualized guns blasting and felt ropes tangled around his body.

Several days passed. Still, the same nightmare came with the darkness. Custis felt trapped in the house. Out in the barn, he knew where the rifle was hidden. He'd kill them all first, then saddle a fast horse. He'd be scared, but he'd do it anyway. No more fear or harm would come to the ranch. Everything could be back to normal. But then he'd be on the run for the rest of his life. He would never see Sarah again.

He wouldn't be able to go to school. Colleges don't accept murderers or horse thieves.

Custis snuck out of the house and ran to the barn. His makeshift bed was made of straw and horse blankets. He fell asleep to nature's night sounds with Hatchet wrapped around his head. He woke to Sarah's voice.

"Custis? You out here?"

"Yes. Over here."

He felt Sarah sit down next to him. "I can't sleep either."

Custis handed her a blanket. "Here, rest on this. It will keep the straw from coming through."

"Father is still real mad at me for getting kicked out of school again."

"I wish I could go in your place."

"Me too. I'd ride all day long then."

"How do you get kicked out, anyway?"

"Well, it's called expulsion. Miss Rogers was asking about how many percentages she had left if she sold two-fifths of her apple cobbler, then gave one-third of what was left away. I told her she'd still have a whole pie because no one would buy her pie in the first place. The old bat told me to sit down and be quiet, then asked me if I wanted to teach the class. I said, 'Well, yes, I do,' and so I tried. Now I got Mr. Henne again, the tutor. Today I learned about rhetorical questions."

"I love math. It's the secret to most things."

"God knew I'd be too powerful if I could do arithmetic."

"I can't wait to go to school. I've been thinking, Sarah. When I go off to school, and you go off to your school, we won't be able to see each other. I'm going to start writing you letters right now just in case I get too busy with my studies."

"That's the stupidest thing you've ever said. My school is close by, so I'll get to come home on weekends, and I'll be here for the summers, too. Your school is too far away. Father said you might have to stay there but come home at Christmastime. Your school will be different from mine. But we still have a lot of time."

x x x

Custis fed and watered the horses and cleaned the stalls; by morning's light, he was back inside the house, waiting for Mary.

At night he'd read aloud in the kitchen, just to be close to Mary. He liked the way she made him feel good inside. She was always talking, humming, or singing. She worked hard, just like his momma. Custis decided he must love her, yet Sarah was right—his life would never be the same.

But as of late, ever since the men from town came out, Mary acted differently. It was referred to as "the incident" whenever it was mentioned. Mary was scared. Custis could hear it in her voice. She wouldn't let Custis or Sarah get out of her sight. She stopped going into town for provisions, something she had always enjoyed. Now, she was easily cross at Buster and James when they failed to get the correct supplies. Mr. Tennison, too. He acted tired and wary. Custis knew he was pretending to not care, but the gun in his waistband indicated otherwise.

One evening, Martin walked into the kitchen and asked Mary for a cup of coffee. He sat down next to Custis.

That's odd. Mr. Tennison usually has his evening coffee in his library or at the parlor table. He looked happy, so maybe all was good.

"I've been wanting this cup of coffee all day. Finally a moment. Smells good. How's your reading coming, Custis?"

"Really good."

Martin cleared his throat and interlocked his fingers. "I was talking with Buster today. He said you're spending a lot of time out in the barn, getting the chores done real early."

"Yes, sir."

Martin picked up one of Doc Lyman's books and began thumbing the pages. "You know, I don't think we'll ever see those men coming back to the ranch. Things seemed to have settled down in town. I can't promise it will last, but word going around town is Ewald is selling his place and moving away." Martin placed the book back on the table and looked directly at Custis. "We're strong people. We've had too much loss already and come out the other side to let something like this take us over. We can't keep on borrowing other people's problems. We can't let them keep us afraid anymore. Why, we even found out that we had friends we didn't know we had. We can be smart, have plans, and be as careful as we can, but if we allow them to keep us scared, they triumph."

"I don't want them to win anymore."

"Good."

Martin paused. He turned his coffee cup but left it on the table. "I've been thinking about something, and I need your help. Building on to the barn. An office, a records room for the horse sales and breeding accounts. We're running out of space in here. I was hoping to get your input, Custis. Maybe you can help me design it."

Custis looked at Mary. She was smiling and nodding. *I can't believe Mr. Tennison is asking for my help.*

"Looks like James will be down for a week or so. Hurt his shoulder trying to get one of the thoroughbreds to behave. I sure could use your help with this."

"Yes, sir. If you really need me."

"All right, then. We'll do it."

"Mr. Tennison? Is Mr. James gonna be all right? Me and Sarah have been using Stardust around the thoroughbreds because she seems to calm them all down. We just pull her alongside."

Martin tilted his head. "Does she, now? I'll let James know, although a little too late. And you're not supposed to be handling those horses, anyway."

Martin stood, winked at Mary, and left the room.

Mary picked up the cup of coffee from the table. "He took nary a sip of this."

Custis helped design a small two-room office addition to the horse barn. He spent several days in the house library, assessing various engineering manuals and construction books. Custis developed a plan, drew out the schematics, and presented an inventoried list to Martin. Two hundred twenty-five square feet divided into two small rooms. It was a lean-to of sorts—one large window on the east side to catch the morning sun, a small window on the south to allow in a cross-breeze, and a small potbellied wood stove in the middle to help with the evening chill.

Martin had a small wood mill set up near the barn, which James and Robert used while Buster designed and made iron clasps, door hardware, and bolts and straps for the headers.

Research, planning, and drawing came easily for Custis. Working with carpentry tools did not. It was the kind of knowledge that could only be gained through experience, kind of like human behavior.

Sarah showed Custis how to hammer. "Choke down on the handle and stop that tap, tap, tap. Swing hard, and you can be more accurate with your strikes."

She showed him how to use a saw. She taught him to use the drill, set the dowels, and nail shingles on the roof. Custis designed a block-and-tackle pulley system to hoist up roofing supplies. Later he fastened the hook and rope to the back of Sarah's overalls and hoisted her up with ease. Up and down and back up into the rafters, just for fun.

With the office addition completed, Martin furnished it while Custis checked the irrigation system on the other side of the ranch. Martin and Sarah then gathered everyone and met up in front of the barn when Custis returned.

"Custis, we thought we'd all have a grand opening for the new office. Why don't you lead the way?"

"Of course I will." Custis opened the door and let everyone in. A desk made from loblolly pine sat in the front portion of the room. An iron bed, complete with bedding, was in the back room, along with a nightstand, lantern, and bureau. Neatly stacked books in a variety of colors filled the new shelving. Two chairs sat in the corner, facing the potbellied stove.

Custis looked surprised. "I thought this was going to be an office, Mr. Tennison. Whose bed is this?"

"It's yours, Custis."

"What do you mean?"

"We all made this for you. It's a surprise, right from the start. Mary made up the bedding, the pillows, and she even made these curtains for you. James and Robert knew all along it was built for you."

"It's mine . . . you mean this is all mine? This is my own desk?"

"Just for you. You sneak out here and sleep in the barn anyway, so I thought you might like a room a little closer to the animals. Can't get much closer than this. And besides, after you go off to school, I'll change it into an office for the ranch hands. With you and Sarah gone, I'll need to hire a ranch manager, and this will be perfect."

Martin walked over to the inside wall. "Look here, Custis. This was Sarah's idea, and Buster made it for you."

He twisted an iron knob, and a small, secret opening appeared. "A hidden window so you can check on the animals in the middle of the night. Don't even have to get out of bed. Hatchet likes it too. Had to throw him out a couple of times already."

Mary nodded and shook her finger. "I still expect my coffee to be on when I come down in the mornings, though. No forgettin' about that."

Custis turned, almost in a complete circle. He wished his mother could see. No more daylight peering through the walls with wadded paper attempts to trap the cold air. He had a genuine store-bought bed, real curtains covering real glass. He looked down at his feet. A wood floor. No more sweeping musty dirt. He remembered his momma, how she worked so hard for everything they once had. *Always look in your own heart, Custis. There be a reason for everything.* A motive for all things—good or bad. Maybe that's why Custis loved mathematics—it had reason and resolve and no personal opinions or feelings.

"Are you sure it's just for me?"

Martin smiled and placed his hand on Custis's shoulder. "Of course it is, Custis."

𝓍 𝓍 𝓍

The rains finally came. Persistent and unrelenting. Mary had always called them "the promise of tomorrows." The rivers flowed fiercely, ponds were full, and the two reservoirs on the ranch were carefully watched for incremental releases. The weather kept everyone inside for the most part. Custis read book after book in his new barn room. Martin worked in his library, while Sarah put up with Mr. Henne, as promised.

Three years had passed since Custis had been at the ranch. He lay on his bed with an open book across his chest. Time seemed to pass so slowly, but each book brought him closer to going to college. Nothing would get in his way. He closed his eyes. *I'm going to do it, Momma.*

The sound of the rain was enough to soothe even the thoroughbreds. An indulgent percussion softly tapped the roof above. Gentle plumb rain, obeying gravity, falling straight down to earth—always humble in its purpose.

A fast knock came on his door. *It's probably Buster, needing a hand.*

He opened it to find Sarah, drenched. Her hair hung straight down, both arms to her side.

"What's happening?" Custis stepped toward her. Her eyes were red, and he could now differentiate the tears from the rain.

"Stardust—she's hurt."

"What's wrong with her?"

"I think she's gone lame on her front. It's swollen. She won't put any weight on it."

Custis opened the stall gate, touched Stardust's face, then bent down and rubbed her leg. "It's swollen badly." Custis stood and pushed the horse back. "Go on, girl, back up, back up." Stardust hobbled and stopped. "Maybe something is in the shoe and she's got a little infection."

"No, I already checked. I checked everything. She's lame." Sarah slid down next to Stardust and wept. "She wasn't this way yesterday, and she's been in her stall all night."

"It might be from an old injury. The weather's got it all acted up. My leg hurts when it gets real cold too." Custis squatted down again and felt the leg. "It's warm, inflamed." Custis hugged Stardust around her face. He patted her head and said, "It'll be all right, girl."

"No, it won't, Custis. It's been hurting her before, and I've always nursed it back. It's never been this bad. It's the same leg that got caught on the train track, and she's hurt it again somehow. We have to put her down."

Custis watched Sarah run from the barn, through the rain, and into the house. He kissed Stardust's muzzle and closed the gate. He hated death, he hated sickness, and he hated knowing that more was coming.

Custis thought of his mother, the night she died. What she looked like, what she was doing, and even what she was wearing. Her last words seemed so casual, so unknowing. *"And don't forget to say your prayers, thank God for all that he has given us."*

"I will. Just one more chapter. It's at the good part."

"Even thank God for Mrs. Herman. There be a reason for everything, son. Did she try and cheat you again?"

"No, Momma, she didn't cheat me." His last words to his mother were about a woman he didn't even like. Why couldn't he have said, *"I love you, Momma?"* Custis wanted to change it all.

Custis turned back to Stardust and rubbed her face. "Thank you, Stardust, for saving my life. You are the best horse in the whole world. Horses go to heaven. You'll be just like Pegasus. Tell my momma that I love her. She knows that, but just tell her anyway."

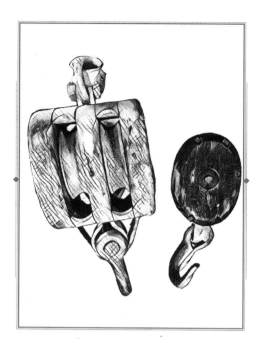

Custis prepared himself for what would come. He'd help Martin dig the hole, harness the mule, and drag the dead horse into the looming pit. He would do it for Sarah.

Through the rain-smeared glass, he saw two distorted figures walk from the house. They moved together unhurriedly, heads down. Custis sat at his desk with a notebook in front of him. He pressed the pencil down hard, nervously breaking the tip. Custis got up and solemnly walked to the entrance to the barn.

He watched Martin enter the stall. Stardust was completely still.

She looked so forlorn and helpless with her stance unbalanced. Martin reached out and rubbed her shoulder. He lowered himself as his hand touched the forearm, knee, cannon, and fetlock, and down to the pastern. Now on his haunches, he moved his hand up to her knee then back down to her hoof. Stardust fussed, picked up her leg, and tried to move away. Martin stood, stepped back, and let her settle. Sarah lifted Stardust's head to hers. Stardust softly nickered as Sarah cried.

"She's in pain, honey." Martin's voice quivered. "We need to put her down."

Sarah kissed Stardust on her muzzle and softly whispered, "You're the best pony I've ever had." Her words were barely audible. "Such a good girl."

Stardust nudged into her as if asking for help.

Sarah kissed her again.

"Go on, into the house, Sarah," Martin said softly.

"No, Father. Stardust took care of me, and I need to take care of her. It's my job, not yours."

Custis watched Martin. It was a moment so powerful that it should have stopped movement and time. But Custis's voice broke through, "I know how we can fix her."

Both Martin and Sarah turned around. Martin looked directly at Custis. "She's lame now, Custis. We need to put her down."

"Mr. Tennison, I know I'm not supposed to argue, but I have an idea. We need to keep her off her leg, let her heal."

"Her leg is compromised. She'd be too weak and will only come up lame again. She can never be ridden. The weight will break her."

"Yes, sir. I have that figured out, too."

Sarah looked at her father, then back at Custis. "Do you really think we can help her?"

Sarah grabbed Custis with one hand and reached for her father. "Please, let's listen to his idea. Just listen, then we can decide."

"I can put together a big block-and-tackle pulley system, maybe two systems. Buster can help with the hardware. Hang it from the barn rafter and connect it to a wrap that goes around and under Stardust's belly."

Custis looked at Sarah. "Just like putting overalls on a horse, or like a fisherman's net. Let her hang until she heals. And just so her leg muscles won't atrophy, we can hoist her down gently, each day, just for a little while, and let her stand on three legs. I can make three wooden shoes from the ironwood trees that are inches higher than her hurt one. Raised shoes. They would allow exercise, standing weight on her other three. She won't be able to touch down with the other. Then after her muscles are exercised, we'll hoist her up again."

"But still, Custis, she won't be any good for riding, even if she heals. And this is a working ranch. We can't keep what will not produce, or this entire place would be a menagerie."

"Yes, sir, but no, sir. Stardust is not a regular farm animal. Stardust is a friend, a companion to Sarah. She is dust from heaven. Remember? And she will be useful; she'll be a good associate horse for the thoroughbreds."

"An associate horse?"

"Each time we put the thoroughbreds out in the runs, they tear the fencing apart and hurt themselves and the other horses. We can't even ride out of the barn without them going crazy in the stalls. Remember when James pulled his shoulder out, trying to get ol' Major to behave? They're all nervous and such. They don't like being by themselves, but when they're together, they get all flustered too."

"That's the breed, Custis. That's why they're fast. We can't change what's in their blood."

"But Stardust is just the opposite and has a calming effect on them. She's their companion."

Custis walked closer to Martin. "You see, I've been reading on thoroughbreds. Their eyes . . . they're so tall and powerful. They look like they want to run right through me. They scare me to death." He looked at Sarah. "Actually, they *all* scare me, but mostly the thoroughbreds. Stay right here—just a second."

Custis darted back into his room and quickly returned with an opened book. "I've been reading about how to temporarily stabilize their anxiety and edginess. Companion donkeys are being used down near Kentucky and Georgia. I figure Stardust could be our associate donkey, after she gets better."

Sarah stood next to Custis and faced her father. "Father, Stardust already calms the stallions down just by being in the stall next to them. I think it's a wonderful idea. We have to try."

Martin shook his head. "If . . ." He paused and cleared his throat. "If you two are committed, I think we need to give it a go."

Custis had just influenced the course of someone's life. It felt so strange—the roles had reversed. Mr. Tennison had listened. Sarah believed in him. Custis sensed the weight of responsibility. Perhaps it was pride. But this was different from the pride his mother had spoken about. This felt warm and healthy, not coldhearted or mean. He'd make it work. If anything, it would buy him time to think of something else.

Sarah grabbed him and squeezed him tightly. He could feel her skin on his. She kissed his cheek and hugged him tighter. A purposeful touch, but this time he only thought of her happiness. Sarah laughed and cried and embraced her father, but he didn't get a kiss. Custis had his first kiss from a real girl.

x x x

Throughout the night, they all worked on the plan. Custis drew out schematics for a double lift and a threefold purchase pulley as Sarah salvaged large chunks of ironwood from the woodpile.

Custis looked at the wood. "It's going to take too long. We need to use what we have for now. Double up on the pulleys. We can make a better system once she's off the ground. I can start making her raised shoes tomorrow, once she's up."

Buster stayed up half the night and fabricated hooks, straps, and sheaves. Mary helped reinforce two large horse blankets, which would act as the six-point lift.

At first, Stardust was a little skittish, but she settled down after a couple of days, coming to terms with her new light-footedness. Buster helped Custis and Sarah release the tension three times a day and allowed Stardust to stand on three legs for about a half hour, or until she became fidgety—then up she would go.

Mary made ice slurries in a bucket. Custis and Sarah applied the cold wraps to the injured leg four times daily. "Not too tight," Custis said. "Don't want to cut off any circulation; just want to reduce the inflammation."

"How do you know all this stuff, Cus?"

"I read about it. Cold for fresh injuries, hot for old or chronic injuries. That's what Doc Lyman did for me, remember? Cold to reduce inflammation, edema, swelling. It'll subsequently decrease her pain. It's called thermal therapy.

"Heat therapy will come later, in a week or so. It, too, decreases pain while increasing local circulation. It accelerates healing. But no more than 113 degrees Fahrenheit. We'll need a thermostat. Then, before we allow her back in her stall, we'll soften the floor. I haven't got that part worked out just yet."

Sarah filled a bucket with oats and hay and fed her horse. "Do you know how to fish?"

"Fish? Of course I know how to fish. What are you talking about? We have work here, with Stardust. We don't have time to go fishing."

"No. I mean, do you know how to fly-fish?"

"Oh. I've read about it. Once I saw a rod and reel in the window of Mr. Pete's store."

"I can teach you if you want."

"The river is too far away. I still need to read the last batch of books Doc brought out, anyway. I'm learning more about physics."

"We can practice out front."

"Now I know you're crazy. There's no fish out there, Sarah."

Sarah went into the main house and returned with a rod and reel. "Come on, I need help."

Under Sarah's direction, they both pushed, rolled, and levered five large rocks to the edge of the lane just down from the barn. Sarah strategically moved each one into its final place. She paced off forty feet. "Here, Custis, stand here. Imagine you're standing upstream. The water is coming from behind. The trout usually hide behind the boulders and rocks in the stream, just like those rocks. Notice where the sun is. They hide in the shade. They rest and take a break from the current. See what I mean?"

"Yes. The first one is at twenty feet, the last at forty."

"You want the fly to act normal, like what a live fly or bug would do. It's going to float downstream. You want to place the fly above the rock in moving water and let it momentarily float down and around. If the fish doesn't bite straightaway, pull it back. It'll make him mad, and he'll be more inclined to take it the next time. So, you do it all over again."

Sarah picked up the fly rod, adjusted her line, and began to cast. She worked the line back and forth, releasing a little at the time. "Be gentle. Pretend you're part of the line. Close your eyes and imagine the pattern, then imagine the lead doing the same movement." Sarah reeled in the line and handed the rod to Custis.

Custis let out some line, tossed it toward the rock, and jerked it back.

"No, Custis. You're too rigid. Do it softly, like it's you, yourself, just touching the surface. Don't look at it. Feel its effort through the rod—look at where you want it to go to land softly."

Sarah stood behind Custis and leaned against him. She placed her right hand on top of his. She jiggled the rod. "Lighten up; ease up on your grip. It's not a horse."

"Why can't we just hook on a worm and wait for a bite?"

"Anyone can do that, Cus. This is an art, a science of nature. Sometimes you can hear the movement of the line and know it's going to be the perfect cast even before it alights."

She moved his arm forward and back, forward and back. "It talks to you. It changes you forever once you understand its complicated beauty."

"Yeah, I can hear it. The fish are laughing."

Custis practiced for hours a day but never saw anything resembling beauty. He listened with intensity, but it never talked to him like Sarah swore it would. What was he missing regarding this connection between humans and nature? He had conversed with chickens and bonded with a cat. He had a good relationship with Stardust and a mediocre rapport with the other horses.

Fly casting was not an art or anything close. It was a rhythmless tangle of line that ensnared itself around his feet and latched on to fence boards, tree limbs, and cows. Something was missing. Custis never gave up, though. Sometimes in the early morning, when the fog was low in the pastures, he cast again and again into the soft, white, fishless, waterless sea.

15

"I have something for you, Custis," Martin said, placing a stack of assorted papers and books on Custis's desk. "You have two years to decide. Pick one."

Custis took the top booklet into his hands, then quickly examined the spines and covers of a few more. "Colleges and universities." Custis fingered through the pile without lifting his eyes.

"Whatever you choose, I'll stand behind you." Martin's voice was resolute.

Sometimes, Custis never wanted to leave the ranch. But there was always a feeling pulling at him, leading him elsewhere. It never went away. It was like trying to hold back the wind. "My momma told me God had plans for me. When she said that, it scared me. I just wanted to be a boy who could play with others, a boy that could go to school." Custis cleared his throat. "I'd like to send away for the tests right now."

"Let's just give it another year, at least. There are schools out there that we don't even know about yet. And besides, some don't require an examination at all. Doc said some colleges will just accept you based on your application letter and interview."

x x x

Custis was determined and focused. He wrote to prominent church pastors, government agencies, and colleges and universities around the country requesting further information on any educational opportunities available.

Custis could obtain a prestigious medical degree from Howard or esteemed law degrees at Tuskegee and Morehouse, but Wilson Place in Ohio offered the most in the disciplines of science, engineering, and first-year physics.

Doc wrote reference letters stating that Custis was the smartest young man he had ever met. He wrote, *Years of reading and studying came easily. He has an eidetic memory and a work ethic far above anyone else.*

Wilson Place College for Negros accepted Custis just before his eighteenth birthday.

It was autumn 1883 when he left. At the train station, Mary hugged Custis goodbye, then straightened his black tie. Martin and Doc Lyman shook his hand, while Buster smiled from a distance. He was sure that Sarah was out there somewhere too. She never liked goodbyes, and he couldn't blame her. He felt heartache, fear, and excitement all at the same time. One more emotion would have split him wide open, and seeing Sarah now would surely bring him to tears. He had practiced for months what he was going to say to her. But now he was sure he would have messed it up anyway. He waited for Sarah, down to the last possible moment. He imagined kissing her goodbye like a full-grown man would do.

Custis carried his bag and walked down toward his car, closest to the engine. He felt the locomotive's vibration under his feet. The idle was deafening and easily silenced the voice of the engineer yelling at the fireman. Heat radiated all around, while bursts of dissipating steam slickened footholds and handholds. The mechanical marvel and sheer power of this immense machine symbolized only a fraction of the capabilities of man. He felt dwarfed by its force and girth as he looked down on the distant curvature of the tracks.

The same rails that had led him home as a small boy were now the tracks that would take him far, far away. The constant, never-changing steel working in perfect unison would lead to the rest of his life.

x x x

Wilson Place College sat between two rounded hillsides clustered with flamboyant fat-leafed trees. A grand four-story white brick building stretched upward into the blue, silent sky. Striking arched doorways, harbored under large verandas, seemed to protect whatever was inside.

The surrounding grounds consisted of an array of supplementary buildings, some two stories and others only one. Many smaller structures were light brown, the shade of dirt pastures after being tilled and dried by the sun. Graveled paths created a labyrinth as they circulated through the campus, circumventing intermittent trees while linking each building in well-groomed unity.

Two hundred first-year students filled the orientation auditorium—students that looked like Custis. He studied the faces of the men surrounding him and felt overwhelmed with fellowship. Martin was right—Custis had lived an isolated life. This campus would now become his home among these strangers, a stream of young minds all driven by an insatiable craving for knowledge. They were his community, his brothers, his family.

Over the following weeks and months, Custis attended classes. The rooms were modest, with worn-out desks. Textbooks were tattered and scarce. Students shared and worked out a schedule of who-will-get-what-when. Custis studied in his dormitory, but with twenty roommates, it was more like an open bunkhouse. He worked late into the night, hunched over a flickering oil lamp, while the others slept. Sometimes, he'd take advantage of the privacy and pen letters to Sarah. He'd write about the latest news from the North, updates on his classes, and sometimes about the unbearable freezing weather.

Sometimes, before morning's light, the campus is buried in a low, thick fog like the river we fished, back home. But now, white covers everything. It's so quiet here when it snows. When the others are asleep at night, I walk the grounds alone. Sometimes, if the night sky is clear, the moon lights up the fallen snow as if it was competing with the sun. Specks of sparkle blanket like the soft white frosting on Mary's layered cakes. And complete quietness seems to overcome the entire world, and all are at peace. Sarah, did you know that two inches of snow can absorb 60 percent of ambient noise? The air trapped between snowflakes attenuates vibration.

He wrote about how much he longed for the ranch, the peacefulness. *And I miss my Sarah.* His pen would stop midthought, hanging over an incomplete sentence as he contemplated what he couldn't say. He loved Sarah. He loved everything about her.

x x x

Friendships were slow to evolve. A cautiousness consumed most underclassmen. The majority had hardships, but no one was without discussing their dreams and the societal changes they wanted to see. All had different stories. Most were one generation removed from slavery, and several were mixed-race sons of wealthy White planters, while others were from manumitted parents.

Custis spent his first Christmas away from Sarah since he had known her. He was not alone at the university. Other students stayed as well. Some had no homes to go to. One of the professors carried a small fir tree and stuck it in a corner of the study hall. He tied a red bow on the top and decorated the limbs with strings of vivid pink crab apples.

Most of the professors, fervent Black men who seemed to have overcome their own hardships, inspired Custis even more. He saw their selfless dedication to the education of others, most of the time at their own expense. He befriended Professor Babbage, a man from Minnesota. The professor was impressed with Custis's mathematical skills, aptitude in chemistry, and prowess in agriculture sciences, but especially his familiarity with Grimm alfalfa seeds.

"I would like to offer a proposition, Mr. Custis." Professor Babbage was tall, broad, and bald. His beard was thick and resembled the gray-green Spanish moss that hung down from trees back home. He had deep-set eyes, an unbending reputation, and exacted no nonsense. "The administration would like to see you on our faculty someday. Soon."

"Professor, I've just started."

"Your academic level now is far above that of others at this institution, even some that teach. Next summer's special session, as a trial, if you will. Your commitment now could relieve any financial hardships you may have in the future. Subsequently, you can return to your regular schedule in the fall without worry. Do not think we are trying to manipulate your circumstances. Many here need help paying the nethermost tuition and must depend on sponsors or find work outside academia. A few selected students have contracted to stay on after they graduate. The Methodist Episcopal Church owns the university and is pioneer in the nation to have all Black proprietors and staff. We want to be the first to have the youngest professor in the country."

For the first time Custis could be financially self-sufficient. The thought was overwhelming. Custis felt giddy inside.

"Pardon my astonishment. It is an honor. My thoughts have only gone to obtaining an education in physics."

Custis knew Wilson Place lacked a full discipline in physics, and no other edifice that did would accept him.

"That is a specialized field not many students desire. Wilson Place, of course, would like to see more of our community obtain their education in the more customary domains our school can accommodate. We are establishing quite a reputation for success. The Church works tirelessly to procure funding through scholarships, donations, and even from the federal government. Unfortunately, our administration cannot keep up with the protracted workload. Summer sessions will be our attempt to reach out to as many students as possible.

"We will talk soon. Think about your opportunities here with us. Having a professorship will provide unforeseeable opportunities."

Consequently, the university offered Custis a full professorship upon his graduation. Custis graciously accepted. *Unforeseeable opportunities*. In the meantime, Custis would need to complete his current studies while teaching and tutoring during the summer months.

x x x

In his second year, Custis moved into a smaller campus dormitory with only one roommate. Benjamin Cobbler was in his final year. He was from New York, studied fiercely, and pursued political science with passion. He appeared to be a mixed race with light brown skin and eyes the color of ditchwater. He was confident in his studies and seemed to have the energy of three men. He'd leave the campus a few nights during the week only to return, sometimes disheveled, in the early morning hours.

"You need to come with us, Custis. It's noble work. We're making progress. We now have another Black man about to become a member of Congress."

But Custis rarely left the university. He did not deny the difficulties, indignities, and discrimination outside of the campus gates, but rather, he believed his toil was to honor the university and obtain his professorship. It could be the door that would finally open into the world of physics.

Another spring came. Ben would graduate in June.

"I'm going back to New York. You should think about going there, Custis. Lots of people, lots of change. You could go to Centennial University. I hear the physics department is premiere, world-renowned."

"Whites only, my friend."

"That's what they think too."

"What are you talking about?"

"I'm just saying, change is coming. New York City is bulging at the seams with people from all over the world. It's easy to get lost and never found."

"You're not making sense. You been drinking again or are you just out of your mind?"

"Come with us tonight. You'll see. It will become clear."

"I can't. In the morning I'm presenting plans to Professor Babbage, and they have to be perfect. It's an idea I've been working on for years. Next time."

"Suit yourself, brother."

Ben grabbed his satchel and jacket and left the room. Custis went back to his work but thought about Ben. His activities were intriguing, confusing, and worth more explanation.

x x x

Professor Babbage's office was on the second floor of the administration building. The conference was in its second hour.

Custis had spread out his papers and charts on a large table. He had answered every question the board had asked, even the nonpertinent.

"We appreciate your work," Professor Babbage said. "But we are incapable of taking on such a fantastic project. We have not the equipment nor the facility."

"Nor the minds," a board member added.

"This would take thousands of dollars, maybe millions. This radiation probe may be in the future of medicine, but not here. We cannot financially sacrifice hundreds of students from their education on a single futuristic gamble. It is our resolve here to offer an education to as many students as possible, and some begin with only rudimentary skills. Your request is beyond our capabilities and our morals."

Although he had failed to persuade the college board to fund his project, Custis was more assured of its possibility. It was empowering to present his case and inspiring to hear others converse on its potential. Custis would somehow make it happen.

x x x

Word of unrest in nearby cities filled the hallways. Uprisings, buildings burned, train tracks sabotaged, and people killed. Benjamin Cobbler had yet to return to school. The university reverted to a closed campus. More dormitories were constructed, and all students were expected to live on campus.

Letters arrived from Sarah, sometimes two or three each month, and during the rainy season, some from Martin. Sarah attended Rosemont Hill University and unsurprisingly hated the women's curriculum.

My dear Custis, God help me. I now know how to teach elementary school children, provide a physician with the necessary tools to set a broken bone, and keep a secretary's account of earnings and losses of various fictitious businessmen. I have also become proficient in washing clothing, a requirement from and for the nearby men's college. It has been suggested that I disguise myself as a man in order that I may attend the classes of my choice. But alas, my uncontainable hair would have to go. My only relief, it seems, is summers and holidays back with Father. He has donated two hundred acres of the ranch to Rosemont Hill to be used as demonstration fields for various crops, except tobacco. Astonishingly, this has allowed me that illusive exposure to education only afforded to those who have the correct appendages.

Over months of correspondence with Sarah, Custis helped design a large warehouse to accommodate new equipment, classrooms, and a small bunkhouse and kitchen for resident students. He sent schematics for a mechanics shop next to the warehouse and a list of associated equipment. Sarah would write, *Please come home, Custis. It would be so good to have you back.*

Sarah wanted to raise horses and breed a new type of cattle dog. But most importantly, her letters stated she wanted to extend her mother's alfalfa seed studies and experiments. Custis wrote about someday working in physics—understanding the power of matter and energy—and no, he couldn't come home just yet. Sarah graduated with honors, while Custis earned three degrees—mathematics, chemistry, biology—and took on the full professorship position.

Over the years, the letters to each other shuffled through their lives on pieces of paper. Sarah's words were boundlessly filled with poetic narrative—the ranch, changing seasons, and unfettered dreams. It was as if her hand came out and held on to his. *Paper, it's just plain white paper.* Custis kept each letter organized by date, tied with jute, and tucked away in a box. Time had not eased his yearning to be with Sarah. After seven years, her written words still brought him back to the ranch, to her, and made him feel as if he had been there all along.

One day a letter arrived. Seeing Sarah's handwriting on the envelope made Custis smile. He'd read it later, alone, after he dismissed his class. Evening came, and Custis returned to his campus studio. His finger caressed the return address—the closest thing he had to Sarah. He delicately pulled open the seal.

I have good news. Sarah wrote she had been asked for her hand in marriage—a schoolteacher.

Custis sat there, stunned. He loved Sarah. The secret, hidden deep inside, safe from society, never stated aloud. He had lived on fantasies, and now reality sucked his breath away. *Married?* Shock turned his thoughts into blunt, ireful notions. He was the one who loved her, not some schoolteacher. Yes, she had mentioned the lusk before, but he was only a friend, Martin's friend. *I'm the one she loves.* Maybe Custis had misinterpreted superfluous exchanges and redundant business advice as something more. *No, there is more. She loves me. I have all her letters. Why would she have written to me if she didn't love me back?* He felt the weight of unspoken emotions crushing his chest.

For days, he tried to extract infatuation from the equation. What had he expected? He was a Black man forbidden to marry outside of his race. Five hundred miles away, a seven-year separation, and both with different dreams and goals.

There was no solution. Custis wrote and gave his congratulations. He tried to sound light. He told her to hold out for an attorney, as they needed one in the family for his inventions. He vowed to return for the wedding to see what man could have managed to harness his childhood best friend, the one with the wild hair.

PART II

16

1890

I t rained the day Mary died. It was the kind of rain with big fat drops that splat on the parched leaves of September. Unlike spring rain that bounced and pinged off taut green foliage, the transitioning reds and yellows absorbed the dulling sound until they bore wet with silence.

Custis held the letter in his lap as he read it again. The paper had lost its crispness, folding easily with almost a memory of its own. One hundred thirty-eight words folded into seven-and-one-half square inches: the sum of twenty-five years of his life. He remembered the day he left the ranch. Seven years seemed like a lifetime ago.

The letter was from Martin Tennison. His handwriting was artful, his words almost poetic. He had found her in the garden. A spilled basket of harvested greens lay next to her. He carried her to the house. Sarah held her hand. She spoke of her boys.

Our Mary has passed peacefully.

He sat alone in the rail car, but as the train lugged itself farther from Ohio, it filled with various itinerant souls searching for somewhere else. The assigned car for coloreds was without sleeper berths, luggage racks, food services, or a proper toilet. Water was sporadically available, and the toilet area was rarely cleaned. A ten-inch round hole in the floor served as the toilet repository, allowing a clear and unobstructed view of a passing blur of rail timbers. Sometimes the holes were equipped with a knife-valve, but that was an exception. It was supposed to prevent frigid air coming inside or a foot and leg going outside.

As Custis relieved himself, he looked at the black-and-white porcelain sign hung on the wall just below his eye level. *Use Prohibited When Nearing Towns.* A written notice, hung in a train car designated for people forbidden to read.

Custis slept sitting up, sometimes leaning his head against the window. He used his coat for a pillow, hoping to protect his skull from sudden jolts against the glass. His thoughts jostled with each sudden movement. He thought of his project and ran through new possibilities. He'd need to leave Wilson Place. He wondered about his friend Ben Cobbler and his cryptic behavior. But when he thought of Sarah, everything else went away. He tried to imagine what she would look like now. He remembered her pink dress, standing next to her father while taking on the town mob. He closed his eyes and chuckled as he imagined the same little girl threatening to disguise herself as a man to outsmart an entire university system.

For five days, Custis fell asleep alone but woke up sitting next to strangers. Everyone seemed to be looking at him. Children stared at his eyes. Their parents studied his clothing, and ne'er-do-wells scrutinized his bags and belongings.

The porter entered the car. "Ten minutes. Ten minutes to next departure."

Seven years and ten minutes. He felt an uninvited nervousness stirring in his stomach. He gathered his belongings, put on his bowler hat, and checked his reflection in the window glass. He rubbed his unshaven face, the whiskers too short to be called a beard. *Not good.*

In the remaining nine minutes, memories flooded his mind. Reality jarred itself into priority. For him, analysis had always been his strategy. What would he say first to Sarah, to Martin? He had gotten taller, maybe put on weight. His voice had deepened. He was no longer the gangly kid Sarah saw last, but a professor at Wilson Place. He was still in love with the eighteen-year-old girl who couldn't say goodbye.

Sarah was betrothed to another man, a man Custis did not know. How could he face her and profess to be perfectly happy about the engagement? How could he pretend he didn't love her anymore? What would she say to him? He'd tell her she was beautiful. No, that wasn't on the list. He had written things down he wanted to say, but excitement took the words away. He quickly patted his pockets. *Where did I put it?* He'd meet the driver, then be taken to the ranch. He still had time to make another list, but no means to shave.

The train dragged to a stop. His car would be the last to disembark, the farthest away from the platform but closest to the obnoxious engine. He stepped to the door and looked down the line of cars. Small portable stairs were on the platform. The porters and the conductor assisted passengers down to the wooden landing while bags and luggage were brought out by employees and stacked nearby. Custis looked at his shoes. He rubbed each top on his pant legs, seeking to find the shine again. Two questionable wooden steps attached to welded metal stair-stringers descended to one big leap onto the jutted rocks below.

The train engine was still panting and wheezing. Some people meandered, trying to find their loved ones. Others walked away with purpose. Some chatted and laughed, while others hugged and cried.

Custis walked down the edge of the line, carrying his own bags. The jagged and uneven rocks kept his eyes downward. He'd momentarily pause and look forward, wondering how he'd find his driver. Maybe he would be found first. By the time he reached the platform, the steam from the engine had receded to barely a wheeze.

At the other end of the station, he noticed a woman wearing an exquisite hat. People darted back and forth in front. She stood still, opposite the surge of anadromous travelers. Custis placed his bags on the platform and easily lifted himself onto the deck. He straightened his jacket and tie. It felt good to walk, stand, and breathe in the fresh air. By now, most people had dissipated, along with their luggage and families.

The woman in the hat had not moved. He could see her now out of the corner of his eye. Custis wanted to turn and stare but abided his discipline and looked away. He was back in the town that had killed his mother and had wanted him dead as well. And from what he understood, nothing much changed. The pain of losing his mother had eased with time—the hatred from others had not.

The woman wore a long flowing dress, maybe a tiny print that gave off a light shade of blush. Her hair was pulled up neatly but allowed just a strand down on either side of her face. She was beautiful. Custis couldn't pinpoint what it was about her. He had never been good at social cues.

He wanted to steal a glimpse but forced a blink and kept his head turned away. *The driver must be late, might be inside the lobby.* Custis picked up his bags and walked to the opened doors of the station. The woman was closer now. He glanced in her direction. He wanted more but was afraid. Why was she not moving? He couldn't help but stare at her now. There was no mistake.

Custis dropped his bags, landing with a thud. He took three steps toward her, maybe four. He didn't know for sure.

"Sarah?"

"I had forgotten how striking your eyes are, Cus. They're mesmerizing."

Custis could not stop staring at her. This moment, a lifetime of rules, no longer existed. Her smile was genuine. She stepped closer to him, now only two feet apart. He wanted to reach out, take her into his arms, and hold her close. His childhood best friend, who once towered over him, wearing britches and a sweat-stained straw hat, had unequivocally metamorphosized into an entirely different being. He didn't know what to do with his hands. He breathed in. At least he remembered to do that.

He saw Sarah's hands trembling. She started to reach out to him, then stopped. She looked around and then lowered her head as a single passerby gawked.

"Sarah," Custis whispered, "you are so beautiful. I almost didn't recognize you." He removed his hat. *There, one hand is now occupied.*

Sarah laughed. "So you mean I was ugly before?"

"No, Sarah. You've always been beautiful to me. I mean . . . I mean, you are. You are just stunning."

"Well, my friend, you have turned into quite the handsome character as well. I didn't expect you to be so tall. And so fetching."

Custis smiled. He wanted to say something noble. To say something that could sweep her away. "Six foot three. I need to find the driver your father arranged for." *Well, that wasn't so noble. That didn't even make sense.*

"He's around back; I just wanted to come along for the ride." She smiled. "Come on, Professor Custis. Let's get you to the ranch."

Custis stepped toward Sarah. He felt like a giddy puppy with no plausible direction other than to aimlessly follow.

"Get your bags, Cus."

He followed Sarah to the back of the station to an awaiting covered buggy.

"My, my, my. Just look at you. All grown up," the driver said.

"Buster? I didn't expect to see you until we got to the ranch." Custis reached out to shake his hand but hugged him instead.

"I'm doing a lot of driving nowadays. That horseshoeing and all, well, it's for younger men."

Custis helped Sarah into the carriage and began to close the door.

"Oh no, Cus. You ride with me, back here."

Custis looked at Buster.

"It's all right, Professor Custis. Miss Sarah picked this buggy out special. Got the good top on, deep on the sides."

Custis looked around. No one seemed to be watching. He smiled as Buster closed the door. The beam never left his face.

"Buster, let's go through town on the way home. Show him every-thing he's missed."

Buster tilted his head and touched the brim of his hat. "Will do, Miss Sarah."

Custis looked out on his side. He felt odd. The ranch had once given sanctuary from this town, and Wilson Place College had done the same. He had lived in isolation in both worlds. He felt wide open again, cast back in time, into reality, returned into the certainty of non-entity. He felt split in half, not fully belonging in either one.

"It'll be all right, Cus. Just lean back in the seat and keep your hat on."

17

The town had grown up as well. Asphalt and macadam roads had replaced the clay streets in some parts, still mainly cobblestone, with a rare sighting of timber planks in the low-lying areas near the outskirts. Trolley lines ran down the middle of the main street. Cement had replaced the wooden sidewalks. Some buildings were now five stories high, bursting with commerce. The roadway was noisy, raucous at competing levels, fluctuating octaves, unlike the monotonous clacking undercurrent of the train. A wagon driver yelled at a passing motorized bicycle to slow down as his horse startled. Another man hollered across the street at someone else. A trolley bell rang. Boys played ball. Gas streetlights had been replaced with electric. Arteries of wires and telephone lines strung overhead traversed to those who could pay.

It seemed as if it only took a handful of minutes for the hour ride out to the ranch. The archway was still there: *Tennison Ranch*. Custis stretched his neck out the window, looking up at the sign as they passed beneath.

"I'd like to walk up the lane, if you don't mind."

"Of course." Sarah smiled. "Buster, can you hold up right here?"

The buggy stopped, and Custis had the door open before Buster had a chance to help. "Stay right there, Buster. I got it."

Custis took Sarah's hand as she stepped down. He didn't want to let go. Custis wanted to be a different man, one without filter or explanation. He yearned to gently kiss the top of her hand and stare into her eyes. He felt himself guiding her closer to his chest. She didn't smile. Maybe he was misconstruing her now as he had with her letters. Perhaps over the years he had fabricated mutual adoration from a trembling pen stroke or words unsaid. But now it was no longer two-dimensional paper. Custis thought he felt her fingers tighten on his. Holding her hand came so easily; it was truthful and unconditional. She looked in his eyes, smiled politely, and took back her hand. He could have easily felt rejected, but there were too many other signs revealing the opposite.

"Thank you, Buster," Sarah said.

"All my pleasure, Miss Sarah. Professor Custis, I'll see to it that this luggage all gets up to the house." Buster headed up the lane.

"I don't like being called that."

"Being called, what? A professor? You are. Get over it."

Custis looked at the ranch. It was magnificent. He saw new buildings, horse corrals, irrigated pastures, and a working therapeutic walker with a circular alley next to the barn. Thoroughbreds dotted the green runs, segregated by fresh board fencing. Their shiny dark coats glistened, accentuating perfect muscle form as they romped with their associate donkeys.

"I'm amazed, Sarah. I knew this was all here, but you just don't appreciate its wonder until you see it with your own eyes."

"I'll take you to the classroom tomorrow. But for now, there's a couple of people waiting for you."

They continued up the lane. "It smells like home. There, sweet alfalfa and oat hay from the barn. And the river, I can smell it from here. Oh, my goodness. Full of trout, I suppose. We need to fish, Sarah, promise me. I've been practicing."

Custis paused and looked at the pump and water trough. He recalled another time. Memories filled his head of watering the horses after a long ride, fetching water for Mary, and Mr. Tennison protecting his family, his values.

"It still works, but we have several more wells now. All automated. Come on. Father is waiting."

A black-and-white dog ran from the barn. It barked at Custis and circled Sarah. She bent down, patted the dog's side, and kissed its head. "This is Ollie. She's our border collie. Wait until you see her work the cattle."

"Hello, Ollie," Custis said. "She's the third generation now?"

"Yes. All blue ribbons."

"Of course." The dog stood between Custis's legs, wiggling her tailless butt as she garnered rubs to her chest.

Custis and Sarah stepped up onto the porch. Custis looked at the rocking chairs. "As beautiful as this place is, I'd forgotten about so many of the little things."

Sarah pulled on the screen door. It screeched open.

"Even that."

Custis and Sarah walked into the library.

"Father, look what blew into town."

Martin stood from his desk and quickly walked to Custis.

"No, not this young man. This couldn't be our Professor Custis."

They shook hands and smiled.

"Good to see you, sir."

A voice came from the other side of the room. "Ronald Custis the First."

Custis turned and smiled broadly. "Doc Lyman! What a surprise. I didn't expect to see you here. I must apologize. I need to clean up. Five days on the train ... you can imagine."

Sarah looked at Custis. "Come on, I'll show you the way, just in case you've forgotten."

Doc Lyman nodded his head. Martin agreed. "You go on up. We've got lots of time."

Sarah pulled at his coat sleeve. "Come on. Father had a bath put next to your room."

She led him upstairs. Custis carried his bags and looked at each thing he passed by. Some were new, but it was the familiarity of the old that silently escorted him back in time.

"I've been living a bachelor's life with four wooden walls and bookshelves for so long, I've forgotten what a home should feel like."

"I'll go down and get you something to eat. You must be starving."

"That I am. I've been so anxious to get here, I haven't eaten since yesterday. I need to talk with you, Sarah, tell you something."

"Let me go get you some food, then we'll have plenty of time."

Custis took inventory of his surroundings. His mind burst with excitement. He wanted to see, hear, and experience everything. He placed his luggage on a rack at the foot of the bed. With both arms, he reached in and swooped up one big pile of clothing against his chest. He carried the load to the side of the bed, turned, and sat down. The soft mattress felt luxurious.

An oil painting above the bureau in front of him caught his eye. A skyscape of clouds with barely a horizon below looked as if it could have been a plein air painting of the sky standing sentry over the ranch. He leaned back on the bed, taking the armful of cloth-ing with him. He stared at the medallions and intricate woodwork that bordered the ceiling. He closed his eyes. For the first time in five days, he could lie supine. There was no more rocking or jarring of the train. Unadulterated silence had replaced the constant clacking of the wheels. His muscles seemed to meld into the mattress, the quality of which he had not felt in years. What an extraordinary feeling it was to experience the velocity of time—time that had taken Mary away, time that was pressing to alter his life, and time that was luring Sarah away. He slowly spread his arms out, clothing following, cascading all around, and fell asleep.

𝓍 𝓍 𝓍

As was his custom, Custis awoke before the rest of the household. He walked into the darkened kitchen and lit the stove. He put on the coffee and waited alone in the darkness. He recalled the summer days making blackberry jam, helping Mary with the recipe, boiling and stirring to the accurate consistency, the exact point of coagulation. He imagined Mary sleepily coming downstairs. Maybe even cursing at him for giv-ing her a start. He could almost hear her steps. They sounded so real.

A scream! A loud female's cry broke the darkness. It filled the kitchen with chaos. Custis jumped to his feet. A woman was in the kitchen. She grabbed a frying pan from the counter and swung it at Custis. Custis yelled. He held up his hands, trying to protect himself. She shrieked again and threw the iron skillet directly at his face. His forearms took most of the force, but the handle thumped into his forehead. He fell solidly against the table, ricocheted to a wooden chair, and broke it to pieces.

Custis woke up on the kitchen floor, with Sarah leaning over him. Martin handed her a wet cloth. A strange woman was crying in the corner.

"Raise his legs, Father. He may have fainted."

For a moment Custis thought he was back on the train. His head was going in circles again. "I didn't faint. She hit me on the head with a skillet." Custis sat up, squinted his eyes, and lay back down. "I think I have a concussion." He felt his forehead.

"You don't have a concussion, Custis. You fainted."

"Do you not see this lump on my forehead? She hit me. Who is she, anyway?"

Martin stood up straight. He was still in his bathrobe. "Good to have you back, Custis." Martin smiled. "You'll be fine."

"That's Layne. She's taken Mary's place."

"Mr. Tennison, I didn't know it was him."

"It's all right, I forgot to tell you he gets up early and sits in the dark," Martin said. "I'm going to get dressed. You all can figure this out now."

Sarah helped Custis to a kitchen chair. "Layne, can you get some ice for Professor Custis's big head?" She looked at Custis and smiled. Her face was only inches away from his.

Custis rubbed his forearm. It was tender to the touch. It had taken most of the blow; maybe he had fainted after all. Never would he admit it, though. He rubbed his face, closed his eyes, and moaned. "It hurts pretty bad. You'll have to keep an eye on me for the rest of the day. Check my pupils." He moved even closer to her.

"You're kind of a big baby now."

He felt her strong yet caring hands on both sides of his head. She leaned into him and stared into his eyes. He could feel her breath on his face. Her thumbs pulled up his eyelids. She examined his pupils, back and forth.

"Your pupils are fine." She abruptly let go of his head. She may have even pushed him back a little. She probably knew he wasn't really hurt, but seeing her reaction gave Custis a chuckle inside. "Next time, stay in bed like normal people."

"I am normal. I just like the quiet mornings."

Layne handed him an ice bag.

"And this morning was anything but." He placed the bag on his head and winced. "By the way, nice to meet you."

"I am sorry, Professor Custis. I had no idea it was you. I thought you were a burglar."

"Well, we should all sleep soundly knowing that the house is well protected."

"I'm so sorry."

"It's all right. I'll feel better when it quits hurting."

It was well into the afternoon before Sarah finished showing Custis all the ranch additions and improvements. They were never alone. The ranch was full of activity. He met with four students from the university and seemed to enjoy their projects with the demonstration fields. Custis offered suggestions regarding chemical makeup and fertilizer reactions, leaving them with possible solutions through mathematics, chemistry, and applied and pure formulations. He stayed with them into the night, working on their hypotheses and experiments.

The following morning, Custis stayed in his room until after sunrise. He loudly walked down the stairs. "I'm going to walk into the kitchen." He entered. He was alone. A plate of food on the table waited for him. *I thought no one got up early around here.* He sat down and ate cold eggs and ham.

Custis felt the coffeepot. It was still warm. He poured himself a cup, walked to the porch, and sat in one of the rockers. As he sipped his coffee, he looked out over the front of the ranch. The grounds were manicured. Everything seemed to be in perfect order—even the five large rocks. The same five rocks he and Sarah had rolled next to the lane years ago, where they had practiced fly casting.

Custis smiled. Today, he would find a way to be alone with Sarah. It could wait no longer.

Beyond the rocks, two horses and riders rode up the lane in the distance. One was Sarah, the other, a man Custis did not know. He was most likely Sarah's fiancé, the teacher in shining armor riding upon his steed. He rode behind Sarah's horse. The knight hadn't ridden much from the looks of it. Custis tried to smile. He felt his chest rise. Reality had returned with a cold burst of acuteness.

18

Sarah rose in the saddle and waved at Custis. She moved in flaw-less unison with her horse. Her hair cast away to the breeze they made. She was back in her britches and tall leather riding boots. Custis gestured back and forced a courtesy smile.

Both rode close together now, turning toward each other, talking and laughing. Custis stood next to the porch railing and waited. The cowboy hat shaded the man's face; most likely he was going bald, overweight, soft—maybe it was his jacket. His clothing looked fashionably new; it probably would show no sign of wear or stain. Most likely he wasn't used to being outside much. In just another minute, they'd be at the porch railing. *Better think of something nice to say.* Sarah looked wonderful. Her smile was genuine, and her eyes sparkled in the morning sun.

"Good morning. I see you found the coffee. Any more random assaults?"

"No, and apparently I was left completely unsupervised as well."

"Custis, this is Phillip Lucas. Lucas, this is Ronald Custis the First."

Custis looked at Sarah. "You always call your friends by their last names?" He barely nodded his head at Lucas. "Nice to finally meet you, sir. I've heard a lot about you. Congratulations on your capture of this extraordinary human specimen."

Lucas smiled as he dismounted, then handed Sarah the reins. "Well, I'm not quite there yet. She won't give me a matrimony date."

"Hard to pin her down."

Sarah shook her head. "Well, as you men decide my fate, I've got work to do." She led the horses away and disappeared into the barn.

Lucas stepped on to the porch as Custis extended his right hand. Lucas paused. He squared off as he looked up at Custis's face. Custis didn't move. It felt as if the moment had frozen, his arm and hand perpetually extended.

Lucas removed his hat, exposing a full head of hair. He wiped his forehead with a handkerchief. He smiled and shook Custis's hand. "I have heard so much about you. Any friend of Sarah's will always be a friend of mine. My condolences. I know Mary must have been very special to you."

Lucas was probably a fine man. He would have to be. "Thank you. Yes, she was. I'll be going up to the cemetery today. Sarah said the baptisia are in bloom down under the river birch. I thought I'd go there first. Mary's favorite."

Lucas was a big man. Broad shoulders made the rest of him appear triangular. He looked older than Sarah. Handsome enough— his hands uttered academics. Sarah had described him as being misjudged on the outside while being kind and considerate on the inside. Sometimes, she wrote, he could act quite intimidating, which he used to his advantage to control unruly students, and sometimes to regulate a parent. He was strict but always rewarded the students appropriately, and the school board loved him. Custis stared at his face. *Obviously manipulative, too.*

"Sarah tells me you've been traveling with Mr. Tennison to the West Coast during the summers. Railway designs," Custis said.

"Yes, it's the only time I can leave. I enjoy the extra work. Too bad I didn't study civil engineering. But I do what I can."

"Never too late to go back for a degree."

"No, I enjoy my young students very much. I like staying here, close to the ranch, for much of the year. Sarah and I want to build a house right over the hillock. There." Lucas pointed out over the pastures.

"It's a beautiful spot. You can see that area from the third story, the attic."

"Martin wanted us to stay in the house, but I would rather have a small home—well, big enough for a passel of children."

Custis smiled politely. He had thought about this before, Sarah having children. Of course, that would be expected, typical. But now, at this moment, the reality of Sarah being with Lucas for the rest of her life was galling. He wondered how long she had been in love with him. Maybe she wasn't. She had written about Lucas over the years, but it always seemed platonic. She wrote about plans, her desires, her future, but Lucas was never mentioned as her potential husband.

Lucas slightly tilted his head, as if waiting for Custis to say something. Custis realized he was lost in thought. "I'm sure it will be a wonderful home."

Sarah and her father emerged from the horse barn. Martin cupped his hands around his mouth and hollered. "Custis, come see the new foal."

"Well, let's hope it's not a thoroughbred." Custis stopped and looked at his old room on the side of the barn. It was cluttered with numerous boxes and crates, appearing to be an office and storage room now. Custis looked in the far corner. He moved some boxes and exposed his old loblolly pine desk. Custis gently rubbed the top edge. Still smooth as the day it was given to him. He uncovered the top and squatted down in front of it. He touched the legs, worked the drawers, and caressed the hardware. Still solid, still perfectly beautiful.

Custis felt a gentle hand on the top of his shoulder. He knew it was Sarah. It was a comforting, intimate touch, and he didn't want to disturb it. He couldn't be sure if she were alone. He turned his head. Only Sarah.

Custis smiled. His voice was almost a whisper. "Want to see something?"

"Sure."

Custis pulled open the smallest drawer, released the catch, and turned it over. A rudimentary carving was on the bottom—numbers inside a heart.

Custis stood up and showed Sarah the bottom of the drawer. He rubbed the numbers with his fingers. "I did it with the pocketknife Mary gave me. She made me pay a penny for it. Said it was bad luck to give a knife away."

"Sixteen and six. I don't know what that means."

"Those are atomic numbers for weight on the periodicity of the elements scale."

"I still don't know what it means."

"It's how they're organized. The atomic number sixteen is sulfur. Six is for carbon."

Sarah studied the carving. "S and C?"

Sarah's stare suddenly lifted. Custis felt as if something deep inside of him had just been set free, impossible to recapture. The carving was from a schoolboy, but now he stood as a man in love with her—a Black man, a generation away from being enslaved. Sarah would now realize he had been in love with her for years. Maybe she was in love with him. He had to get ahold of himself, calm his insides. He was a Black man, and that would never change. Maybe she would laugh, *silly children*. Perhaps she would turn and run away. Custis began to reach out with his hand. He whispered, "Sarah, please don't marry him."

"Come on, you two, come meet our newest addition." Lucas smiled as he came through the door, jarring Custis from his thoughts. "Come on."

Sarah seemed to startle but just as quickly returned a smile to Lucas. "Coming, my love."

x x x

Custis was the guest of honor at dinner. He beamed, shared stories, laughed, and sometimes nearly teared up. Lucas smoked a cigar as Martin and Doc Lyman drank a whiskey and peppered Custis with questions regarding his schooling and professorship at Wilson Place.

"I wish you could stay in Carolina and be a part of the faculty here."

The room became quiet. Custis looked at Sarah and Lucas, then at Martin. "Mr. Tennison, it's different in the North. There is no negro faculty allowed here, at Rosemont Hill. Actually, not even Black students."

No one said a word. Sarah glanced at Custis. She looked as if she were about to cry. Reality had crept back in. Lucas looked downward, his fingers fidgeting with his cigar.

Martin looked disconcerted. He spoke clearly and methodically. "I know. I was just wishing it was different. I don't want to pretend to be color-blind, Custis. I see and appreciate you for who you are, where you come from along with all the experiences you must have gone through. I just want you to have what we all have."

Custis cleared his throat. "My college does not have a doctorate program in physics or science, which means I can go no further. Most Black universities only offer industrial arts curriculums. There are some where I can get a law degree, a doctorate in education or economics, an architectural degree, mathematics, or be a professor in any of those disciplines. I am not allowed to attend White universities with graduate programs that can accommodate my work. Because I am a Black man, my work, my research, stays locked up in a closet."

Martin shook his head. "I am sorry, Custis. My naïveté is appalling at times. I have given so much to our university here. Maybe I can make some contacts."

"Thank you, but no. I'm afraid it is beyond your influence. I would enjoy helping with the students here on the ranch, but agriculture is not my desire. Your work here is noble. It not only provides for the students, but you are making a difference in the state and, hopefully, the country very soon."

Sarah looked confused. "What is your work that's locked up in a closet?"

"Medical research and physics. I want to design a machine that can look inside the human body—a live human body—without breaching the skin." He looked at Martin, then back at Sarah. "A machine that can discover cancer in its infancy. I dream of attending Centennial University in New York, where my work in physics can continue and be recognized as such. There is talk of Centennial becoming desegregated, but it will only allow industrial arts degrees, and even that will be off campus. I've spent the last four years looking in the North, South, out West, and even overseas. I've been in correspondence with a university in Belgium. It's a possibility, but Centennial is a perfect match for my project. They have just begun working with radiation—the only place in the nation. Their laboratories are avant-garde. I'm not going to give up, but right now, I have taken it as far as I can."

"We can build you something here, Custis," Sarah suggested.

"No, although I appreciate your gesture. I've already tried to build my own laboratory. My needs will take hundreds of thousands of dollars, maybe millions—laboratories, equipment, supplies, research assistants . . . the list goes on. Some of my research will take me into working with radiation. It will need to be sanctioned. Only an established research university can help me now. And Centennial has the laboratory I need." Custis briefly made eye contact with each person around the table. "Unfortunately, they are more interested in my skin color than what I can accomplish in the medical arena."

After a long, silent pause, Doc Lyman said, "We need to find a way. There's got to be some means to get you in."

After supper, Custis accompanied Doc Lyman on a walk down the lane. The evening air was full of autumn, the aroma of oncoming rain, a slight breeze that compelled a chill up the spine, and the prolific minstrel of the night birds' songs. Custis slowed his pace and made sure he didn't rush. The seven years of being away showed on Doc. His hair had thinned and grayed, his steps were more deliberate, and his voice had turned a little velveted.

"Sometimes, Custis, I feel as if doctoring has passed me by. Seems all I'm good for anymore is birthing babies and stitching folks up. Can't imagine the work that's being done now—inventions, new tools and techniques, and drugs, too. I'd like to hear more about your work."

"The mechanics of radiation—I have this idea. I can feel it, see it, hear it. I just don't yet know how to get there. A radiation probe, but invisible. It needs something to travel through a conductor, maybe water. A range far above human sight, though. Atoms can travel into a patient, through the body, if you will, and bounce back when they reach different types of tissue. It opens up the entire body, so to speak, all without incision."

"It sounds fascinating, but dangerous, too."

"Yes. All my research on paper leads to radiation damage. I must develop something similar but not so lethal. Maybe some form of electrical stimulus. I can't get it out of my head. I can't sleep at night. When

I was little, I saw the pain and hurt in Sarah over the loss of her mother. Sarah once told me her mother was the strongest woman she ever saw. She watched her dwindle away to almost nothing. Cancer seems so common. Why is that, Doc? Why can't we figure out how to get to the cancer before it gets to us? I see the formulas for my machine over and over again. It's obsessively coming out, bit by bit. There is more to an atom than originally thought, and it has something to do with how it will work. Somehow, it will come. There is research being done in Germany right now that can take a photograph of a human bone, but my work will be different."

"You said something about Belgium?"

"Yes, they are very interested, but they cannot confirm they will have access to the complete necessities. Centennial in New York has what I need, and the money to fund it, but as soon as they see my alma mater, my application will be rejected, regardless of my degrees."

"What can we do?"

"The impossible."

19

artin and Custis drank their morning coffee in the library. Custis admired the books and looked at framed schematics of railways and roundhouses. "You know, Custis, all night I was thinking about you staying for a while. I've got to leave for a few weeks this coming month. I'm putting in a new locomotive roundhouse in central California. I need to look at some of the surveying first hand. Too bad you couldn't stay and help run the ranch for a couple of weeks."

"I need to get back to Ohio. They are expecting me."

"You've been going gangbusters for seven years now. Maybe it's time to take a short sabbatical. Finalize your thoughts about your work. Lucas has been doing that, taking a break from his teaching. He's been coming along, working right beside me, learning the business."

Custis listened to his words. Lucas was going to be Martin's son.

"He loves Sarah. He works hard, trying to fit in. He knows that she'll never leave the ranch, so I guess he's come to terms with living out here. It's funny, though. Sarah gets this faraway look in her eyes, and I don't know where she goes. I thought the wedding would be last spring, but she finds reasons to postpone it. She will marry him, I have no doubt. She just needs to work something out in her head, I suppose."

Custis felt his muscles tighten. He had given Martin no indication that he was in love with his daughter. Maybe Martin had picked something up from Sarah. *What is he trying to say?*

"The happiest day in my life was the day I married her mother, and I want Sarah to have that type of love. And I'm sure Lucas will be that man."

The words hit hard. They were not true. No one could love Sarah the way Custis did. The ranch had always offered sanctuary; Martin had provided him a life, but Sarah—she had given him the inspiration to live again. Custis needed more data. He needed to know what was real and what was illusory.

"Sarah's been doing a fine job running the ranch. With overseeing the demonstration fields and classrooms, it's hard for her to do it all alone. We've been looking for some help, but no one seems to be able to keep up with her. It would only be for a month or so, just until we get back."

Sarah came into the room, carrying a cup and saucer. "Oh, dear, what are you two scheming?"

"Your father just proposed I stay for a few weeks." The idea of a month with the most beautiful woman his eyes had ever seen just over-rode reality.

Of course he could take a sabbatical. "I'll have to send a telegram back to the college." Custis couldn't stop smiling. He kept his eyes on Sarah. He waited for her reaction. Would she jump for joy, clap her hands, and beg him to stay?

Sarah set her cup and saucer on the desk, kissed her father on the cheek, and walked out of the room. Custis was still. He felt his smile disappearing. How could he mask the look of devastation that must be on his face? He looked at Martin. Martin shrugged his shoulders.

Custis yelled, "Where are you going?"

"Into town to send a telegram to Wilson Place before you change your mind."

It took everything that Custis had to constrain his happiness—Martin would be watching. He thought he felt his body leaping up and down. *Elation, a month alone with Sarah!* Completely unsupervised, free to roam 1,032 acres in the middle of nowhere with the woman he loved. Time for unfettered conversations. Custis swore he felt his body rising, floating in air. *Euphoria.* The feeling of bodily well-being and hopefulness such as misplaced presentation in the final stage of terminal illnesses. *Oh, my God, I'm going to die.*

Both heard the front door slam. Custis dropped from the ceiling. Martin put on his reading glasses and picked up the newspaper from his desktop. "Well, I guess that settles it."

x x x

Martin and Lucas left for California the following week. Custis worked at the demonstration fields and tutored those falling behind or those who could not afford to travel home for the weekends. He toiled consistently on his research hypothesis and devotedly helped Sarah with anything she needed. Custis learned more about animal husbandry than he cared to. The breeding, feeding, and tending processes were unyielding. He watched calves being born, helped deliver a litter of puppies, and put an old dog down when Sarah could not.

In the evenings, Sarah and Custis sat in the porch rocking chairs and took turns reading to each other. Custis adored listening to Sarah. Her voice had a poet's soul. It had the power to transform make-believe, soothe his consciousness, and steal away reality. He wanted to stay right there, next to her, forever. He imagined being close enough to feel the vibration of her intimate words. He closed his eyes and leaned his head back on the rocker. It would be a dangerously impossible relationship.

"Why don't you marry him, Sarah?" Custis asked.

"I will someday soon. He's a good man."

"Someday. Soon. An oxymoron? What is it, exactly?"

"It's exactly what it means. Someday soon. In the future. Soon."

"And children."

Sarah closed the book. "That is out of the blue, but yes. I'd like to have daughters. I want to see them be able to have a great education. Maybe veterinary school someday. After college, I tried to go. I wanted to specialize in veterinary medicine, but none allowed women. Iowa State, Chicago, Minnesota, St. Louis, Harvard—I tried them all, even the University of South Carolina. My father was so angry. He threatened to sell off some of the land and put in his own school. Even wrote to the state representative."

"Someday, Sarah, women will be running this country."

"I can't even ride into town without the fear of being arrested for wearing trousers. I can't imagine how you must feel at times. I guess we're both outcasts." Her distant stare lingered as they sat in the twilight in comfortable silence, the kind where the absence of words nurtured contentment. The sort of silence that came so effortlessly between friends.

"You have been a great friend to me, Sarah."

"We have the same faults in common. What more could we ask for?"

Custis stood from the chair. He walked to hers, bent down, and kissed her softly on the cheek. His lips remained on her skin for only a moment. She closed her eyes. She didn't breathe. Custis rested his cheek next to hers and kissed her again. He felt no movement in return. "Good night, Sarah," he whispered.

Custis turned and walked away. He felt lightheaded. He trembled inside. His heart felt out of rhythm. He thought he might faint. He was out of control. *What have I done?*

"Cus?"

He paused. Forgotten childhood memories streaked by like a fast-moving train. A cardinal sin—the voices were clear and cruel. He remembered the merciless blows to his body, appalling laughter, and running as fast as he could in urine-soaked clothes. But this was different.

He had touched Sarah before. *But never like this.*

He waited for her words. Would they be kind, or had he crossed boundaries and severed their relationship? He could leave in the morning and never come back. She could marry Lucas and have his children. He couldn't look at her. He stood motionless.

"Tomorrow is Sunday. The crew doesn't work until early Monday morning. Maybe we can go riding, just the two of us."

His mind had taken free rein with either end of the emotional spectrum. It was seizing control of his entire nervous system. He couldn't speak. His eyes felt swollen. Tomorrow, he would leave nothing unsaid. He tried to swallow but only managed to nod his head. The screen door screeched as he pulled it open.

Custis found himself lying in the dark on top of his bed. He was back on the train. The room was lurching out of control. His thoughts were a horizontal blur. He dreamt, not of figures or conjectures, hypotheses, or solutions. He dreamt of being with Sarah.

x x x

Custis was in the barn before sunrise. He had slept fitfully, replaying events in his head. It became a visual distortion of colors, an embellished vision anticipating what the day would bring. He changed his clothing two different times and shaved closer than usual.

The animals were fed and watered. Not knowing which horses Sarah wanted to take, he combed out four of her regulars. Three were working quarter horses. The fourth was a feisty Tennessee Walker named Firecracker. He wiped down the bridles and saddles and packed water and food to take along. He sat in the barn and looked up at the house. Still no sunrise. Still no Sarah.

Custis raked the loose hay back into the stalls as Hatchet II supervised from a rafter. Every few seconds, Custis glanced out the door. He wondered if she had overslept. Maybe she also had a restless night. He walked to the slider, took in some air, and waited.

A figure emerged from the darkness.

"Good morning. I saw you from the house. Brought you some coffee."

Sarah handed Custis the cup, the steam still rising. His fingers purposely touched hers. He smiled and took a sip.

Sarah had pulled her hair up under her canvas fishing hat. This was when she looked the prettiest, Custis thought. Loose strands fell to her jacket collar. Her eyes glistened. "How is it? The coffee?"

"I couldn't sleep last night."

Sarah stared, not saying a word. Custis's mind ran in tight little circles. Why was she not saying anything? She just stood there, looking at him. He wanted to close his eyes and silently pray for guidance or forgiveness, whichever was applicable.

Custis felt her hand in his as she took his coffee cup and tossed it into the hay pile. She leaned her body into his, placed her hands around his face, and kissed him on the mouth. He kissed back passionately. He believed it was real this time.

x x x

Late morning, they found a spot to rest near the river. Sarah tied the horses to a dead-fall maple. The meadow grass was deep and dry. Custis retrieved the lunch he had packed; he had no desire to eat but thought Sarah might.

They sat on a slight rise in the meadow, shoulder to shoulder. Custis's arms rested around his raised knees, his hands locked together. They watched the horses, the clouds in the sky, and passing cranes. Custis waited for Sarah. *A touch is all it would take.* He wanted to breathe the same air, feel her head on his shoulder, feel the warmth of her skin on his. But Sarah's words never came. He reached over and took her hand.

Custis broke the silence. "Do you love him?"

For a moment, Sarah was still. She squeezed his hand, looked out toward the river, then down to the ground in front of her. She took a long breath. "Yes, I love him. But—I am *in* love with you."

Custis sat motionless. He recited the words in his head. He needed to say something, move, react with intensity. Sarah was waiting. He wanted to burst out, yell at the top of his lungs that he was in love with Heather Sarah Tennison. He wanted to run through the field and stand on the highest hill.

"Phillip Lucas is a good man. But I've been waiting for you, it seems, my whole life."

"Sarah, I love you. I love you with everything I have. I've been wanting to say it out loud my whole life. I feel like you have just given me a breath that is saving my life again. I didn't know what to do. I am so scared of what may happen to you and your father. The enormity of what could be ahead seems so insoluble."

"We can live on the ranch. No one will ever know."

"What about your father, Sarah? How will he really feel about his daughter with a Black man? He raised me as his own son."

"Well, son-in-law is good, too. I've been hurting, aching, since seeing you step off that train. Each night when I fall asleep, I dream of you. And then, at that moment between sleep and awake, I pretend I will find you lying next to me."

"I want that as well. What about Lucas? What will he do?"

"I'll have to tell him. He deserves the truth."

"No one can know about us, and certainly not Lucas. It's too dangerous, and the penalty will be death for me. We need to think this through and be smart, Sarah."

"We can move to a different country. You said Belgium will accept you."

"They will accept me, and they will accept you, but not *us*. You can travel in first class, and I'll be in steerage." He smiled. "We can get there, of course, but we have no place safe to be together. We will never be received as a couple anywhere we go. We would have to remain at the ranch forever."

"And you could never finish your future work, your experiments. I can't think straight. Right now, Cus, I just want to live in this moment. We have that for sure."

The breeze was warm. The waist-deep grasses waved in rows of passing unison—the dry shafts colliding in concert. Custis turned toward Sarah. He reached up and cupped her face in his hands and kissed her deeply. Her hair fell to her shoulders as Custis removed her hat. He gently pulled back, looked into her eyes, and kissed her again. Sarah gathered him against her and gently pulled him to the ground. The tall grasses offered sanctuary from the breeze and a brief reprieve from a condemnatory world.

It was near dark before Sarah and Custis returned home. The barn was quiet except for a pair of doves in the rafters. Custis unsaddled the horses while Sarah fed and watered the others. Both worked in silence. Custis glanced at Sarah every chance he got. He watched her watching him. Without a word, Sarah turned the lights out, one by one. She paused at the last lamp, stared at Custis, and turned it off. He felt her approaching. He held out open arms and brought her in. With Sarah in his arms, he had never felt so absolute, so perfect, so consumed by anything before. There, alone in the darkness, nothing else mattered.

x x x

The summertime days passed instantly with Sarah next to him, and nights were almost without sleep. He was in love with the most beautiful girl in the world, and she was in love with him. Custis had never felt so unrestricted and spontaneous in all his life.

Layne was awake at daybreak. Coffee was hot by the time Custis came down to the kitchen.

"Good morning, Layne. I think summer's about to get over. It feels different in the mornings now."

"Yes, it does. Telegram came yesterday for Miss Sarah. She must have missed it by the time she got in last night."

"Hope everything is good. We'll make sure she sees it this morning."

"Sees what?" Sarah said as she entered the kitchen.

"Telegram, Miss Sarah. Came yesterday afternoon."

Sarah rubbed her eyes and fingered her hair back from her face. She opened it slowly. It must have been brief. She looked at Custis, then back down.

"What is it, Sarah?"

"Father and Lucas will be arriving in two days. They look forward to seeing us." Sarah cleared her throat. She placed the telegram on the table. The envelope fell to the floor as she turned and left the room.

Custis stared at the yellow paper. He wanted to pick it up and read it with his own eyes, but he knew it was true. Two more days until reality ruptured back through, invading his enchanted fairy tale.

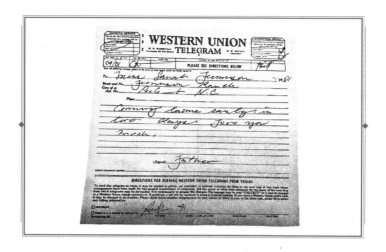

L ayne picked up the envelope from the floor and placed the telegram back inside. She handed it to Custis. "You and Miss Sarah got some thinking to do."

Layne's words hit Custis like a shock wave. He felt so foolish, perhaps even arrogant, that he'd really believed no one would ever find out.

"You've been here a month now. I see the way you look at her, and I see her smiling back. Now, I know Miss Sarah pretty well. Known her way before Mary died. I don't know for sure what's been going on, but if she's got herself all mixed up with the likes of you, then you must mean the world to her.

"She has everything possible she could ever want—her daddy, an education, the farm, and Mr. Lucas. Now everybody's in jeopardy here. You're gonna get yourself arrested or killed, or both. You're putting

Miss Sarah in a real bad situation. You're forgetting about Mr. Lucas? He may just kill you himself before word ever got out that his future wife was with a Black man. No one would ever know what happened to you. Maybe never even find your body."

Custis found Sarah in the barn. He soundlessly watched her brushing down a mare. She had been crying. She wept as she spoke softly to the horse.

Sarah stopped. She didn't look up. "I knew you'd come out here."

Custis walked into the stall. "When I'm really scared, in my head, I work mathematical equations over and over again to disguise what's really going on inside of me. I have endured pain for most of my life, whether physical, emotional, or psychological—after a while, it all feels the same. It never quite goes away. But when I'm with you, it's different. It's the worst pain of all."

Sarah turned sharply, her swollen eyes looking into his.

"It is a bottomless pain, an intuitive awareness that I can never have what I truly want—to go far, far away with you by my side. I no longer want to live in a fantasy. I want to live in the real world with you as my wife."

Custis stepped toward Sarah and took her hands. "You ready to go figure this out?"

Sarah sniffed, then smiled. "Of course I am. Two days. Two thousand eight hundred eighty minutes." She stared at Custis. "I've been practicing my arithmetic. Come on, let's go."

Firecracker and Sheba were already saddled. Custis shook his head. "You're so predictable."

He watched Sarah as she tightened the saddle's leather strap around the fishing rods. Her long, slender fingers meticulously pulled the cinch and double-checked the buckles and ties.

"I am *not* going to ride Firecracker. Last time, he tried to kill me," Custis declared.

"He did not try to kill you. Take Sheba."

Custis took the reins, patted Sheba's neck, straightened her fore-lock, and kissed her on the muzzle. "Hello, girl. Ready for a ride?"

"I'll take the rods, and you take the basket Layne filled for us. Let's go."

An hour's ride took them to where the river bent south, a place that, if only for a moment, allowed the world to slip away. The water opened up right before the bend and formed a large, quiet pool that didn't have a name. The pond edge was shallow enough for the horses to drink, kick, and scare any fish. The surface ripples spread out wide, finally dissipating into the distant current.

Until the river turned to freestone several miles downstream, the land on either side was on the Tennison estate. Except for the company of an occasionally lost squatter, this place was solely theirs to share.

Custis unsaddled the horses and tied their leads to a rope already stretched between two trees. Here they had been secured many times, under the shade of the maples where they could graze.

"There you go, Sheba. All you can eat, now." He rubbed her back, wet with sweat where the saddle had been. *How it must feel to have an entire life completely unencumbered.* He smiled and turned to Firecracker. "What are you looking at?"

Sarah was just entering the pond. Her clothes were neatly folded and placed near a quilt she had spread beneath a sweetgum tree. From a distance, Custis watched her walk deeper into the river. Not a breath of air could be found. The water slowly wrapped around her naked body. A flawless body, now being embraced and kissed by the sun.

She sank under the surface, then slowly reappeared. "Come on, Cus!" She let the water clear her hair from her face. She sank back down to her shoulders and waited.

Custis sat down on the quilt.

"I'll stay right here," he said firmly. Custis rested his arms on his knees. He wanted to look around, make sure it was safe, but he couldn't manage to take his eyes away from Sarah. His thoughts were lost in the sun-speckled surface of the water. He felt as if he were drowning. The water wrapped in, keeping him from the air he needed.

"Professor Custis! The cool water will do you well. It will take all that weight off your shoulders."

"That's exactly what I'm concerned about. It's too dangerous out here, Sarah."

"Come on!" She smiled at Custis as she caressed the water with her arms. "I love you twice around the world, you know."

His body screamed for oxygen. He wanted to gasp for air, but if he did, the water would fill his lungs. He'd slowly and effortlessly sink to the bottom of the pond, where he would never be found. "Only 49,802 miles' worth? What happens after that?" Custis smirked. "But the meridional circumference would be more. So, which is it, since you've been practicing?"

Custis lost sight of her in the sunlight. He lay back and stretched out on the blanket. Warm bits of dappled sunlight danced downward through the sugar gum leaves. His mind descended deeper under the water. He dreamt of when he was young, walking beside Sarah as she rode bareback on Stardust. He recalled, even then, wishing to ride up there with her. Over fields of tender new grasses, he had imagined his arms straight out to his side, lifting on the breeze—unencumbered. He'd listen to her laugh and feel her wild hair blowing back, tickling his cheeks.

Custis stirred to the sound of squawking crows. *Caw–caw–caw.* He eavesdropped on their chatter. *Caw–caw–caw.* It was a disparate sound without music, unlike the melody of the cardinals, the distant call of the chickadee, or even the lulling beckoning of a titmouse. *How is that possible, a bird with no song?* Custis abruptly sat up, his eyes scanning all around. It was an alarm! Had someone arrived at the pond? An intruder? *Where's Sarah? Her clothes are gone!*

The horses swished their tails as they grazed about aimlessly. The meadow was motionless except for the gossamer webs drifting horizontally in the air. Leaves rustled above as the crows deserted their perch and flew away to wherever they wished.

She was fly-fishing, almost waist-deep in the pond. The surface was perfectly still except for the minute drops of water falling from the line as it was cast forward and back. Weightless water-striders skimmed the surface on their long, spindly legs, leaving no trace of their existence. Dancing above the meadow and illuminated by the long afternoon sunbeams, autumn's gnats flew like tiny daytime fireflies.

Custis watched Sarah effortlessly orchestrate the connection between man and nature. The precision flight of the line, forward and back, was lulling, mystically addicting, an ellipse repetitively lassoing the atmosphere. If he could hear the movement itself, Custis imagined an unhurried cello sonata performed by experienced hands, her hands. In Custis's mind, the movement was a mathematical equation, a heuristic process of control and beliefs accompanied by rhythmic sound waves he couldn't quite hear.

Back and forth, over and under. The movement of the line, an experiment trying to imitate nature with an artificial invertebrate teasing the limbless, cold-blooded dupes harbored just below the surface. Custis was that fingerling trout hiding in the shadows of rock, tormented by things he wanted but couldn't have.

Custis was lost in his comfortable world of scientific assessments where time and reality vanished easily. Sarah sat down next to him. He was startled by her touch. In the honesty of the moment, he reached out and pulled her close. But he had lost track of time, the sense of his surroundings. Someone could be near, watching from the distance. Custis abruptly drew away. He scanned the river, the edge of the woods, around behind; the meadow was clear. He had unintentionally dropped his guard. His nerves had taken hold and wouldn't let go.

"Custis, we're fine. No one is here. We're on the ranch."

He turned quickly and looked back toward the river. "I know, I know. I'm just making sure."

Sarah took his hand and pulled him back down. She kissed him three times, the last resting on his lips.

For Custis, the heart of mathematics was simple problem-solving—the nature of chemistry, matter changed but never lost. The problem was the color of his skin, a constant. He and Sarah had started as strangers. Then their relationship changed into friendship, grew into passion, and evolved into love. Custis turned his logical thoughts into a relationship of symbolic algebra, a conjecturing and convincing formula. He wanted Sarah to be happy, have a family, a future. Most of all he wanted her to be safe.

Custis lowered his head. "At night, when I close my eyes to sleep, I see you with Lucas. I know you love me." He looked into Sarah's eyes. "But that vision is destroying me on the inside."

"I am going to tell Lucas the wedding is off. He'll move away. We'll be safe here on the ranch for a while. I don't want you to stop your work. Your invention, I know how much it means to you and the world. What if your machine really could save lives? It could have saved my mother, prevented her suffering, saved a lifetime of heartache. I will not ask you to give up your dream."

"And I cannot ask you to give up this ranch. It runs through your veins just as deeply as my work runs through mine."

"I will wait. You can finish your work and can travel back to the ranch whenever you can. We can live here after your work is complete, or we can go to California. My father has business out there. Custis, I will wait for you."

Sarah paused and kissed Custis again.

"You don't understand. It's the same everywhere. Laws are differ-ent from state to state, but the prejudices remain. We couldn't even ride in the same train car or stay in the same hotel or eat in the same restaurant. I can't walk with you on a public sidewalk. In some cities, I can't vote unless I own land. We can't even be buried in the same cemetery."

Custis pulled away. "I've thought about this every possible way. I am not willing to live without you. We need to stay together. But it won't be possible when we use conventional baseline data. We need to change the formula in order for this to work."

She shook her head. "What do you mean?"

"Listen, Sarah. I've been working on a plan. It finally came together on the train." Custis lowered his head. "I wasn't going to mention it to you until I had everything worked out. It's illegal. If we get caught, I could be arrested or killed. But now, this stupid telegram. We don't have much time left. We must do it."

"Do what?"

"I am going to apply to Centennial in New York. The university. For my research."

Sarah let go of Custis. "It's for whites only."

"Yes. I am going to try and pass as a White man. I've heard others have done the same—all over the country, in fact."   .

Sarah quietly repeated some of his words. "Pass. Pass?"

"The world is not changing fast enough for us. The New South? It's getting worse. You said you'd wait for my work to be completed, but that may be years. I can't live that long without you."

"Have you met someone who has done this, who has passed?"

Custis stood to his feet. He tightly paced, then squatted down and took Sarah's hand. "No, not in person. But people do. At Wilson Place, I had friends that were involved in the underground. They came back from New York with documents for others. Perfectly fictitious. A Black man is right now serving in the State Assembly, and no one knows. There have even been Black women married to White men. It's the only way we can be together. I am going to pass, and you will be my wife. I want to walk down the sidewalk with you rather than behind you, to hold your arm in public.

"We can live in New York while I attend the university. Four years of study, then the laboratory will be all mine. Graduates have full access. It's what I've dreamt about since I was a little boy. My research will work. I will make a difference. After that, we'll move and buy a ranch. With a new identity, we *can* go to California, raise our children there. If it is possible for me to pass as White, then our children can as well. Please, Sarah. The only thing is we can never come back here. You can rebuild your ranch in California. We'll bring your father, start all over."

"Do you really think you can pass?"

"Look at me. Look at my light skin, my eyes, these same green eyes that disparaged me for years. Do you know how many times I was told that 'God has a plan' for me, that I'm 'special'? This is the *plan*, Sarah; I'm going to pass. Remember your letter to me a long time ago—how you were going to pretend, disguise yourself as a man to get into the school you wanted?"

"I was only joking, and I certainly wouldn't have been killed for it."

He helped Sarah stand, then pulled her close, face-to-face. In this moment, he was no longer a scientist or mathematician. His mind no longer held encryptions or formulated data. His eyes teared.

"I heard about a man, a Black man, who passed as White. He attended Georgetown University, got his degree, and is still teaching there. Several more stories of the same, in different cities, mainly on the East Coast. Some stories come out of Chicago."

"I remember something about Chicago," Sarah said. "When I was at Rosemont Hill, we heard of some type of revolt. Black people were killed—they were hanged for pretending to be White businessmen."

"They got caught because they weren't smart, Sarah. I am. I've got a chance to get into Centennial, to finish my work. My machine will save others. We're so close. I have a chance, and I'm going to take it. I'm doing this for us."

"But what if it doesn't work?"

"It will have to. This is the only way we can have it all."

Sarah shook her head. "We'll never be able to return to the ranch. This town has too many eyes and ears."

"No, we can never return. We'll have altered identities, a different life away from here. But wherever we end up, we can send for your father. That is, if he agrees."

"But my mother . . . my mother is buried here. And our Mary."

"My mother as well, somewhere in that unmarked grave. I'm afraid this may be harder on you than it will be on me. You have history, lineage, family and friends, and business connections that must be forever severed. I've worked hard in Ohio, purposely focused on academics, my work, and inventions. No one will miss me except a professor or two who may wonder whatever became of me. I can no longer hide my love for you. I want to scream out loud that I'm in love with you. But I can't tell anyone." Custis swallowed to clear his throat. He eased his grip on her arms. "I can make an entrance appointment. Next month."

"Next month? That will give me time to talk with Lucas."

"You cannot tell Lucas the truth, Sarah. He will be humiliated and may do something to stop us. Please, Sarah, not a soul can know. I need to leave, go back to Ohio, and clear up a couple things at the college. Then I will go on to New York. After I get things settled, I'll send for you."

"Send for me? How long will it take to get settled?"

"I don't know—maybe six months, maybe a year. It's better than having you wait here all alone for four years, then even more after that. When I get to New York, I'll write to you and let you know where I am. We just need to make sure Lucas is gone and won't intercept the letters. We have to be deliberate and measured. We have too much to lose. This is an identity that will go on for as long as we live and, eventually, our children will be part of it as well.

Sarah was silent. She looked deep in thought. "I can't imagine what my life could have been had Mother lived. People kept telling me I'd be all right. But I wasn't concerned about me. It was her. I still see her face when she was so desperate. On the outside, she was convincing; she even smiled at me. But I know on the inside she had such a profound sadness about leaving me, not knowing what would happen, who I'd grow up to be. I only wish she had known that I would grow up and marry the man who fought this bastard cancer."

Sarah looked directly at Custis. "I know you can do it, Cus. You need to go. You've got to be careful, so very careful. We can make this happen."

Custis wrapped his arms round Sarah and gently rocked her back and forth. Custis wiped his eyes, laughing and smiling as he brushed away the tears from Sarah's face. The setting sun backlit Sarah. Custis smiled; she looked like an angel.

Hand in hand, they walked through knee-deep grasses back to the horses. The last of the daylight fireflies seemed to understand their elation, parting the way, then falling back in behind, protecting them as one.

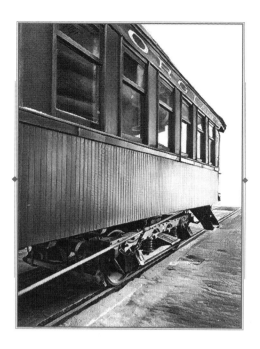

21

It was dark when Custis and Sarah reached the barn. A single lamp lit the interior. Lucas stood in silence. He had come home early.

Custis was unprepared. He looked at Sarah and primed himself to see her fear. His priority was to protect Sarah and shield their plan. But she waved and feigned a smile. "Hello, darling. When did you get home?" Sarah dismounted and quickly walked to Lucas, who remained in the partial shadows.

"About two hours ago."

Sarah quickly hugged him and kissed him on the cheek.

"I've been worried."

There was no anger in his voice. Lucas stood relaxed and motionless, as if conserving his heartbeats for a long battle. His eyes were that of a cobra, still and focused just before the deadly strike. Whether Lucas knew of the totality of the relationship, Custis was now unsure. Custis knew one thing—Lucas had been waiting for them.

"I knew you'd get here sooner or later. You all right?"

"Yes, of course. We went for a ride and checked out the upper reservoir, then checked on the timber growth. Custis helped me with the calculation of board feet. Then ol' Firecracker bucked Cus off and ran into the woods. We just lost track of time after that."

"Let me take care of your horse, my darling. I'll make sure to brush him down. Your father is up in the house. He has some exciting news for you."

As Sarah left the barn, Custis offered Firecracker's reins to Lucas. But he declined with his eyes.

"We caught an earlier train. I came home early to be with Sarah. When I couldn't find her, I went for a ride." Lucas looked at Firecracker, then back at Custis. "Put him away." His voice sounded resolved. Lucas fidgeted with something in his pocket, maybe coins.

Custis led the horse into the stall, removed the tack, and patted him down. Custis glanced at Lucas through the slats in the stall. From the shadows, he watched Lucas remove two shotgun shells from his pocket.

Lucas studied the shells. "How long have you known me, Professor Custis?"

Custis fought away the tremble in his hands. The quiver in his voice would be harder to disguise. Layne had predicted this day might come. Lucas would kill him, and no one would care, nor even know. Custis straightened his shoulders. His clothing was damp with perspiration. A cold shiver forced a sharp breath. He tried to calculate exactly how much blood was rushing through his head and at what velocity. His stomach prepared to heave with bile. *How long? How long have I known him or known of him? He knows. He went for a ride. He saw us at the river. He knows.*

Custis looked for the shotgun. It had to be nearby. But there was none. His eyes returned to the shells in Lucas's hand, then noticed his clothing. Hunting attire.

"Sir?"

"How long have we known one another?"

"A handful of weeks."

"Six and a half weeks, to be exact." Lucas paused. "I have known Sarah for five years now. I asked her to marry me a year ago. I have been waiting for her. She is all that I have."

Custis heard the burden in Lucas's voice. "I have given up part of my teaching so I might tailor into this family, to be closer to Sarah. I have traveled the country, learning to survey and draft to help her father. I know what kind of man you are, Professor Custis. You have a brilliant mind, evidenced by your education. You have the work ethic of a finely tuned machine and the strength and mettle of twenty men. I've seen you with Sarah. I have seen the way you look at her."

Custis stepped from the stall.

Lucas rotated the shells in his hand like he was playing with a deck of cards. "You know, suspicion is a hideous thing, the way it erodes connection and understanding. You will leave this ranch in the morning. Say your goodbyes and find an explanation to never return for a long, long time."

Custis wanted to sit down. Not because he felt weak but rather to keep his emotions masked. The sound of the words should have severed through the darkness with the precision of a scalpel plunging deep into his chest. They were absolute, irrevocable. But the thought of having a life with Sarah filled him with power. His plan was perfect, the only plan that could work, and he had something Lucas would never have—Sarah.

Lucas turned and stopped with his back toward Custis. "I will marry Sarah, Professor Custis. As for me right now, I shall go make passionate love to my beautiful fiancée."

Custis watched Lucas walk through the darkness and into the house. Custis would leave in the morning, but it was on his own terms. The plan had already commenced.

x x x

Before morning's light, Custis had packed up his belongings. All was quiet except for the squeak of the screen door. The only light source was the moon and stars overhead. He set his luggage on the front porch and walked out to the barn. It would be the last time he saw the ranch, the last time he'd walk down the stalls. He hoped he might see a distant relative of Hatchet, but the only animal that stirred was Firecracker with a swift kick to the wall.

Custis leaned over the half-door and whispered, "You won this time, Firecracker."

The horse walked over to Custis and stood completely still. Firecracker's eyes were calm. There was a glint of gentle wisdom, deep inside, a calmness that Custis found comforting.

"Are you saying you're going to miss me? I forgive you. You're a good boy." Custis reached out to pet his muzzle. Firecracker abruptly lifted his head and tried to bite Custis's fingers. Custis jumped back into the aisle. "Son of a bitch!"

Martin silently walked into the barn. He made eye contact with Custis and cleared his throat. Martin took off his hat and nervously toyed it in his hands. "Last night after Lucas came in, he said you'd probably be headed out today. I didn't sleep much. I was hoping to spend more time with you."

Custis wanted to reach out, hug Martin, and share words of joy and excitement. But no, this would have to be up to Sarah. She would be the one to know the opportune time.

"I need to get back. I didn't plan to stay this long, but I'm so glad I did."

"Me too. You coming back down for the wedding?"

"I don't think I can. I mean, I already took all these weeks." Custis was repulsed by his own lie. He wanted to tell Martin the truth. He wanted to believe that Martin would join them later and start a new ranch elsewhere. This was the part that required difficult lies.

"You know, after her mother died, Sarah was so empty. I thought she might die as well. You made her so happy. You gave her friendship, companionship. You gave her a zest for life itself, something I never could do. When I picked you up in that field so long ago, I felt an angel helping me. I believe it was my Heather. I want you to know this was all meant to be."

Custis pulled an envelope from his jacket pocket and handed it to Martin. "Please give this to Sarah. I'd appreciate it if you did it discreetly."

"I understand. I'll have Buster drive you to the depot."

"I was hoping you'd say that. Please tell her goodbye for me." Custis tried to smile.

Martin smiled. "She doesn't do well with goodbyes, does she? When she does that, it means she loves you." Martin paused. "I'm sorry the world is the way it is."

For a moment, Custis thought Martin might be trying to encrypt his words.

Martin reached out, shook Custis's hand, then hugged him. "Know that you will always be in our thoughts, always in our prayers. You did something for me, Custis. You gave me my daughter back, and you gave me a chance to raise a son."

"Thank you." Custis could barely form the words. Soon, he would take his daughter away all over again.

Martin looked straight at Custis. "I wish my Heather had known you. She would have loved you as well."

x x x

Custis fished his way through the train depot crowd. He carried a kit-bag strapped around his shoulder. His thoughts were raw and elsewhere. The side of the bag bumped into a few people, all giving him disparaging looks. Custis paused. He turned around and looked at the platform bursting with noisy people trying to talk above the engine's sound.

All strangers. His searching eyes combed over the crowd. He recalled years ago, being on the same platform, leaving for Wilson Place with Sarah refusing to see him off. *Maybe she came this time. Maybe Sarah is there, in the back, hidden within the movement of the herd.* But he knew what was happening—his emotions were overriding logic. *Breathe, just breathe.* He closed his eyes and listened just in case she was calling out for him. He imagined the conflated voices of the strangers turning into a great circle, whirling upward and away, leaving only Sarah standing on the platform.

Custis felt someone abruptly push against him. He opened his eyes to a man passing by.

"Get out of the way!"

Custis left the platform and found his car down the line. There was no conductor, porter, or steward to greet him or take his bag. Custis pulled himself up and found his seat in the middle of the car. He started to sit facing toward the back of the train but then changed to a forward-facing seat. He didn't want to say goodbye either. Not to Sarah, nor to the land he had grown to love. He wanted to remember the hills, meadows, and pastures, evident in his mind as if he were still there with her. It was the land he had to forsake so that another future might take hold.

His mind churned with plans. His cash would last a year if he was careful. Living arrangements would be the costliest until he was able to live in the dormitory. He had already researched the tuition and had set that money aside. Food and everyday expenses could be manipulated depending on the circumstances. The only thing he needed to do now was figure out, precisely, how to pass, establish himself, then send for Sarah.

A father, mother, and little girl sat down in the seat in front of him. The train lurched upon its departure. Custis leaned his head back on the seat and pulled his hat down over his eyes. He heard the little girl talking to her mother. She must have been looking out the window.

"Momma, horsey."

The little girl watched a stately Tennessee Walker. It was ridden by a beautiful woman with long, flowing reddish hair, chasing after the train until the curvature of the tracks faded her from sight.

PART III

22

1891
MANHATTAN, NEW YORK

C ustis had been in Manhattan for just over a week. He felt anonymous among a thousand faces. People moved like shoals of fish avowing to find the ocean. The current didn't stop for obstacles. Its members swirled round, separating, then effort-lessly merging again.

Buildings towered on either side of the harried street. Most were cement and steel, others grandiose with sculptured facades and porticos. All rose in a beige sky thick with smoke, amalgamated with rising clouds of white steam bulging from factory stacks. Water storage tanks silhouetted the skyline, perched atop each building like resting seagulls on dock posts.

There was no sanctuary or silence here. Streets were chaotic, with carriages, trollies, and cable cars all seemingly competing in different directions. Wayward pedestrians left the safety of the sidewalk and darted into the street. They dodged horse-drawn buggies and streetcars until they reached the adjacent side, disappearing into the flow again.

Custis found an empty space near a lamppost. He stopped and looked around. Passing whiffs of strong perfume and body odor meshed with the smell of horse manure piled near the sidewalks. It felt as though the earth itself was a colossal radiometer. He was one of a million tiny bustling molecules bouncing, ricocheting, fighting for space in response to invisible currents of light, heat, and shadow. As people splayed around Custis, some stared at his eyes, others scanned his clothing, but all moved past silently. Maybe it was an undercurrent, a fluke tide that permitted him to be close among strangers.

Custis made his way down a side street. Horseless wagons and wooden carts overflowing with goods crammed the roadway. Street vendors and peddlers hollered in a kinship of banter. The movement was slower now, with people milling about, examining the wares, and consuming pinched food samples. Intensified colors of yellows, reds, greens, whites, and purples all filled the carts in graduated levels. Fruits and vegetables stacked high, and flowers were so thick they seemed to blossom right out of the asphalt. The metropolis was alive and breathing.

Custis had secured a room in a small second-story flat. He hadn't eaten a complete meal in days—he didn't want to. He was too excited.

x x x

Custis wanted to find Centennial. He walked for miles. Up hills, through neighborhoods and industrial areas. The people seemed to change frequently along with the landscape of buildings and residences. It was clear where one class stopped and others began. At times he was sucked in, evaluating his surroundings, forgetting his way. Neighborhoods turned into cluttered tenements that seemed to have no end. Maybe he was walking in circles.

He passed through an Italian area and tried to listen to their language. When some spoke English, he could barely understand but a word or two. He navigated a transaction for a loaf of bread. It would hold him until he returned to his flat somewhere on the other side of the city.

The campus was settled on an allotment of land surrounded by what looked like a proper borough. Custis walked the entire perimeter, imagining the day he would soon be inside. His mind was exhausted, his eyes still burning from stagnant neighborhood smoke. An iron bench was just ahead. He sat and rested. His leg muscles were fatigued, and his mouth was parched.

As he chewed on a piece of torn-off bread, Custis cataloged the sights in his mind. It was strange, these different neighborhoods. Areas or zones, districts, or whatever they were called seemed to be independent of one another. Custis mapped out the different neighborhoods. He had found an Irish community near the docks. They seemed welcoming, but their accent was such a lilting brogue, Custis could not break through. He walked through a poor Polish quarter and was approached by numerous children attempting to sell him useless empty oyster shells.

Other neighborhoods he dared not enter. The air smelled of coal smoke, dead fish, and sewage. Structures left over from the war were now ramshackle commercial buildings combined with clusters of squalid shanties held together by a prayer.

Narrow roadways severed through brooding buildings on either side—their tops still connected high overhead by ropes, wires, and airing laundry that needed to be washed again. The wharf, down farther, displayed hopeless arrangements of slips and adjacent wooden wharves backdropped by stockyards loaded high with boxes and bundled supplies. Men and their equipment scurried about like squirrels, not sure which way to go.

He had read about New York and its immigrants from around the globe, but nothing could describe what he was seeing with his own eyes. In the segregated city, Blacks had been given more freedom here, but prejudices still surfaced. There were Black elites, rich and influential, who were still not afforded complete liberty. The city, its politics, and its population functioned on classification and money, with classification taking priority. But all the money in the world still would not allow a Black man to obtain a degree from Centennial University.

Custis wandered into a small community several blocks away from the main street. It was poor but not as dilapidated as some closer to the port. He was unfamiliar with the people's language. Their woolen clothing design was intricate but odd. Wooden carts with tiny wooden wheels were pulled by fat goats tied together with frayed ropes. The handwritten signs on various vegetable carts were not letters but rather symbols, marks, and dots. *Greek, of course.* Ancient Greece, the foundation of education. As he examined the street wares, he eavesdropped on their conversations. It was a strange cadence full of syllables squashed together. He heard a man's voice yelling. Custis turned and saw a man looking directly at him, speaking to him.

The man continued and motioned for Custis to join him across the street. By the time Custis crossed the road, he saw two other men struggling to move a large, broken-down wagon. Custis helped push the wagon over the raised threshold of a warehouse door. Once inside, the men began to laugh and seemingly congratulate themselves as they placed chocks behind the wheels. The first man approached Custis, still talking and smiling. He shook Custis's hand and continued talking, then reached out to a nearby food cart and grabbed a small wedge of cheese. He smiled, spoke in his language, and handed the wedge to Custis.

"I speak English only. English."

The man looked surprised, said something in return, then called for someone else. A young girl approached and spoke with the man.

"My papa, he say thank you. He gives you goat cheese, but he wonders why you no Greek."

"Greek, I see." Custis smiled. "Because I am an American. Tell your papa thank you for the cheese, but there is no need to pay me."

As the girl spoke with her father, he looked confused as he glanced over at Custis.

"Please tell your father thank you for the offer. Your language is beautiful, and someday I will learn it."

Custis caught himself smiling as he left the neighborhood. The men and girl had thought he was Greek, a real Greek. He could pass as a Greek man. He could learn the language, but how long would that take? Clothing, presentation, comportment, and speech would be crucial, and maybe a closely manicured beard might lend attention to his green eyes. He went back into the neighborhood, and from a distance he examined the men, their mannerisms, and their clothing. Most had dark hair and long handlebar moustaches. Some had slicked-back hair, and others sported broad, floppy hats. A few buttoned their shirts tightly to their neck, while others had rolled-up sleeves and wore thick black belts. There was a kinship about them. They stood in groups, old and young, all acting as family. Custis felt like a voyeur, covertly intruding into their lives and stealing away a part of their privacy.

For the next two afternoons, Custis returned to the neighborhood. He'd watch from a distance. At times he'd walk down the street and purchase goods from the vendors. He listened to their language, mirroring their cadence and behavior while making purchases of bread *psomi*, cheese *tyri*, and olives *elies*. He introduced himself as Renauldos Custis, and that is exactly what they called him. "Efcharisto, Renauldos Custis." He'd need more time. Immersing himself in this language might take weeks—he only had days.

x x x

Custis watched his reflection in the large storefront windows, subtly maneuvering his posture and adjusting his gait. He studied White men on the sidewalk—how they strolled, moved through passersby, and greeted others. He took note of the businessmen near the banks and law firms, how they tipped their hats and when they did not.

Custis noticed a man walking on the sidewalk in the financial district near the Stock Exchange. He looked familiar. He was speaking to three other men, all expensively dressed. The man held on to a wooden cane topped with a bronze ball, maybe a sculpture of an animal head. Custis couldn't place him. He was young, maybe in his mid to late twenties but completely bald. As Custis walked closer, he could hear the man's voice.

It was Benjamin Cobbler from Wilson Place College.

Custis stopped. He couldn't believe that Ben Cobbler was alive. Word was he had been killed in some kind of political uprising years earlier.

"Ben!" Custis smiled broadly and lifted his arms with welcome.

The man briefly adjusted his head but continued his focus with his associates.

Maybe he had made a mistake. No, it was Benjamin. It was his voice. "Ben, so good to see you."

The man stopped talking and looked irritated as he scowled at Custis. "Excuse me, but I do not know you."

"Of course you do—I'm Custis, from Wilson Place; we were roommates."

Custis held out his hand and stared at Ben in amazement. Ben did not offer his hand in return as Custis awkwardly lowered his.

"No. I have no idea what you are referring to. You have made a disconcerting mistake. My name is John Sterling, and my alma mater is Centennial University. You may know my photograph. I am the deputy mayor of New York City."

Custis was stunned. He looked at the other men. White businessmen.

For a moment Custis retained eye contact with Ben. Ben remained stoic until he glanced at one of his companions, smiled niftily, then looked back at Custis.

"I'd like to have your support and vote, assuming you are a landowner, of course."

"Of course." It was the only thing Custis could manage to say. Benjamin Cobbler had passed as a White man, and his light skin and shaved head had afforded him the ability to do so. Custis felt the corporality of possibilities, a sudden surge of energy. He felt neither gleefulness nor excitement, but rather a sense of assurance and accountability. This jolt of reality placed him one step closer to having a life with Sarah. Custis nodded his head, touched the brim of his hat, and turned away.

Custis walked back to the main street just in time to see a parade of wagons and horses and marching brass bands passing by. *This may explain the crowds.* Custis watched the ensemble go by, followed by groomed horses and fancy carriages. He could hear more commotion coming. It couldn't be a circus, not in the middle of Manhattan, and certainly not with a hippopotamus. His mind returned to a colorful poster on a drab wooden fence. The memory was now only a millisecond of his life, powerful enough to alter his course and propel him down paths others said would be impossible.

Two motorized bicycles came from behind the carriages, followed by a three-wheeled electric motor contraption. It was driven by a solo man sitting on a box between the back wheels. He seemed to control it with a handheld lever system without any pedals. It whizzed right past Custis.

The crowd roared and clapped. Custis tried to get through the onlookers but couldn't keep up. He needed to see the engines, look at the designs. They were fantastic, the way they moved with speed and precision. The sound was high-pitched and whined higher with the increasing speed. The riders wore goggles, and one wore a leather cap. They played to the onlookers and turned in circles.

The horse-drawn carriages yielded and stopped closer to the sidewalks while people filled the roadway for a closer look. The crowd's applause incited competition. The three-wheeler shrieked and broke out of the circle. The bicycles followed; the mob cheered. The parade, now transformed into an unsanctioned race, ran down the middle of the main roadway.

A blaring horn spooked a carriage horse. It reared and bolted into the roadway, leaving the driver panicking as he pulled on the reins. Onlookers dispersed. One of the bicycles swerved, avoiding the horse, but crashed into the raised curb. The rider flew over the handlebars and landed on the sidewalk. His head hit hard. Unlike the dirt paths and fields on the ranch, cement encroached upon every remnant of nature with its unforgiving surface. He began to moan. A small swarm gathered around the downed rider.

No one was helping. Custis made his way through the onlookers and squatted down next to the injured man. He was writhing, holding his arm, and bleeding from his head. His left arm and shoulder were limp and looked misshapen.

Custis heard a man's voice from the crowd. "Somebody better get this fool a doctor."

Custis hesitated to touch the rider. The crowd might turn on him. But he couldn't leave him there, helpless and in pain. "What's hurt?" he asked.

The onlookers focused not on Custis but rather on the hurt man. Maybe it was just excitement or curiosity.

"My arm. I think it's broken."

The crowd shrieked and scattered as another three-wheeler came back up the street heading straight toward them. It was out of control. The driver screamed and flailed his arms. "Get out of the way, get out of the way!"

The driver jumped free and rolled in the street as the three-wheeler crashed into a lamppost at the edge of the sidewalk. Custis and the injured man were directly in line with the iron pole. The globe burst, spewing shards of glass downward as the column teetered from its base. Custis grabbed the man by the back of his coat and pulled him out of the way as the streetlight crashed to the ground. The electrical line at the base sizzled and snapped as it tore loose from the sidewalk.

The sound of a police whistle filled the air. Onlookers dispersed. A few remained. Custis saw the driver of the three-wheeler standing with two police officers. He looked shaken. Custis focused back on the rider. He had touched a stranger. "I'm sorry, I had to pull you out of the way."

His hands were still on the man's shoulder. The offense was irreversible. *No one is helping him. Might as well continue.* More remarkably, no one seemed interested in a Black man touching a White man. Custis palpated the man's arm with his fingers. He stared at the forearm, then the elbow. He focused his eyes and imagined his sight penetrating the skin, following the texture of red muscles upward, through the white network of nerves and over the bluish veins and arteries until reaching the proximal end of the humerus. Custis felt the deformity, the humeral ball outside of the shoulder socket. Dislocated. The rider screamed.

"Can you move your arm at all?"

"No! My shoulder, it's bad."

"You'll be all right."

Custis glanced around. The police were busy with the other involved racer. *Where are the doctors in a place like this, anyway?* The rider was in excruciating pain. Custis was almost sure his shoulder was only dislocated. He could easily stop the man's agony by resetting it. He had read about the process. It all seemed so logical, and he could easily help make all the pain go away and maybe prevent future nerve damage. But if he was wrong, he might cause additional injury. Custis silently asked God for help. "This is going to hurt for a couple of seconds more."

"It's killing me!"

Custis levered his foot against the man, picked up his wrist, pulled, moved, and twisted his arm. The man screamed. Custis slowly released his arm. The man's cries changed to heavy breathing.

"Pump your fist?"

The man made a fist and started to smile. "God, it hurt so bad. What did you do?"

"Let me see you move your elbow. The head of your arm bone popped out of the socket of your shoulder blade. Nothing to worry about. I just pulled it back in. Simple." Custis looked at the man's fingertips and nails. He imagined the hand without its protective skin. He saw the blood circulating through muscles, nerves reacting and tendons stretching as the fist closed and opened. Custis smiled. "Nothing looks broken."

The man sat up and rubbed his arm. He had a large abrasion on his forehead.

Custis offered his handkerchief. "Here, your head is bleeding."

The man looked around. "Did I win?"

"Pretty sure you both lost. Can you stand up?"

Custis helped the man stand to his feet.

The man patted his forehead with the handkerchief and looked at the blood. "Do I need stitches?"

"No. It's an abrasion. You'll live. Just don't carry anything heavy for a while. At least ten weeks." A sequence of memories flashed through his mind of Stardust in the barn, supported in the overhead sling as Sarah iced down the horse's knee and pastern. "Might try a sling for that arm."

"Thanks, Doc."

"I'm not a doctor—not a medical doctor, anyway."

"How did you know how to fix my arm?"

"I read about it."

"That would have been good information to have before I let you pull on it. But rather impressive, as it is. I could use a drink. Can I buy you a beer and some dinner? Least I can do."

Custis brushed off the knees of his pants.

"I'm Conrad Preston Langmuir IV, by the way. My friends call me Preston."

"But we're not friends, and—"

"Yeah, but we could be. Hell, you just plugged my arm back in its socket. Thank you." He ran his fingers through his tousled hair. His goggles had been lost in the collision. He smoothed the front of his suit and tugged on the bottom of his waistcoat.

Preston extended his hand. Custis hesitated. A seriousness returned to his face. Preston smiled and extended his hand even farther. Custis was about to shake a White man's hand in public. He reached out and took Preston's hand. "I'm Renauldos Custis. My family is from Greece." There, he'd said it. The plan was activated. He wasn't quite prepared—he'd have to be careful.

"I sure am glad to meet you. You do not sound Greek, nor from around here."

"Yes, no. I am not from here. My father immigrated to America from Greece."

Preston paused and slightly tilted his head. Custis needed to adjust. Maybe this was not working. Change the subject.

"I have a master's degree in science."

"Science?"

"Yes. Natural science with a mathematical analysis degree. A professor."

"I see. We need that beer. Come on."

Preston slapped Custis on his arm, looked back at the driver of the three-wheeler, and yelled, "Hey, meet up at Ace's."

After getting a thumbs-up from the driver, Preston tugged on Custis and said, "Let's go. There's a pub a few doors up. They make a pretty good steak, too."

"No, I appreciate the invitation, but I better get going."

"Come on. What kind of accent do I hear?"

"I'm from North Carolina."

"I was guessing Tennessee."

Preston turned and stepped up to the front door of a tavern called the Ace of Pubs Club and pulled open the door. Custis remained on the sidewalk. He looked upward at the tall brick structure that housed several retail businesses on the bottom level and what looked like residences starting on the second story. The door and front windows were topped with tattered canvas awnings where pieces hung down like long lichen in the trees back home. Maybe the windows needed cleaning, too.

"What's wrong?" Preston asked, propping the door open. "My place isn't good enough for you?"

Whites only. Custis was about to commit a crime with intent. A silent second seemed like minutes, and Preston had noticed the pause. "Just look at me. I can't go in dressed like this. Why, look at you," Custis said, faking a smile. "You're all fancy-like in that impeccably expensive suit."

"Oh." Preston pressed his lips together and furrowed his brow. "Yes. I see what you mean." Preston grinned. "Come on. I'm their best customer. You'll be all right; you're with a Langmuir." He grabbed Custis by the coat sleeve and pulled him through the door. He nodded at the bartender, held up two fingers, then pointed to a table in the back corner.

Custis followed and sat down.

"You say you're Greek? A Greek with an annoying South Carolina accent."

"North Carolina."

"You're just a hillbilly. Professor Hayseed Plowboy from North Carolina. Don't say a word now. Just nod if people talk to you. I shouldn't be seen with you." Preston burst out with laughter. "I'm just kidding."

Custis smiled.

"Explain something to me. How are you without a Greek accent? Do you even speak Greek?"

"My father and mother immigrated to the United States and ended up in the Carolinas. My father prohibited my mother from teaching me Greek. He said we were Americans and should act like it. I went to school, upon his insistence, had my own friends, I guess. My father worked the land and put me through school."

Custis wanted to look around. He had never been inside a bona fide bar and felt a bit queasy about the commencement of his scheme. Fear and excitement coursed through his body, fusing together as one big stomach full of jitteriness.

"Tell me, Renauldos, are you a professor here at the university?"

Wilson Place College for Negros. Custis felt the flutter of his nervousness.

"No, back home. Rosemont Hill." Custis was surprised with the words coming out of his mouth. *Rosemont Hill—no, I should not have been so specific.*

"What are you doing here in New York, then?"

The bartender brought over two glasses of beer. "This is my good friend Renauldos Custis. He's from Greece. This is Andoe," Preston said.

Andoe was big. A thick gray beard was neatly trimmed in a half circle perfectly framing the lower half of his round face. A flat cap might have been covering a bald head. Lines at the corner of his eyes indicated a propensity for laughter. His cheeks were chubby and poised for merriment. "Welcome. Sorry to see you've friended up with this here fella." Andoe placed the glasses on the table.

"Come on, Andoe, he's new in town."

"I'm fresh out of ouzo for ya, lad, but I can certainly add it to my stock. What's your specialty? What are you studying? I assume you're attending university here with Preston."

Custis nodded and then looked at Preston. Custis had never heard of ouzo and needed to respond. *Say something, Preston.*

"Orthopedics," Preston said matter-of-factly. "We met on campus. He's acclimating to New York. I'm helping him out a bit."

"Well, welcome. First one on the house for ya. But everything else is cash or on Preston's tab."

Preston seemed perfectly charming. He was definitely practiced— or maybe wily. Custis needed more evidence to determine an accurate hypothesis.

Custis smiled politely while Preston laughed out loud. "You know my tab is paid up every month. If it weren't for me, you'd be sweeping the streets."

Andoe laughed deeply. "You mean if it weren't for your father."

A perfectly charming and spoiled son of a rich man.

"Aw, now, come on. It's the least he can do for his son, the doctor."

And a doctor. Why can't he pay his own tab then?

"You boys let me know if you need another now." Andoe looked at Custis, winked, and turned away.

Custis waited for Andoe to get out of earshot. "You're a doctor, and you didn't know how to set your shoulder?"

"I'm a medical student. I don't like it, and I'm not good at it."

"Why, for God's sake, are you doing it then?"

"My father wants me to." Preston picked up his glass. "Well, here's to you and your endeavors."

Custis looked down at the beer in front of him. He had never been to a tavern, let alone drunk alcohol. "I've never had a beer."

"What?"

Well, that was the wrong thing to say.

"I never drank a beer before."

"I heard you. I just can't believe it. A country bumpkin teetotaler. Try it."

Custis picked up the glass, drank a gulp, and placed it back down on the table. He wiped his lips. "That's dreadful."

Preston laughed. His own glass was already half empty. He refilled it with Custis's beer and took a long drink. "I'll get you a happy salmon, then. You'll like it."

"Happy salmon? That sounds even worse."

"It's something that Andoe makes. Lots of tomato juice and a wee bit of vodka."

Custis noticed two men across the room, staring at him. "They must be deliberating on my lineage."

Preston looked at the men. "They must not be familiar with Greeks." Preston raised his voice and held the stare until the two men looked away. Preston was not a physically large man, but nothing so far indicated he would ever walk away from a confrontation. He spoke with sureness and resonated with confidence, perhaps compensated with attitude when necessary.

Custis looked around the room. His stomach ached for food. He smelled garlic and bacon, the aroma coming from the kitchen in the back.

Preston watched Custis. "You hungry?" He held up his hand, got Andoe's attention, and mimed eating with a spoon. Andoe nodded.

"I can't afford to eat here. Dinner will be waiting for me when I get back to my room."

"It's on me. I insist. You look like you're starving."

Andoe brought over two big servings of stew, bread and butter, and more beer. Preston mainly drank, and Custis did most of the eating.

Custis wanted to slop up his plate with the bread, but manners and self-doubt got the best of him. Preston sat legs crossed, stiff-backed and proper.

"You are studying at Centennial University?" Custis asked.

"For a long time now. Just not sure I want it. I started in something different, changed my course, and then changed it again. It's what I'm doing currently, I suppose. What about you?"

"I want to apply to Centennial University. I want to—well, I *need* to—go to Centennial for access to research materials. I have degrees in mathematics, applied and pure science, and chemistry. I worked in physics as well."

"But you have not applied to Centennial yet, correct?"

"No, not yet. I have an appointment in nine days."

"And what, pray tell, are you going to say?"

"I have a presentation regarding my project. Once they understand my work and see what I have done and the possibilities—"

"Wait, just stop." Preston placed his near empty glass on the table. He leaned in and looked directly at Custis. "Centennial is not going to accept some hick from South Carolina."

"North Carolina."

"With this university, it's all about who you know and how much money and acclaim you can bring to them. Sorry to tell you, but you are not exceptional enough for ol' man Adams or his board."

"It must be Centennial."

"Now, say, if you were some esteemed student from a prestigious, world-renowned university like University of Constantinople or

Athens or wherever the university is over there, that's another story. They'd smell publicity on that ten miles away. Centennial is all about its reputation. Just look at you. You're socially awkward, you look scared to death, never even had a beer before, and you sound like a waif. And why Centennial?"

"All graduates from Centennial have access to the research labs. I have no sponsorship. The cost of research could be phenomenal. Centennial is the only university in the United States with access to some of the equipment I need to develop my machine. I need their laboratories, assistants, finances, and support to go forward. I have all my research papers. After they see my plan, my work, they will absolutely want me on board."

"Wait—wait just a damn minute." Preston sat back in his chair. "Your appointment is in a handful of days. What are you going to say when they ask you for your credentials for this grandiose secret machine? Show them you graduated with honors from Rosemont Hill? You're an idiot, a damn idiot."

Custis was quiet. Maybe he *was* a fool. Reality once again had slapped him hard in the face. "I could tell them my education comes from Greece, and the documents were lost in the emigration process."

"It will be easy enough for them to obtain records, or lack thereof, through correspondence. And, what about your *Hey, y'all* Tar Heel accent? What is your work, anyway? What would be so fantastic that could compel the university to accept you on no other merit?"

"Radiation and movement, such as using a passageway to look inside a human body without breaching the skin." His voice quieted. "Imagine the possibilities. We could have an entire road map of the interior of a living human being. We can calculate and create schematics of broken bones, tumors, cancers. Identify issues before they become problems. Before they cause death. I believe it will change the world of medicine. Maybe other things as well. I just don't know the full extent of its capabilities. My hope is the university recognizes the possibilities."

"Hope is not a strategy. Where are you staying?"

"Right now, I have a room near 126th Street, which includes one meal per day, except on Sundays. I can stay there until I can get into the dormitory on campus. It's all I can afford."

Preston shook his head. He stared at Custis. He bit his lip and shook his head slightly. "I'm telling you, make another plan. Can you meet me back here tomorrow? I've got some friends that may be able to help."

"Help with what?"

"I've got an idea. Let me sleep on it, figure it all out, and let's meet back here tomorrow. In the meantime, just lay low and stay away from the campus. Here, tomorrow. Five o'clock."

Custis couldn't quite figure out Preston's motive. He was quick to lie, good at talking, and experienced with small doses of intimidation—everything Custis was not. Custis knew the scheme for passing was his only route into the university. Even though Preston was unaware of the plan, he had inadvertently exposed weaknesses that could scuttle everything.

23

C ustis was early. He had calculated one block per minute at a comfortable pace but allowed additional time for unplanned delays.

Custis stood in front of the tavern, pulled the watch from his waist-coat pocket, and checked the time. Ten of five. The chain was too short. Links had been replaced with rusted wire, and the face was discolored and cracked. It was mostly accurate, though.

An open carriage stopped at the sidewalk. Preston paid the driver and stepped out. He carried his coat over his arm, exposing his pinstriped vest and his white shirtsleeves, sharp with new creases. His derby, black and lint-free, was a perfect fit.

"Why are you out here and not inside?"

"Because I still talk like a rube."

Their same table was empty. Andoe gave them a nod and started to pour a beer.

"Let's try one of your happy salmons today," Preston hollered, then turned abruptly to face Custis. "Here's the plan—"

"Lower your voice!" Custis hissed.

"Sorry. I think you can legitimately pass for someone with an exotic background with your suntanned skin, your green eyes. But you have to change your attitude, your clothing. You need to be and look more cosmopolitan."

"What's wrong with my clothing?"

"You look old and poor."

"I am old. I'm twenty-five."

"And poor. We must get rid of that accent. I have a buddy studying linguistics, a brilliant man. He can help, I'm sure."

"Go on."

"If you want to get into Centennial, you have to change your mind-set completely. You have to be someone else 100 percent of the time. You have to lie about your degrees from Rosemont Hill. I mean, we will not change any of your work, classes, or degrees, but we will change the college name. Once they see anything about some hick school in North Carolina and hear your voice, it's over."

"Let's just present that I have studied at the University of Athens."

"It's too simple to confirm or deny if you studied in Greece. It may take months for correspondence, but you will be found out eventually. Listen, I've got connections at Simpson University here in New York. We will transfer all your records to indicate you attended Simpson. It's perfect. The classes will match seamlessly. It's not that your records from Rosemont Hill will be destroyed. There will be no reference to you having ever gone there. They will believe you are from Greece with an American education from Simpson. They will have no reason to check with Rosemont Hill."

"Forge documents?"

"Yes. You're willing to lie about being from Greece. Forging documents is the same as lying, but just in writing. Do you want to go to Centennial or don't you? We're only changing the name of the school. If you don't, you will never get in. You may never see your work completed."

"I don't understand how we can do this. I mean, all the documents and certificates. I have eight more days until my appointment."

"Change it. We need another month. There is too much we still must set up. I have someone who works in the records department at Simpson. She owes me. We can trust her. I kind of saved her life; I believe you can do this, Custis, but you need to fully commit, because now it will involve other people—me specifically. In the end, I want to be able to say I played a small part in your success. Listen, you seem like an honorable man, but you owe Centennial nothing—no respect, no loyalty. It's an institution, not a person you need to revere at the cost of everything. Do this for your project, your life's work."

Custis nodded. "I'll postpone the appointment."

Andoe set the drinks on the table. Custis looked up and gave a quick smile.

"Any food for you boys today?"

Preston took his beer. "We've got some friends coming in. Better wait for them. Make them pay for their own drinks this time." Preston smiled and winked, then looked at Custis.

As Andoe walked away, Custis took a sip of the happy salmon. He wasn't sure what to expect, but it certainly did not taste as good as sweet tea back home. Custis caught his thoughts. *Sweet tea back home*. Preston was right—he had to change 100 percent, even on the inside. Custis was lost in delight. He had a secret, an ally, and a strategy. Preston continued talking, but Custis didn't entirely hear all the words. His mind was on Sarah.

"Look at it this way: All the information, the grades, the classes, and the degrees will be exact. It's not like we're lying about that. You earned those degrees, and you need to continue."

"I have worked harder than others to get where I am today. It seems so wrong, but I must do it."

"To me, I think you could save lives, maybe change the world. And the one thing that stands in your way, Professor, is the name of a school on your degrees. Everything else will be unaffected. What do you say, Renauldos Custis?"

"I can't figure out why you're doing all this."

"Listen, you have no money. Look at your suit—it's nearly thread-bare. You're too thin, starving yourself to death in order to pay for a room in the slum tenements. How long before you come down with tuberculosis? This is reality. You come into this city all starry-eyed, thinking you can be accepted in one of the most prestigious universities in the nation with just an idea? Let me advise you, my friend, this is all about money. Greed is imbedded so deep in the bowels of academia that the stench will outlast all of us."

A man grabbed Preston around the shoulders as a second man looked on. Preston looked startled but quickly smiled as the man slapped him on the back. "Brother Langmuir! Let's hear more about this incredible favor," the man said.

"Hey, Marshall. Meet my friend Professor Renauldos Custis."

Marshall smiled widely and shook Custis's hand with enthusiasm. "Eugene Marshall, good to meet you."

"And this is Dee McKay. He attended Simpson before Centennial. He's got all kinds of information for you. I filled them in last night.

And Marshall here is a linguistics specialist, known around the country for his work."

Marshall looked at Custis. "Now, don't tell me where you're from. All I need is a minute or two of listening to your dialect." He looked back at Preston. "Wager? My tab here?"

Preston smiled. "I know you're good, and I know your bar tab is always high, so that sounds like a sucker's bet to me. But if you can narrow it down to the state and a specific region, the bet's on."

Preston and Marshall shook hands as both guzzled their beer.

"Renauldos, let me have it," Marshall said, wiping his mouth with the back of his hand.

"And no mention or indication of your home, or the bet is off," Preston added.

Custis was intrigued with the openness of their friendship. Why would strangers be so perfectly kind? He wanted to play, but his brain needed more time. Confusion meant that his subconscious was finding its way to the surface. Or he was simply hungry and wanted to eat their lies.

"Come on, give it to me."

Custis recited a poem, the only thing that came to mind. "*I inhale great draughts of space, the east and the west are mine, and the north and the south are mine. All seems beautiful to me.*"

Marshall smiled and rubbed his face. "Walt Whitman would be proud, but I need something not recited, please."

"As a child, I read to my mother each night. Her favorite was Charles Dickens. Mine was *The Last of the Mohicans*. She used to make the best blackberry cobbler. Horses scare me to death. I used to have a cat named Hatchet. And a girl named Sarah taught me to fly-fish. She's the most beautiful girl in the world, and one day I will marry her. And I'm rather good at it now—fly-fishing, that is. Is that enough?"

"Yes," Marshall said. "Definitely Carolina. North Carolina."

"And?" Preston asked.

"North Carolina has the most dialects per region of all the states." Marshall sipped his beer. "This is difficult. I hear a bit of Piedmont. At first, I thought it might be Sandhill, but I think it's got to be the plateau region. Piedmont."

Custis kept eye contact with Marshall. He started to smile but stopped himself.

"Well? Is he correct?"

Custis smiled. "That he is. Exactly."

The group roared with laughter.

Custis shook his head. "Amazing."

"Well, I guess I'll have to pay off your tab."

McKay was the smaller of the men. He was dressed sharply and seemed polite enough. "He'll need different clothing, and that hideous accent—atrocious."

"Marshall can fix that. It will take some time. McKay, I need you to work with Custis regarding Simpson University. He needs all the professor names pertinent to the field. Names of halls, campus orientation, etc. Anything he may need to know about the school if he's asked."

Custis shook his head. *There's so much information involved.*

It was the proverbial tangled web wrapping itself around and around.

Andoe interrupted with platters of steaming hot food. "There ya be, boys. The missus made it up special."

Marshall took a plate and set it down in front of Custis as the others began scooping food into their mouths. Their arms crisscrossed in front of Custis, reaching for butter and bread. Mouths full of food, still talking and laughing. Custis looked at the plate in front of him. It had been so long since seeing such bountiful food, he felt blessed again. He closed his eyes and whispered, "Thank you for this food and all that you have given us . . ."

McKay stopped eating. His arms rested on the edge of the table, one hand holding a loaded spoon, the other a biscuit. He looked up over his plate at Custis, then quickly leaned over to Preston and quietly asked, "Who's he talking to?"

Preston smiled and placed his hand on Custis's shoulder. "Listen, you have more degrees than all of us put together. It's all in your head. All we have to do is get you into the laboratory.

"Marshall, we need you to work on his speech. Figure out where he's from in Greece, and then educate the hell out of him. People may ask about his homeland, and he better be prepared. We can do this. We can make it happen. The goal is four weeks."

"He needs a mustache with stiff ends. Change his hair. It's going to be a lot of work," Marshall said.

"He better have a good memory," McKay added.

"It is, and he does. It will all be worth it, my brothers. Here's to our pact, here's to the future. No backing out now, Renauldos."

Custis's mind was in a whirlwind; his brain was being pulled apart with centrifugal force by unproven influences he shouldn't trust. His mind formed ledgers, columns, and a logical hypothesis. Preston, Marshall, and McKay: a mathematical vinculum. They were part of the formula. And as a formula, they were constituted with symbols— tools for a probable solution, maybe the only one. Preston stood up and swallowed the last gulp of beer from his glass. "I got rounds to do. Custis, meet me at the back door of Saint Angeline Hospital tomorrow night at ten thirty."

24

Saint Angeline Hospital sat humbly, surrounded by newer buildings nearly three times as tall. Behind the hospital, a back street severed the block in two. Custis stood at one end of the alleyway and listened to the conversations of those who passed by. He surmised some were doctors and nurses, but most seemed to be students.

It had rained earlier. Puddles of water had collected in dips and low seams on the sidewalk. Custis heard dripping from the copper leader box overhead. Gutters were clogged with summer debris, obviously forgotten about. *Some rains are like that,* he thought, *sneaking up into the last bit of summer with surprise.*

The alleyway was empty now. A streetlamp illuminated each end of the passage. A single light hung over the back door. Custis looked at his pocket watch. Ten forty-two. Perhaps the scheme had been rescinded.

Too complicated, too chancy. Why would strangers put their careers at risk? Maybe Preston had set him up; maybe he was playing a joke. He had been duped. They were somewhere having a beer, laughing at him. They had been no better than callous bullies.

The back door of the hospital opened. Preston stepped out, still holding on to the handle. He waved and motioned Custis to come inside. Custis gave a hesitant nod and walked toward Preston.

"Come on in. It's downtime right now. We'll only have a few minutes before I must get back." Preston wore a white doctor's coat and held another in his hand. "Here, slip this on. I want to show you something. Leave your hat here. And don't talk to anyone. Come on, this way."

"What are we doing here?"

"I want to make sure you have something to remember."

"Remember for what?"

"For those moments when you have second thoughts and want to back out, leaving the rest of us hanging out to dry. All of us could be kicked out and lose our degrees if you break."

Custis followed Preston into the hospital, through equipment-narrowed corridors, and up two flights of stairs. They entered a large room with banks of west-facing windows, most likely designed to catch the sunlight but now surely blocked in the shadows of surrounding skyscrapers. Dim sconce light fixtures lit the opposite wall.

It was a nursery. Two iron bassinets separated by a rocking chair were next to the door. Both were empty. One long row of small iron beds with chipped white paint lined the windowed wall. The wall plaster showed signs of wear, rubbed raw in places. An empty dark wooden chair sat at the foot of each small bed. A nurse's desk was at the end of the room, where a desk lamp solemnly illuminated neatly stacked papers and charts.

"We have to hurry. The charge nurse will be back soon."

The floor must have been cement. Their footfalls echoed sharply. Preston approached a bed near the nurse's station. A small girl with dark hair lay awake.

"This is Emma." Preston reached down and stroked her forehead with the palm of his hand. "Emma, this is my friend Renauldos."

Custis never considered that Preston would have a tender side to him. It was strange to see, uncanny to feel.

"Hello, Doctor Renauldos." Her voice was whispery. "Are your eyes made of looking-glass?" She took a breath. "You must be an angel!"

Custis bent down, lowering his upper half over the bed. "No, my darling, I am not an angel, but I can be your friend."

"Yes, I would like that."

"Is this your baby doll?"

"Her name is Adaline."

Emma cuddled her doll and closed her eyes. Her breath was labored.

Custis pulled the blanket up close around her. "What's wrong with her?"

"Let's go out."

Custis followed Preston out into the hallway. "Where are her parents?"

Preston looked up and down the hallway.

"Where are her parents, Preston?"

"Her mother will be here in the morning. She works at night cleaning offices to pay the hospital bills. During the day, she works downstairs in the laundry. She's here any chance she gets."

They walked down to the ground floor and toward the back door.

"Will she be all right?"

"She has cancer. It had spread throughout her entire body by the time it was discovered. It may have stopped had we detected it earlier. But there's no equipment that will do that. Can you help her? I mean, with the knowledge you have already, your machine?"

Custis processed the crippling words. He stopped walking, unable to think about movement. He had just looked into the eyes of a dying child. A beautiful and faultless child.

"She is going to die, Custis. Your project may be the answer."

"There's not enough time, Preston. She's on her deathbed."

"I just thought we might expedite the work."

"Expedite?" Custis unbuttoned the white coat, pulled it off, and rolled it into a ball. "You think I can magically get into a laboratory and wave my wand around and make a fantastic machine, all before she dies? No wonder you're a terrible doctor." Custis shoved the coat into Preston's chest.

χ χ χ

By the next day, Preston's motive had become clear. His interest and eagerness for Custis to be accepted into Centennial and the success of his machine was on the hospital's fifth floor. Preston was a good man after all. The image of Emma was indelible.

At ten thirty the next night, Custis waited at the back door of the hospital. Finally, an exiting student. The hallways were deserted. He opened the first few doors, hoping to find a closet, praying for a white coat. He stumbled into a janitor's storeroom, looked around, and took off his jacket, tie, and waistcoat. He rolled up the sleeves of his white shirt, put on an oversized apron, and grabbed a mop and bucket.

Custis retraced his steps from the night before. He carried the mop and bucket down the third-floor corridor. He watched the nurse exit the nursery and turn in the opposite direction. Custis hesitated and made sure she was out of sight before continuing. He slowly opened the door. The room was quiet. He looked around, took in a deep breath, and stepped inside.

Custis pulled a chair up next to Emma's bedside. In the dim lighting, he watched her breathe, her chest rising under the blanket. Her face was flushed as if she had been playing outside on a warm day. He thought about death, its irrefutable permanency, and his helplessness to intervene. There was no rescuing her from a creek or casts to mend broken bones. Death was already inside her, waiting for life's last heartbeat, its last little breath.

Emma opened her eyes. Her voice whispered with surprise, "You came back."

Custis smiled, nodded his head, and pulled his chair closer. "Yes, of course. We are friends, remember?"

"Yes." Her words were soft and unhurried. "I was worried I might never see you again. I have something to tell you." She looked into his eyes and smiled. Her stare did not break as her expression became solemn. "Your momma must surely love you. I see her. She's with you all the time. She's right there behind you."

Emma became quiet. She looked at peace, her eyes still locked on Custis. "You don't need to be afraid anymore, Doctor Renauldos. I think you are an angel after all."

He leaned in closer and whispered, "Emma? What do you mean? About my momma?"

There was no more labored breathing. No more pain. Little Emma was gone.

Custis reached over and gently closed Emma's eyes with his fingertips. A shiver ran up his arm. He instantly cupped his hand around her cheek. He felt her forehead. She was cold as ice. He adjusted a small directional light at the top of the headboard. Her skin was pallid, almost translucent. He immediately stood straight up and started to back away. His panicked mind was searching to understand why she felt so hard and cold when she had just been talking. He reached back down and felt her cold and rigid arms just to make sure.

The nurse's dictatorial voice jolted through the darkened room.

"What has taken so long? I sent for you near an hour ago. She needs transport to the basement." The nurse wheeled a metal cart next to the bed.

Custis drew in a deep, stammering breath. "Basement?"

"The morgue. Are you new, orderly, or are you just dumb?"

It would have been easy to rationalize. Maybe an illusion, imagination, or even a dream conjured by his exhaustion.

"You'll have to get her; I can't lift." The nurse was curt. She turned and went to her desk.

Custis didn't take his eyes away from the child. He had just spoken with an angel. He thought how eminently close to God he had just been. He repeated Emma's words in his head, over and over. It would have been easy to leave, but Custis could not bear to leave this child all alone.

Custis pulled the blanket back up over her arms and tucked it softly around her shoulders. He lifted Adaline and slipped her in closer. He covered both with a small white sheet, then gently picked them up and placed them on the cart.

The nurse returned to the bedside and handed Custis some paperwork. "Here, you'll need this."

Custis wheeled the cart out of the room.

The basement hallway was dank, empty, and soundless except for the rusty wheels striving to rotate on the cart. He found the morgue door and sounded the bell. The buzzing was harsh and rebounded throughout the corridor.

Custis leaned down and whispered, "Tell my momma I know what I need to do. I will make it happen. She made me strong for a reason." He straightened up, breathed in, and let the air out quietly. *It's so hard here, Momma, it's so hard. But I will no longer be afraid.*

x x x

Custis walked in the darkness. The streets became narrower as he neared his boardinghouse. He thought about his life, all the random steps that had led him to this place—the painful, the joyful, and the misunderstood. They were all connected, fitting together perfectly—not accidental at all, just like the mechanics of a human body.

The lock on his door had been busted through. Inside, his belongings had been riffled and disheveled, the blankets on his mattress stolen away. *How can I live like this? Everyone here is so poor.* It was no longer about who he was. It was now about food, shelter, and survival.

Custis removed his canvas money belt from his waist. He counted out four envelopes inside, each marked with coinciding labels: food, rent, tuition, misc. He recounted the money and removed a few bills from each envelope. He rolled up the currency and placed it deep into his front pants pocket and secured the belt back around his waist.

The next morning, Custis returned to Saint Angeline. This time, he went through the front door. He hadn't slept all night. His clothing was disheveled, his hair uncombed. Step by step, he looked for directional placards. *Whites. Coloreds. Wait Here. Administration. Nurses' Lounge. Lavatory for Coloreds. Kitchen. Bookkeeping.* He opened the accounting office door and addressed a man wearing small round eyeglasses. Custis nervously cleared his throat. "I'd like to pay a bill."

The man sized up Custis with his eyes. "You will have to wait your turn."

Custis was the only person in the room other than the clerks behind the desks. "Of course. Sorry." He stepped away, holding his hat in his hands. He looked around—no chairs.

Custis watched the clock. Nine minutes had passed.

"Next."

Custis returned to the window.

The man, never lifting his eyes from his desktop, asked, "How can I help you?"

"I would like to make a remittance."

"Name?"

"Renauldos Custis."

The clerk searched a ledger. His beady eyes followed his crooked finger down two columns. "I have no Renauldos Custis listed."

"I am sorry . . . I am Renauldos Custis; I was confused."

"What is the name of the *patient*?"

"Her name is Emma, a child up in the nursery."

"Last name?"

"Again, I am sorry. I do not know."

The clerk set his pencil down flatly on the desktop and looked up at Custis. "Step away from the window." He placed a placard on the front of the desk. *Closed*. "I will have to contact upstairs."

Custis waited nearly an hour. The clerk returned, holding several papers. Custis placed his hand into his pocket and felt the currency. It was the right thing to do. He could find work somewhere, replace what he was about to spend.

"It appears that account has already been paid and closed." He removed the placard and plopped down into his chair.

"Please, may I ask who paid it?"

The clerk huffed as his fingers moved through the paperwork. "Preston Langmuir."

"Thank you, sir. Thank you for your time."

Custis walked outside and stood at the curb. He ran through the possibilities of why Preston Langmuir would pay the hospital bill. Could it have been that Preston was only purporting to be an uncaring, manipulating soul? Maybe it had been Langmuir III who had paid the account. Perhaps he owned the hospital.

Custis found human behavior curious and unpredictable. He had never been exposed to such diverse classes. Carolina seemed to be either White or Black. Wilson Place had sheltered him safely within its walled campus. But here in New York was the nucleus of class order—from the wealthy elite and professionals to laborers and immigrants to Blacks. The lower the caste, the more difficult the mobility, all marked by disparities in income, education, and living conditions. The common denominator was revenue and gave no value to character or integrity—money could easily buy that.

25

There were no trees in any direction—just buildings and roadways. Custis wondered if the people here appreciated the color of quivering autumn leaves or the tinkling sound they made just before they fell. *Have they forgotten the sound of their crispness as they skip across the ground, spinning with* the *breeze?* The only thing that fluttered now was a nearby wind-torn flag and paper advertisements attached to the lamppost. Custis sat on a black iron bench across from the Ace of Pubs Club. He looked upward at the sound of another flutter. A seagull screeched overhead, perhaps returning to the outdoor market.

Each afternoon he waited. On the fourth day, Custis saw Preston enter the pub. His back stiffened as he breathed in. The next sixty feet Custis was about to walk would change his life.

Preston sat at his regular table, sipping from a glass of beer. Custis sat down next to him.

"What's on your lip?"

"I'm growing a mustache."

Preston laughed. "All right, then. We've got some work to do, don't we?"

"Lifestyle and history will be easy. Language is another issue. I'll also need to learn to write it. I'll need access to the library."

"No library. You can't take a chance of someone seeing a supposedly educated Greek man researching Greece. We'll bring you what you need. After we do this, you'll need the library for your work, and you don't want to be recognized from before."

"I have no source of income at the moment. What about the cost of a new wardrobe?"

"Some of the items we can gather for you. Don't worry about it. Everything else I can cover until you get back on your feet. Another thing—you cannot live in a tenement building. It's not safe, and you need to be closer to campus."

"It's a room on top of a restaurant."

"I'm working on a place—as soon as you can lose the accent. You need to have access to Marshall straightaway."

"I know nothing about Greece except for ancient history."

"That's better than nothing. McKay already has a study plan for you. I'll need your transcripts from Rosemont Hill. Then I'll get them over to my contact at Simpson so they can be duplicated."

Rosemont Hill was part of the lie. All records would show Wilson Place College for Negros.

"That will be a problem in this short amount of time. All my records from Rosemont Hill, along with other luggage, were lost during the move here. I've already submitted a requested for replacement, but I'm afraid it will take too long. I have everything memorized, though."

"Good. There's a building on campus, on the far side. It's been shuttered for years. We can use the attic. It's not much, but it can manage to be a study hall for now. But first, you need your new clothing and a lesson or two from Marshall just in case someone stops you on campus. Meet here tomorrow, same time. Bring your records."

x x x

Custis was the first to arrive at Ace's. He picked a table in the back. Preston entered, carrying a small luggage case, followed by Marshall and McKay. Preston handed Custis the case.

"Here. These are the things that I had. From now on, only green neckties, the brighter the better, vivid patterns. We need to accentuate your green eyes. Makes you look more cosmopolitan. Some different stickpins, too. No more flat caps unless you're playing sports or selling newspapers. There's a pocket watch in there as well. It doesn't work, but the chain is bright, unlike the cord you're using now."

"But mine works."

"Doesn't matter. Later today, I'll take you to my tailor on Fifth. But before that, Marshall needs to make a couple of adjustments on you."

"Just a few for now," Marshall said. "Before we venture out, we need to work on your attitude. Your body language yells introvert. Greeks shake hands firmly, smile, and maintain direct eye contact. Good friends embrace and may kiss each other on each cheek. Friends often slap each other's arm at the shoulder. You need to learn how to lie, Renauldos, just lie."

Custis had been walking the streets of Manhattan for numerous days without confrontation. This would be his first time with a specific cause and the direction to intermingle and exchange. Custis was a performer now, consciously aware, needing to reverse an ingrained behavior with nothing more than an attitude, determination, and luck.

Custis made his way back to the conversation as Marshall continued. "Here is a list of phrases to add and words to eliminate. From now on, you will become Renauldos Custis from Patras, Greece. You will articulate methodically, think systematically. Pause before you speak. People will assume you are thoughtful and smart."

McKay handed Custis a leather case. "Here is a package of information on Simpson. Commit it to memory. I will have more on specific professors as soon as we go over your records from Rosemont Hill."

"Here," Preston said as he handed Custis a new square crown hat. "Marshall will shadow you down the street. I'll meet you at DiGiordano Clothiers at five."

Custis put on the hat. He turned toward Preston. "Afternoon, ma'am."

"Oh, please." Preston laughed. "Don't say anything. Just try walking down the street and looking at people. Greet them only with a smile. Here, put on this necktie." Custis removed his worn-out black necktie and replaced it with a new silky emerald-green cravat.

Custis walked down the street with Marshall following. "Tip your hat; do not look away. I'll be here just in case you're questioned or stopped."

"This is all it takes? A new hat and tie?"

"Don't be glib. You will be learning to speak a new language, educating yourself about a complicated country, and then an entire university system you know nothing about. You will soon be mingling with some of the smartest minds in the world, and you better be convincing or you'll be kicked out on your ass and most likely arrested for fraud. So, no. This is not all it takes."

Custis walked five blocks. He no longer looked ahead or up at the buildings but rather at passersby. Some smiled back. Some even responded to him first. It was like being able to see or hear for the first time. He felt as if he had suddenly been given an additional sense. He moved in slow motion, while the energy of everything else accelerated straight through his body.

It was just before 5:00 p.m. Marshall found an empty bench near DiGiordano Clothiers. "Let's sit and wait here."

Custis looked at the stores across the street—stores that prohibited his entry.

"You look like a cowboy about to wrangle. Cross your legs and keep your shoulders back."

Custis sat quietly. He had just walked over fifteen blocks while greeting strangers. It was empowering. It was also manipulation, and it came with an agonizing sacrifice.

He felt anonymous inside. He had given away his identity, the only thing left from his mother. But she was the one who refused to talk about Custis's father. She had shrouded the man away, deep in secrecy. Who exactly was he? Had his father been a good man, a man so deeply loved by his mother that she couldn't bear to speak his name? Or was his father a White man, a slave owner? Was Custis a product of rape? Or was he a creation of forbidden love? He thought of Sarah and the deep love he had for her. He hoped his mother had been able to feel the same passion sometime in her life.

"You need to smell of cigar."

"What?"

"You need to smell of expensive cigars."

"I don't smoke."

"Do not use contractions."

"I do not smoke."

"Then start."

Marshall looked at his pocket watch. "No contractions. The Greek language does not have vowels like the English language. Vowels and syllables are all you have to concentrate on for your accent at this point."

"What if I meet someone who speaks Greek?"

"Pray that you do not."

Marshall put his watch in his waistcoat. "Look at it as scientific experimentation. Various vowels do not exist. There is a single 'a' sound. Long vowels like 'peace' become 'piss.' 'Cut' and 'cat,' 'but' and 'bat' sound the same."

"How is that a scientific trial?"

"You are the scientist. You figure it out. 'Close' and 'claws' sound the same because the long 'o' does not exist. Fewer vowels are the problem. 'Her' and 'hair' sound the same. Greeks have a hard time with 'sh' as well. 'Ash' becomes 'ass,' 'ship' becomes 'sip.' Horrendously difficult for them, 'sh' is. 'Sheep' becomes 'seep.' Avoid words with 'j'; you won't be able to do those correctly. And 'm' and 'p' as in 'lamp' are pronounced 'b.'"

Marshall pulled a set of folded papers from his jacket pocket. "Here are some rules to get you started. You can work on the syllables first. They are simple and will give you an advantage as soon as you start. All syllables are pronounced and given the same weight, the same length. All vowels are pronounced equally. 'Choc-o-late'—all syllables are flat and even. 'Fam-i-ly,' 'com-for-ta-ble' . . . flat, no rise, no emphasis, no shortcuts."

Marshall pulled Custis by the coat sleeve. "Come on. There's Preston. When you go into this store, I want you to overenunciate your words. Leave out articles. Pronounce every syllable slowly, equally, and methodically. The owner is Italian and has his own set of problems. He won't notice. Try it out."

Preston was already in the store, speaking to the proprietor. Custis was stiff and hesitant. Marshall nudged him from behind.

Preston smiled. "This is my friend from Greece, Renauldos Custis. This is the best tailor on the East Coast, Azie DiGiordano."

Custis paused, cleared his throat, and took a step forward. "I-am-plissed-to-have-meet-you."

DiGiordano smiled broadly. He placed his hands together like he was about to pray. He spoke with a heavy Italian accent. "A friend of Preston Langmuir is a friend to me." DiGiordano kissed Custis's cheeks.

"I-am-in-need-green-tie. Cigar."

"And a couple of new suits," Preston added. "And colorful, shiny, vivid-patterned waistcoats. Lots of green, my friend."

"Yes, yes. Of course." DiGiordano stepped back, his eyes pausing on Custis's drab, threadbare jacket. "Yes, this hurts my eyes." He huffed, smiled, and measured Custis, turning him around and around.

Custis was fitted in a new jacket, waistcoat, and green tie. He studied himself in the full-length mirror. Superficial clothing, demeanor, social intellect, and performance ability had surreptitiously placed him into an entirely different race and class. His ethnicity was arbitrary and biologically meaningless. For the first time in his life, he realized, but for the color of a man's skin, no meaningful differences separated whites from Blacks. He, a Black man, son of a slave, had manipulated societal prejudices steeped deeply for ages. It was all a big fat lie.

"No brown. Just gray, black. Some red neckties as well," Preston added. "Better get an overcoat, too."

"Oh, yes, it will be beautiful. But those boots. Atrocity." DiGiordano placed his finger over his lips, stepped back, and shook his head. "Not with my beautiful suit, Signore Langmuir. Please, no."

"We will address that issue, Azie." Preston laughed. "Let me know when all is ready to be picked up. Or better yet, send it to my home. I'll keep it there for Custis until he has a permanent residence."

Preston paid the bill in full.

x x x

Late in the evenings when his head was exhausted and his muscles ached, Custis wrote to Sarah. He agonized over the thought of one of the letters being intercepted. He had no way of confirming when Sarah had spoken with Lucas or what had taken place after she told him the wedding was off. Surely, he would be gone by now. But still, his words were cryptic, never quite saying what he wanted to say. Subtle and metaphorical expressions masked explicit language making sure he never referenced Centennial.

I want to apprise you and your father of my living arrangements. General delivery, Manhattan, but only as I briefly navigate life's mysteries. Dreams are coming true, and I have a respite from the ordinary. I have taken a sabbatical from Ohio to accept a temporary position of tutoring a young man whose father and I commiserated with while at Wilson Place.

Custis wanted to express his love and excitement, share his progress on passing and how close he was to being accepted at the university. He wanted to tell Sarah how it felt being treated so inversely, but he would be patient and wait for her direction. He had left her a departing letter under the care of Martin, confirming point by point. Both would need to stay the course, work the plan to each small detail.

Every morning he'd wake before sunrise. Sometimes he walked or rode an old, salvaged bicycle, but on bitterly cold mornings, he'd take the electric cable car to his first daily task—the post office to check general delivery. But there was always nothing.

Custis learned more about Greece than he had expected. History, locales, culture, industry, trade, and agriculture. Even weather patterns were committed to memory. The most challenging undertaking was linguistics, losing his own accent and picking up another. Custis converted pronunciation, inflection, and intonation into mathematical modeling. A recurrent pattern, a formula, a calculated uniformity, a measured explanation.

He spoke only with a Greek inflection, and when his Southern accent popped up unexpectedly, Marshall immediately corrected him. He memorized the names of professors, classes, and even the layout of Simpson College. Quizzes and mock interviews were held daily. He even carried a wallet containing Greek drachma and small crumpled photographs of unknown Greek families.

His identity had been completely replaced. He had a mother and father, a sister, brother, and cousins. Custis was close to achieving his life's dream. A student, a research scientist, and an inventor at Centennial University, the finest school in the world. It was at his fingertips and soon would come to fruition.

But at night, when things would settle from the day and sleep would close his eyes, he'd see his mother, never pretending to be someone she was not. *"No one here on this earth is any better than anybody else, and that's the truth. One thing we all got in common is we all gotta die someday, and nobody can do nothing about it. Can't buy or fight your way out of it."* He and his mother had experienced impenetrable hate and bias. But now, he, the son of a slave forbidden the slightest of education, would infiltrate the nation's most prestigious university.

26

Custis ventured out farther into the city each day. One day Preston showed him the attic in the unused building on the far side of campus. It would become Custis's makeshift office and study hall. They covered the windows at either end of the room to keep the cold out and the lamplight in. Preston paused. He looked around the room, then back at Custis. "What's wrong with you? You look like you just swallowed something alive."

"My appointment with the chancellor is Thursday afternoon."

"You're ready, my friend. Don't worry about it. No one has suspected anything."

Custis sat down on a wooden crate. He didn't know if it was his empty stomach or the burst of reality rushing into his head that made him feel weak. All he had worked for was now resting on what would occur Thursday afternoon. Years of work suddenly became a reality: a sweet relief or wretched end. A mathematician breathes to solve theorems. Chemists exist to investigate the nonexistent. And scientists thrive on demonstrating the impossible. But now he was also an imposter, a play-actor performing for the rest of his life.

"You need some fine-tuning for the interview with Chancellor Adams. But in the meantime, this will be your room. After you get this place cleaned up, we can bring the rest of your new wardrobe here. Bring everything from your flat here to the attic. We'll start fresh in the morning."

Custis looked around the room. "Good. I've been here for several weeks without going to school or working. That was not in my plans. I barely have enough money to pay for the first two semesters and a couple months' worth of food." Custis patted his waist. "Right now, it's helping me keep warm."

"You keep all your funds on your person? You need it in the bank," Preston said.

"It comes with me, wherever I go. I never leave it in my room. As it is already, I had to pay extra to safeguard my books. People go through the rooms like rats. They'll take anything."

х х х

Old doors on wooden sawhorses became tables. Reclaimed chalkboards, miscellaneous office supplies, and limited equipment mysteriously appeared. Preston seemed to be the only one not baffled.

Custis's entire project, his life's work was laid out on seven dilapidated doors. Preston stood over stacks of research papers, thumbing through a pile of sketches.

"I know this will work. Its value will be tremendous. I cannot comprehend how you get there, though."

"Right now, I'm not getting anywhere. My fingers are so cold, I can no longer write. I've looked at the boiler in the basement. It's beyond repair. Probably why this building isn't used anymore."

Custis had one last trip to make back to his room. He looked up into the night sky. There were stars above in air so cold they could shatter into a million pieces at any moment. Custis's eyes watered, his breath visible, and his fingers were so numb he couldn't feel the skin sticking to the metal handlebars. The campus was dark and quiet except for the squeaking bicycle wheels and the tires' thud sounding on the cobblestone. Lamplight ahead lit the path. City streetlights on the corners were brighter than on campus. He would be there soon . . . not much farther. He should have left earlier. It was too cold, too dark, and too dangerous. But at night he could travel faster, without interference.

The streets seemed to grow wider. Furrows of horse manure lay in wait next to the sidewalk, along with wooden crates of refuse at the curb edge. The sidewalks were empty of people, and the darkness provided safe harbor for rats and an occasional scruffy dog, all scavenging for the same scraps.

Custis concentrated on his pace. He watched for icy spots, slipped on some, but regained his balance. In the alleyway ahead, a dark frozen trail drained into the gutter. It looked treacherous. He slowed to a stop, straddled the bicycle, and looked back at the campus. Maybe he should go back, wait until morning for the last load.

Custis felt a rush of movement coming from the darkened alley. An arm-bar hold from behind clinched around his neck. He felt his body heaving violently off the bicycle. Air stopped at his throat. It happened so suddenly there had been no time to prepare, to fill his lungs with oxygen or hold his breath. His neck would break. Custis pushed his back into the assailant. Both fell to the pavement, the vice still holding tight. Two more men in dark clothing dragged him deeper into the alley shadows. Fists pummeled his midsection. They held him down and tore at his waist. A solid hit to his face, and all went black.

Custis slowly regained consciousness. He lay flat on his back with his hair partially frozen to the ground. His jaw ached, his head throbbed, and his eyes blurred. A rat gnawed on the bottom of his shoe. Custis recoiled and kicked at the rodent. It leapt upward and scurried under a nearby debris heap. His clothing was partially stuck to the pavement, and he heard it rip as he stood. The front of his jacket hung open. His vest and shirt were torn apart, exposing his bare chest. Custis pulled on his pants. The waistband had been cut. Someone had slashed open the side of his trousers. The money belt was gone.

The morning air inside the attic was colder than outdoors. Preston opened the door and stepped into the room. "Brother Custis! You in here? Why's the door unlocked? Renauldos?"

Custis was in the corner of the room, squatted down with his back against the wall. He wiped his eyes with the heels of his hands. "My money is gone," he managed to say.

Preston stepped farther into the room. He looked around, as if trying to follow the sound of the voice.

"What on earth are you doing? What happened?"

"They took my money belt, my bicycle."

"What?" Preston sat down on the floor next to Custis. "You all right? Are you hurt?"

"No, I'm not all right. I have nothing now. I have no money left. They took the belt completely off me. But they left my wallet full of drachma."

"They must have known about the belt, then."

Custis purposely kept his eyes closed, his hands on each side of his head. One look at Preston, and Custis would be on his feet, grabbing

Preston and accusing him of stealing the money. But it couldn't have been him. It didn't make sense. Preston did not need money.

"No one knew, Preston. About me. About the money. No one except you."

"You think I did this to you? You know what, for someone so smart, that is a stupid thing to say." Preston shook his head and abruptly stood to his feet. "Why would I want your money, you ungrateful son of a bitch?"

Custis held up his hand motioning for Preston to stop.

"I told you to get out of that neighborhood. Someone knew you had it or assumed you had one. All of them are thieves, ne'er-do-wells. They watched you go back and forth from the moment you got here. Of course they knew you wore a belt. How many times did they pilfer through your room looking for money? Where else would your cash be? You think you're the only one who wears a belt? You're so naïve."

Preston was right. He had no reason to assault Custis. He was a supporter, colleague, and friend. Preston had financed the plan and had put himself and his reputation at risk. Custis felt a tinge of remorse for his irrational thoughts. Stress, it was only stress.

Custis looked up. His face and hands were streaked with filth, and his eyes were red, watery, and puffy. His left cheek was swollen and scraped. Preston looked horrified and bent back down.

"I need to get you some ice." He gently turned Custis's head and examined closer. "We've got to get you cleaned up. You have a cut, and it will get infected. And you stink."

"I have to postpone my appointment. I can't go in looking like this."

"No, you are not. You'll keep it. We have too much riding on this. I'll loan you the money for now, and we can figure it out later. Get up. You're coming with me to my place. My father is gone until spring. By then, you'll be living on campus, in a room with a heater."

"No. I'll stay right here. If you can just spot me a bit of cash, enough for my first semester. I've got someone in Carolina that can help me. I'll write to them and will pay you back when I get the funds."

"Listen, don't contact anyone right now. Let's just get you through the appointment, and then we'll go from there."

"I will pay you back."

"I know, so get your ass up and get cleaned up. Then let's get to work preparing for Chancellor Adams."

27

Twenty-four granite stairs ascended to the portico of the chancellor's office. The first step was seven and three-quarter inches high. For one hundred years, great men had climbed these stairs. The granite treads gave Custis a similar steadfast feeling as the steel train rails and timbers in North Carolina had. But these steps, carved from stone by unknown men, free or indentured, lay in the same place for longer than anything Custis had ever seen. With each step, he imagined walking in the exact tracks of noblemen he would never meet.

High above the colonnade, the stone pediment stretched across the face of the building. Sculptures of allegories filled each side and abutted three large carvings in the center. Custis translated the Greek letters. Koios, God of Curiosity, on the left and Sisyphus, God of Perseverance, on the right. But in the middle, a female figure: Aidos, Goddess of Humility, able to give reverence or shame to restrain men from wrong. A sacred goddess ruling over an institution where women were not allowed.

Once at the top, Custis turned and looked out over the campus. He stood in the moment that held the rest of his life. He removed his hat. Men dashed from one place to another while others walked solemnly. They resembled white mice in a giant maze scurrying to find their reward; some were confused, while others seemed barely concerned at all. All his fragmented and disoriented paths, swirling collectively, had led him up these stairs.

Please, God, you've given me all I can just about take, and I still got this far. Just don't let me foul this up.

Custis turned and stood before the enormous door leading into the chancellor's office. He entered an empty anteroom, and the great door echoed shut with a reverberant acoustic.

He was alone. Overstuffed wingback chairs lined the two walls. He chose the chair farthest from the entry door and silently sat down. He looked around at large, dark paintings of men he did not know. White men with thin gray hair. Bearded faces and some clean-shaven. All with surly eyes refusing to shift their glare, each examining the man that sat at their feet.

A door, secreted within the millwork design on the wall, slowly opened. A man, younger than the men in the paintings, even younger than Custis, stepped into the room. "This way," he said.

Custis picked up his case and stepped through the door.

An old man, looking disproportionately small, was sitting behind a large, ornate desk near the far wall.

Tall, dark bookcases reached to the coffered ceilings high above. Small lamps illuminated paintings among the book collections. A single wooden chair sat empty in the middle of the room, facing the desk.

"Mr. Custis. Sit." The man did not look up from his papers. The top of his head was bald, and his skin was in want of sunlight.

Custis nodded once, sat down, and placed his case and hat on the floor next to him. The chair was uncomfortable. The chancellor placed his fountain pen on the desk and folded his hands. An indication of gray hair wrapped around the sides of his head. His necktie was too tight, or maybe his shirt had become too small. His eyes studied Custis in awkward silence. Custis recalled Preston's advice. *Remain quiet. Most people cannot handle the silence and start talking, saying things they should not. It's a test. Remain silent until he speaks or asks you something specific. Do not be tricked.*

"Mr. Renauldos Custis."

"Yes, sir, Chancellor Adams."

"I see that you are from Greece."

The chancellor put on his reading glasses, resting them on the end of his nose. He looked down at the paperwork neatly aligned in front of him. His eyes, the only part of him that seemed to move, returned to Custis. Deep creases lined his forehead, reflecting years of repetitive practice. He opened a folder and began to read. His head moved slightly side to side, his index finger leading the way. Another page was turned, read, and flipped over.

After another moment of silence, the chancellor asked, "What can you tell me about a Ronald Custis?"

"Sir?"

"A Ronald Custis from North Carolina."

Chancellor Adams stood from his desk. He walked to a nearby wooden filing cabinet and removed a large file. He returned to his desk and sat down with a thud and an accompanying grunt. He opened the file, retrieved two papers, and held them side by side.

"It seems that you may be the same?"

A million thoughts burst into Custis's mind, but only one mattered. The chancellor knew the truth. *But how does he know? What is he reading? This is how it all ends.*

Custis would not be admitted. He'd lied, conspired with others, and falsified records. He would be arrested. His work would go uncompleted, and he would be a failure. But worst of all, he could never be with Sarah. Custis felt his body going limp. He concentrated on his fingers gripping the wooden armrests on either side of the chair. He tried to move, but his muscles were immobile. It was going dark. He saw a small girl wearing lavender cloth. Custis heard soft tapping. He glanced down at his hand gripping the end of the chair air. It was his finger, tapping a small black riding boot in a muddy creek bed. Custis breathed in deeply, allowing oxygen to refresh his blood.

He had come so far—from that muddy creek bed to convening before the chancellor of one of the most prestigious universities in the world. He thought of his mother, of reading to her by candlelight. He thought he heard her voice. *You are as smart as God makes. Someday you're gonna be the best scientist on this earth.* Custis felt her presence. His fingers loosened their grasp on the arms of the chair. He looked directly at the chancellor.

"Yes, sir. I resided there for some years. My name was changed. Renauldos versus Ronald. The intent was to be American, to fit in, I suppose."

"I received a letter earlier in the year from a source requesting anonymity. Apparently, this unnamed source holds you to be a genius. Specifically, 'with brilliance and fortitude far exceeding all normal limits.'" Chancellor Adams looked up from the papers. "He seems to think that our university would have adverse beliefs or unsympathetic practices against allowing you to attend. Why would he think that, Mr. Custis?"

Custis wanted to clear his throat, but that would give his nervousness away. *Think through the problem. White males only, period. It is the law. It may be simple, then—race versus ethnicity. Do not yield. Remember the accent.*

"Mr. Custis, why would this anonymous man harbor belief that we would be unwilling to permit Greeks into our university? Is that not odd when one thinks about the Lyceum or Plato's Academy, Socrates, and Aristotle?" Chancellor Adams paused. "Of course, he, the anonymous source, is from the South. I surmise that is to be expected, then."

"My father and mother immigrated here, to New York. He was a genius and had studied agriculture and life sciences. He took my mother to North Carolina to farm and invested his life savings into the land. He quickly learned North Carolina has a different caste system regarding immigrants. Those from foreign countries, such as the Greek Isles, are believed to be inferior. I can assure you, I am not."

"Are you from the Isles?"

"No. I am not."

"You hail from Patras." Again, it was a statement, not a question.

Chancellor Adams meticulously turned each page in the folder. He glanced at each, top to bottom. "This source has attached payment, which encompasses the fee for the first three years." His eyes moved up over his eyeglasses to Custis, then back down to the paper.

Chancellor Adams closed the file. He placed his glasses on the desk, rubbed his eyes, and leaned back into his chair.

"Including monthly incidentals. He has also made a large endowment to the research of cancer with the commitment of quittance for the future chair sponsorship specific to that field."

The information led back to Martin Tennison. *Do not show emotion. Stay calm.* He concentrated on his facial muscles. He felt sweat forming on his forehead. He wanted to wipe it off with the back of his hand. No, better to use the handkerchief in his jacket.

"Are you nervous, Mr. Custis?"

"Of course I am. This is one of the most important events in my life."

"Good. I do not trust those who act otherwise." The chancellor appeared to wait for Custis to return the handkerchief to his pocket.

"Apparently, his wife passed from cancer some years back. Quite understandable."

"Yes. Quite." *Don't give up information. Keep answers short. Less to get tripped up.*

Chancellor Adams flipped through the paperwork. "I see your records from Simpson are exceptional. I have received an endorsement from"—he paused as he adjusted his glasses up, then back down to his nose—"Professor Bates. He states you were one of his best students. Maybe even his protégé. You desire to continue and even repeat your schooling here? I do not understand."

Custis's thoughts stopped on the name Professor Bates. Bates had been listed in the Simpson University dossier.

"Yes. I wish to obtain additional training. I aspire to work with the mechanics of radiation as it pertains to medicine. Centennial has the laboratory I require to complete my theories. No other institution offers the equipment and capability to meet the objective. Most importantly, no other institution presents the resourcefulness and courage Centennial possesses. This institution takes uncharted possibilities and turns them into reality."

"We will be interested in your progress, of course."

Chancellor Adams was silent. The room was soundless except for a ticking sound. A loud tick that Custis was hearing for the first time. He didn't dare move. *There it is.* It came from a large mantle clock directly behind the chancellor on the bookshelf, just above his head.

Tick. Tick. Tick.

An odd place for the chancellor's clock. He'd have to stop, turn, and stand to see the time. The clock sat solitarily on a shelf while books and paintings besieged all the others—the mahogany shelving, hard and dense, perfect for sound reverberation. Custis visualized the movement inside the clock. He saw the verge escapement mechanism and imagined the foliot, alive and breathing.

Tick. Tick. Tick.

The purpose of its position was not for the chancellor but rather the casualty sitting alone in the middle of the room. Time was running out. He watched as time passed before his very eyes. Custis had not said enough, and his responses had been too short. He needed to adjust, have more conversation. He felt compelled to talk. But that was part of the game. The clock had a role, to make people uncomfortable, to throw them off. To make them think that time was up, and life was passing by.

"We have students from Greece, albeit not in your field. A few are transfers from Simpson. You may know them already."

"Yes, sir. I have not had the time to maintain friendships, unfortunately." Custis realized he may have said too much. "My studies consume all of my time."

"You have no family here? Nor friends?"

"No, sir. Not many. I have a new friend. Preston Langmuir."

"Preston Langmuir. Langmuir, of course. His father is very committed to our institute. Graduated here himself. With honors, I recall." Chancellor Adams stood, picked up the folder, and mumbled as he walked to the file cabinet. "Rather strange how things seem to skip a generation." The enigma of the ticking clock working against its own creator. His voice was now direct and firm. "It would behoove you, Mr. Custis, to keep your head grounded in books and resist the temptation of lollygagging with your life's progression."

Custis quickly filed away the words. "Yes, I am very anxious to get started."

Chancellor Adams firmly closed the file cabinet drawer. "Be not anxious, Mr. Custis. Be excited. Your caliber will be compared with those great men who came before you. Do not disappoint us."

The plan had worked. A Black man was about to be accepted into a world-renowned all-White institution. Custis looked downward. Joy surged within, and his eyes would be the first to divulge emotion. His hands trembled. He felt the warmth of blood capillaries pulsating through his muscles. Custis was at his mental threshold. He slowed his breathing and imagined the calmness of a hawk, aloft and soaring on warm afternoon thermals.

"I can assure you, Chancellor Adams, I will not disappoint you."

"I will put you in contact with Professor Alger. Orientation will commence on January 5th. He will assist you in confirming your courses. Professor Alger may be a great resource for you. He has family ties in Greece as well."

The charade was far from over.

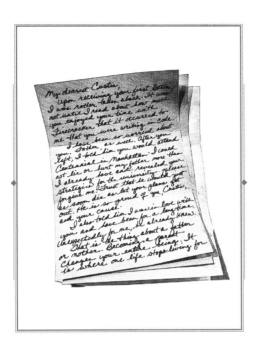

28

C ustis returned to the attic and opened the door. He was so excited he could barely keep a straight thought in his head. Preston, Marshall, and McKay played cards on one end of the table, drank whiskey, and smoked cigars. All three had covered their shoulders with blankets.

Custis dropped his case to the floor, landing with a loud thud. They turned with sharpness. Custis feigned dejection. "It's over."

Their laughter stopped. Preston rose to his feet. He looked like he didn't know what to say. McKay and Marshall fidgeted with their hands.

Custis could no longer hold in his prank and burst out laughing. "I'm joking . . . I'm in! January 5th."

The men looked at one another and tossed the playing cards into the air as blankets hit the floor.

Custis could barely get his words out. "I've never been so nervous in all my life. I'm not exactly sure what happened after Chancellor Adams said, 'Please sit.' But I am in. I'm in for three years, all paid for." Custis pulled a paper from his coat pocket. "I have a monthly stipend for food." He waved the check. "This is my funding for the first half of the year. I can buy food. I need to go to the bank. Open an account."

Preston looked stunned. He said nothing. The man with the grandiose scheme, the one who had counterarguments and wiles for all occasions, stood speechless.

Custis grabbed Preston by the front of his shoulders. "What's wrong with you? Didn't you hear me? We're in, and it's all paid. I'm sponsored. And why didn't you tell me about your father knowing the chancellor?"

"Of course, I'm elated. In shock, but elated. What do you mean, though? Who is paying?"

McKay interrupted. "Doesn't matter. Unbelievable. I knew you could do it."

"We need to celebrate," Marshall yelled.

"No, you boys go. I'll catch up. I need to sit down for a while." The room was cold, but he hadn't noticed. He held his hand out in front. "Look, I'm still shaking."

Preston buttoned his overcoat. "Who paid? Who would do that?"

Custis knew it had been Tennison but couldn't reveal that part of his life. "I'm not sure. But who is Professor Bates?"

Preston smiled across his entire face. "He owes my father a great deal. *Daddy* comes in handy sometimes." He wrapped his scarf around his neck. "Meet us at Ace's. A happy salmon will be waiting for you." Preston closed the door.

Custis moved to the nearest chair. Its upholstery was worn and tattered, but its bones were still strong. He leaned his head back and closed his eyes. The room was perfectly still, as if time had stopped. A pathway to his life's goals had emerged. He felt his muscles sinking deeper into the ragged padding of the chair. Soon, he could be with Sarah. He could no longer hold in his tears.

Custis covered his face with his hands and gave thanks for all his blessings. He had pried open the doors to another world and would stand in the footsteps of those he had only read about. He imagined leading his mother off the dirt floor of their cabin and walking arm in arm onto the grand white portico of Centennial University.

All he needed now was Sarah. His mind untangled columns of logical facts and assumptions. *How did Martin know?* Sarah had told him, confided the plan. Now he could write to Martin—Lucas would never intercept his letters. He had to let Martin know he had been accepted and was already staying in a building on campus. Now, he would be able to secure a more suitable place with Sarah. Most importantly, he needed to know if she was safe and Lucas was gone.

χ χ χ

In this megapolis called New York, time must pass differently. Its vastness of merging populations connected only by intersecting streets must work as a labyrinth in slowing down time. Two months without hearing from Sarah felt like years. Sometimes, Custis traveled so deep within himself he perceived arteries and veins as never-ending streets and paths he must travel.

His first Christmas in Manhattan would be soon. Spending an hour in line at the post office was not unusual. The postmasters had become familiar with him, shaking their heads even before he reached their respective windows. But not today. Custis achingly looked at the postmaster, the one with the gray mustache partially concealing a shiny tooth. He smiled and held up a letter.

For a moment, Custis did not move. He stared at the envelope. *Sarah*

Tennison. He recognized the perfect connecting strokes. *Renauldos Custis, General Delivery, Manhattan Isle, New York City*. He heard his own voice, "Renauldos." She had received his letters. Custis was hesitant to touch it. He didn't want to wake up and realize it was some unkind dream.

"Go ahead. It's real," the postmaster said as he tapped it on the countertop as if to prove its legitimacy.

Custis took the letter and forgot to acknowledge him.

The postmaster chuckled and nodded his head. "Next."

Custis carried the letter in his hand as he ran, walked, and ran again back to the attic. Intermittent sprinkles of rain forced him to protect the envelope under the front of his jacket. But he never let go of it. He felt his constant smile tire his cheeks. He laughed and sometimes wanted to cry. Once there, safely inside, he lit the lantern and opened the seal.

> *My dearest Custis,*
>
> *Upon receiving your first letter, I was rather taken aback. It was not until I read about how much you enjoyed your time with Firecracker that it occurred to me that you were writing in code.*
>
> *I have been so worried about you. Father, as well. After you left, I told him you would attend Centennial in Manhattan. I could not lie or hurt my father more than I already have and revealed your strategies for the university. Please forgive me. Trust that he would just as soon die as let your plans get out. He is so proud of you, Custis, and your cause.*
>
> *I also told him I was in love with you and have been for a long time. Unexpectedly for me, he already knew.*

The three sheets of stationery quivered in his trembling hands. He placed the letter on the table and flattened out the creases. He tried unsuccessfully controlling his tears and used the back of his hand to wipe them away. Martin knew. He had sent the funds for sponsorship. He was supporting the plan. It all was coming true.

That is the thing about a father or mother. Becoming a parent changes your entire being. It is where one life stops living for itself and willingly lives without compunction for another. It is only now, my darling, I understand and know this to be true. When my mother was dying, I remember her face. Now I know—it was not the fear of death in her eyes, but rather, it was her seeing and feeling the fear and confusion in the face of her own little girl, her flesh and blood. She must have been so worried about leaving me without a mother.

I am with child, Lucas's child. Shortly after you left, Father found me in the barn. I thought I had fallen from the horse. But Doctor Lyman found it differently. There is no question about this life inside of me, and soon, Lucas will be a doting father. I have seen the pain in your eyes and felt the anguish in your heart for not knowing or under-standing your own father, an aching, as you told me, that shall never go away. I cannot allow the same to befall this child to come.

We married up on the hillside behind the house. Father stood next to me as he always has. It took me days to come to terms and weeks to find the courage to write to you. There is a profound sadness within me, a gaping hole that shall never mend. I have loved you all my life and shall continue to do so, quietly.

I revisit moments and wish we could have them once again. The memories provide comfort but also intensify the pain of navigating through such longing. Acceptance of my future life does not mean my pain will ever disappear. Nothing can be written or said aloud to make my child's fundamentals come before my own desire.

I do not have a right to ask for your forgiveness, but I do hope in some small way that you understand. You now stand on the cusp of making a difference in our world. Your remarkable mind and unlimited heart are destined for greatness. You will have more glorious accomplishments than I could ever help foster. There is no doubt about your achievements, and I will await to read great articles about your work and discoveries.

When the white Dutch clover returns to the pastureland, and our lives are full of spring and new beginnings, I will meet my child and read to him great stories of adventure and lore. And in the early autumns of each passing year, know that we will stand amongst the turning leaves and breathe in the promise of tomorrows—and I will think of you.

Sarah

x x x

Custis walked aimlessly for miles. At times he'd stop, find an alcove, a bench, or an empty alleyway. He wanted to believe the child was his and Lucas had mastered control over Sarah. He read the letter over and over, but the vernal equinox of spring did not calculate. *I was there in September.*

Sometimes, the streets buzz and rumble in every direction. Sidewalks are full of a murmuration of strangers, all seemingly without objective or intention. They have no leader. Their intensity must work for safety, constantly maneuvering to the center of the flight, avoiding the risk of being absconded from the edge. Why is it that when death occurs, the world continues to move and breathe and quickly forgets about the broken heart that remains? Is it a humble reminder of the impermanence of life or proof of the profound impact another soul has on our hearts? That is what it felt like—a death, a horrible and unexpected death.

For days, Custis flew in a torrent of chaotic emotions—a storm moving from the depths of sorrow while feeling brief moments of relief in knowing Sarah would be safe. He could never stop loving her. But now it must be a conversion, a transformation he must accept. He summoned strength from the knowledge that the undeniable necessity of a mother's love and sacrifice would last until the end of her days. And it was a choice etched with a permanence that would define the rest of his.

29

ustis sat in the upper rows of the physics theatre. The bird's-eye view felt like an advantage. Below, Professor Alger stood confidently in front of a wall of chalkboards donning a leather apron rather than a white lab jacket. Stacks of books spilled out of the shelving onto the desks on either side of the stage. He was younger than Custis had imagined.

"Seventy-three percent of you will fail this class." Professor Alger looked around the room. His voice was without intonation. "Of the remaining students, 18.25 of you people will quit; 8.75 of you will remain. Prove me wrong."

Two men sitting next to each other stood up and left the room, followed by one more. Custis stood, collected his belongings, and stepped into the aisle. He walked down and took a seat in the front row.

Professor Alger watched silently. His hair was full and black with no sign of graying. "What is your name?"

Custis stood. This would be his first time publicly addressing his professor, a Greek professor. Custis cleared his throat. His accent had to be perfect.

"Renauldos Custis."

"Mr. Custis. What now is the number for success?"

"It remains the same. It appears we just lost three of your 18.25 quitters."

"Sit. Anyone else wish to leave? No one? Good."

Classes and associated work were redundant for Custis. Studying for exams was unnecessary. He easily passed without opening a book. He attended all lectures, but his head churned with other ideas. He refreshed his studies of anatomy and medicine on his own. In the future, he would need that knowledge to merge with the development of his project. He dedicated his evenings and weekends to the laboratory. Sometimes he'd work through the night, not realizing the time until students arrived for morning class. He slept in the attic where he could study and work at will and come and go as he pleased.

During holidays, he seemed to be the only one left on campus. While others had left for homes and families far away, Custis slept on the soapstone countertop in the lab. He made coffee in glass beakers, kept provisions in the pharmaceutical icebox, and warmed food on Bunsen burners.

Custis craved guidance from his professors. He wanted to present his work and ask for their help, in the hope of accelerating his project. But at the cost of being discovered, he chose, rather, to sidestep any signs of fellowship, dodge invitations when he could, and make sure he was never available for student social functions. Preston was a regular pest, wanting to drink and find girls. Custis couldn't be distracted. The loneliness drove him even deeper into his work. He often wondered how Preston managed to lollygag through school and life. The chancellor's words that sat uneasy in Custis's mind. Preston was without bearing and didn't seem to mind. It made Custis uncomfortable, since it wasn't something he could understand. Marshall and McKay seldom had the occasion to be on the science and technology side of the university. But they all met every third Tuesday at Ace's. They called themselves the Vampire Club. Not because they killed anyone but because they all consumed Happy Salmons, which made them look like they were drinking blood.

"Andoe," Preston yelled, "another round."

"Not for me. I've got to get back to work." Custis stood.

"Wait, you can't leave just yet. I've got a proposition for you."

Marshall and McKay laughed. "Oh, God, here we go again," Marshall said.

Custis shook his head and reluctantly sat back down.

"I'm looking to change my field. Medicine just isn't the road I'm looking for. I want to do research work like you're doing, Custis. I'm tired of seeing death and blood."

"Have you lost your ever-loving mind?" McKay placed his empty glass on the table. "You're crazy! To start all over is just insane."

Marshall shook his head. "We're about to graduate, and you want to do this?"

"It's not starting all over. It's just changing course a bit. Listen, it's already underway. I agree. I need to get serious about what is best for me. I've helped everyone at this table. . . . Just forget it." Preston abruptly stood. "Thanks for all of the support."

"Wait, don't get all indignant. We support you," McKay said.

Preston placed some money on the table and walked briskly out of the bar.

Custis looked at Marshall, then at McKay. "What's going on here? Do you think he's serious?"

"Yes. Preston is a professional student," McKay said. "His father pays for everything. Preston doesn't have any deep interests except for alcohol and women, it seems. A regular saga boy."

Marshall added, "He doesn't want to work out on his own. He's afraid he will fail. Fail in front of his father."

"But he's so intelligent. He's brilliant, actually," Custis said.

Marshall nodded. "I wouldn't take it that far. He rarely studies. Always passes, though."

"And he can talk a snake out of its own skin if it's important to him. He needs to be a politician." McKay giggled.

"But he'd do anything for you, obviously. He's a good man, just has issues with his father, I suppose."

"And rightfully so," Marshall said. "His father expects nothing but perfection and will use all his power to clear the way for his son, no matter how much it costs or who it hurts. The wrath of Conrad Preston Langmuir III. The man has no scruples."

Custis took a drink from his mug. Identifying and categorizing social behaviors was never Custis's strength—Preston had many layers hidden away. "Listen, Preston went out on a limb for me. You all did. And for that, I cannot be more indebted. Whatever his issues, we need to stand by him."

McKay nodded. "Political science is actually a good idea."

Custis recalled the tender side of Preston, the hospital nursery and Emma. The side of Preston deeply hidden away from others.

"Tell me something," Custis said. "Does his father own the hospital?"

Marshall answered, "He may. I know that he's on the governing board."

30

C ustis spent his second New York Christmas alone. Thoughts
of Sarah came easily and only dissipated with deliberate effort. He walked the empty stairwells, never needing
to yield, always staying deep in thought. Vacant hallways gave great
echoes. Resonated footfalls of a singular stride invisibly filled the
chamber, flowing like fluid into arteries. All was quiet and wrapped in
stillness. Even the sun had been given a respite.

Custis worked freely on his prototype apparatus in the laboratory.
Deep calculations filled his head as he wiped his brow with his arm. He

placed both his hands on the top of the machine and strummed his fingers as if waiting for answers to magically appear. *It's not there. Something is missing.* He slammed his fist on the top then tossed a pile of paperwork to the floor. He turned around and threw his wrench, shattering into glassware across the room. He rubbed his head then pushed a file cabinet over to its side, then stood silently with his hands on his hips. It was the wrong path, once again. The number sequence had turned into scattered logic and frustration. He looked at the paperwork strewn about the floor. "Well, this is unproductive," he said out loud.

After collecting his papers, he began to sweep up the broken glass on the far side of the room. His eyes caught movement outside in the quad area. He looked out the window and rubbed the glass for a better view. Far below, a light layer of snow covered the ground. A man and woman were holding hands, both bundled up tightly. Graceful snowflakes fluttered down as two small children, a young girl with dark hair and a little towheaded boy, played nearby.

Custis looked out farther onto the campus. Not another soul in sight. They were an ideal family in a perfect postcard photograph. He smiled as he watched the boy amass an inventory of snowballs. A fight would surely ensue. The boy took cover behind a leafless tree. Snowballs flew toward the girl, one after another. The man laughed, then launched some of his own at the boy. The boy retreated as the girl commandeered his stockpile. The woman clapped her hands and laughed at all three.

The memories of Sarah took Custis far away. He pictured her more beautiful than Christmastime itself. She would be doting on her father, maybe her husband. He refocused his eyes. The man stood still now, looking up and facing the laboratory. He waved at Custis. It was Professor Alger. The little girl stood next to him, also staring up at the building. Custis was startled and wondered how long the professor had been watching him.

I've been in a trance.

x x x

By New Year's Day, the snow was nearly a foot deep. The campus remained deserted. The air was profoundly quiet except for the sound of an occasional celebratory blast coming from nearby neighborhoods. Custis was startled at the sound of the laboratory door opening.

"Mr. Custis, I thought I might find you here."

Custis quickly stood from his desk. "Professor Alger. What a surprise."

"I saw you working earlier in the week."

"Yes. Merry Christmas and Happy New Year to you. I thought I was the only person left."

"My family and I live here on the campus, faculty housing. It's not much, but the proximity is very convenient." Professor Alger took off his overcoat. "For us fledgling professors with young families, we are grateful for what is provided."

"Yes, I saw you and your family in the snow last week. Surely, you are a blessed man."

"Thank you." Professor Alger looked around the room. "Everyone seems to defect this time of year."

"I find it rather peaceful. I can concentrate and accomplish so much more when it's quiet."

"You are diligent, Mr. Custis. I have watched you with curiosity as well as with concern. Sometimes you stay and work late into the night and are the first to return in the mornings. And here you are, alone. Very assiduous." The professor walked closer toward Custis. "I would surmise that you are working on something entirely different than what you are assigned to do. Is that correct?"

"Only in my spare time, sir. My assignments always take priority."

Professor Alger stepped closer. "I believe it is the tradition of the university to allow alumni access to the laboratories, but you have yet to graduate. However, I do not take negatively to anyone who has such dedication such as yourself. And apparently, neither does Chancellor Adams. I recall he indicated you would have a project of your own. I do not fully understand you, Mr. Custis. I have examined your records. It appears you could teach any class here in physics, chemistry, or even mathematics. You could even have my position. You come highly recommended by Professor Bates from Simpson."

"Do you know him?" Custis asked cautiously.

"I know of him. He is quite the plunger. But you know how rumors grow. It is best to disregard them at times."

"My work is very important to me, and this laboratory is a crucial component. I am developing a theory regarding radiation, hopefully safe radiation. Every week it seems I find a small piece of the puzzle. I believe it can revolutionize preventative and diagnostic medicine. I hope that my work, someday, will be representative of this institution."

"I would like to look at it. But for right now, I come here at my wife's request. She insists you join us for New Year's dinner."

"I am deeply appreciative, but I cannot leave my work."

"It is only my wife and the children. I was never one for parties and such. Your work will not miss you for one evening. Please. I insist."

Custis turned and looked at a contraption on the table, then looked back at the professor.

"My children call you 'the man that has no smile,' locked up in the castle like Rapunzel." Professor Alger handed Custis a small card. "Here is my address, not a far walk at all. I hope you will join us, Mr. Custis."

After the professor left, Custis looked at the card. The professor's offer to share his personal life and family was generous. Professor Alger might hold the answers to Custis's missing link. And right now, he could use another open door.

Custis found his cleanest clothes, brushed them off, and dressed appropriately. It took him fifteen minutes trudging through the snow to find the address. Custis knocked on the front door of the cottage. His hands were red with cold, his feet numb in wet leather shoes. He should have worn a pair of galoshes, but it seemed that remembering such minutia came easier to other people.

The door opened. A small blond-headed boy held on to the knob while leaning his head into the gap. "Friend or foe?" His voice was playful but resolute.

"Friend."

"What is the secret password?"

"Abracadabra?"

"No." The door slammed shut.

Custis stood there, unsure about whether to knock again, then the door opened widely.

Professor Alger stood in front of the boy. "Please come in. Excuse the entry interrogation."

A woman stepped next to the professor and touched his arm. Her smile grew in gentle motion and seemed utterly unpretentious. Her dark eyes beamed as she reached out to Custis. Her hand was soft but firm. She stared into his eyes.

"This is my wife, Gladisen."

"Thank you, Mrs. Alger, for the invitation. It is very kind of you to share your home."

"Thank you for coming, Mr. Custis. We are so excited you are joining us," Mrs. Alger said.

"And these are our children. My son, Ellis. And this is my daughter, Caroline." Ellis wore short pants and a formal shirt. Caroline's dress was a velvety emerald-green, matching Custis's necktie. She wore a paper tiara and what must have been her mother's long white gloves.

Custis bent down to the small boy's height and shook his hand. "How do you do, Ellis?" He looked at Caroline and nodded once. "And Caroline, what a pleasure to meet you as well." He took her hand, clicked his heels, and kissed her gloved hand just like a handsome prince would do.

"Are you the sad man in the window?"

"I am afraid I am. But I am not really sad at all. I must concentrate on my work. But for you, I will smile more, I promise."

"Yes, please. That would be kind of you."

Professor Alger seemed to brim over with happiness. "The adage that children should be seen and not heard—I do not believe in such ideas. My children have a voice. They have thoughts, reasoning, and logic. I rather like conversing with them." The words resonated with Custis. It would have been the way he would have treated his own children with Sarah.

"Yes, we may learn something great from them, do you not think?" Custis asked.

"Let me take your coat," Mrs. Alger said. "Children, Mr. Custis is from Greece."

Ellis leaned into his father's leg as Caroline stared at Custis with infatuated eyes. "Are you a prince from the kingdom of Greece?"

"No, my dear, but I wish I were. Then we could all go for a wonderful sleigh ride, right outside, and eat *bougatsa* and drink hot chocolate."

"Come, sit down." Mrs. Alger led him to the table. "I hope you are hungry."

"My great-grandfather is from Greece. Do you know him?" Caroline asked.

Custis felt Caroline's innocence. "Probably not. Greece is a vast place. Many islands, over two thousand."

The table was perfectly set. The food was abundant, and Custis found it easy to believe in his own charade. He smiled effortlessly and listened with relevance, looking at each face. He had forgotten how it felt to be surrounded by family. His thoughts muffled the sounds around him. Laughter from the children teasing each other, Mrs. Alger tapping the serving spoon on the edge of the dish, and even Professor Alger's voice was soundless. Custis smiled inside as he evaluated the visual language of those before him. He did not need sound to confirm the bond between siblings, the devotion of a mother, or even the adoration of a husband who looked at his wife as if she breathed life into his soul. *Silent sound.*

Custis felt a hand on his. It was warm and soft, just like Sarah's. His smile disappeared as sound returned to his head. It was Mrs. Alger. She had a disarming kind of stare, looking beyond the surface but rather deep into his marrow, wrapping around softly with offers of grace and contentment. "Please, tell us about you. You must have quite the story of immigrating to our country. Do you have a family?"

Custis cleared his throat and patted his mouth with his linen napkin. "I have no children. I left my family to come here, to New York. To work and attend school." An unintentional moment of comfort caused Custis to fall back into the truth. He must remain cautious and display only his best impression.

"That must have been very difficult," Mrs. Alger said. "You have left your parents, one life for a new one here in America."

"Yes, my parents—both are gone now. What I mean, my distant cousins, I consider family. Unfortunately, I lost track of them some years ago."

Caroline politely interjected, "My great-grandfather lives in Santorini. He is an olive granger. Have you been there? Maybe you are friends, after all."

After all. The exact words little Emma said before she died. Custis looked at Caroline. His stare, vibrant with color, seemed to seep directly into hers. She had the same dark eyes as her father and her mother's kind smile, so genuine it would indeed have the power to melt the hardest of future hearts.

"I have not been there."

"Yes, your accent seems like you would come from farther north."

"I'm doing my best to lose the accent, Professor."

Professor Alger looked at Custis with curious eyes. "Maybe from the Epirus region?"

"Not quite that far north. The western region is known for hot summers and mild winters. Exporter of agriculture." Custis stopped abruptly. It sounded as if he had just read a passage from a book. "Patras. A good place to grow up. That is where I call my hometown, my birthplace."

"Patras. Yes, of course. Regional spoken dialects exist side by side. I was born here in America. My father immigrated from Crete before I was born. I have always wanted to go back. Someday I will take this family of mine. First, I will have to refresh my mind with the Greek dialect. My father spoke very little Greek to me. Only when he was angry, it seems. Maybe you can help me with that, Mr. Custis."

"That was a tumultuous time for the Greek kingdom. It must have been challenging for your father."

"He escaped through the Samaria Gorge, evacuating with others into Egypt. Eventually, he came through New York and spent a year in the infirmary. But that is a story for another time. I would like to hear about your work."

"I am afraid it will bore these children to pieces."

"I have two very precocious children, Mr. Custis," the professor said. "Even though we live in America."

"Curious. Why do you qualify that statement?"

"This surprises me that you do not see the American and Grecian educational differences."

Custis had faltered. "Yes, of course." He needed to redirect. "In comparison to America, Greece has a longstanding tradition of valuing academics. For your son, there will be no impediments. Europe's first secular institution was the University of Constantinople, founded by a woman in AD 425."

"As you know, Mr. Custis, in your homeland, women can and are expected to attend higher educational institutions. My grandmother was an architect. But here in America, only men are considered for academes. Yes, there are female seminaries here, such as the Seven Sisters, of course, but they only offer teaching degrees."

Professor Alger looked at his daughter. "What if she does not wish to become a teacher? Maybe she will wish to be a physician or scientist such as yourself. My own university here will not allow my daughter to attend. So ludicrous."

Custis tried to digest the professor's words. Analysis sank deep into his mind, maybe a surreptitious code. *It's an offer of support.* Custis was living proof of hateful witlessness.

Custis looked at Caroline and smiled. "She will be victorious in all she chooses."

"I am already a proud father. I cannot wait to see her future."

Custis stood. "I should probably go before the next snowfall hits. The regular students will not be back for several more days. It will be my honor to show you my work if you find the time."

Mrs. Alger helped Custis with his overcoat as Ellis motioned with his index finger to come closer. Custis leaned down as Ellis cupped his hand around his mouth and whispered in Custis's ear, "The secret password is 'Doctor Frankenstein.'"

Custis whispered back, "Oh, dear, I shall always remember that. Thank you very much, my friend."

"Yes. It is about an unorthodox scientific experiment."

"I have heard about it," Custis whispered in feigned astonishment.

The sharp crunch of snow beneath Custis's footsteps was the only sound left on campus. The night air was so cold Custis covered his mouth and nose with his scarf to keep his lungs from freezing. He thought about his friends. Each would be with their families, warm in front of a fire, laughing and singing. Preston, at a large celebration, probably inebriated by now. He'd be making trivial toasts to the New Year, undoubtedly surrounded by young women. He thought of Professor Alger and his family, their generosity and kindness.

His mind drifted to Sarah. Was she inside, sitting in front of a warm fire with her son, maybe her daughter? Was the family drinking hot apple cider and making their New Year's resolutions? He wondered if he could ever write back to Sarah or if the words would only cause more pain for both. He could separate his feelings, converse with superfluous chatter, but for what reason other than to pretend his heart was not broken and life easily restarts.

The snow was deeper than Custis realized. He lifted his knees high, his arms out for balance. Out of breath, Custis laughed at himself. He was no longer used to strenuous activity. Not much farther now, he could see the attic in the distance. In the moonlight, surrounded by leafless trees and partially covered in winter's ivy, it appeared as if Doctor Frankenstein himself should live there.

Custis stopped. He leaned forward, squinting for a better look. Black smoke was coming from the upstairs window—a fire in the attic.

31

"No!" Custis screamed. He lifted his feet and trounced through the snow as fast as he could. Stockpiles of research material, the backbone of his work, were being destroyed. He couldn't keep his eyes off the building and fell face-first. He tumbled again, then ripped off his long topcoat and threw it aside. Smoke billowed out of broken windows. Soon the heat of the fire would break out the other windows, the flames lapping up the oxygen. The entire structure would be engulfed. Bottles of chemicals might explode. People could get hurt.

Custis burst through the first-floor door and ran up the stairs. He had locked the attic door. The key was in his overcoat, which lay discarded in the snow. Custis rammed the door with his shoulder. Maybe he could salvage his drawings, take the most valuable, the irreplaceable. Schematics, calculations, conclusions.

Another heave into the wooden door. The frame busted inward. The door flew open. Custis landed on the floor. The light was on. People were standing next to the window. It was warm inside.

Preston looked down at Custis. "What are you doing? Just open the door, for God's sake. It wasn't even locked."

Custis was in shock. No flames consumed the room. No fire, no soon-to-be explosion. The room was just like he had left it. Except now there was a coal-burning stove near the window. A metal stovepipe from the top of the stove led out of a small-paned frame of broken-out glass.

Marshall and McKay, both amused, helped Custis to his feet. Each could not stop laughing. Preston outstretched his arm toward the stove. "Look what we did for you. Happy New Year's, buddy." Preston drank from a whiskey bottle as he swayed back and forth.

Had Custis not been so relieved, he would have hit Preston in the face. "I saw the smoke. I thought the place was on fire. Oh, dear Lord, I thought I'd lost everything." Custis yanked his arm away from McKay. "It would have been nice to know about this, before I almost died of a heart attack."

McKay sounded confrontational. "You're forgetting your accent!"

Marshall held on to Custis's shoulder for balance. Custis could smell the whiskey on Marshall's breath. "We were gonna tell ya. You just weren't here. I thought we were gonna break a leg getting it up here, up the stairs, in the middle of the night. But now I think I got a hernia." Marshall snickered.

"We wanted to surprise you," McKay said. "I think Professor Bates will be the most surprised when he returns to his cold classroom."

"You stole this from Professor Bates at Simpson?" Custis asked.

McKay was unsteady on his feet. He looked up to the right, like he was deep in thought. "Well, kinda, I guess, if you put it that way."

"But the smoke, fellas. You can see the smoke from the outside." Custis walked toward the stove. He put his hands out and rubbed them together. "I can't believe the heat it puts out."

Preston glanced solemnly at Marshall and McKay. They looked embarrassed, as if they were children caught in the act. "Smoke, we never thought of that." All three smirked and burst into laughter. McKay dropped to the floor.

"Not funny, boys. I'll be discovered at the light of day," Custis said.

"Just use it at night then," Preston suggested.

"What do you think it is right now? And clearly, I saw it."

"Yeah, but people don't usually come to this side of campus."

"It feels so warm. Maybe I can make a governor, a screen of sorts for the stovepipe, to filter out the smoke."

"Of course you can." Preston swayed back and forth. "We just stuck it out the little window that was already broken. We tried to get on the roof, but we kept slipping, so we just adapted. Stuck it out the little window that was already broke because we couldn't get on the roof."

"Because we kept on slipping," Marshall said.

"All right, you guys are gonna stay here with me or you'll end up getting arrested for sure or find yourself enlisted in the military. I'll make you some strong black coffee on my new stove." Custis looked down at McKay. "See, he's already asleep."

x x x

Professor Alger met Custis in the laboratory the following weekend. "Do you ever rest, Mr. Custis?"

"Professor Alger, I was hoping you would come by." Custis yearned for a colleague, someone like-minded with whom to confer and debate. It was a gratuity he had not been afforded. He would have to be careful.

"Of course. I would like to see your work. Finally."

Custis smiled. "I am sorry, Professor. I am afraid that this is only part of my project. Most of my machinery is here, but I believe I need to start you elsewhere for you to have the entire perspective. My charts and schematics would take up too much space here. Up for a stroll?"

"You have certainly piqued my interest now."

Custis and the professor walked across campus. Trees dripped melted snow, and the sun made what was left glisten like specks of broken glass.

"My work involves radiation—a tiny part, that is. I believe I can look inside the human body, so to speak, without breaching the skin."

"X-rays? I think you are a little late. Germany has us beat."

"Better than X-rays. I hope to differentiate soft tissue, masses, even the flowing of blood. Can you imagine the possibilities?"

The attic was just ahead. It was just an old, dilapidated, abandoned building during the daylight hours rather than Doctor Frankenstein's laboratory.

Professor Alger looked forward. He paused. "This is the old Vanderbilt building. The boiler blew up years ago, and it was never repaired. Too far away from the rest of the campus to bother restoring, I guess. I've never been in it. Is it sound?"

"So far, except for the occasional raccoon brood searching for safe harbor."

Custis opened the door to the first floor. The inside was cold, damp, and smelled of mold. It resembled a ramshackle greenhouse or abandoned conservatory rather than a grand ballroom, alive with society couples. "The staircase is here. It's all upstairs."

Custis unlocked the attic door. The long metal key slipped deep into the lock and turned with a hollow click. Custis allowed the professor to enter first. The room was warm and smelled of coffee. Downward rays of sunlight came through the small panes of glass like dispersions in a prism. Every wall was alive with schematics, graphs, and charts. An old sofa and two wingback chairs sat in front of the coal stove on the far sidewall. A metal boxed contraption was fastened to the stovepipe just before it exited the lower broken-out windowpane. Every space seemed to have a well-ordered purpose. For anyone with a scientific imagination, it was overwhelmingly beckoning.

Professor Alger removed his hat. His eyes, wide open, scanned the walls. He slowly walked the perimeter, examining the charts and graphs, sometimes stopping, leaning closer, and reading the small print. He did not ask questions, nor did Custis offer explanations.

A bookshelf encircled the room above his head. Professor Alger looked at the shelving. He turned in place, his body following his eyes. Walking around each of the seven makeshift tables, he picked up a small stack of papers, sat down in one of the chairs, and crossed his legs. He looked overwhelmed. Custis, still standing near the door, knew there was no going back. He would continue to keep his identity a secret, but now his motives and work had been revealed.

"I am amazed, Mr. Custis. I would like to learn more."

Custis sat down on the sofa. "I keep what I can here. As you can see, it requires so much room. I wanted to perfect all that I could before presenting it to the university board."

Professor Alger listened quietly. His eyes still scanned the room, as if he were taking inventory.

"I am missing a component, a linkage. I know there is one. The first mechanism came to me when I was a boy."

"That does not surprise me. Direction or maps leading to our life's purpose come from childhood aspirations."

"I wanted to look inside a horse's hurt leg, to see how to fix it. Then, thoughts of finding a cancer before it had a chance to metastasize. But right now, without the last modus, I feel it's just drivel."

"Inglorious drivel." Professor Alger smiled. "Sometimes the very nuclei of brilliance and discovery, Mr. Custis."

Professor Alger placed the papers back in their respective stacks as he glanced over another mound of drawings. He picked up the top piece and examined it. "What is this?"

"That is a new furnace I designed for this building. I thought of it in my sleep. I call it the Cephalopod. Its metal arms are designed to wind into multiple rooms on both floors. The heat travels equally, employing a fan intake. The entry port is inside the room, not outside. Inside air is returned to the furnace through one route while being forced out of another after being reheated. But the marvelous part is that it is no longer hydronic. Nor is it hand-fired from coal. The furnace uses gas, like a Bunsen burner.

"Professor, I am preparing a presentation to the university board to ask for help. I have taken this as far as I can. All of this work has been conducted independent of my required classes. I can no longer work in secret or by myself. I am still considered a student here."

"So you will bypass the physics department and go straight to the board? Not to mention mechanical engineering and medical units? You will make enemies. You do not seem to be able to trust others."

"I trust you, Professor. Everyone here, including yourself, sir, has told me I should be a professor rather than a student. I am wasting precious time with this requirement of repeating what I already know in order to have laboratory privileges. I am a scientist."

Professor Alger returned the paper to the neatly stacked pile. "Get me a list of everything you may need to see your project through to operation. Do you understand?"

"Sir, with all due respect, know that I want this project's completion more than my own life. But I do not wish any problems for you."

"You must learn to appreciate the unexpected. Unforeseen problems sometimes may incite unforeseen resolutions. Sometimes, even from unforeseen people."

Professor Alger walked over to the stove and looked at the metal box on the stovepipe. "What is this contrivance?"

"I designed a filter of sorts to eliminate the black smoke on the exterior. I didn't want to be discovered here in the building."

"Hm." Professor Alger placed his hands around his back. "Aesop proves to be correct once again. Necessity, the mother of invention."

As the professor left the room, he paused and faced Custis. "Your project needs to be sanctioned. I will need the list by Tuesday. In addition, I will need the schematics on Squidly."

"Cephalopod."

"Yes, and your smoke-filter device."

Custis's ally had been there all along.

32

Spring could not come soon enough. Custis had grown tired of slushing through snowdrifts, wearing wet shoes and clothes that never seemed adequately warm enough. Nippy mornings gave way to warmer days. He missed seeing the green countryside of Carolina with its widespread, unencumbered views of rolling hills and mountains. On campus, spotting an occasional crab apple, dogwood, or blooming redbud ignited recollections of the ranch. He found Central Park to be an illusion of naturalistic terrain intended to represent a rural landscape for people who could never leave. It was deception surrounded by obtrusive buildings, a mere affectation of natural geography.

Custis deviated from the well-traveled park roads for smaller paths, sometimes forging his own. A dirt trail serpentined through perfectly imitated tree groves and reproduced meadows. A rock arch bridge crossed above a streamlet of water connecting large ponds. The stones formed a perfect arc and gave rise to an elevated view. Custis leaned against the large center keystone and looked out over the sullen-looking, stagnant ponds. In the distance, he saw a man fly-fishing. It had never occurred to Custis to fly-fish in anything other than a moving stream. But it made sense now. Manhattan, surrounded by seawater and brackish streams, was an island. The few freshwater streams were now underground and referred to as polluted nuisances, most serving as sewer passages.

Custis watched the rhythm of the casting, its silent tempo back and forth. Its arc was flawless. He closed his eyes and imagined the sound of the line no one touches. He thought he heard the droplets of water falling from the tippet. *Sarah.* He imagined her below, standing near an unblemished water's edge. A summer's blue sky overhead, the soul of all scenery, mirrored on the water's surface. Her experienced hands orchestrating the line to dance gracefully. How could he now ask God for her return after being granted the strength to survive without her in the first place? Time had elapsed, allowing her life to unfold on the ranch and his, to live as another with freedom and liberties. He opened his eyes. The fisherman was gone. Left behind was a distant gray haze infused with dark, puffy flumes from the industrial wharfs. Thick pollution robbed color in the distance yet was invisible at close range. Far into the haze, layers of buildings with their undefined edges and silhouettes of chimneys and water towers interrupted the horizon.

Custis returned to campus and found Professor Alger sitting on a black iron bench near the Vanderbilt building. Custis smiled. "Good day, Professor." After passing so many strange faces in the park, it was good to see a friend again.

"I looked for you in the laboratory and in the attic, then came here."

The professor did not stand up but motioned Custis to sit down next to him. "I knocked on the upstairs door to no answer. I even tried the secret password."

"I took a walk to clear my thoughts. Sometimes I feel so close to finding the answer to my work, then get so frustrated each time I hit a dead end. I hope you haven't waited long."

"Not at all. Actually, I have enjoyed sitting still and doing nothing." He reached for his leather case, opened it, and pulled out a handful of papers. "I need to talk with you, Mr. Custis. Share some information." Professor Alger turned serious.

Custis panicked inside. He glanced at the documents—forged papers. He removed his hat, hoping to disguise any nervousness. Pretending to be composed came easily. He had practiced it his entire life.

"We need to stop this charade."

Custis's heart dropped. He wanted to lower his head, squeeze his eyes shut. His mind wound tightly over thoughts of Alger discovering falsified documents, the lies about his race. Custis had finally felt safe, but now it was all slipping away—his project, his inventions, even his liberties. Alger had known all along.

"You are no longer going to attend classes here."

The charade. It was finally over. There would be no more privileges and liberties to relish by pretending to be someone he was not. No more benefits or scientific endeavors. Custis was losing everything, everything that he once held in his hands. It was predictable. Profound grief would surely follow. All his struggles, his glories, burdens, and blessings fell to the ground in front of him.

"You are correct in your assessment of yourself. It has been decided to allow you to graduate two years early, this summer, if you can pass the final examinations. Clearly, that will not be an issue. You already possess the education of a tenured professor. The chancellor has agreed. We are wasting time."

Custis was no longer concerned about his physical or emotional composure. He held his head in his hands. The words ran through his mind, twirling with nowhere to land. He saw his emotions as once being a solid substance that had transformed into a gas, now converting itself to liquid, never quite lost. *Is that how I am, God? Never quite lost? Is all this necessary?*

"What do you mean? What does this mean for my project?"

"Your project will proceed, Mr. Custis. Just not in its current application." Professor Alger broke into a smile. He exuberantly shook Custis's hand. "Congratulations. The chancellor and the board of trustees have authorized the annexation of this Vanderbilt death trap to the physics department. We have allocated funds for complete construction and refurbishing. No pains have been spared. It will be a laboratory—an auxiliary classroom, to some extent. The second floor will be renovated into a dormitory. Your dormitory, Mr. Custis."

Custis sprang to his feet and paced back and forth as if deciding what to do, or maybe which way to run. He rubbed his face, then his head. "I don't understand. Where did the money come from?"

Professor Alger cleared his throat. "Please sit down. You are making me nervous."

Custis sat on the bench and rested his elbows on his knees. He hung his head down to gather oxygen. Professor Alger breathed in deeply.

"I have been meeting with Chancellor Adams. He recalled your admissions interview. Called you a peculiar individual. I showed him the schematics of your two inventions, then advised him of the potential of your current project and projected costs. It did not take copious efforts to convince him that the patents might subsidize the cost of the annexation. Not only financially but also statistically. He does enjoy bragging about the list of successful patents that originated from his university. I took the liberty and submitted your Squidly or Cephalopod and the Smoke Emanation Sieve under the name of the university.

They are now patent pending. I hope you don't mind. I thought the means would, in fact, justify the end."

"Of course, of course. I am sorry. Can you please say it all again?"

Professor Alger placed his hand on Custis's back. He smiled sincerely, leaned into Custis, and quietly said, "We have funding for your project."

Custis looked at his trembling hands. He leaned back and breathed in deeply as tears filled his eyes. He shook his head, trying to process the information. "How did you do it, Professor Alger?"

"I did nothing. You did. I was just the messenger." Professor Alger nudged his elbow into Custis. "And Mr. Preston Langmuir. It was he who approached me and offered to help with the patent submissions. He is in one of my classes and shows an interest in being a laboratory assistant here in his spare time."

Sometimes, divine navigation has many hands. "Yes, he is a good man," Custis managed to say.

"I thought it was brilliant. Divide and conquer—not in a military sense, but rather, divide the undertaking and conquer the goal. Construction will commence the day after graduation this June."

x x x

Keeping track of time had never come naturally for Custis. Other than the planting and harvesting seasons, the calendar months did not require much thought. Now every day mattered. Had it not been for his daily entry of black Xs in his almanac, he was sure June had been cast back onto Jupiter.

Finally, June arrived. Custis's equipment and property had been packed and stored away. Professor Alger found Custis in the basement, disassembling the old boiler. Custis was covered in dirt and smiling like a little boy with a new toy.

"Look who I found lurking about," Professor Alger said.

Custis looked up from his work and saw Marshall, McKay, and Preston standing at the bottom of the staircase.

"We're not here to work. Just wanted to say congratulations," McKay said.

Marshall shook Custis's dirty hand. "Yes, we're so excited for you. McKay got hold of me and said we must come back and celebrate."

Preston broke between McKay and Marshall and placed his arms around each one. "Yes, celebrations are definitely in order."

Marshall laughed. "You've been celebrating since spring."

Professor Alger had walked over to a nearby shelf. He examined the old dusty and cobwebbed items. Wooden boxes of glass containers, some broken, dirty burlap bags barely covering the contents, sooty buckets, and pieces of old hoses lined the shelves.

"I'm afraid I've gotten myself into a pickle." Professor Alger's voice was too restrained to be heard by the others. "Renauldos," the professor said a little louder, "I am in quite the situation here." The professor stood with his back to the group, head down.

Custis stepped toward him. "I'm sorry, what did you say, Professor?"

"I'm afraid I've gotten into a bit of a dilemma." He didn't move, not a muscle.

The professor held an old wooden bucket. His head was still down, looking at the contents. Custis looked in the container. Sticks of old dynamite, crystallization coming through the oily dust. The professor slowly looked up at Custis.

"Don't move, Professor."

"Obviously."

McKay and Marshall started to walk over. Custis held up his hand and told them to stop. McKay and Marshall continued and looked in the bucket.

"Oh, God," McKay said.

"Nobody move."

"It's just nitroglycerine deposits. Alkaline degradation. This basement remains cool throughout the seasons. It's a perfect environment. No telling how long it's been down here. Just look at it, wispy-like hairs. Resembles mold on cheese. Quite beautiful, really." Custis looked up at the others. All were motionless.

"Does anyone have any vodka?" Custis asked.

No one said a word.

"I am being serious. Does anyone have any vodka?"

"Have you lost your mind? Even I wouldn't drink to this," Preston said.

"No, I need alcohol. Preston, you carry a flask." Without taking his eyes away from the box, Custis tapped Preston's chest with the back of his hand. "Give it to me."

Preston slowly reached into his coat pocket and handed him a silver flask. Custis carefully poured the contents into the bucket. "I need more. Give me your other one."

Preston didn't move.

"Now."

Preston fumbled into the other breast pocket and handed him another flask. "Alcohol desensitizes, therefore neutralizes, the nitroglycerine. With chemistry, you never lose anything. All changes into something else. Just like our emotions, even our bodies, eventually. Like ashes to ashes, dust to dust, I suppose."

McKay and Marshall reached into their coats and each handed Custis a flask.

"Here, take mine. It's whiskey."

"And mine, here's mine."

Custis poured all the contents into the bucket. "Nitroglycerine has combustion-promoting oxidants and fuel built into the same molecule, unfortunately. That's what makes it so sensitive, the highly exothermic triggers. Heat, shock, and friction—not good. Well, that ought to do it, if you can just hold that for a few more seconds. Make sure it's all absorbed." Custis turned and walked back to the boiler.

The professor looked shocked. "Wait, where are you going? Renauldos?"

"I've got to get this boiler torn apart. Oh, you can take that bucket with you. Put the contents in your garden. It's mainly ions of ammonium and nitrate now. Makes good fertilizer. Just dump it out and till it in. You'll have wonderful tomatoes."

x x x

Construction crews gutted the building, including the basement. Custis oversaw the fabrication of Squidly but strategically managed to avoid publicity whenever possible.

"Part of this plan is your exotic presentation for the school," Preston said. "You can't keep avoiding it. It's what you need to do."

Two separate lies to two different groups of people. Managing the storylines was taxing. Custis could not take the chance of any photographs or articles reaching anyone from Wilson Place College. One slip could ruin everything.

"I don't like the politics of it," Custis said. "You're so good at it, the extrovert. I'm just fine being the introvert."

Marshall and McKay were invited back for the grand opening while Preston, somehow, was assigned to be the master of ceremonies. He introduced the board of trustees along with Chancellor Adams. All posed for the photographers in front of Squidly, with Chancellor Adams always at the center.

Preston called for more photographs outside the building, specifically from the *New York Times*. Custis stood at the sideline with Marshall, McKay, and Professor Alger. They watched Preston line up the board members and the chancellor in front of the entrance for one more photoshoot. Preston squeezed in next to Chancellor Adams. "All right, fire away."

McKay snickered, "Good job, Preston."

Custis smiled. "Let him have his day. It's fine. I'd rather be right here."

"It's for Daddy," Marshall added.

"By the way, Custis, what happened to the coal stove?" McKay asked.

"Quite obsolete now, don't you think?" Professor Alger said. He paused and placed his hands into his pants pockets. "I donated it to Simpson University," he said firmly. He raised on the balls of his feet, then back down again. He looked directly at McKay. "Along with a year's supply of coal."

All stood guiltily silent, watching people they did not know posing for the photographer. Over their heads, carved in stone above the doorway, were the words *Mater atrium necessitas*, bordered on one end by a raven and a vase and acorns on the other.

Professor Alger abruptly moved sideways. "Oh, you startled me, my dear."

Caroline had wrapped her arms around the side of her father's waist. "Mother said I might join you here for a moment."

"Of course. This is a spectacular day to share. Mr. Custis has a new laboratory. See here." He guided Caroline in front of him and placed his hands on her shoulders.

Custis saw Caroline. "Caroline! I am so happy to see you. Would you like to see inside?"

"Oh, yes. Father, may I go with Mr. Custis?"

"Of course." He looked at Custis. "If you don't mind. I have a few hands to shake."

"Not at all. It will be all my pleasure."

Custis bowed and held out his arm. "Miss Caroline."

Caroline's smile consumed all of her.

33

Custis and Preston were alone in the Vanderbilt laboratory. Both hunched over the machine. Custis repetitively adjusted knobs, tightened valves, inspected hoses, and rechecked the electrical components. Preston held a clipboard and worked numbers recited aloud by Custis.

Custis heard the laboratory door open and close. "Good morning, Professor Alger. Come, Preston wants to name our machine."

"Of course he does. Give it a sense of humanity."

Professor Alger examined the contraption. He kept his hands behind his back as he walked around the table, viewing all sides. "I have a question for you, Mr. Custis. Yesterday at the dedication, you showed my daughter the laboratory. Did you teach her anything specific?"

"Sir? I suppose I did, maybe inadvertently."

"I ask this at the request of my wife, who referred to an 'unladylike mannerism.' What about this whistling using her fingers?"

Custis tried to keep his smile at bay. "As a parent, you, sir, create memories, teach life skills, and instill values—impressions on her heart and soul that will be lasting. We should approach life as curious and insatiable learners. Developing skills which prove useful in life is imperative, Professor—such as an intrinsic sense of direction or whistling with fingers in your mouth. Whistling is an excellent skill to have. It is a measure, an uncommon octave far above what is natural than most man-made sounds. It serves as an alert to other people, a call for help."

"Hm, I see. Or getting the attention of a newsie, or a vendor in the park," Professor Alger added. "Could come in handy at some point, I suppose. I will relay this data to my wife."

x x x

At times, Custis felt sorry for Preston. He was working as Custis's lab assistant, but his genuine interest lay elsewhere. He mainly managed the paperwork and documentation. At times, Preston oversaw the fabrication of parts and participated in experiment documentation. He designed a darkroom in the laboratory and became proficient in developing film.

Custis worked through the weekends by himself. Fridays turned into half days for Preston, and eventually, Mondays turned into sick days. It wasn't until near midweek that Preston started displaying a pleasant disposition. Preston's lack of discipline and drive was annoying at times. Custis struggled to hide his frustration. He became short and curt with instruction and expectation. But Custis was indebted to him. Preston had been instrumental in the university admission process and had only offered Custis friendship and respect. Without Preston's direction and guidance, Custis was certain he would never have been admitted. But now, Preston was becoming a liability.

x x x

Custis had been granted a professorship and worked in substitute status for the physics, chemistry, and mathematics departments. It was only a handful of hours per week, and Custis enjoyed the fresh, eager minds.

Early mornings, before the campus was alive with activity, he savored the moments before sunrise. Strolls down unfilled walkways still shadowy from overhanging trees and across empty greenbelts brought calmness to his soul. The morning light made the buildings more prominent, their architecture more pronounced, and even made their empty hallways seem endless.

Custis reserved the first Monday of each month for chemistry exams beginning at 6:00 a.m. The early morning hour was brutal on his students but allowed Custis to return to the laboratory for most of the day.

On this particular Monday, Custis carried his leather portfolio, unlocked the chemistry wing, and propped open the door. He listened to his footfalls on the tile floor as he walked down the corridor. Each step clicked loudly. *Step. Step. Step.* Like the ticking of a clock. He counted the clicks. They matched his heart rate. Another click, now out of sync. A double echo. Custis looked upward. The sound reverberated off the ceiling. High above, the top was arched, lined with tile and stonework—an echo of the echo. Custis stopped, but the sound of the footsteps continued. He turned and saw Professor Alger coming up behind him. He waited.

"Good morning, Professor Custis. Empty hallways have great echoes, do they not?"

Custis stared at Professor Alger. He stood motionless. The professor's words—it made sense, it all made sense. *How could I be so stupid?*

"Renauldos, are you all right? I did not mean to startle you."

"What did you say? What did you just say?"

"That empty hallways have great echoes?"

"Yes. Yes! Exactly!"

Custis brushed past the professor and started to run down the hallway, heading outside. "Professor Alger, please . . . chemistry . . . 703," he called over his shoulder. "Can you please proctor for me?" Custis spun back around and tossed his satchel to the professor. "I think I've got it. The missing component."

Professor Alger fumbled with the bag as he watched Custis run out of sight. "Of course."

Custis ran across the still-sleeping campus. The sidewalks were his to cut corners, take shortcuts under the maples and through the cedar grove. He burst through the laboratory door.

Preston was just putting on his lab jacket. "What in God's name?"

Custis was out of breath. His face was red and wet with sweat. "I got it! I think I have the answer! Wait. Why are you here so early?"

"I couldn't sleep. Answer for what?"

"I have the missing component. It's empty hallways! It's a ticking clock! It's the repetitive clanking of the train! It's the horse's hooves pounding on the prairie! *Dig-ah-dig, dig-ah-dig.* It's whistling with your fingers at annoying octaves!" Custis tried to whistle. "Listen, high pitch." Nothing came out except short bursts of air. Custis stopped to catch his breath. "Octaves. The rhythm. It's the ripples in the water."

Custis rested his hand on a desk, bent forward, and breathed in deeply. He shook his head. "It's silent sound. It's been here all this time." Custis felt crazy with happiness. He tried to smile, but it interfered with his air intake.

"What are you talking about? You're acting like a madman."

Custis grabbed Preston by the shoulders. "Listen. Just listen. Do you know how to fly-fish?"

"I guess so, yes. Why?"

"Good, let's get your rod and reel, and I'll show you exactly what I'm talking about."

"But it's at home. What's gotten into you? Have you been drinking?"

"No! Let's go! Let's go get your rod, and you'll understand everything. We need to show Professor Alger. It's the underpinning of everything."

Custis and Preston hurriedly left the campus, jumped on a streetcar, and headed for Preston's home. All the while, Custis mumbled to himself as he wrote down figures and information in his pocketbook as fast as he could.

"By the way, there's nowhere to fish around here."

No response.

"And even if you do catch something, it won't be edible. I'm not even going to get near the water."

"Shh! Don't talk to me. I'm thinking. Sound waves are only mathematical equations, don't you see?"

"You just told me to shut up, but no, I don't see."

Preston lived in a high-rise, on the third floor of a stately building. Balconies on every other floor overlooked the busy street below.

The doorman opened the front door and tipped his hat. Preston led Custis to the elevator, where the liftman nodded. "Third floor, Mr. Langmuir?"

"Yes. Thank you."

The liftman closed the door. Custis glanced at his reflection in the polished brass wall paneling. Without turning, Custis glimpsed to the right and met the attendant's stare doing the same. His skin was dark; his expression was cheerless. His dull, cloudy eyes examined Custis in the reflection, from his shoes up to his face. Their stares converged in a mirrored image. Custis was first to break the contact, lowering his head, pretending to look at his shoes. It had been more than just a casual assessment. Custis had rejected his own race, condemning his heritage for the benefits of whiteness. Custis had been given the ability to re-create his entire existence, while the liftman had only been allowed to renegotiate specks of his own. *Luck or curse?* The line between empathy and shame melded as one. The elevator grumbled to a stop.

"Here you are, Mr. Langmuir."

Preston hurriedly led the way down the short hallway to the only door in view. "Come on in. Father's out of town."

Custis impatiently looked around. The room was large, open, and expensively decorated. He needed to compliment but not right now. A set of French doors led out onto a balcony. Preston walked out of sight and returned holding a fishing rod. "Here, this is my father's."

"Oh, it's beautiful." Custis took the rod and carefully flexed it into movement. "I've never seen one so superb."

"Can you now tell me what the hell is going on?"

Custis opened the doors to the balcony. "Here, you stand out here. Watch me below. Tell me what you see."

Custis turned and rushed back to the foyer. As he flung open the door, Preston yelled, "I see a crazy man! That's what I see."

Custis ran down the hallway to the staircase. He could run down three flights of stairs before the elevator could even pick him up. Custis burst out onto the sidewalk. The roadway was teeming with pedestrians, streetcars, horse carriages, and delivery wagons.

Custis ran into the street, carrying the rod. He held up both arms, waving as if he were stopping an oncoming train. He looked up at the balcony and saw Preston leaning over the railing.

Custis yelled at the drivers as he waved. "Stop. Stop. It will only take a second! Please! It's a matter of our future! Please, it will only be a second!"

He unreeled the line. He began forward and back, slowly letting out the line. His back was toward Preston. His hand went up intermittently, trying to keep traffic at bay. "I promise, just a few seconds!"

Preston cupped his mouth. "You're certified crazy now! You're gonna get yourself killed!"

Bells clanged and horns honked from the trollies. Men yelled, and women held on to their children as crowds gathered on both sides of the street. Custis worked the line. Finally, the rhythm was perfect. Back and forth, back and forth. "What do you see, Preston? Do you see it?"

"See what?"

"The pattern of the line. Watch the configuration the line makes!"

"You mean the design?"

"Yes! What pattern is it making? What pattern do you see?" Custis worked the action, loading and unloading, letting out more line while stepping backward.

A man's voice came from a motionless car. "Get the hell out of the street, you idiot."

Preston yelled even louder, "I don't know! Maybe serpentine?"

"The motion! Look at the motion before I get killed."

"Ah, vibratory? No, wait, harmonic motion?"

Custis stopped. He was out of breath. The line went limp. He turned around and looked up at Preston. His arms fell downward. He smiled as he breathed in. He held his arms out to his side with the rod still in his right hand, the line entangled around his lower legs.

"It's sound waves, Preston. It's the same pattern sound waves produce."

People on the sidewalk looked confused. A young boy began to clap. He must have thought it was a street show and wanted more. Slowly, his mother began to clap. Soon more and more people joined in. Bells clanged. People smiled and cheered, all except for the man who had called him an idiot.

Custis reeled in the line and stepped onto the sidewalk. He turned, waved, and bowed. In a perfected Greek accent, his words flowed effortlessly. "Thank you all for your momentarily disrupted day. You have just witnessed history in the making. A day which I shall remember for the rest of my life. I grant you safe passage." He looked at the angry driver. "To all of you!" Custis kept smiling. He practically flew up three flights of stairs.

Preston popped a bottle of champagne as Custis ran through the door. "I have no idea what just happened, but it seems like it calls for celebration!" Preston grinned as he poured two glasses.

Custis couldn't talk. He was gasping for air but took the glass of champagne.

"Here's to sound," Preston toasted. "Not quite sure what it all means, but you look pretty excited."

"All this time I was thinking radiation. But it's a different radiation. The radiation of sound. Sound vibration *is* radiation." Custis took a gulp and choked. He handed the glass back to Preston as he covered his mouth, trying to regain himself.

Preston patted him on the back. "You all right?"

Custis, still coughing, held up his thumb and covered his mouth with his other hand.

"Here, the lavatory. Take a minute. You're turning blue."

Custis tried to clear his throat and managed to say, "Wrong way down."

"It's all right. Looks like you're getting air."

Custis coughed his way into the lavatory and closed the door. He cleared his throat several times as he looked at himself in the mirror. He cupped his hands under the running water and flushed his face. He looked for a towel as he turned off the spigot. The countertop was clear, other than a soap dish. He flicked the water from his hands down in the sink. He smiled at himself.

He wanted to laugh out loud. The answer had been with him all these years. He saw Sarah in his mind. She was standing knee-deep in the pond, the rod in her hand with the lead softly controlled by her fingers. Her movement was graceful perfection—the unencumbered line creating a sound that no one could hear.

Custis was rhapsodic. He laughed and covered his mouth with his hand, trying to control his loopiness. He wiped the tears from his eyes with his fingers and leaned toward the mirror. "Sarah, it was you. You knew all along," he whispered.

Custis twisted his mustache, realigning it. He stepped to a nearby cabinet. It was full of neatly folded linens. He grabbed a towel, patted his face dry, and stepped back to the sink. As he straightened his tie, he glanced at an object in the reflection. In the linen closet, it was behind him, oddly hanging down from the top shelf.

Custis stared at the reflected object as he methodically folded the hand towel and laid it down next to the sink. He tilted his head. It looked familiar. It belonged to him. His smile disappeared. Custis turned and stepped back to the opened linen closet. He reached up and touched the dangling strap. He rubbed it between his fingers and thumb, then pulled it out between a set of folded sheets.

It was his money belt.

Custis held the belt in his hands. He slowly opened the flap. It contained currency. It was his money, along with the photograph of his pseudo family.

Custis remembered the night. It had been cold and shadowy. An arm from behind, blocking air to his lungs. Violent pain to his head. He could still smell the odors, the filth of the pavement. But how had his money belt gotten here? To his friend's house? Custis felt as if he were deciphering an impossible equation filled with sophisticated trickery. He forced his mind to slow. A heuristic approach. *The simplest explanation is usually the correct answer—Occam's razor.* One thing for sure, Preston knew the attackers.

Custis slowly walked back into the living room.

Preston was still chattering while pouring another glass of

champagne. "We should call Marshall and McKay, plan a great celebration. And Professor Alger, too!"

Custis was still. His arms hung straight down by his sides. His right
hand held the money belt, the straps touching the floor.

Preston looked at Custis. "What's wrong? It looks like you've just
seen your dead grandmother."

Custis glared at Preston. He tossed the money belt on the sofa.

Preston's eyes followed the belt. The playfulness vanished from his
face. He set his champagne glass on the table. He glanced at Custis,
then stared at the belt.

"It's just how I left it. The money is all there. All the same order and
increments." Custis did not take his eyes off Preston. "What did you
do to me? Why?"

"Now, look. Don't jump to conclusions. If you remember, you were
about to give up. You wouldn't accept my money, and you were living
with rats, for God's sake. I knew you had a great idea. I wanted to help
you. It was the only thing I could think of."

Preston stepped toward Custis. "I wanted you to live in this house
with me. So you would be protected. So you would be able to complete
your work. Only one thing that kept you from doing that, and it was
your money, what little you had. I thought that if I took your money,
you would come to live here, where it's safe. You're too proud a man to
do otherwise. You wouldn't have survived the winter in your shithole. I
swear to God, that was the only reason."

"You have no idea what that did to me. You left me for dead. Did
Marshall and McKay help you beat me until I was unconscious? Take
my bicycle, my only transportation?"

"No, of course not. They had nothing to do with it. They know
nothing about it. Listen, I paid someone to take your money. I told
them not to harm you."

"You must have paid them very well for them to bring back all of
my money."

"They didn't expect you to fight back so hard and had to knock you out. That wasn't planned. I swear."

Custis felt his body tense. "After you took my money belt, you left me in that alley and let the rats crawl over me."

"I didn't know they did that—I swear."

Custis lurched at Preston, both falling to the floor with Custis landing on top. Preston tried to fight back. Custis's anger exploded into uncontrollable rage. There was no more looking the other way, turning the other cheek, or running away. "Why did you do this to me?" Another punch to Preston's face. "Why? Tell me the truth!"

Custis pulled Preston's upper body up by his shirt.

"I had planned on paying the enrollment fee for you."

Custis screamed through his clenched teeth and punched Preston in his face again and again.

"Listen to me. I help people all the time. I send food down to the tenements when I can. I pay hospital bills for other people who couldn't pay. I would never harm anyone."

Custis stopped. For a moment, his grip eased. *Hospital bills.* Custis clenched back down with his hands and shook Preston by his shirt. "You are disgusting. You care about no one except yourself. Saint Preston, paying everyone's bills, buying friendships."

"I didn't buy you, and I didn't buy Emma."

Emma? Emma? Hospital bills. Custis felt his hands clamping down even stronger. "You know nothing about Emma." Custis heard Emma's words being whispered. He was sure he felt his mother's hand on his shoulder pulling him away. Custis felt an eeriness wrapping around his body. "You know nothing."

Preston's hands covered his face. "You don't understand. Stop, stop! Emma was my daughter—she's my daughter!"

Custis was motionless. *Daughter. My daughter?* He leaned to the side and fell against the sofa.

Preston rolled to his stomach and quickly crawled away as if his life had just been spared. "You don't understand."

Custis wiped his sweaty face with his arm. His knuckles were bloody, and he struggled for air. Preston was just about the most disingenuous person he had ever met. "Emma. She died. You weren't even there. You're her father?"

Preston pulled himself up against a chair. He breathed in and sniveled. "No one knows about her. I didn't even know about her until she was hospitalized. I mean, I knew about her at first, years ago." Preston was bleeding from his nose.

Custis's eyes were watery, the color simmering away. "She died alone, in an indigent hospital ward. What's wrong with you? How could you do that?"

"Father said to walk away, that Emma's mother wasn't worth it. Father said he didn't want some third-class ragpicker breeding itself into Langmuir blood and fortune." Preston covered his face with his hands. "He said he didn't want a waif for a grandchild. My life was just beginning, and I had to concentrate on my studies. It was a mistake, a one-night mistake. Father got rid of her. Sent her away to Chicago. He said we couldn't be so sure the child was mine anyway and didn't want any interference with my future, or his.

"Then, after all those years we got word. She was back for more money. That's what Father said. I saw her at the hospital, working in the laundry. She didn't notice me. I did some checking and found out she had admitted her daughter. Her age . . . it all added up. She came back for help, for Emma. I couldn't bring myself to step in. The cancer was terminal; there was no question. At that point, there was nothing I could do."

"Why did you take me to her? Why would you do that?"

"I felt so alone, a complete failure. You told me about your machine. I thought you could save her. I was going to tell you that night. I had no idea your machine would take an eternity to create. I thought you could save her, buy me more time to figure things out. That's why I helped you in the beginning. I was grasping at a possibility, but it was too late. Marshall and McKay had no idea. They were just returning a favor to me.

"But when I saw your interaction with her, how natural and genuine, and then her reaction to you. . . . My daughter looked at you with absolute adoration in her eyes, like she had known you all along. It should have been me, but I wasn't man enough to cross my father. I actually hated you for doing that. The great Renauldos Custis does it again."

Preston pulled himself up and sat in the chair. He stared into nothingness as if every thought had perished from his mind. His spirit was gone, his energy abruptly depleted. He looked like a sickly old farm animal, now without value, waiting to be put down. "Father said I needed to go away. He wanted me to run his overseas company." His voice was limp. "Some say war is near, brewing. Austria, Serbia, the Balkans, and more." Preston turned his face toward Custis. His eyes looked fearful. "But Father says the war won't concern us. I am his only son, and I have become an embarrassment for him.

"I would have been a complete failure, once again. I wanted to stay here in New York. He said he was done with me squandering my education and that he would be pulling me out. This is my last year at the university. I've already spoken to the chancellor. I will graduate with several bachelors of science degrees and a preliminary medical degree—which, by the way, does me no good since I faint at the sight of blood. I'm afraid that after all this time, Father expects nothing more out of me. I told him I wanted to work with you, that your project had such a lucrative sound. Believe it or not, I do have a great business mind."

Custis shook his head and quietly huffed. "So it all comes back around to you and how you feel. You're a narcissistic bastard."

Preston wiped his face with his wadded-up handkerchief. "I was only trying to help you by taking your money belt. You'd be dead with tuberculosis by now. Then the anonymous donation came in, and everything was for naught. I am so sorry.

"By then, I was invested in you. My God, Custis. You were a dowdy plowboy without a clue, with no plan of any background support. You were just going to pop in and show how wonderful you were and hope for the best. Not good, Custis. For you supposedly being so smart, that was the most nonsensical, idiotic thing you could have done. But wait, let's not forget about your big anonymous donor, your mysterious endowment. Who is that, Custis? How did that happen? You accuse me of not being truthful. Let's talk about all *your* lies."

Custis was silent. Preston could not have known the truth. *Remain quiet, it's a test.*

"And now, look at you. A professor, a great scientist, on the cusp of an invention that has the possibility to revolutionize the entire medical world."

Custis pulled himself up to his feet. His arms hung down to his sides as if they had been emptied of all the strength. "I have to think about this." He looked down at Preston. Nothing sybaritic remained in the sight of this broken man sinking into the luxury of his ridiculous home. Custis walked toward the door.

Preston wiped his mouth with his handkerchief. "I planned on giving it back to you, explaining it all. But as time went by, it became harder for me to justify. I was just too afraid to tell you what I had done. I have never lied to you, Custis. You are the smartest man I have ever known." Preston wiped his eyes. "Except for that first plan of yours." He tried to laugh. "Your mind is acute, photographic. You can do anything you choose. I hate my life here."

Custis turned his back on Preston. He stood in front of the door, turning the handle, listening to it click. He wanted to hate Preston.

Custis was no longer a little boy being cheated out of pennies for eggs. His livelihood had been stolen away; it had almost cost him his dreams and nearly taken his life. Custis had been played. *Played*—like he had played others, taking advantage of his prowess and their ignorance, lying and manipulating others for his needs. Custis was no better than Preston. But morality was no longer black and white but rather all mottled together. Custis thought of his own life, the people who truly loved him for who he was. People who had risked their lives so that he should live.

Custis felt his insides shaking. He wanted to leave Preston to his own miserable devices. This was a moment his mother said would someday come. Custis felt her presence. All the lessons of turning the other cheek had finally congealed. It was an opportunity to have strength. *Stand up for what you believe and continue to share. We are not to get revenge; we are not the punishers.*

Custis cleared his throat. Preston needed boundaries. Maybe that had been the source of all his issues. Without turning around, Custis calmly said, "About the money belt. You did what you thought was right at the time. Certainly not how I would have processed a solution. But everyone is different, are they not? I still need help in the laboratory. We have lots of work before us."

"I'd like to forget about all of this. I should have been honest with you from the beginning, and I am truly sorry."

"I'll need three weeks to set up a new lab and be ready to work. I'll leave it up to you."

To forgive was so much easier than forgetting. Both were supposed to work in tandem. Custis had torn up the proverbial promissory note but was keeping the wastebasket where it had been thrown.

˘

34

On the first floor inside the Vanderbilt laboratory, Custis fabricated a five-hundred-gallon cistern approximately three feet high and twice as wide. Its metal sides were corrugated into an oblong shape and welded into the bottom metal plate. Custis was bent over inside the tank, making additional concave fillet welds to the seams. He heard a voice, looked up, and removed his welding glasses from his dirty face. It was Preston.

"Are we building an aquarium or a public bath?"

Custis turned off the gas and stepped out of the tank. "Could be either one if my idea fails." He reached out and shook Preston's hand. "Ready to get back to work?"

"Listen, I need . . ."

"No. It's over and done with. We have lots of work to do."

Preston nodded. He walked around the tank, touching the top and examining nearby equipment. He pulled lightly on the side of the tank as if testing its strength.

"It's a water tank. Sound travels at a faster speed through water than air."

"You couldn't have figured all this out with a smaller tank?"

"We will need its size for the rest of the equipment—and the patient, of course. Grab the hose and connect it up to the bib. Should take a couple of hours to fill."

As the tank filled, Custis showed Preston additional apparatus. "High-frequency sound waves and their echo techniques are like the echolocation used by bats. Bats use sound waves for spatial orientation, sound that we cannot hear. This apparatus produces sound waves of a frequency in hertz."

"So it's painful?"

Just as the tank was almost filled, Professor Alger walked into the laboratory. He smiled as he looked around. "I read your findings, Renauldos, and just wanted to check on your progress."

"We're about ready to start. This was the biggest piece of equipment, but the easiest to fabricate. That's about five hundred gallons."

The professor walked around to the back of the tank. He looked at the floor and raised up and down on the balls of his feet. "Water weighs about eight pounds per gallon, is that not correct?"

"I know what you're thinking," Custis said. "About four thousand pounds. I reinforced the structure, underneath in the basement, with ten-inch solid beams. It shouldn't be a problem. Sound waves are similar to light waves, both originating from a definite source and can be disturbed or scattered. But sound waves can only travel through a medium, the fastest in water. Water is denser and more elastic than air, and sound waves can propagate more efficiently through it, resulting in a higher speed of sound."

Preston stood in front of the tank. "There's a small leak here, a little pool of water."

Custis threw him a rag. "Maybe just a fissure. I can fix that with a weld."

Preston bent over and wiped up the water as Custis examined the hole. "Yep, just a little pinhole. It's fine. Just put a bucket here."

Preston grabbed a nearby metal bucket.

"It's more than just a little pinhole," Preston argued. "It's in a seam. Even I know that's not good."

"It will be fine for now. I don't want to empty out all this water."

Custis walked back over to the counter and glanced at the schematics again. "This is just the preliminary testing."

The sound of a sharp, metallic pop darted through the room.

The metal vertical seam in front of Preston burst open with an ear-splitting bang. The strength of the water gushed out, forcing Preston off his feet and slamming him into a fixed wooden cabinet. The wall of water covered him steadily for several seconds. Just as quickly, the gush subsided and ended with the entire floor covered in water.

Preston wiped the water from his face, gasped, and looked around the room. He dropped the bucket to the floor. "Well, that was ill-advised."

Custis stood motionless, not knowing what to do. He turned toward Professor Alger, who stood with his hands still in his pants pockets. He was watching the water recede from around his ankles. Professor Alger breathed in, exhaled deeply, and began to walk away. "You boys keep me apprised of your progress."

Custis nodded and waved goodbye to the professor.

"Who taught you to weld, Custis?"

"No one. I read how it is done."

"Therein lies one problem."

"One? One problem?"

"Yes. The second problem is that you, the brilliant Renauldos Custis, need to admit *you* need help. You might want to involve more people. Just off the top of my head—industrial arts students?"

x x x

A frozen rat. A live frog. An anesthetized mouse. All too small to differentiate the internal organs from blood and bone.

"Now what?" Preston leaned over the lab table for a closer look.

Custis shook his head. "I know it's there. It needs modifications. Different lengths, amplitude, frequency, time period. The velocity is just too much. The frequency of sound waves depends on the speed of the source."

"It's got to be something else. We've been doing this for six months. It's not improving."

Custis abruptly looked up from his work. "But it is. Each time we get closer and closer. Look at your numbers. Bit by bit, it's getting there. I'm pretty sure it has to do with the velocity level."

"We need a larger specimen. What about a dog?"

"We're not going to use a dog. We need a human who can communicate the symptomology."

"Do we need permission for that?"

"It will take too long, maybe weeks." Custis looked at Preston. "I can do it. You'll have the controls, and you'll need to tell me the exact readings, levels, saturation, and what you see. I'll tell you how it feels."

"I can't do that. I'm the scribe. I might kill you."

"We need a third person. Professor Alger may not allow it just yet. We'll have to wait."

Preston walked around the machine. He inspected the interior components, rubbed his jaw, then combed through his hair with his fingers. "I'll do it. I'll be the guinea pig."

Custis wanted to smile, but the seriousness of the experiment overrode any enthusiasm. He knew Preston had ulterior motives, whatever they may be. In the past, everything Preston did was not out of selflessness but rather came from a place of need. But maybe it was different now. Together, they had both come so far. "I'll need to strap you down so there is absolutely no movement."

Preston removed his lab coat and nodded his head slightly. "Just give me a second." He walked to his desk, opened the bottom drawer, removed a bottle of vodka, and took a long swallow. Then another. "All right. I'm ready. I'm putting my life in your hands."

Preston sat down on a stool and methodically removed his shoes. He pulled off his socks, stuffed each into either shoe, then positioned them neatly against the wall. Maybe he just wanted them out of the way, or perhaps he thought he might never need them again. His hands trembled with the sort of fear Custis understood—the kind disguised by inventing false courage. The kind one chose to experience in the name of friendship.

Real courage is being afraid, then doing it afraid. Custis kept his thoughts to himself. *A mechanical wave. The physics of waves. The process of which sound is produced, travels, and is received. Produced by objects that are vibrating, a disturbance from point A to point B.* He looked back up at Preston.

Preston pulled himself up on the long table. He lay down on his back and looked up as Custis buckled the leather straps. "Will it kill me?"

"Some of the waves get reflected back, while some travel on farther until they reach another boundary and then get reflected."

"But will it kill me?"

"I hope not."

"Will it hurt?"

"I hope not."

"Will it scar me for the rest of my life?"

"I hope not."

"Will it prevent me from ever having children?"

"I would think there is another component in that equation, but it shouldn't stop you from trying."

"Well, then, let's proceed."

"We'll start with your legs."

"Start? I thought the legs would be it!"

After four hours, Custis had projected thirty-eight schematic plates of his lower legs, each one methodically examined. He recited the control number and findings as Preston logged the information into the ledger.

"I can clearly project bone placement. Look at this one, Preston. My God, I think I can see an artery. This graph here must be the blood flow. Give me the levels on this overlay, Exhibit R C 724, R L M."

Custis modified the equipment one more time before strapping Preston down again. "The relay back to the machine is off. The calculations of the distance from the transducer to the boundary and the speed of the echo return—I'm missing something. Let's move upward to the heart."

"Let's think about this. Start with a kidney. At least I have two of those."

"We need to show Professor Alger. Let's get more plates first in case he shuts us down for unauthorized human experimentation."

Preston and Custis worked through the night. A few times, Preston fell asleep while still on the table.

"This is amazing," Custis said. "Absolutely fascinating. Preston, do you feel no pain? Preston! Wake up."

"What . . . what?"

"Do you feel all right? Do you feel any pain?"

"No. Just a little vibration, maybe a little warmth, but I think it's just in my head."

"No pain? The sound radiation wraps around all sides. I can intensify the electricity."

"Well, at this point, let's just reevaluate what we've got," Preston said.

"All right, let's call it. We should have enough for this round."

The graph plates were examined, dated, and logged by the following afternoon.

Professor Alger entered the laboratory. He carried an open box full of paperwork and three rolled-up blueprints under his arm. Custis was busy with machinery. Dark, protective glasses covered his eyes as he worked a weld. Preston sat at a long desk near the bank of windows, his back hunched over stacks of papers and ledgers.

Professor Alger smiled as he slammed the box down on the countertop, then fumbled with the blueprints, one falling to the floor. Custis abruptly stopped the welder and turned off the gas as Preston looked up from his desk.

"You have another year of full funding. I reassured the board that you are near and the results will be nothing short of blockbusting."

"That is fantastic! We are so close," Custis said.

Preston raised his arms, his fists into the air. "Yes! That is incredible." He grabbed Custis, patted his back, and then shook the professor's hand. "It would be my honor, sir, if I could continue here."

Custis had forgiven Preston for his past behaviors, but they had yet to be forgotten. Maybe it was time. "Yes, I could not continue without Preston. He has meticulously documented our progress and has managed a complete financial accounting. I would trust no other."

Preston added, "Professor, I have already crafted a cash-flow forecast, current balance, and a complete record of all financial transactions and acquisitions listed and tallied down to the cent."

"I am familiar with your accounting prowess, Mr. Langmuir. Two different degrees in business and economics, three in science, is it?" Professor Alger smiled. "I would not have this team any other way. Congratulations, men. Oh, by the way, they requested your presence before the board, to see your exhibition. I convinced them that your time was more valuable here, in the laboratory. Expect a visit in the near future."

"Yes, we will." Custis smiled broadly. "We have something to show you, Professor," Custis said. "We were hoping you'd stop by." Custis pulled out a graph plate. "Look, Professor."

Professor Alger looked at the plate. "What is this? What am I examining?"

"The grid images and calculations form crackling shadows, and highlights will come into definition for you. Just keep looking at it. This mark and this one." Custis pointed with his finger. "Reflected waves are picked up by the probe and relayed to the machine. I calculate the distance from the probe to the boundaries in a series of graphs. These overlays of grapheme represent the fourth and fifth ribs. But look deeper, beyond the grid."

Professor Alger studied the plate. "I see something. I can see the definition now. But what is it?"

"That is a graph of a live human being's own beating heart. It's Preston's heart!"

"Astonishing, simply astonishing."

Professor Alger leaned in for a closer study, then suddenly stared at Preston.

Preston laughed. "Yes, Professor, tangible evidence that I do, in fact, have a beating heart."

"We need further development into a processing unit for photographs rather than just charts." Years of work had finally presented a glimpse of triumph. Custis was on the verge of making history. Ideas ricocheted in his head as he struggled to control his emotions. "Once we graph a controlled human body, a known healthy specimen, then we can find anomalies in another."

Professor Alger returned his gaze to the graph display. "Is this the only one?"

"One out of 132. A couple more have a good definition but are not nearly clear enough. This is just the beginning, Professor. It needs more work, but we have the concept now."

Professor Alger looked at Preston. "We do not have the authority to experiment with human beings to this degree."

Custis handed the professor another graph. "It's safer than X-rays. We're using sound waves. There is more danger in the development of nitrate plates. We just need a step further, changing the numbers into a two-dimensional picture that anyone can understand. Maybe some type of graphical recording."

The professor clasped his hands together and paced back and forth. He looked at Custis. "I will be stepping in and covering your classes. You must dedicate all your time and energy to this project and nothing else. And another thing, no one comes into this laboratory without my permission. Is that clear? No one. The doors are to remain locked as of today."

"Of course," Custis said as Preston nodded.

"And both of you, you look exhausted. Get some sleep. Start fresh in the morning."

Custis felt momentarily exonerated from thinking the end justified the means. He had never experienced a level of exhilaration to this degree. He placed his head in his hands and tried to organize the chaotic thoughts of his labor—from beginning to end. Every person who had touched his life had their purpose. He had only been the vessel.

1901

The new year brought word from Stockholm, Sweden, from the Royal Swedish Academy of Sciences. Professor Renauldos Custis I had been nominated for a Nobel Prize for his work in the mechanics of sound radiation. In celebration, Preston hosted a black-tie event held in a grand room on campus.

Custis felt undeniably successful. He was overwrought with the attention and craved only to be back in his laboratory working on the next phase.

Strangers surrounded him. Beautifully dressed women accompanied university department heads, city officials, and the governor. Women Custis did not know fawned over him while friends teased. He was glad to see Marshall and McKay. The last ten years of repetitive, painstaking work had taken over his life. His dream had turned to reality.

Custis was surrounded by success, intellect, wealth, affluence, and power—a social caste system gathered from across two continents. But his heart was elsewhere, back on a ranch in North Carolina. He had everything now—except for Sarah.

Custis had already written the letters, sealed them, and placed them atop his bureau—one to Sarah, the other to Martin. He was waiting for the formality of receiving the official notification of the evening's ceremony. He thanked them both and explained how their influence would change the world. But in Sarah's letter, he added that she would forever be a part of him. All this success, recognition, and future possibilities were because of her, and no one could ever take that away. It was now part of history.

McKay shook Custis's hand. "Congratulations, my friend. I've never heard of the Nobel Prize, but from the looks of this party, it must be astonishing."

Preston grabbed another glass of champagne. "They say it will be an annual event for the rest of time. This is its world inaugural."

Marshall sipped from his champagne glass. "You better not mess it up, then."

"How could I? My accent is perfect, thanks to you." Custis paused and pulled Preston to the side. "I am concerned, worried about the publicity. What is the probability of the truth emerging from one of these investigative reporters? What if they research more thoroughly?"

"If anyone starts snooping around, we'll take care of it."

"What does that mean?"

"It means there is no reason to worry about it unless it happens. Then we'll deal with it."

"I never fathomed this would be so public."

"Your records are with Simpson. And besides, they have already passed a tough test by getting you here in the first place. It's been ten years. They're not going to travel to Greece to research your parents. Why are you so paranoid all of a sudden? So what if they discover you're a hillbilly? You think they will now expel a Nobel Prize nominee? Settle down."

But Custis was not worried about the lie concealing his birthplace. He was concerned about the lies Preston did not know. Word and publicity would travel to Ohio, his alma mater. His last name was the same. Any published newspaper article could raise suspicion. Worse, published photographs would be disastrous.

Preston looked around the room. "We'll make it all about Centennial anyway. Be humble, a man of few words. Try to stay away from the cameras. I can help with that. Let me do most of the talking. I'll direct their attention back to the work itself, rather than just to you. We didn't plan on you winning a Nobel Prize. You can't worry about it now. What's done is done. You'll be fine."

Custis managed to find his way to the back of the room. He tried to shake the thoughts of being discovered out of his head. He thought about the paths that had led him and people who helped along the way. He thought of his mother and Mrs. Cramer, who taught him to read under the threat of being arrested. The love bestowed upon him from Mary. He thought of Sarah and Martin and Doc Lyman. He even thought of the veiled support of Sheriff Abbott. Here he stood, in a black tuxedo without any of the people he cared about the most. Custis felt lightheaded. He breathed in deeply, briefly closed his eyes, and exhaled. Sounds began to thicken and slow. He needed to get out of the room and wondered if he would ever outgrow his impulse to run.

Custis found Professor Alger outside on the back patio. He stood alone in the darkness.

"Well, Renauldos, what now?"

Custis smiled. "I don't know, to tell you the truth. I guess I need to turn around and help those coming up behind me." Custis took a deep breath. "We still have so much work to do."

"Yes, and tomorrow will be waiting for you. Funny, everyone has the same number of minutes in their day, and yet we all seem to come out with different results."

"I wish I was in the laboratory right now instead of here."

Professor Alger laughed. "This is just for the nomination process. Wait until you win the prize. Then you will be standing amongst the most brilliant minds in the world. Of course, there you may feel more comfortable, yes?"

Custis nodded his head. "I appreciate what is happening here. I just can't seem to grasp the politics of things."

"Good. You need to stay that way."

Professor Alger reached for Custis's hand. "Congratulations on your work. You carry a weight others will never understand. The weight of a genius. Come, let's get back to your party."

The two turned and began to walk toward the opened glass doors of the ballroom. Several people were surrounding an older gentleman entertaining those who were listening. He was a large man, tall, balding, and dressed in long black tails. He was doing all the talking. The cigar in his hand was nearly gone. He gave it to a waiter, dropping it onto a silver platter of food as he passed by. He took another from his breast pocket without missing a beat. Professor Alger touched Custis's arm. "Speaking of politics."

"What do you mean?"

"Have you not met Preston's father? He is, after all, the one sponsoring your congratulatory party."

"Preston's father? No, I mean, I thought Preston was giving the party. Conrad Preston Langmuir."

"You are partially correct. Conrad Preston Langmuir the Third is your host. Our Preston is the Fourth."

"I just assumed it was Preston. Is his father in politics? I thought he was just some wealthy bully businessman who doesn't like his son."

"He is retired, so to speak, from politics. But his hand is still in the pot of many politicians down the East Coast. Once a politician, always a politician. Money buys just about anything, Renauldos. And he has been very successful. That is why I encourage you to not get entangled in politics with any future scientific pursuits. You are too honest to be a politician, and you will lose badly. Come, I will introduce you."

Professor Alger and Custis walked back into the noisy ballroom. Now, at the back edge of the room, Custis saw Preston standing next to his father.

"That's him," Professor Alger said.

Mr. Langmuir was plump and boisterous. It might have been his height over Preston that made him look as though he were berating him. Preston stood next to him with downcast eyes. Two people intercepted Custis, introduced themselves, and shook his hand. The professor and Custis made their way to the center of the room, where the group was assembling. Preston was gone.

"Mr. Langmuir," the professor said.

"Now, Professor, I've told you to call me Conrad." His eyes turned to Custis. "Tell me, is this our guest of honor? I'm Conrad Langmuir, son. I've heard a lot about you."

Custis shook his hand. "Yes, sir, Mr. Langmuir. I cannot thank you enough for what you have done. Your son, Preston, has been instrumental in our work. You should be proud of him. I could not have done it without him."

"So I hear. I must be honest with you—when Preston first told me he was going to be a lab assistant, I was not thrilled. With his education, he should be able to operate any laboratory in this country. But he assured me it was the specific project that interested him. I allowed him to stay. He has a propensity to select the easier road—your coat-tails, I presume."

Custis recalled Preston's comments about his father wanting to send him to their overseas businesses. "Yes, he has been a good confidante."

"I suppose if it were not for Preston, you would not be here."

"Sir?"

"He's a Langmuir. My money precedes him. He should have been a full partner in this type of venture, if not the leading catalyst. Not a good business formula."

Custis needed a moment to digest the implication, but he didn't have time. "He has worked very hard."

"Of course. I find it interesting that he appears to have humbly taken a back seat to all of this."

Custis was beginning to see the surface of Preston's obfuscated life. A man approached and whispered in Mr. Langmuir's ear, then walked away.

"My apologies. We need to talk later about what's next, but right now, I must meet with Senator Fulton. He's the lead on a Southern delegation I'm working with regarding railroad business. They want to take some photographs."

"Yes, sir, of course."

Mr. Langmuir shook hands, turned, and hollered at his concierge. "Where's Preston now? He needs to get in these photographs."

It was an odd conversation, and Custis was glad it was over. He watched Mr. Langmuir part the crowd toward the back of the room. Custis's gaze stopped on two men talking and laughing. "Professor Alger, who are those two men, there in the back next to the draperies?"

"That is Mayor Van Wyck and his Vice Mayor, John Sterling."

It was Ben Cobbler. Custis could sense panic rising. He could feel his heart pound and momentarily lost direction. His mind would revert to tunnel vision, and mistakes would be made. He breathed in and turned his back toward Cobbler. Custis forced his thoughts to slow and reevaluate. Cobbler would pose no threat—he had more to lose than Custis. *Settle down.* Still, Custis felt vulnerable and wanted to avoid an awkward interaction.

"Professor, if you don't mind, I need to slip out of here."

"Oh, of course. Baby steps, Renauldos. You have a long, illustrious career waiting for you. Your introverted personality is quite charming at times. I wish I could do the same."

$x\ x\ x$

Custis ran up the stairs of the physics department in hopes of catching Professor Alger before class began. He hadn't slept all night, still full of excitement from the night's celebrations. After three hurried flights of stairs, Custis chuckled to himself as he slowed down and reached for the handrail. He glanced out the window as he took the last two steps to the landing. On the path below, he saw Chancellor Adams walking alone. The chancellor walked over to a somewhat secluded iron bench and wiped off the seat with his handkerchief. He sat down, pulled out his pocket watch, and looked around. He lit a cigar and remained on the bench.

The door to the classroom was open, and class was already in progress. He could hear Professor Alger's lecture, but Custis remained at the window, looking below.

"Mathematical reasoning is defined as the process of reaching a decision or solution by using critical, creative, and logical thinking. Be curious. Be collaborative, resourceful, and resilient. Scientific reasoning is problem-solving, a manner that includes critical thinking relative to content, procedural, and epistemic knowledge. It involves an awareness of certain aspects of reality. Without it, understanding physics would be impossible."

Custis watched the chancellor. Still sitting alone on the bench, he looked out of place. A man approached the chancellor and offered a handshake. The chancellor declined and remained seated. Obviously, the man was not in good graces. His outstretched arm awkwardly lowered as he turned and sat down next to the chancellor. It was Preston.

Custis could not help feeling uneasy. It was a surprising yet odd occurrence with no logical explanation.

Custis turned and stood in the open doorway of the classroom.

"The epistemic dilemma on the board, top right. It will need a solution within the hour."

He caught Professor Alger's attention and motioned to him.

As the classroom fidgeted with their undertaking, the professor walked out and greeted Custis. "Good morning, Renauldos."

"Sorry to disturb you. I was hoping to catch you before class started. I just wanted to say you thank you again for all that you have done."

"Of course. But it was you, all your years of discipline. You never gave up."

Custis stepped back over to the window. "Look, Professor. What do you think of this?"

Still on the bench, Chancellor Adams was unmoving, while Preston appeared demonstrative. Preston looked around as if to check for anyone watching. Custis felt unease rise and quickly tugged Professor Alger back from the glass.

Professor Alger resisted the movement. "Is that the chancellor and Preston?"

Preston pulled a large, folded envelope from his front jacket pocket and handed it to the chancellor.

"Yes, and it looks like Preston just gave him something he was not supposed to. Maybe money."

"Perhaps paying for a graduating degree?"

Chancellor Adams opened the envelope, thumbed through the papers, and paused midway.

"It does not look like cash. How long have they been there?"

Custis and Professor Alger watched as both men stood and shook hands before walking away in opposite directions.

"Just for a minute, right before you came out. Look, Professor, now he shakes his hand. He did not when they first arrived. He must have collected something of value."

"Last night, at the party, Preston left abruptly. Did you not see how his father treated him?"

Custis nodded. "Preston was supposed to be in the laboratory with me early this morning. When he never showed up, I thought he must have been too hungover."

"Strange indeed. It may be very innocent, but I think not. Keep this to yourself. You may be able to use it to your advantage. I need to get back to class. I will meet you this afternoon in the laboratory. Be cautious, Renauldos."

Custis stayed in the laboratory for the rest of the morning. He watched the clock, eyed the door, and scanned out the window, unable to concentrate on his work—distraction was the better opponent. *Conjecture. Facts. Hypotheses.* Neither Preston nor the chancellor wanted to be seen in the admin building. The chancellor did not shake his hand at first, indicating dislike. Preston had covertly provided an item of value. *What is that value?* Undiscovered fundamentals had been part of Custis's existence—seeking out patterns, formulating new surmises, and establishing truth by deduction. But this was more than the disciplines of science and math. It was cast in the intangible and mysterious performances of human behavior.

Custis heard the laboratory door open and close. "Professor?"

There was no answer.

"Preston?"

Custis walked out into the laboratory. Three men stood side by side.

"Can I help you?" Custis asked.

"Mr. Custis?"

"Well, Professor Custis, but yes?"

"Your services are no longer needed here at the university. You are to leave immediately."

Custis was not sure he'd heard correctly. Who were these men? "I'm sorry. What? Who are you?"

"I am William Brock, Esquire. I am the vice president of this university. This is the sergeant of arms, and our local constable. You are to surrender your keys, any and all property belonging to the university, and gather your immediate personal items; you will be escorted off this campus. You are no longer allowed on said property. Here are your termination papers, cease-and-desist, and intent-to-prosecute warrants."

Custis felt the air leave his lungs. *Am I hallucinating, or has Preston instigated an elaborate joke?* Surely at any moment, Preston would rush into the room, laughing. But no one came in. This was all too hateful to be a silly prank put on by a drunken fraternity mate. Custis took the papers. His eyes saw printed words *Fraud and Embezzlement*, but his mind could not comprehend. He shook his head. "No. This can't be true."

"It is true," Mr. Brock said. "No coloreds are allowed here."

Words that had become distant now reemerged with noxious precision. Suppressed memories severed through his thoughts of defense. "I have no idea where you are obtaining your information, sir, but I am from Patras, Greece." Influencing others by maneuvering facts or statistics to expose a different viewpoint or consequence always came easily for Custis. But no amount of intelligence or wit could disguise his blatant lie and the deception that was now surfacing.

Mr. Brock moved directly in front of Custis, standing face-to-face. A full head shorter, he placed his arms around his back like a mean schoolmaster subjugating classroom children. Custis knew the game. *Don't say a word. This is what they do to make you nervous.*

Mr. Brock squinted. His lips tightened as his arm flayed around, slapping Custis hard on his face. Custis took the hit. A hit from a coward, a bully, not man enough to deliver a punch to the gut but rather, a repressive slap to inflict the deepest sense of obedience.

Brock's voice was deliberate and monotoned. "If you insist, I will take you into custody forthwith." Brock took a handkerchief from his pocket and wiped off his hand. "Let me repeat myself. There are no coloreds allowed here."

"What about my work? My machine?"

"That is the property of the university. Get only your immediate necessities."

Custis scanned the room. His life was scattered everywhere. "My clothing, it's upstairs."

"Sergeant, escort Mr. Custis upstairs to gather his belongings."

"Yes, sir," the sergeant said.

Custis gathered an armful of clothing, some small personal belongings, and his bankbook. He didn't know what to take, what he would need, or even where he was going.

It was over. After years of work, sacrifices, and accomplishments, he no longer had value. He was without a history and now without a vision or mission. He felt hollow. *I've lost everything.*

Custis loaded up a metal milk crate with smaller boxes of sketches and notes, several ledger books, and anything nearby. His hands shook. Randomly he picked up a glass ashtray and placed it on top of the box. He stared at it. *Why do I want this?* It was an object of no value or utility. He put the ashtray back down on the table and exchanged it for a handful of pencils and a fountain pen. *Why am I taking these?* He slung his clothing bag over his shoulder and picked up the crate. He quickly placed it back down on the desk and opened the center drawer. Custis reached for a small, scuffed photograph of Sarah. She had given it to him years ago. Her faded handwriting on the back read *To Cus.*

The sergeant slapped his leather sap across Custis's back. "No. That is quite enough."

The hit forced Custis to wince and lean forward. He braced himself on the desk with his hand. "It is only a photograph."

The sergeant pushed the hard edge of the sap on Custis's forearm. "No. Enough."

The pressure of the sap dug into his muscle. Skin pinched and nerve endings began to tingle. Custis pulled his arm back and picked up the crate.

The three men escorted Custis out of the building and across the quad. Custis looked up toward the physics building. There was a figure in the window far above. The same window Custis once had looked down upon a young family playing in the snow. Professor Alger was watching. Custis could not see his face. He needed Professor Alger to know the truth, the logic and reasoning of how and why. Custis tried to pause, to briefly convey respect by nodding his head, but he was strong-armed into moving forward and out the campus gate.

36

Custis walked for blocks without direction. He hated feeling so confused. He imagined it as a parasite eating away his brain. Custis knew he needed to step away, gain perspective, a wider angle, rather than trying to take small pieces and push them all together. The day's circumstances had taken their toll, consuming all thought, forsaking sustenance. His conscious brain was unable to process, fighting to understand while the subconscious mind quietly played along.

Custis sat alone on a sidewalk bench, exhausted and weary and lost. He watched people pass by, come and go from businesses, laughing and talking. He looked at the storefront next to him. A new canvas awning, clean large glass panes, and a bright fresh sign. *No Coloreds. Whites Only.*

Custis stared at the placard.

Custis had altered himself except for the color of his skin. He had been accepted as a White man based on a portrayal, a ruse, no more than a made-up social experiment that could be turned off and on with only a notion or influence. Custis was mad. Good and mad. He stood, walked over to the sign, ripped it from the wall, and threw it on the ground.

Custis picked up his crate and bag. He looked left, then right. Preston's house was southbound within a half mile. The storekeeper bolted out the door, retrieved the sign, and threatened to have Custis arrested. But anger had made Custis feel indomitable. He turned and walked away.

The paperwork from the university had cited fraud and embezzlement. Custis did not yet know why this had happened, but he did know who was involved: Preston. *How did Preston know?* He must have checked records at Rosemont Hill. There would have been nothing, maybe leading to more suspicion. Maybe the chancellor had hired Preston to research the anonymous donor. But so many years had passed, so why now? Why wait until after the awards ceremony? It didn't make sense.

Custis stopped. Benjamin Cobbler had been at the awards ceremony. But Ben would have nothing to gain. It would have been too dangerous to divulge information.

Custis's arms ached desperately from the weight of the crate, and the leather strap of the bag dug into his shoulder. He was almost there.

Custis knocked on the door. For the first time that day, tears filled his eyes. Expended anger turned to pent-up stress and flowed out effortlessly. He knocked again. The door opened.

"What in God's name are you doing here? Why are you coming in the back door?" Andoe said.

"I'm sorry, Andoe, I had no other place to go."

Andoe stepped back. "Get yourself in here. Let's go upstairs."

Andoe looked up and down the alley. He saw a drunkard going through a crate of empty liquor bottles, and then he closed and bolted the door. Andoe took the box from Custis and motioned him to go up the narrow staircase. The small apartment was overly furnished. He could hear muted voices and laughter coming from the downstairs bar. A large dog lay on the floor. His coat was white, black, and brown, and very thick. The dog was the size of a small pony. He stood, stretched, drooled, and lumbered toward Custis.

Andoe reached out and petted the dog. "This is Sam."

"What is he?"

"Sam? Well, he's a Saint Bernard."

"I've never seen one before. My God, he's huge." Custis continued examining the dog. "He must weigh 150 pounds."

"Aye, and he eats me out of house and home. Be easy, Sam. This is our friend."

Custis let go of Sam and watched him walk away. *I miss having dogs.*

A redheaded woman appeared from the next room with an apron tied around her midsection. Her blue eyes smiled until they met Custis's.

"This is my bride, Stella."

Stella looked taken aback. She abruptly stopped and stared at Custis's face while wiping her hands on her apron. "Oh, my. It's been a long time since I've seen eyes like yours. They're so beguiling. You must be from the old country too." Her smile returned. "We weren't expecting company at this hour. Please excuse the mess."

"Your home is beautiful. I am the who needs to apologize for the intrusion. My name is Ronald Custis."

Andoe set the crate on a nearby table as Custis lowered the shoulder bag to the floor. He stretched out his back. "Stella, it looks like he could use some supper. Do you mind?"

"Be my pleasure." Stella left the room.

"Sit down, Custis. Tell me what the devil is going on."

Custis sat on the sofa, dropping lower than he had expected. Worn quilts of several colors and textures covered the back. Another quilt lay on the seat of an overstuffed, frayed chair adjacent to the sofa. Custis rubbed his shoulder and wiped his face on his sleeve. "I've been terminated, fired from the university. They said they were going to pursue criminal charges against me."

"Good God."

"Fraud. And I'm afraid that part is true. I am not who I purported to be. I am not a Greek, Andoe. To be accepted as a student for my work, I lied about being from Greece. Then it just remained as fact after all these years.

"Last week I received notification that I had been nominated for a Nobel Prize in science. Last night was the reception party at the campus, in celebration. Today, they rescinded the nomination. All my work is gone. My dream—I left my family for it. I have no plan B."

Andoe huffed. "Wait just a damn minute now. What? What do you mean you're not Greek? Are you Italian? Surely you're not Irish? You know our plight. How we're treated, what people think of us."

"Andoe, I am a Black man. I am prohibited from attending the university."

"Oh, thank God. I thought you might have been Irish there for a moment." Andoe laughed, deep and hearty. His hands wrapped around his ribs as the rest of his body joggled along.

For the first time that day, Custis smiled. How could several small, simple words create such immediate comfort? Words were a stimulus for specific interactive responses by activating different brain parts. But these words, from such a man, triggered not the brain, but Custis's heart.

Andoe suddenly turned somber, his eyes serious. "I'm not one for schoolbook education. Oh, I know enough to barely run a business, but life seems to be my better teacher. Some men are educated beyond their intelligence, and they seem to be the ones telling people like us what to do. Sadness is upon me, Custis."

Custis leaned back and sighed as Andoe sat in the ragged chair. Sam crept up on the couch, sank down, and lay his head on Custis's thigh. Custis rubbed Sam's ears, then kept his arm around the dog's shoulders, just as a loyal friend might do.

"I'm not sure how Preston found out, but he's lied to me from the beginning." He looked at Andoe. "I need facts to add up, and I can't make them. I thought he was my friend."

"You listen to me now. I know you're friends with Preston, but all things by him will always have an ulterior motive. What's best for him, as it were."

"Yes, and I am no longer his friend."

"His father does great business with me and has done some wonderful things in this town. I couldn't have made it without him. Sometimes a man like me has to look the other way when it comes to taking care of his family. But you need not trust them all the time. Or even like them, for that matter.

"Preston has been berated his entire life by his father. He is very powerful. The Third has underhandedly shaped this city, including eminent domain of hundreds of acres of land, right here on this blasted island. He was part of the government seizing Seneca Village. Eight hundred forty-three acres of eminent domain left hundreds homeless. He still has his clutch on the politicians clear down to Georgia. A lot of his money came from railroads. Now he seems to be in the land business."

"I don't know what comes next, Andoe."

"No one really does, do they now?"

Custis was quiet. It felt good to sit, to be in a quiet room.

Andoe sat up straight. "Did anyone see you coming around back tonight?"

"No."

"Are you sure now?"

"I walked all over. I didn't notice anyone."

Stella returned to the room carrying a platter of food and drink. "Here you go. I took it upon myself and straightened up the office for you. It's just a small bed. My Andoe uses it when he's in exile for snoring too loud. It's all yours for however long you need."

Andoe pulled up a small wooden end table, took the platter from Stella, and set it in front of Custis. "Sam, get down now. You know you're not supposed to be up there. Let the man eat in peace."

The dog reluctantly obeyed and returned to his bed, landing with a heavy plop under the window.

"Here, this warm drink will help clear the fog while you relax. Clarity will come. You are safe here with us," Andoe said.

Custis heard Andoe's words. *Safe. I thought I was safe. But Andoe is different. He has no connection to the university, nothing to gain, nothing he could want, and there is nothing left to take.* Custis imagined himself standing amid a pile of crumbled bricks and stone—dust consuming the last particle of air.

Custis began to eat. The food was warm and delicious. "I'm sorry for my manners. I've forgotten how famished I am."

"It's quite all right. Stella will certainly enjoy your enthusiasm."

After Stella returned the empty platter to the kitchen, she brought two small tin cups. She handed one to Custis. It was warm and smelled of heavy spices. Andoe smiled and reached for the other cup as he breathed in the aroma. "Mulled cider and whiskey. Irish, of course."

Stella laughed. "Well, now, I didn't know there was any other kind. I think I'll leave you two fellas to yourselves. I'm off to bed. It is so good to have you here with us, Mr. Custis."

Custis stood up. "Thank you, Mrs. Andoe, for your generosity and kindness. I am grateful."

Stella kissed her husband on the top of his head, then pulled his ear. With a firm voice, she admonished, "No more whiskey for you tonight, hear me?"

Andoe smiled as Stella left the room. He leaned in toward Custis and whispered, "Drink up. It will warm your soul. And we have plenty more."

Custis sipped from his cup. He noticed a small Bible on a table next to Andoe. "When I was small, my mother and I collected books. Any books we could get our hands on. She couldn't read, so I read aloud to her every night. I had to hide the fact that I knew how. It was illegal. People were killed for it."

"It must have been horrible. I've been pretty lucky—luck of the Irish, I suppose. I was born here in America. My father was not. Sometimes, though, it didn't seem to matter. We lived in a shantytown—us Irish, living in shacks cobbled together out of discarded lumber. Sanitation was lacking, open ditches at best. We were faulted for spreading diseases— typhus, tuberculosis, cholera. They called us ignorant bogtrotters, but we really were just souls looking for a better life. We all tried to hide our heritage—even the Black Irish. We changed our names and tried to live here like all the other folks. Regular. I just wanted to grow up to be a regular American."

Custis unknowingly nodded his head. As a small boy, he had wished similarly.

"Sometimes when my father would drink, he'd tell stories of his life before he met my mother, when he lived in the old country. The famine, how diseased crops turned to rot. People starving. He'd describe his neighbors as hollow, with faces as empty as their stomachs.

"After she died, my father jumped a converted cargo ship with hundreds of fellow countrymen, all running toward a better life. It took four and a half weeks of suffocating on fetid air overwhelmed with human soil and vomit, his clothing drenched in it. During the daylight, he volunteered to work on the ship just so he could breathe fresh sea air. At night, he helped take the dead, drop them overboard in nothing but their clothing. He once told me he could still hear the splashing of the bodies when he closed his eyes to sleep."

Andoe looked as if he were in a trance. Sounds and smells, two bodily senses so powerful to conjure memories back to life and resistant enough to be passed down through generations.

"He didn't know what America might hold, but he knew it would be better than what Ireland had turned into. Landing on the shores here in New York, most of them stayed here. No farther from walking distance to the docks. The lucky ones, like my father, were stevedores. He married my mother, just barely a woman. It saved her from a life most others could never understand—a netherworld robbing innocence first, then life itself. She had four of us. There's only me now. Tuberculosis. It's evil. Makes you linger. It wants you to feel every minute of the wickedness it has planned for you."

Custis was quiet on the outside, but thoughts of his childhood inundated his mind. The physical pain had dissipated long ago, but the humiliation, shame, and fear were as fresh as a new day. He remembered his mother's hands, rubbed raw from washing other people's laundry, her knees swollen from scrubbing floors, and her voice quivering when saying grace. "We all have our own unique stories. Sometimes there are no words to describe the challenges. Maybe as time passes, each generation will prove easier. My mother showed me how to be strong, strive after the impossible, and never give up. I feel, at this minute, as if I've lost everything. All has burned to the ground again."

Andoe took the last sip of his whiskey. "Your mother was wise. You're not in this life alone, and you can be sure of that."

Custis looked up at Andoe. "She has been with me all along." His mother was the angel guarding her son who was clashing with devils. "She will not leave me now. They can't take away what is in my heart, nor in my head. I have the knowledge now. I know the mystery."

37

Professor Alger organized scattered furniture and boxes on the lawn in front of his home. Students hurriedly walked by and appeared absorbed in their own needs. Alger looked at his pocket watch. *They're going to be late.* Their lives continued as usual while Alger's life was being packed up and stored away in trunks and crates. He watched the tardy students. It was easy to differentiate the freshmen from the upperclassmen just by the way they walked and how many books they carried. All so young and full of hope and excitement.

There was a commotion farther down the sidewalk as a figure of a large man emerged through the students. Things that transpired in the scientific world were sometimes difficult to explain: the perfected architecture of a spider's web, the luminescence power of fireflies, or the mysterious command of a mother's instinct. Then, some things happened that could be called oddities. The sight of a sizeable, white-bearded man in formal Celtic dress accompanied by a massive dog walking through a university campus was one such abnormality.

While the students on the sidewalk parted way, others stood in the distance, watching and whispering, some even smiling. Whether stares were derived from the sight of a grown man wearing a kilt and shiny black shoes topped with silver buckles or a dog the size of a small horse decorated with a collar of green plaid scarves, it didn't matter.

The army of one, plus dog, strode with purpose. As they approached the cottage, Professor Alger stared at the procession.

"Head forward, Sam. Pay no never mind to 'em. Stick with me now. Be not afraid." They stopped and faced the professor. "I am trying to locate a Professor Alger."

"Yes, that is me."

Andoe gave a quick nod. "I have a letter for you. From Custis. Professor Custis, that is."

Professor Alger looked confused for a moment. He brushed his hands together and hurriedly walked to Andoe. "You must be Professor Custis's friend from the bar, Mr. Andoe."

"That I am. And he is a good friend of mine as well. He asked me to give this to you. He is no longer permitted to be on the property. Not quite sure what it all says, whether all is explained or not, but Custis said he trusts you will understand."

Professor Alger took the envelope and asked with concerned eyes, "Is he all right?"

"He will be. He's on his way to Ohio. Wilson Place College. He's hoping to take his professorship back. Sorry to see him so lost." Andoe looked back into the campus, appearing to momentarily forget his assignment. His shoulders relaxed; his eyes saddened. "This university tried to take the life out of him."

Professor Alger nodded. "If you can, please let him know that the university has reconsidered going forward with the criminal proceedings, as well as the demand of reimbursements. Clearly, the reality of negative publicity outweighed their ego."

"I will get word to him. I am sure it will be a load off his heart. It was important to him that you know the truth. He greatly admired you as well as your family. Of all the things he lost here or was taken away from him, Custis was concerned the most about you."

Andoe watched Professor Alger look down at the envelope in his hands. His shoulders sank, and his voice softened. "I have never seen a man with such spirit, Professor. Here he has an axe thrown upon him. They've cut his dream right from his hands, and he still stands tall."

"It is attestation of something bigger in his life. We all have gone through trials and tribulations, it seems. Maybe him more than we can imagine. I fought for him, challenged the university."

"The university does not see him as a human being. He knows that. It's their loss, really."

"I am leaving myself. Taking my family to the west. There is a university there, in California, where I have been offered a position. Stanford. Very promising. My daughter will be able to attend when she is old enough." He looked back up to Andoe. "Just a few more years for her, but really, just a blink of an eye in the context of life." Professor Alger smiled. "It was founded by a woman and her husband who were not afraid to outgrow old thoughts and ways. It seems so simple, doesn't it?"

Andoe nodded and composed a tight smile. "My bride has been reading about places in Oregon where the fishing ports are overrun with busy canneries and overloaded boats. Docks with bustling trades but run shy on pubs where opportunity and favor awaits. Where the fir and redwood trees grow right outside your front door, branches so high you can't nearly see the tops and are green twelve months of the year. Where the sky is still blue, as blue as the ocean, where it's hard to tell which is which if it weren't for the whales and dolphins leading the way. I might even try my hand at fishing."

"Sounds like we may become West Coast friends someday. But you'll have to get a big enough boat for the both of you."

Professor Alger petted Sam's head. "I've never had the pleasure of meeting a Saint Bernard; I've only read about them." He softly took hold of Sam's head, bringing the dog in close to his waist. He rubbed Sam's ears and admired his eyes. "His head is bigger than mine."

"Aye. Sam here, he's ready for a change too, aren't you, boy?"

"Embracing new things whether we want to or not. It is uncomfortable getting to the other side of being uncomfortable. But I am afraid that sometimes it is the only way to find our individual peace."

Andoe offered his hand. "The best of luck to you and your family."

"Remember, Mr. Andoe, Stanford University. Please let me know where you land. I will look forward to your letters."

"Of course; my bride will be obliged. I never took to school much. Always believed life gave the greater lesson."

"Most of the time, it seems."

Andoe snapped to attention, turned, and beckoned, "Sam. Fall in."

The dog heeded and stood by his side, waiting for the next movement. Andoe cleared his throat and took the first step forward on the empty sidewalk. "On with it, boy."

Andoe walked stiffly, as if keeping time with an imaginary regiment, his shoulders drawn back, his arms and legs synchronized with the nonexistent beat of bodhran drums and soundless bellowing bagpipes of Ireland.

x x x

Custis stood inside the New York Central Railroad terminal and waited his turn. Two pieces of luggage sat at his feet. He had no companions to see him off or wish him well. Alone, this is what he needed to do—repair all the damage, begin all over again. Custis watched the travelers move about. They were conversing, laughing, bumping into others as if they had no concern that he had died inside. He felt the sweat beneath his clothing. The air was dreadfully hot. It smelled of stale body odor—maybe it was dead as well.

Custis placed a few worn bills on the counter. "One ticket to Ohio. Columbus, please." His voice was without passion, his movements—deliberate.

"Round trip?" the ticket agent asked without making eye contact.

"No."

Custis watched the man's fingers separate the bills. "That will get you to Buffalo."

Custis reach into both pants pockets. He retrieved some coins and another wadded-up bill and placed it with the other cash.

"That's to Cleveland."

Custis opened his jacket and pulled out a leather wallet from the breast pocket. His fingers thumbed through a stack of bills but pulled out only one.

"Akron. Third class."

"Close enough."

Custis returned the wallet to his jacket. He looked at the money on the counter as the agent filled out the ticket information. Custis's vision began to blur. He closed his eyes and briefly felt the cool relief of darkness. Voices began to merge and rotate until the sound became a loud drone. He imagined the drone becoming visual, turning and twisting into a set of steel tracks, gently rising and snaking with the trajectory of invisible hills—the hills of his home.

"Wait." Custis raised his hand and covered the bills with his palm. He looked at the clerk. Custis felt tears welling. "I want to go home."

PART IV

38

1901
NORTH CAROLINA

Morning had passed quickly. Overhead, the sun was hot, but the breeze brought a dismal promise of relief. Even with her eyes closed, Sarah knew the alfalfa windrows were almost dry from their heady scent. Long, winding rows lay slightly raised, forming faded green stripes across the pasture and over the rise. New growth, already shooting bright green through the stubble, was a futile offer for one last harvest before autumn brought its rain.

From a distance, Sarah watched a horse and buggy approach the ranch gate. She couldn't make out the driver. She squinted, waited, and tried to tell if it might be her father, but he wasn't due for hours. Something was strange. The carriage stopped at the gate, turned, and drove away. The rig was too small to be her father's, and it was only one horse, maybe a palomino. Probably someone lost.

Sarah rode to the back acreage near the reservoir. "Owen." Sarah waved her hand.

He gestured with his hat and rode toward her.

"Morning. Or afternoon. Just inspecting the water level. Been so blessed hot I was worried about evaporation levels. But it looks real good. Actually, better than last year at this time."

"That's great. I wanted to check on the alfalfa. Make sure everyone is on hand. It's close, I think."

"Yes, ma'am. We got the students from down below all ready to go. They're real excited about the Sudan grass, too. Waist-deep now, and they just planted it the first of July. Eighteen pounds of seed per acre, and they're betting on an exceptional yield. We've already got early milk stage on the seed heads. Should be five feet high in another month."

"Yes, let's hope so. I thought I saw a dry spot the other day. I'll check the irrigation before I go in. I wanted to let you know we have a broken top rail in the number-four run. The post is fine, still solid."

"Danged ol' Colorado again, most likely. I'll get to it today so no one gets scratched up."

"Colorado needs a girlfriend, I'm afraid. I'll go and check on the water flow, get it going again."

"I can do that for you, Sarah. Should be getting close to the girls coming home."

"I've got a couple more hours. Father is picking them up. He promised to take them to the grand opening of the library. Then for ice cream, I have no doubt, or anything else they can lure him into."

"They sure love their grandpa. They're fine girls, Sarah. The best."

"Oh, they're a handful, as you well know."

Sarah turned her horse and smiled. Owen was just about the kindest man she had ever known. He was handsome, too, with mirthful eyes, always smiling, which sometimes posed a bit of a problem when supervising others. At first, his younger age had been an issue with the cowhands, but his apparent skills quickly corrected that. The girls loved him. They saw more of Owen Brannon during the summertime than their own father.

Sarah stopped her horse, turned, and looked at him. "Owen?"

"Yes, ma'am?"

"Thank you for all you do."

Owen grinned. He took off his hat and brushed back his dark hair. "It's my job, of course, but also my honor. You're welcome."

His voice was always smooth. It had a reassuring key and made Sarah feel safe. "No, well, that too, but thank you for what you're always doing for the girls. They adore you."

"Oh, my goodness. You know I just can't get enough of those little rascals. Your family has shown me nothing by kindness. You know I'd do anything in the world for you and your father. Not many men like him left in this world."

Sarah nodded, turned her horse, and rode away toward the front portion of the property.

Sarah tied her horse to the fence railing and patted his neck. "Not this field, Jack. It's not ready for you; you'll make yourself sick."

Sarah removed a short shovel from a saddle tie and hung a leather satchel over her shoulder. She easily pulled herself over the fence. Her arms were strong and tanned. She walked the irrigation check until she found the dry area. The grass was much shorter, and the ground had cracked from the heat and lack of water. Sarah dug out and reconstructed the dirt check. She wiped her brow as she watched the water flow freely.

Sarah bent down to her knees, collected a dirt sample in a glass vial, and secured it back into the satchel. A gust of wind moved the grass. She stood and looked around. Yes, just a gust of wind.

The grasses moved in concert, seemingly to melancholy music she could not hear. Sarah removed her leather gloves and hung them in the front of her waistband. She closed her eyes and held her arms out straight, just above the top of the grasses. The milky seed heads brushed against her fingertips. She turned in a slow circle and listened to the rustle of the grass.

Sarah suddenly stopped. There was a different sound now. She opened her eyes and twisted around. She didn't move and held her breath. No one was there. In the distance, the arch over the front gate was barely visible. Another gust of wind blew the grasses in the lower field. Something was there, down by the entrance. She waited for the breeze. The grasses bowed and waved again, but nothing was there— just her imagination.

Sarah collected a few samples of seed head and walked back to Jack. As she climbed over the fence, straddling the top rail, she had a better view of the archway. Nothing was there. Jack snorted, nostrils flared. His ears moved front to back as he scraped at the ground.

"Easy, boy. You feel it too, don't you? We'll be all right."

Sarah secured the equipment on the back of the saddle, mounted the horse, and turned. She sat high in the saddle, looked down the lane, and saw movement at the gate. She couldn't see what it was, though. Maybe a steer had gotten out. It made her uneasy. Sarah galloped her horse back to the barn and retrieved a leather holster and revolver. She spun the cylinder, confirmed it was loaded, and hung it on the saddle horn.

Sarah looked around. Owen was still on the far side of the ranch. He probably had the rest of the men back there with him. She slow-walked the horse down the lane, pretending to inspect the pastures. Maybe she should get Owen, after all. But what if it was something silly, just a steer or a cow? Perhaps it was a wayward dog. The sun was bright, and the heat was relentless. A bit of a mirage, perhaps. She'd get a little closer, where the property dropped a bit. She'd have a better view. She felt odd. She had never been afraid of confrontations—just the opposite. Her father told her it was part of her charm. But this time, it was different.

The figure of a man standing under the archway slowly came into focus. She couldn't see a face. A hat first, then a white shirt and dark pants were all she could discern. She held the reins in her left hand, and her right she kept free, close to the revolver. She didn't move her head but scanned the area as best she could. Sarah had the advantage—she had a horse to flee back to safety. *Keep your distance, she silently warned.* The figure did not move. He faced Sarah. There was something next to his feet. Maybe a box.

Sarah kept the horse at the slowest pace. "Easy, Jack, stay easy now."

Sarah suddenly stopped. Her voice whispered, "Whoa, Jack."

She didn't turn her head. Her eyes stared straight ahead. The man eerily resembled Custis but looked too thin. He stood the way Custis did, balanced and sure. He even held his hat in his hands just like Custis would have done. Tears began to well, and she tried to blink them away. Sarah opened her mouth and took in a deep breath of air. She dismounted and let the reins hang free, without looking away from the man.

"Stay right here, Jack." She stood facing the man. He still didn't move. He was just outside the open gate. Sarah slowly stepped forward. Tears came freely now. She covered her mouth with her hand.

It *was* Custis. He was crying too.

x x x

Sarah's hat fell to the ground as she began to run to Custis. Her hair, tied from behind, fell loose. Custis wiped his eyes hard with the heel of his palms. Sarah stopped ten feet away. Her eyes glistened. Custis wanted to slow down time, confirm reality, gather his emotions. He stepped toward her slowly, not taking his eyes away from hers. He felt her arms wrapping around his neck. She felt so light and free. She must have jumped into him. Custis embraced her closely and rocked her side to side.

"Here, let me look at you." He let her slide down until they were face-to-face. Custis held her head and brushed away her wildly loose hair.

Sarah hugged him tightly. "I thought you were gone forever."

Custis took her face into his hands again, looked into her eyes, and kissed her on the cheek. "I've been out here most of the day, just waiting. Trying to figure out what to say."

"Why didn't you come up to the house?"

"I was scared to death."

She wrapped her arms around him again and squeezed.

Custis held Sarah tightly in his arms. "I'm so sorry, Sarah, I'm so sorry."

Sarah didn't let go.

"I didn't know I was pregnant. I didn't know. I would have told you."

"I know."

Custis nodded and tried to smile.

"I married Lucas, but I wanted to marry you, Cus."

Custis took her arms from around his neck. He held her in front of him. "I wanted to marry you the first time I saw you. We were ten years old then." He wiped away the tears on his shirt sleeve. "The world hasn't changed, Sarah. If anything, the government has gotten worse. New laws and more to come. So much crueler."

Sarah took her neckerchief and wiped her face. Custis forced a smile and tried to laugh. "Just look at us now. You are more beautiful than I ever remember."

Sarah tried to laugh. "And I see you never really recovered from that brain injury. I'm not sure why you're here, Custis, but I'm glad. Father will be absolutely ecstatic to see you. Lucas, probably not so much."

Both giggled.

"Oh, yes, Lucas. I need to remember that."

"He's away on business."

Custis felt a little relief. One less confrontation. He'd have more time with Sarah.

"He's my husband. I love him."

"Well, let's give that some perspective. Do you love him more than your horse? This ranch?"

"You haven't changed. Always requiring illustrative facts. And your accent, you don't have to pretend anymore."

Custis nodded. "Ten years of talking with a bogus Greek inflection has become second nature. Hopefully it will be easier to lose than it was to gain."

"Come on. You can't stay out here all night." She took a step away, and he began to follow. "Get your bag, Custis."

Of course. Custis reached down and lifted his leather case.

"Let's get you cleaned up. You need to meet my children."

"Children? More than one?"

"Three. Three girls."

"Oh, dear. That sounds like a better story than the one I have."

Sarah reached for Custis's arm. Both walked side by side until they got to the horse. Sarah took Jack's reins and pulled him along.

"Just look at this place. It's so beautiful. It's gotten so big. More barns. What is this? It looks like corn."

"That's Sudan grass. Another month and it will be ready to harvest. Good silage."

"Oh, my, your home. It's beautiful. It's right where Lucas said he wanted to build it."

Custis stopped and tugged on Sarah's arm. "I don't know what to say to your father or Lucas."

"Lucas is away for another week. He's traveling to New York, then Raleigh."

What business would Lucas have in New York? Custis's thoughts flashed to *New York*. The city was fickle, consuming ten years of Custis's life. It had offered profuse opportunity, granted sanctuary, and fulfilled dreams only to renege and leave him for dead all over again.

"Sarah, something awful happened. I had no other place to go. No friends. I just needed to come home. I needed to see you, if only for a moment. I didn't know what else to do. I don't know how long I can stay."

"Let's get settled, and then when you're ready, you can tell us all about it. This is your home, and you are safe."

Sarah held Jack's reins, and Custis tugged with the weight of his bag as they walked side by side toward the horse barn.

In a way, Custis wanted only idle conversation. It kept him from falling apart. "What is Lucas doing in New York?"

"He's a state representative now. He loves his work—adores the public life."

Politics was not something Custis wanted to contemplate right now, but he heard the glee in Sarah's voice.

"The catalyst was Jessy, our daughter. He thinks Jessy will be the veterinarian in the family, and by the time she's old enough, he wanted to make sure women would be allowed to attend the University of Veterinary Medicine."

Admirable. Custis couldn't help but think that maybe he himself had been the shining example of how bigotry worked. But then, no. Sarah had been prohibited from attending such a school. "He sounds like a wonderful father."

"He is. When he's home with us."

Sarah unsaddled Jack and put him in his stall. Custis walked down the center aisle and looked at all the horses. *Maybe I'll see some old friends.* Sights, sounds, and smells brought back scenes he had long forgotten. Custis felt as if he were being replenished with life. He stopped, turned, and watched Sarah brush down Jack.

"Tell me more about your children."

"Jillian is nine. Audrey and Jessy are six. Twins."

"Twins! Amazing."

"Jillian is the homebody. She was first born and in charge. Miss Priss. She doesn't like getting her hands dirty. Reads like a maniac. Audrey is book smart too. She loves her daddy and follows him everywhere when he's home. She'll probably be another politician in the family. Jessy would sleep in the barn if I'd let her. Loves her puppies and horses and cows or anything that seems to have lips or beaks. She's the one that needs no direction on hard work, cleaning stalls, or keeping everything fed and watered. She'll be the veterinarian." Sarah walked over to the aisle and stood in front of Custis. "What about you?"

"I need to be fed and watered too."

"I mean, do you have children?"

"No. I'm afraid my life has been all work."

"Custis, I'm so sorry for everything. I planned on meeting you in New York and spending my life with you. When I found out I was pregnant with Lucas's child, things fell apart. I couldn't leave the father of my child. I couldn't let my child grow up involved in that kind of lie. I hated myself, but I loved the child within me."

Custis heard a scream inside his mind, a shriek no one else could hear. That's how pain and grief operate. On the outside, all appears calm, maybe sweaty palms and a few reckless tears. But on the inside, it devours both heart and brain.

"I grew up not knowing who my father was, and I will die without knowing. I understand how that feels and what it can do to a person."

Custis needed to keep the painful and despairing emotions at bay for a little longer. The time would come, but at this moment, nostalgic sights and sounds gave him a fresh breath of life. For a moment,

Custis felt empowered. He had achieved the unachievable. Nothing could change that fact. He had a lightness about him, a peculiar sensation of freedom. Custis wanted the feeling to last forever, but he knew it would be impossible. He didn't want to hear himself talk. He didn't want to think anymore. "Come, introduce me to your friends here."

"This is Colorado Sly. He's the current stallion and thinks quite well of himself. He's only in this stall because he damaged the stallion barn and it's in repair. It's being reinforced with rubber padding. The bay is Coosanova Tidings. Paradise Pride, daughter of Gruenig Girl, the roan is Charlotte Peak, and Norman is right here. She's our only Tennessee Walker."

"Norman is a mare?"

"Yes. Seventeen hands. She's one of our favorites. That's why I keep her in Stardust's old stall."

Sarah stopped. She rested her arms on the top rail and looked at Norman. "We kept Stardust as long as we could. Father and I couldn't bear to put her down. It was right after you left the last time. Lucas said he'd help, but I couldn't live with myself for allowing someone else to do it. She was mine. She saved my soul, saved my life. She belonged to me. It was my responsibility."

Custis watched Sarah. Ten years had passed, but he saw the pain still fresh in her heart. He wasn't surprised. *This is what honest people do*, he thought. *They keep the aching deep inside, nurturing it until it becomes a memory. They are loyal to the pain but manage to go on, and sometimes, they are willing to do it all over again.* Being away from such truthfulness made Custis realize he loved Sarah more than he even remembered.

"And over here is Sparkler."

"Sparkler? Any relation to Firecracker?"

Sarah laughed. "No. Jillian named him Sparkler when he was born. She said his eyes sparkled."

"Oh, thank God. Where is ol' Firecracker?"

"He was sold to a place down near Charlotte. A young girl accompanied her father here. They were looking for a new line of thoroughbreds. We were out in the runs, looked around, and found the girl in Firecracker's stall. She fell in love with him. Firecracker took to her and wouldn't settle down until she was next to him again. She wanted to ride him, and it was the strangest thing. He was an angel to her. He threw a fit when she left. Two weeks later, the dad came back and talked me into selling him. Said his daughter was beside herself and couldn't live without him. He wrote later that they were two peas in a pod and it was the best thing he'd done."

"I like happy endings."

Sarah seemed so content now. Married with three children growing up on the ranch was a perfect life. Custis thought of his years being away. He had learned to go on without her, feel joy for others, and even find gratefulness within the vile hardships along the way. He had settled into the rhythm of time by quantifying days and nights, holidays, and seasons. He had accomplished what he set out to achieve. Now he understood it was all at a cost he could never recoup. Society's ugly prejudices had been forced out into the open. But Custis knew there was one place where it had never really mattered. Not in Ohio. Or New York. It was here, in Sarah's heart.

39

Sarah and Custis walked out to the front of the ranch near the runs. The afternoon sun had turned the main barn into a silhouette. Custis turned and scanned all that he could. The hay hoist still hung in the prow. The cupola perched on the ridge cap still supported the large iron weathervane Buster had crafted.

"Buster? I'm afraid to ask."

Sarah took a deep breath before she answered. "He died, Cus. He got to hold Jillian but wasn't here for the twins. He never knew what became of his family after the war. We buried him up next to Mary."

"I'd like to go up there, if you don't mind. May give me some perspective. Tomorrow? That is, if I can spend the night. If not, it's not a problem. I can stay in town."

"Custis. Don't be silly. You're staying here on the ranch."

"I would love to meet them . . . the girls."

"Of course. They'll be home, along with Father, soon. I know someone who would love to see you right now. Come on!" Sarah took Custis by his arm, up the lane and toward the main house.

Before they reached the top of the porch, the front door opened, and Layne stepped out. "Oh, my Lord. Custis, is that you?" She hugged his neck, then stood back and looked at him. "My, oh, my, aren't you pretty. You're so handsome." She hugged him again, then pushed back and slapped him hard on his face. "That's for never telling me goodbye. Shame on you. After everything Mr. Tennison and Miss Sarah did for you, you just up and leave."

The slap really didn't hurt. It was more of a surprise. "I'm sorry, Layne. I should have done a lot of things differently." He looked at Sarah. "Better than an iron skillet."

"Don't you ever do that again. You get any idea of leaving, I need to be the first to know."

"Let me give my notice right now, so there will be no mistake. I can't stay forever. Just figuring some things out, Layne."

Layne raised her arms and stepped toward Custis. He winced and prepared himself for the next strike. Layne hugged him tightly and pulled him inside the house.

Custis looked around the room as Layne fired questions and made assumptions. He knew the difficult conversation would come but forced it to the back of his mind. He needed to feel the grace of the house—the home that had already healed him once before.

"Layne, can you make sure Custis has everything he needs for a while? I need to run home and get cleaned up before Father and the girls get here. Cus, your old room is still upstairs."

"I will, Miss Sarah. He looks like he could use something to eat first."

Layne pulled Custis into the kitchen and started preparing food. Custis sat at the table. He looked at the woodstove and imagined a fire crackling on a cold, dark morning. He imagined Mary's hands working bread dough, cutting vegetables, and quietly listening as he read aloud. He rubbed his fingers across the wood top. He saw years of wear. He looked at the open door of the pantry, walked over to it, and turned on the light. The shelves were full of canned goods, boxes, and sacks of potatoes and onions. But in his mind, he saw a small iron bed, a helpless child, and blood. He heard muffled screams, crying, and someone praying.

"Are you listening to me?" Layne said curtly.

Custis turned, startled, not quite sure what had just happened. "I'm sorry, Layne. I must have been daydreaming. What?"

"I said, why are you here, and where have you been? And why are you talking so funny?"

"It's a long story, Layne. I don't know where to start. But I will. I just need some time to sort it all out. I promise."

"I understand. Nothing like being home to straighten the head out."

Custis looked back toward the pantry. "What about Doc Lyman?"

"Oh, he's long since retired. Living up in Raleigh with his daughter."

"Who's running the ranch now? Sarah told me Buster passed."

"Yes, he did. Near six . . . no, seven years ago. Mr. Owen Brannon runs things. He's a real good man. Works hard all the time. Never heard an angry word come out of his mouth or no taking the Lord's name in vain. And, you know, he just loves our girls. He's got some type of special bond with little Jessy. He's teaching Jessy to ride. Every day after he gets off work, he makes time for all those girls. I think he's got a hankering to have kids of his own. I saw him out with Miss Jillian one day, some time back. She was having a tea party and asked him to join her. Well, without a thought, he took off his hat, sat himself down, and pretended to have tea. Little finger and all. Can you imagine that? A big ol' dirty cowboy was having tea. Did it right in front of the ranch hands, too. One strong look from Mr. Owen, and all those cowboys took off their hats and came over for tea. Yes, Mr. Owen is a fine man."

"What about Lucas?"

"Mr. Lucas is so busy. But he loves this place, and he loves Miss Sarah. He's gone a good part of the year."

"And Sarah? Is she happy?"

Layne paused. She wiped her hands dry and looked away. "Those little girls are the sparkle in her eyes, loves them more than life itself."

"What about Lucas? Does she love him?"

Layne paused. "I've never seen her as happy than when you were here at home with her. Ten years ago, now."

Layne's words fell deep inside Custis. After being hidden away for years, the emotions were alive again. He was still in love with Sarah, but boundaries existed even more. His life's path had taken many turns lined with defeat, successes, sadness, and joy, all of which had led him back home to Sarah.

The sound of the front door opening brought Custis back from his thoughts. Layne stood and walked into the living room, and Custis followed.

"That must be Mr. Tennison. Can't wait to see his face."

"No, just me, Layne," Sarah hollered. "I need you to wait here for Father and the girls. Custis, get your hat. We need to go up and check on Owen. His horse came back to the barn without him. Layne, tell Father we're starting at the reservoir."

"Does this involve riding?"

"Afraid so."

"Of course it does. What was I thinking?"

Sarah was already halfway to the barn before Custis was out of the house. A saddled horse stood in front of the doors. Sarah grabbed the reins, looped them around the hitch, and ran into the stalls. Custis helped saddle Jack back up and led him out next to Owen's horse.

"You take Jack. I'll take Spencer."

"But Spencer is smaller. He looks safer."

"Jack is calmer."

"I'll take Jack."

"Last I knew, Owen was at the front reservoir. He probably continued south to the back two ponds. We can start there." Both rode up behind the house and over the ridge.

Within a half mile, Sarah stopped her horse. "There he is. Walking. Looks all right." Without waiting, Sarah rode toward Owen, and Custis followed close behind.

"Well, you're walking. That's a good sign. At least Spencer knew to come back home."

"Yeah, he got spooked by a mountain lion, and I wasn't prepared. Spencer went sideways, and I went straight down. Figured he'd run to the barn."

"Glad you're good. Scared me to death."

"Sorry, Sarah. Not hurt at all, just my pride."

"Owen, this is Custis. He lived with us when he was young. He is back for a visit."

Custis dismounted and shook Owen's hand.

"Glad to meet you, Custis. Thanks for coming to my rescue."

"Not at all. I've been known to require rescues as well."

"Let's get you home. Take Spencer, and I'll double with Custis."

Custis handed Jack's reins to Sarah. "Here, you steer."

Sarah got into the saddle and helped Custis back up. After a few awkward attempts, he sat behind the saddle. He had nothing to hold on to. "This doesn't feel right." Custis recalled the first time that he doubled with Sarah. Down at the river. She and Stardust had rescued him.

"It's fine, Custis. You're just bigger than you used to be."

"This isn't going to end well. I just know it."

"You go ahead, Owen. I'll have to take it slow with this greenhorn."

"Yes, ma'am. See you back at the ranch."

The ride back was uncomfortable. Had it not been for the closeness to Sarah, Custis would have chosen to walk. He tried holding on to the back of the saddle to keep his balance, but it was useless.

"Hold on to my waist, Custis. I won't let you fall off."

Custis wrapped one arm around her. He felt her lean back into his chest, and he leaned forward into her. The closeness was so unpretentious, so soothing, he felt he could ride for hours.

Sarah pushed back even harder. "Custis, we're going downhill. You have to lean backward."

"Oh."

They arrived safely at the front of the barn. Sarah looked down the lane and saw an approaching carriage. "It's Father and the girls."

Sarah swung her leg over the saddle horn, across Jack's mane, and slid off. Custis felt the horse adjust. He thought he was about to fall off, grabbed on to the back of the saddle, and tensed his legs. He wanted to dismount, but he didn't know what to do. The horse bucked. Custis hit the ground hard and landed on his back. All went black.

He heard a little girl's voice directly over him. "I think he's dead."

"He's not dead, Jessy." That was Sarah's voice.

"He's not moving. Yep, he's dead, all right."

"Who is he, Momma?" A different girl's voice.

"It's Custis. The boy I told you about."

"But he's not a boy." Another new voice.

Custis opened his eyes. He saw Martin's face directly above his own. Martin's cowboy hat nearly blocked out the blue sky overhead.

"I'll be damned. It is him. Custis, you've got to leave these horses to the professionals, son."

"I'm fine; thanks for asking."

"Come on, let me help you." Martin extended his hand. "Just knocked the wind out of you. You'll be all right."

"You're so tall," one of the three girls said. "You're so pretty. Your eyes look like marbles."

Jessy looked at him from the top of his head to his boots. "I can teach you how to ride. Owen taught me. He said I could be a famous jockey someday. I don't fall off."

"I might take you up on that, Jessy. Obviously, I could use some help."

"How'd you know my name?"

"Because I'm not dead, and I heard your mother call you that." Custis rubbed the back of his head and dusted himself off with his hands.

"Why can't you ride a horse?"

Sarah placed her hands around Jessy's shoulders and gently squeezed. "Jessy, enough for now. Let Mr. Custis catch his breath."

"No, he needs to go *catch* Jack."

"Jessy, into the house. Jillian, take the girls and help Layne with dinner. Tell her it will be all of us. I'll be in soon."

Custis watched the girls run into the house. "They are so beautiful. Full of your spirit."

"I'm afraid so."

"Sarah, I need to talk with you and your father. But right now, I'd love to just take in all the goodness here. I promise, after dinner. After the girls turn down."

x x x

Martin politely avoided asking Custis any questions regarding his return home. Sarah must have intervened at some point. Custis was captivated by the conversation, camaraderie, and laughter throughout their dinner together. Martin teased his granddaughters as they plotted their next adventure. Custis cherished every second as he analyzed the interaction of the family—how it sounded, how it made him feel warm inside. The girls were flawlessly happy and wholly beautiful. He laughed and stole glances from Sarah at the other end of the table. He tried to keep from being obvious, clowning with the girls, making animal figures by folding his napkin. He wanted the girls to be his children. A terrible sense of futility swept over him. He needed to grieve the whys, the what-ifs, the regrets. They needed to die and go away.

"Can you make a dog?" Jillian asked as she tried to shape her napkin into a form.

"Let me try. I had a friend once. His name was Sam. He was a giant Saint Bernard, all the way from Switzerland."

"What is a Saint Bernard?" Audrey asked.

"Well, it's a dog. But not just any old dog. A Saint Bernard has a thick brown, white, and black coat and is big as a pony. Why, their feet alone are as big as Layne's pie plate and their heads as huge as a pumpkin. There's not a mean bone in their body, and in fact, they are so full of love, it comes out in drool and slobber. Before long, you're sopping wet." Custis folded up his napkin and placed it back next to his plate. "I'm afraid I'm unable to make one."

Little Jessy suddenly perked up. "I have a great idea! You can take us to the new library in town. We can find a book so we can see real pictures of them."

Custis looked at Jessy. Sometimes the sharpness of reality had a way of penetrating and deflating the strongest of hearts. A new library. A whites-only library.

"Papa," Jillian began. "You'll have to take us because Mr. Custis won't be allowed." She looked longingly at Custis. "But, Mr. Custis, we will tell you all about it. I wish you could go. I will even draw you a picture of the Saint Bernard, and you can keep it forever."

"Of course I would love to see your artwork, under one condition—if I may have your signature on the bottom, as you may become a famous artist someday."

"Girls," Martin said, "let's wait until after this harvest, and then we can spend as much time as you like there. We're all going to have our hands full here for the next couple of days." He looked at Custis, forced a crooked smile, and slightly tipped his head.

Custis felt as if he were a little boy again, standing at the doorway of the haberdashery. It was a stark reminder of that habitual invisible barrier. Custis glanced at Sarah. She was already looking at him.

Sarah stood and began to clear the table. "Come on, girls, let's give Layne a hand in cleaning up."

"I can get this, Miss Sarah," Layne said as she came through the door. "In fact, why don't you let me go put the girls to bed, and I can just stay right over there tonight. You take your time, Miss Sarah. Enjoy yourself here. We'll be fine."

40

Martin poured himself a whiskey and sat next to Sarah on the sofa in his library. Custis slowly walked the perimeter, glancing at the books. Some were familiar, some were new, and some were missing. He was stalling. He didn't know where to begin.

He tried to organize his thoughts. There were so many details to thread together to make logical sense. He looked at Martin, the man who had paid for his education. The same education that had been erased from all Centennial records. Custis had practiced for days. On the train, in the coach ride, and even standing alone in front of the ranch for hours. Now his mind was no longer convincing enough to mask his emotions. He cleared his throat. Custis owed Martin the truth.

"When I left for New York"—his voice cracked—"it was one of the hardest things I have ever done. Since I was a small boy, I knew I had a calling, a mission. My mother said it was God's will. Academics was the only thing that came easily to me. I knew if I did not try to get accepted by Centennial, I would have never found completeness.

"That was just the beginning, I'm afraid. I lived in a rat-infested tenement with my wide-eyed dreams of being accepted at the world-renowned Centennial University. I changed my identity and college records so I could get in. I never changed my records regarding classes, experience, or degrees—just the school's name. There was no doubt that once Centennial saw Wilson Place College for Negros, I wouldn't be able to get in the door to explain my work.

"So I chose to falsify my educational records. I stated I was from Greece. I learned the Greek language and culture. Not quite being on the bottom of the caste system, per se, I passed for being White. They would have accepted anyone but a Black man. I lived with privileges and liberties, just as a White man would have."

Custis could barely look at Martin or Sarah. He sat down and held his head in his hands. "When I met with Chancellor Adams, he told me my tuition had been paid. That an anonymous source had already compensated for the position of a professorship as well." Custis looked directly at Martin. "Your donation saved my life, and it saved other lives as well. I will never forget what you have done for me."

Sarah quickly turned her head toward Martin as he looked down. Her face softened as she wrapped her arm around her father and placed her head on his shoulder.

"My true intention was to send for you, Sarah—you know that. After I got your letter, telling me you were pregnant and had married Lucas, I took it pretty hard. I was lost and drowned myself even deeper into my work. I worked for months, then years on my project until I realized that you, Sarah, had my answer all along. Your fly-fishing line was the same pattern that sound waves create. So I used sound waves to penetrate a human body. I just manipulated them to do what I needed."

Sarah and Martin looked at one another, then back at Custis. Sarah covered her mouth with her hand. "Oh my God, Custis."

Martin looked as if he was ready to burst open. "You did it—you really did it. We knew you would; we just knew."

"Last week, I received notification that I was being nominated for a Nobel Prize, international recognition for my work in the mechanics of sound radiation. The sound was based on our lives here on the ranch. It was because of the two of you. I will never be able to explain the experience of finally understanding the paths I was given to travel, the routes that were laid out just for me. It was the purpose for my survival. One of my professors would have called it *deus ex machina*, divine intervention . . . no other explanation."

Custis tried to laugh. "It seemed like my biggest challenge would be trying to figure out some way to be humble. Then within a day, everything was rescinded."

Sarah sat up straight. "What? But why?"

"I got caught. Someone found out I was a Black man and turned me in. They took away everything, even the nomination. Nothing can change the events, and I am truly sorry."

Sarah and Martin hugged each other. They stood and congratulated Custis.

Sarah embraced Custis. "The world has a machine that can look inside a human! Custis! You did it. My God, you did it! I'm so proud of you. You worked all your life for this. You did it, and no one, no one else could have."

"I'm going to get hold of our attorney," Martin vowed. "We'll go after Centennial. I'll rescind everything I have donated. We'll sue those bastards and take them to court."

"No, Martin. You do not need that kind of publicity. The purpose of the machine is to help people, to save lives. And it will do that. I agreed to a scheme. I knew it was wrong."

"We'll get Lucas to contest. The reason he's in state assembly now is to fight for the right for women to attend schools. Why could he not also argue for Blacks? It's the same challenge for all-inclusive universities. End of story."

"You have your children here. A legal battle and a very public trial would put them in harm's way. Lucas could be hung out to dry, lose his constituents. Listen to me. That part of my life is over. That particular machine will go on. I am going to start all over—make a new prototype, one that's even better. Wilson Place has graciously offered me a position. They want me to take my professorship back. I know there is more inside of me, something other than Wilson Place. I'm not sure if that is the path I need to follow again, but that's where I am going to start over. In the North."

"We can build a laboratory here," Martin said. "I'll find investors."

"Thank you, Martin, but I wish it were that easy. I'll still be Black. I walked around New York posing as a White man. I had the freedom to go anywhere I chose. For the first time in my life, I felt limitless. I know how that feels now, and I want it back. I was able to create an apparatus that others said was impossible. Without limitations, I can do more. I pray to God that things will change one day. This last battle just about took the life out of me. I needed time to regroup, recharge. I had to come home to a place where I knew I was loved and respected. But all that stops at the gate down there, where the White laws begin."

Sarah shook her head. "It's bound to change."

"Sarah, it won't change. I left as quickly as I could. I was too afraid to go on pretending. I don't know if I'm a wanted man or not. On the train ride here, it all came flooding back. I sat in filth as White passengers were given refreshments. And when I walked through this town yesterday, I was told to get off the sidewalk as White people passed. I had forgotten. I averted my eyes as teenagers laughed at me. It seems the hatred is generational." Custis paused and took a breath. "So, your offer to build a laboratory here, your support, I shall cherish for the rest of my life. But no, I cannot be successful here."

Sarah eyes were glassy with tears. "I'm so sorry, Cus."

"People have broken souls, Custis. They're plagued with ignorance. I want you to know that I'm so proud of you. My God, I'm proud." Martin shook Custis's hand, then reached out and hugged him. "I'll do what you ask, but I want you to know that I am not afraid of litigation."

"I stand with Father. We will do what you ask."

"Doc Lyman would be so delighted. We need to get word to him. Sarah, let me take the girls to school tomorrow, and I'll send him a telegram in the morning. Custis, I know Doc thought the world of you, and he'd love to hear about your inventions."

"Of course. I owe everyone here my very existence. I guess that is one of the reasons I was so obsessed with my work. I wanted to make a difference for others, as all of you did for me. I wanted to make saving my life worth it. It's time that I wrote him a long, long letter."

Owen walked in from the kitchen. "I saw the lights still on. Just wanted to let you know all is set for the morning. Nearly thirty of us, including the students, are ready for the harvest. Six wagons are lined up for daybreak."

"I can be a driver as soon as I get back from town," Martin said.

"That will be fine. It's going to be an early morning. Just have to make sure we don't get any dew overnight."

Sarah kissed her father's cheek. "I better get home to the girls. Custis, you know where your room is. Father, Custis only has a few days. In the morning, I'd like to take him up to the cemetery, then out to the new acreage."

"That's a fine idea. Owen, can we do without them for just a day?"

"Yes, sir. But they'll have to work twice as hard the day after."

Martin looked at Custis, then back at Sarah. "He could use a break to remember what's important and what's not. A lot of things have changed out there. He may not recognize some areas. Those young new farmers are willing to try just about anything. And don't forget to show him the new kine of your mother's cattle breed."

Owen waited for Sarah to stand and then put his hat back on. "I'll be happy to walk you home, Sarah."

"I'm sure I'll be fine, but I would love your company."

𝒳 𝒳 𝒳

The next day started before sunrise. Owen made a bonfire near the garden. Four tin pots of coffee were brewed for thirty men. A large hole had been dug out in the ground. Laced with kindling and hardwoods, it would barbecue a pig for the rest of the day. Between the bunkhouse cook and Layne, it promised to be a feast. Another hour, and the dew levels on the windrows would be confirmed, and the harvest could begin.

Sarah and Custis shared a cup of coffee on the way to the barn. Sarah pulled out Jack and Charlotte Peak. "I'll take Charlotte. She hasn't been out in a couple of days."

"But Jack doesn't like me. What about Norman?"

"He likes you fine. He just wasn't used to having someone on his rump. You might have squeezed him with your legs and made him jump. You probably owe him an apology."

"Don't you have one named Old Blue or Elderly Edwin or something like that?"

"Come on, Cus. We'll miss the sunrise if we don't hurry up."

The cemetery was over the hillock, behind the house. It was surrounded by ornate black iron fencing. The cast-iron finials were not the usual pointed spikes but small spheres instead. The dry grass was nearly waist-deep, and nearby a grand oak needed rain.

"My mother was the first buried here. Father picked this rise where she could keep an eye on her kine to the north, the ranch back down below, and her alfalfa fields to the west. He said he wanted her to see the sunrise every morning and feel the winds from the south. She would bless them as they passed over her and then send them on across the ranch." Sarah got off her horse and wrapped the reins around the fencing. Custis followed. She caressed the top of the finial, like someone who might touch a bird's egg.

"Father had the balls made special. He said Mother wouldn't want the animals to get hurt on the spears. See this footpath? It's where Father still walks every Sunday."

They walked in through the gate. Custis stepped over to Mary's grave. "Mary Grace Holder," he read. Next to her was Buster's grave. "Buster Russell McAdams. I never knew his full name. Remember when Mary signed my name-change certificate? Three Xs?" He looked over at the third gravestone. *Heather Sarah Tennison.* A bouquet of spent flowers lay at its base. A bare area was worn in the grass in front of the stone.

"Sarah?" Custis turned and looked for Sarah. She was already sitting on her horse.

"Come on."

"Where are we going?"

"To a place far, far away."

They rode over the hill and onto the next ridge. Sarah kept in front. Custis studied her every move. She and her horse were visual poetry—perfectly matched and rhythmic. She was not the horse's master but rather a companion ... deep in a dream but seamlessly awake. He listened to the repetitive connection of the hooves hitting the ground. The sound, the vibration—it was her steel rails of steadiness, determination, and purpose. It was a calming joy, a reassurance that life would go on.

"That's the new property, the valley below. Father purchased more land. He said other than gold, it would be the only sound investment in the future. We're almost there."

They followed a trail down a hillside to a creek. A small cabin was nestled in a grove of loblolly pine and cedar. The old trees created a magical whisper with the wind above. A small corral made of lodge pine poles was attached to one side of the cabin. The roofline extended into the corral and acted as overhead shelter from the sun or rain.

"What is this? Is this part of the ranch?"

"Yes, it's a bit rustic. Come on, let's water the horses."

They rode into the creek. The horses snorted, drank their fill, and pawed at the shallow water with their hooves.

"Owen built it for the girls and me. We enjoyed camping so much, and he was afraid of us not having what we needed. It's our little bunkhouse. I think he was concerned about the bears and mountain lions, really. It's primitive, but it works. Lucas is away most of the spring into the summer. We come here to camp; sometimes Father joins us.

"Before the cabin was built, I came here to camp. I had this awful feeling someone was watching me. Later, I found the spot, just over the hill where Owen was camped. Found the grass all bedded down. He only started his campfire after sundown, thinking I wouldn't see the smoke. Initially, it was unsettling. I spoke with Father, and he admitted he had asked Owen to keep an eye on me at night. They just wanted me to be safe."

"It's a beautiful place. So peaceful."

"Falling asleep to the sound of the creek, the smell of the forest—it washes everything away. It makes you forget about time."

Custis was quiet. He stared into the water. He remembered the hatred and cruelness of the world beyond the gate. He imagined the water sweeping over him, washing away years of struggle. He wanted to drown his memories mercilessly. He wished he had never gotten on that train years ago. But then, there would have been no machine, no recognition by Stockholm or subsequent medical possibilities for future generations. He'd never have experienced absolute freedom or deep and righteous friendships. He thought of Professor Alger and Andoe, and the hundreds of students who had looked up to him and gone on to make a difference. No, he'd choose to keep the bad so he could appreciate the good. Odd . . . he was now experiencing a balance inherent in life. Something he had only read about. *Perhaps it's because I'm home.*

They unsaddled the horses and set them free in the corral. Sarah carried her saddlebag and rifle to the front door of the cabin. Two iron bars were fastened down tightly on either side across the door.

"Bears. They'd push right in without them."

As Sarah unbolted the bars, Custis looked at a painted sign over the door: *In the mountains, we forget to count the days.*

"Jillian made that. She's the artist in the family. The girls call this their magical place. It's only magical because here, homework is not allowed. Chores are limited to watering and feeding the horses. We read stories, hike, collect wildflowers, and fly-fish."

Sarah opened the door and allowed Custis to enter first. "I hope it's not too primitive for you. I'll open the shutters and let in some light."

Custis's boot steps made the wooden floor sound hollow. As Sarah let in the light, he could see the sink at the back and a small table in front of a stove. A set of bunk beds to the right and a larger iron bed to the left filled the cabin. Custis turned and looked at the walls. Just bare studs. His mind watched a small boy crumple newspaper and place it between the two-by-four studs as insulation. He wanted to turn back around to see if his mother was standing at the sink. He looked at Sarah, looking at him.

"It's not much, but it's just what we need sometimes."

"It's perfect, Sarah. You have a perfect life."

"Funny how it always seems cold when we first get in here, even in summer. Must be all the shade."

"I love you, Sarah. I just wanted you to know."

Sarah didn't move.

"I love everything about you. Your kindness, your orneriness. Your eyes when you smile and even when you're mad. Your wild hair. I love the look of your hands, how the strength can turn into soft tenderness without a moment's notice. There is a link between us; it's more than just words or promises. There always has been. Even years and miles apart. I don't know how to fix things so we can be together."

Custis took a quiet step toward her. He placed his cheek against hers, barely touching her skin. He could feel her breathing and waited for her arms. He wanted to tell her it was all right to love him back. They were alone, secluded, and the moment was solely theirs to share. He closed his eyes and whispered, "Sarah?"

He felt her cheek lean into his. *Please wrap me in your arms.* But Custis wanted more than a moment. He wanted to stay with Sarah forever. Everything in his life seemed to have led back to the woman now standing before him. She had been the common denominator all along.

At this moment, the concern was not of race, boundaries, or laws. His body ached to be close, but she was married with three perfect children. He must have come across as entirely selfish, standing in a sacred place with another man's wife.

"I know what is on your heart, Cus. I said my wedding vows to Lucas because I could not say them to you. I am not some schoolgirl with an infatuated crush on a handsome stranger."

Sarah began to cry. Her voice wavered. "It's always been you. You have been part of my being since we were ten years old. After all these years, you are still the true element of my soul."

Sarah touched his chest, unbuttoned his shirt, and fell into him.

C ustis lay on his back beneath a layer of soft, worn quilts as Sarah rested her head on his bare chest. Late morning sun-rays eased through the window glass and illuminated dust particles pirouetting through the air.

Sarah kept her eyes closed as she whispered, "There is a place I want to take you. Not far from here."

"I'm not leaving here. No other place could be better than this."

"We have to start back. The girls will be home in the afternoon."

"Just five more minutes."

x x x

Sarah took Custis to another part of the property where he had never been. They tied up the horses on Sarah's long line between the trees. She removed the rifle and threw the saddlebag over her shoulder.

"They can stay right here in the shade for a while. It's only a short climb to get there."

The sun was hot as they wound their way through the trees to a plateau of meadow grass. Spread out in front of them was a valley far below. It stretched out as far as they could see and merged into a distant blue mountain range. They stood at the edge of the ridge and felt the warm air escaping the basin below. It blew Sarah's hair and tousled it into messy tresses. Beneath, an eagle flew effortlessly, using the warm thermals to glide. Custis felt completely safe. He was standing above where eagles soared, a place where only angels might fly. No other person in the world could see, touch, or hear him. He cupped his mouth with his hands and screamed out over the cliff, "I love you, Sarah! I have always loved you!"

Sarah laughed and pulled him back, away from the cliff. "Sit down before you fall over the edge."

They both laughed out loud as they sat in the tall grass. Custis leaned over and kissed her cheek. "I really do."

Sarah opened the saddlebag while Custis smashed down the tall grass between them. The bruised grasses bestowed their fragrance, while the surrounding tall stems offered a little sanctuary from the breeze.

"Bread, cheese, and apples."

Custis smiled. "It's perfect."

"See way out there?" Sarah pointed outward. "That's the ranch. You can barely spot the barns. And over there, the one single tree, the dark dot. The cemetery just to the left. I want to be buried next to you and my mother."

Custis nodded. "I'd like that. Together forever. Just little specks from up here. Almost insignificant. But down there, it seems it's the entire world."

"When will you leave, Cus?"

Custis paused. He looked at Sarah and shook his head. "I can't even remember what today is."

"See, it *is* the mountains where we forget to count the days."

They paused and took in the moment. *Forgetting to count the days. Prosaic words for such a profound experience.*

Sarah became still. He watched her smile creep away.

"I'd like to have one more day to help Owen with the harvest. Give your father a hand before I have to leave. I need to get back to Wilson Place. I've got a professorship waiting. When I left there, before Centennial, they said they hoped I'd return someday. I wrote to them on the way here and asked to be reinstated—as their new physics professor. They will be expecting me. And you've got a family waiting for you."

"I know, Cus." Sarah cleared her throat. "I forgot the canteen on the saddle."

Custis jumped up. "I'll get it for you. Be right back, my darling."

As Custis returned to the horses, he noticed a path through the trees. Sarah must come here more than she let on. He checked on the lead line and grabbed the canteen. "You ponies holler if you need anything."

Custis trudged back up the trail and reached the meadow. The grasses moved with the gusts as the bright blue sky above layered the horizon perfectly in half. Sarah must be lying down. He didn't see her. Maybe he had taken too long and she had wandered nearby. He scanned left and right as he returned to the spot near the edge of the cliff. Sarah was lying in the matted grasses. She was partially covered by the clothing she had removed. She lifted her arm and pointed up to the sky.

"A pareidolia. I see a grand ship with sails unfurled, right there."

Custis looked up, squinted, and shaded his eyes with his hand. "I don't see it. Maybe I need your view." He lay down next to Sarah. He wriggled in next to her, reached over, and pulled her on top of him. Her clothing fell away, and her hair hung down. He could feel it tickle against his face. He gathered her hair with his fingers and held it back behind her neck. His eyes examined hers, only inches apart.

"Oh, yes, I see it now. Yes, it looks like the *Queen Anne's Revenge*. I see her masts now, the rigging and figurehead." Then he saw her eyes tear up. He wanted to wipe away all sadness, but it seemed to be an unyielding component.

Custis whispered, "How can this not be real? I have never loved anyone as profoundly as I do you. And I know you love me. You are immensely impassioned and fiercely beautiful, Sarah."

She kissed him deeply. He felt her body weight meld into his. Sarah sighed. "You are the only one who can reach deep down inside of me. I can hold nothing back. You have always been a part of me."

At that moment, everything else in his mind dissolved. Custis was completely immersed in the extraordinary woman before him. He wanted to remember each second, to keep each sense alive and breathing. There, on that mountaintop where angels lived, he wanted time to stand still, never needing to leave, never needing to remember what day it was. Every movement between them was choreographed, as if by a skilled artist. Each touch, sound, and scene was indelibly locked away deep inside.

They rested in each other's arms. Custis breathed in her air and touched her sleeping eyes. "Do you hear that?"

"Hear what?"

"The sound of grass when it collides. The stalks. When I was little, my mother told me angels fly over and use their wings to make the wind. The dry grasses bow to give thanks. The sound of the collision is our notice of humility."

Custis looked up into the sky. "When I hear it, I can't help but close my eyes and listen to its rhythm. It's my place far, far away. Like the sea is for you."

Sarah sat up on her elbow and leaned over Custis. "I've heard the same sound before. When you were at the gate. I heard it then."

"The angels must want us to be together, then."

"When we were little, remember we said our mothers were together, waiting for us?"

"Of course I remember."

"Do you think they're still waiting for us?"

"Yes, I do. Time passes differently in heaven. It's been twenty-six years, and they've probably just blinked their eyes."

Sarah gently rubbed Custis's cheek with her thumb. She looked deep into his eyes. He wanted to cry. "I don't want to let go."

She softly kissed each eyelid.

"We need to get back, Cus. I'm so sorry."

"I know."

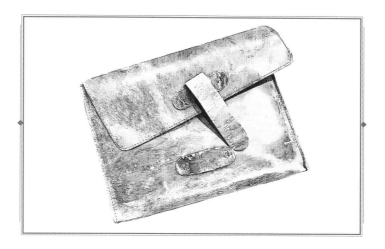

42

The four-point grappling bar required four people to operate—two on the straight line and two to manipulate the hook. A row of wagons, full of loose alfalfa from the fields, lined up under the barn prow. Custis and Owen operated the hook below while Sarah and Martin worked the straight line up in the loft. The barn managed to suffocate the breeze from the south but offered a reprieve from the glaring sun. Custis was wet with sweat, and his leather gloves were wrapped with bandages around both palms.

He ensured the hook was packed with every cast, as a partial load only created an additional lift. With each pull of the line, his mind built a motor and gear unit to hoist the payload vertically, then fifty feet laterally, into the back of the loft. Each heap seemed to get heavier as the day passed. His arm muscles ached, and his neck hurt from constantly looking up to the prow. He couldn't have been happier.

Sarah leaned out the prow and yelled, "Just two more wagons, and we'll have to move to the number-three barn. This one is about full." Just the sight of her standing overhead made him feel a surge of energy burst through his body. She was drenched in sweat, alfalfa scattered in her hair, her face flushed with heat. She looked amazing.

The number-three barn took just over forty wagonloads and the rest of the afternoon to fill halfway. Owen left the north side of the barn empty for the late fall Sudan grass crop.

"I sure am sorry I can't stay and help with that harvest. I need to get back to Ohio to rest. I'm not used to hard labor anymore."

Owen laughed. "I appreciate the work you've given us. Every little bit helps. Sorry about those blisters. You'll need some salve on those palms for sure. Be sure to soak them well tonight. We better get back up to the house. It looks like Martin is pulling the meat out of the pit."

Martin, Layne, and the girls had most of the dinner ready when the sun went down. Outdoor tables had been set out for all the workers and students. The harvest celebration lasted a few more hours until everyone had left, except for Owen and the family. The bonfire waned, log seats had been pulled in closer, and conversation had quieted. Custis watched Sarah from across the pit. Firelight softly lit her face, outlined by the darkness behind her. The fire cracked and popped, sending embers into the darkness above. She held her girls closely as they begged for a story but settled for a song from their grandpa. Sarah sang along and soon was joined by Owen and all three girls. Custis didn't know the words. It didn't matter.

Audrey came around the group and sat next to Custis. She laid her arm across his lap and leaned into his side. Custis wrapped his arm around her shoulder, smiled, and listened to her sing softly. Sarah and Custis locked eyes. In an uninhibited moment, one small, innocent gesture from a child made Custis feel as if the outside world had disappeared. He felt completely at peace. He was in a place meant to be. Custis felt the vibration of Audrey's voice. He looked at her arm across his lap and put his hand on top of hers. Jillian moved next to Owen. He lifted her to his lap as she leaned back on his chest. Jessy sat at her mother's feet as she sang along with her grandfather.

"Can't you stay longer, Mr. Custis?" Audrey whispered.

"I am a teacher, and my students are waiting for me."

The singing died down, and the fire was given back its showcase.

"But you can live here on the ranch and teach at the other school."

"Audrey, Custis teaches at a college in Ohio," Sarah said.

"Then, when I am old enough, I will go to his college."

"Well, I think it's time we get up to the house, girls. Tomorrow will be a busy morning for all of us."

"Tomorrow is Saturday," Jessy said. "We don't have to get up early. You must have forgotten what day it is."

"No, young lady, I have not forgotten. It's been a long, hard day for everyone, and tomorrow is still the harvest. Let's get going now."

"I'll walk you girls home," Owen said. "I don't want any of those crocodiles coming out at you."

Jessy took Owen's hand. "We don't have crocodiles here, silly. Do we, Mommy?"

Custis watched as Owen escorted Sarah and the girls up the hill as they blended effortlessly into the darkness.

x x x

Custis lay awake for most of the night. Lucas needed to go away. It was an impossible, insoluble matter without having excruciating consequences. Three young lives were now involved. The girls worshipped their father and loved their mother. Thoughts spiraled in his head, finally landing in a formulated presentation. The main components were Sarah, the children, Lucas, location, and time. Sarah and Lucas were already growing apart. He was so busy making his way out in the world, so that part of the equation was in progress. By the time the children were young adults, Sarah would divorce him. In the meantime, Custis would purchase land in California, a ranch where Sarah could continue her work. It would be close to a university, where he could teach and maybe the girls would choose to attend. Martin would support and fight for what Sarah wanted, for what truly would make her happy. He could help establish the new ranch. The plan merely needed time—time for the girls to become of age.

In the morning, Sarah would take Custis to the train station. He'd have an hour's ride with her at his side. He silently practiced over and over what he would say.

Custis had breakfast with Martin and Owen. He told Layne goodbye and said he finally had come to terms with forgiving her.

"What are you talking about? Forgiven me for what?"

"For almost killing me years ago . . . with the frying pan!"

"Oh, that. That was a life lesson. You never snuck back into my kitchen again, did you?"

Custis hugged Layne.

"You listen to me, now. Know that you are loved here on this ranch no matter what happens."

"I know, Layne. Please know that I am grateful for all you have done for me." He hugged her again and whispered in her ear. "Thank you for sharing Sarah."

Custis walked outside and set his bag down on the porch steps. He looked at his bandaged hands, white gauze wrapped around the palms. He stretched out his fingers. The balm had eased most of the discomfort. He breathed in the morning air and filled his lungs. He felt his chest rise as confidence filled his mind.

He watched Sarah walk down the hill toward the house and met her halfway. "I spoke with your father, told him how much he meant to me. He's still inside. He said he didn't want to watch me ride away."

"I know how he feels."

"I would like to tell the girls goodbye."

"They'll be coming down soon. Let's get our buggy."

"I've got it all worked out, Sarah. It'll work, I'm sure."

As Sarah and Custis walked toward the barn, they saw a carriage coming up the lane. It crossed under the arch and approached the barn. Sarah waved and started toward the lane. Lucas stepped out and took Sarah into his arms. He kissed her cheek as Sarah hugged him back.

Custis felt the sharp slap of reality hit his face. Two of the most beautiful days in his life were instantly overridden by a man he had hoped to never see again. He watched as Sarah's arms wrapped around him. Custis understood how the embrace felt. He knew the contour of her body and the gentleness of her touch.

"I wanted to surprise you all. I knew we needed more hands for the harvest." He looked at Custis's luggage, then at Custis. "I guess I'm the one who is surprised." Lucas turned to Sarah. "Besides, I missed you and the girls."

"I was about to take Custis back to the train. He came by for a short stay to tell us about his work. He helped with the alfalfa crop."

"I am sorry to have missed your visit." Lucas's words sounded nice enough, but he had no smile. He turned back to the carriage. "Driver, wait. I think we have a fare for you going back into town."

Lucas shook Custis's hand and looked at the bandages.

"We talked him into helping," Sarah said. "I'm afraid we've caused him an acute case of blisters."

"Of course, hard work tends to do that. Custis, you're looking well otherwise."

"Thank you." Custis wanted to wince with the pain of Lucas

squeezing his hand. No, he would take the hurt. "Don't worry, there's still plenty of work to do."

"Sorry things didn't work out up North."

Custis stared at him. It was an odd statement. How did Lucas know things had not worked out? Had word gotten out already? Maybe from Sarah, a telegram. No. Sarah would not have had the time.

Lucas abruptly diverted his focus. "Ah, my girls!" Lucas brushed past Custis and held out his arms to three screamingly excited girls. "I have missed all of you, my princesses!"

"Father, tell Mr. Custis to stay," Audrey said.

"Yes, he needs to stay with us."

"He's afraid of horses. But that's the only thing wrong with him," Jessy said.

"I am sure Mr. Custis has business of his own. Go on, girls. Tell Mr. Custis goodbye, and I will be there in a moment, I promise."

Audrey and Jillian hugged Custis. Jessy shook his hand and said, "I can teach you to ride a horse if you stay. I could do it for two dollars."

"I would love to stay, but I've got work waiting for me in Ohio."

"Go on, girls, I'll be with you in just a moment." Lucas turned and pulled his luggage case from the carriage.

Custis looked at Sarah. Her face was pale. She looked stunned.

Lucas must have noticed as well. "What's wrong, darling?"

"I'm just so surprised to see you. So happy. The girls have been driving us crazy with questions about your return. They have quite the list of things they would like to do with you. You're going to be busy, that's for sure. I'm so glad to have you home safely."

"I'm sure I'm in for a couple of trips into town. Let me help you with your bags, Custis. You need to take care of those hands. Are you still a doctor?"

Lucas took Custis's bags and placed them up in the carriage. Sarah turned and hugged Custis. He felt her tightly against his hollowed chest. He still had so much he wanted to say. He had practiced all night. He had a working plan. Lucas stood next to the carriage, watching and waiting.

"You come back to see us. Let us know how things are in Ohio."

"I will, Sarah. Be sure I won't forget to count the days. It's only time."

Custis walked over to the carriage and stepped up. Lucas leaned into him and said in a quiet voice, "I am not entirely sure of the reason for your visit. Seems you have this uncanny ability to show up when I am not here. This is my family now. It appears you have meddled with my children. That could make a rational man do irrational things. I do not expect to see you again. Do you understand?"

"This is my family as well. You, sir, are the outsider."

Lucas smiled and looked Custis up and down. "And you are not an outsider? Obviously, I am a suitable race. I see you are not much of a chess player, Custis. The game has long been over, and you have lost."

"I try to not use children's game analogies to guide my life."

"See, that is where you have failed. Chess is a game of strategy and skill applied to all battlefield situations. Chess has won and lost wars throughout history. I hope things go better than in New York. Your work, your reputation has been cut down right before your eyes. I might add, in your most illustrious moment." Lucas leaned into Custis. Through his clenched jaw, he quietly articulated, "Check—mate."

Custis knew that Sarah was just out of earshot. He never took his eyes away from Lucas. He felt his insides jitter with adrenaline, his muscles tightening. Pieces of the puzzle ricocheted inside his mind. Lucas was involved with Centennial. He leaned down and looked Lucas directly in the eyes. "You son of a bitch."

Lucas pulled his head away from Custis and grinned. "Yes, that part is true."

Custis watched Lucas walk back to Sarah and put his arm around her. Together, they turned and walked toward their house.

For the second time in his life, Custis wanted to hurt another living being. Rage easily boiled over any scruples left inside. His hands turned into fists filled with hate. New York City had taught him differently. It had toughened him, instilled in him to keep his façade hardened. He was no longer at the mercy of obstacles placed before him, but rather his providence was under the jurisdiction of only himself and God.

"Sarah!" Custis called out. "I forgot to give you my new address." Custis stepped from the buggy, ran up to Sarah, gave her a small address card, and quickly kissed her hand. He looked at Lucas and smiled. "I will see you soon."

Custis turned and jogged back to the buggy. As he rode away, he heard the crackling of the road pebbles beneath the wheels. The birds seemed without song and the wind without breeze, as if both resolved not to like it there anymore. Emotions flooded in and out. He wanted to confront Lucas in front of Sarah. But Lucas could easily deny, explaining away his involvement. Custis's mind worked skillfully. Nothing could be done at this moment. He needed evidence, proof of Lucas's involvement. Then he'd be back.

The carriage stopped next to the train station.

"What do I owe you?" Custis asked.

"Oh, nothing. Mr. Lucas has us on the payroll. We direct bill his office in Raleigh."

"Of course," Custis said under his breath. "Thank you."

Custis pulled his bag out of the buggy. He noticed a thin, soft leather satchel under the seat with an engraved monogram: Rep. P. Lucas. He opened the top, spread it apart, and saw a folded newspaper and miscellaneous business papers belonging to Lucas. "Hmm." *Abandoned property the bastard won't be getting back.* Custis placed the satchel inside of his luggage.

The conductor stood on the platform directly in front of the opened car. His mustache was long and thick, his sideburns bushy gray. As he welcomed people aboard, he tipped his hat at the ladies.

"Good morning."

"Welcome aboard."

"Fine morning."

"Mind the step."

A porter reached down, taking bags from oncoming passengers. Custis waited at the edge of the crowd. He stretched out his bandaged hands and lifted the gauze. Still a spotting of fresh blood beneath. He felt the leather handles of his bags press into the wound as he strapped one around his shoulder and walked into the crowd.

Custis felt like a lost sheep following the herd's movement. He walked up to the car, reached for the metal handrail, and stepped up with one foot. The step made him a head higher. He turned and looked out over the crowd. *Please just let me see her again. Give me a miracle, Lord.*

The conductor looked at Custis. "Not this one. Down the line, down the line. Whites only here."

Custis continued to look out over the crowd. He heard instructions from the conductor but wasn't quite processing what was being said.

"Whites only here. You'll have to get down." This time the voice was firm.

Custis felt the pull on his jacket. His mind snapped back to reality. People were waiting to board. Anxious faces glared at him. "My apologies. I was not paying attention. Sorry, sir."

Custis stepped down and walked off the loading platform until he found his car. He tossed his bags up into the doorway and pulled himself up by the handrail.

He found a seat, stowed his bag tightly against himself, and crafted a plan in his head. Staying in Ohio and getting his professorship back would give him time and money. New York was no longer safe. He'd prove Lucas was behind the Centennial expulsion. Lucas must have planned it for years. Now, it was Custis who would do the revealing to Martin and Sarah. But at what cost? Three young girls were now in the equation. Three young girls who loved the ranch and adored their father.

Custis was spent. The train lugged northward. He forced the thoughts of Sarah from his mind, finally falling into a restless sleep.

Custis woke to a quick jarring and jerking of the train along with the horn blast. It was slowing down and pulling into the next stop. The morning sun was barely up. Custis stood, stretched, and looked at his travel papers. Just a regular stop along the route.

He was able to purchase a ham sandwich and a cup of coffee. Neither worth the money, but it was sustenance in his stomach. The conductor called for the last boarding as Custis opened his case and retrieved the folded newspaper in Lucas's satchel. The back page consisted of miscellaneous articles, notifications, and a couple advertisements. It was several days old, nothing of interest, but it kept his mind from Lucas. He turned the newspaper back to the front and folded it in half. Headlines just above the fold read, *"Local Boy Does Good in Big City."* Custis began to read the first line of the article still above the fold. *North Carolina State Representative Phillip Lucas was instrumental in presenting legislation regarding eminent domain.* Legally taking property from others, usually without fair compensation. What land was Lucas trying to obtain? Or maybe it was the other way around. Lucas was presenting legislation preventing or limiting the government from doing so.

Custis snapped open the newspaper. The article wrapped around a photograph. Three men in black formalwear and white ties.

Custis pulled the newspaper closer. It was Lucas standing between Conrad Langmuir III and Preston.

Custis felt his chest caving in. He fought to control the shock wave reverberating inside. The photograph was taken the night of Custis's party at Centennial. *What was Lucas doing in Manhattan? How did Lucas know Langmuir?*

Custis refocused his eyes and cursorily read the article. He mumbled the words in riffs as if to help him understand. He read it again, this time a little slower.

Custis looked up from the article and strained to recall exactly what had been said that night. A southern delegation. There was a southern delegation Langmuir had mentioned that night. And Sarah stated that Lucas had been in New York for his work. That's how Lucas knew about things not working out.

The article praised Phillip Lucas for his work regarding railway expansion lines between New York through North Carolina and into Atlanta, Georgia. The article explained how new routes would prove to be more efficient, create jobs, and stimulate the economy. Lucas was quoted as saying, "But lastly, a scenic rail route through the most beautiful of all the United States would give those otherwise never to have witnessed it a chance to see the most spectacular part of our country."

Lucas was congratulated along with Conrad Langmuir III, a former politician from New York who was not only pivotal in the development of the line but also financially invested. He and Representative Lucas had worked together for years. Lucas praised Mr. Langmuir as a brilliant campaigner who had been instrumental in his successful election.

The article went on to briefly mention Preston, who would oversee part of the line expansion. Preston had just received a doctorate from Centennial University and was recognized for numerous U.S. patents in current use on campus. Preston Langmuir was currently being celebrated as a "nominee for a Nobel Prize out of Sweden, an inaugural world award of science and humanism that rewards the discoveries that have bestowed the greatest benefit to humankind, for his work in sound radiation."

Custis had not only been betrayed by a friend but also by Lucas, who had managed to infiltrate the Tennison family. From the beginning, it had always been a complex web of deceit, something that may never be completely untangled. Preston, his father, and Lucas—all part of a grand scheme of failure. Why hadn't Lucas just had him killed? Would it have been too hard on Martin and Sarah? It was clear Lucas wanted Custis to fail incrementally to keep him from running back home. Lucas must have somehow crossed paths with Mr. Langmuir years ago while conducting railroad business with Martin. Langmuir had groomed Lucas and was instrumental in his political success. Lucas obliged in return by confiscating land for Langmuir's railroad in the name of eminent domain. Sarah and Martin must have had no idea—that was clear.

The train heaved into movement.

Custis grabbed his bags, leapt down the steps, and out of the train. He ran back to the loading platform, across the deck, and slid into the ticket window. Custis fumbled with his money, finally pulling the correct bills from his wallet, and paid for a ticket back home to the ranch.

"You'll have to wait over there," the ticket master said. "Train won't be coming for another hour and fifty-nine minutes."

Custis paced back and forth, only sitting down for seconds before standing up again. In two hours' time he worked through a series of strategies. He would confront Lucas and show Sarah and Martin hard evidence. Martin could sell the ranch then, and with Sarah and the children, move away from Lucas to California. They could buy property where they all could live, and he and Sarah would raise the children. Lucas was an evil man, capable of even more devastating actions, and theoretically he could do more harm than good toward his own children. Custis could save them a lifetime of false promises, duplicity, and pain from a father who was likely to betray them as well. It all hinged on one factor—whether Martin or Sarah were already aware of Lucas's dealings.

x x x

It wasn't until the next morning that the train arrived back home. Eleven o'clock. Custis rushed to the livery yard carrying one bag on his shoulder and the other at his side. He could see a man inside, mucking out a stall. Custis did not have the time to wait for service. "I need to lease a horse."

"We don't rent out to no negros."

Custis opened his wallet, removed currency, and placed it on the countertop. "Then I shall buy your best horse at twice the going price. That is six hundred dollars."

The man looked at the cash, rubbed his unshaven chin with his hand, and looked Custis up and down. "You pretty fancy, ain't ya?"

"I am sure someone at the saloon across the street would be more than obliged to take the same offer. I am in a hurry, sir."

The man took the cash into his filthy hands. "I got a wagon for hire."

"No. I need a horse."

"Tack is another hundred."

Custis slapped two more bills on the counter and placed his wallet back inside his jacket. The man stuffed the cash into his pants pocket, wiped his nose with the back of his hand, and retrieved a horse.

Custis looked at the mare. "No, she's over twenty years old and won't hold a saddle for long. She can't be more than fourteen-three high." Custis pointed at a different horse. "That one, the gelding."

"But he's feisty."

"I don't care; he's the one I want."

The liveryman grumbled, "Well, don't say I didn't warn ya." He led out the gelding, pointed to a saddle and bridle, and handed the lead rope to Custis.

"Can you keep my bags until I can get back?"

"That'll be another two dollars." He motioned to a dark corner. "Leave 'em there, and I'll make sure they're here for ya. When you coming back?"

"I am unsure."

Custis placed his luggage in the corner, removed the crumpled newspaper, and tucked it inside his jacket. He made sure the bags were buckled closed and set one on top of the other.

"He's just been watered. Here's your bill of sale."

Custis saddled the horse with the skill of an elite horseman. The stirrups and fender were dry and cracked, the horn nearly worn completely through, but the cinch looked good and strong.

Custis mounted the horse, nudged with his legs, and rode out of the stables onto the street. He rode with confidence and proficiency, concentrating not on riding but only on what he would say. He replayed events in his head and formed a cohesive framework of opposition. His last card to be played would be the newspaper.

The horse seemed to know the way to the ranch. Custis had no recall of directing the horse, but he must have along the way. He crossed under the ranch arches and rode up the lane.

Custis tethered his horse on the hitching post next to the barn. The ranch was eerily quiet. He walked through the barn aisles, down one and up the other. He was hoping to find Sarah first, tell her what Lucas had done. He wanted to tell her he would not leave without her this time. He would take her and the children—her father too—to California and buy a new ranch. He listened for voices or the sound of equipment. The stillness was interrupted only by an occasional nicker as he passed by the thoroughbreds. Blood rushing through his veins made him warm, and beads of sweat built up on his face. Directly overhead, a band of rafter pigeons abruptly took to flight. Their united sound of escape sounded panicked and rushed. Custis stopped and looked toward the girders. Just as quickly, stillness returned.

"For someone who is supposed to be so smart, you are very stupid."

It was Lucas, standing in the doorway. A handgun was tucked in his waistband. "I thought you might come back. I saw you riding up the lane. I have already sent a message to the sheriff, expressing my concerns about the possibility of you returning and harming my family." He rested the heel of his hand on the butt of the handgun. His index finger methodically tapped the hammer.

"Are you going to shoot me, Lucas? That's what you really want. I'm surprised you have not already."

"I had to lay my plans first. Now it will be easy to justify the legalities of killing a trespasser attempting to harm my family—my innocent children, mind you."

"Your plan is to kill me before I can get to Martin and Sarah, tell them the truth about you. You don't have to worry about rushing it. I've already written a letter to both of them explaining everything. You know, how you and Langmuir conspired to steal away my discoveries, my machine."

"Why I have no idea what you are talking about. Mr. Langmuir is just a doting father wanting the best for his son. I can certainly relate, can't you? Oh, wait, you're not a father. But thank you for the warning on the mail situation. Easy enough to intercept."

Lucas slowly stepped forward and to the side. Custis followed and stepped in closer. But now, Lucas had changed the plan—it had escalated to murder. Lucas would aim for the gut. Custis's only chance would be to close the distance and knock the gun from Lucas's hand.

"Oh, by the way, Mr. Langmuir was more than happy to learn that you were a negro—and none too happy he was fooled. Well, I put an end to all that, didn't I? You don't know the half of it. I own this property now. Martin signed it over to me. This land is where I shall live out my life with Sarah and my children."

"You manipulated your position and bought your power. You put Langmuir's railroad right through the middle of this ranch by your own corrupt design."

"It was the least I could do. He was so helpful in getting me elected."

Custis had already lost everything. But hearing Lucas boast that he had so cavalierly taken the ranch from Martin and Sarah was unbearable. Custis lost control. He lunged forward as Lucas pulled the gun from his waistband. Both men fell to the ground with Custis landing on top. The gun hit the ground a couple feet away. Custis punched Lucas in the face. Lucas reached for a wooden bucket, grabbed the handle, and swung. It hit Custis on the side of his head, knocking him away. Lucas got to his feet, kicked Custis in the ribs and stomach, then reached down for the gun. Custis swept Lucas's legs from behind. Both men landed hard punches. He pinned Lucas down by his neck while he punched him in the face with his other hand. Custis heard screaming and felt tugging on his shoulders.

"Stop, Custis, stop right now!"

Custis turned and saw Sarah. A punch from Lucas landed solid on the side of his face. Custis lost his grip on Lucas's neck as Sarah pulled him over.

He looked at Sarah. She looked horrified, sobbing, out of control.

"Stop, Custis, I love him. He is my husband. I love only him. You need to leave and never come back!"

"Sarah, you don't know what he's done. It was him. It was Lucas that destroyed me. Lucas stole your land."

Through tears, Sarah screamed, "Leave, Custis. I don't care anymore. Do you hear me? I don't love you. Go, just please go, and leave us. Never come back. It was all a mistake. You can never come back."

Custis stood, trying to maintain his balance. He wiped the blood from his head, then from his mouth. "You don't understand. He has plotted against me for years. How can you do this, Sarah? I love you, Sarah. Please don't do this."

"Because I don't love you. I love Lucas. I chose him! You don't understand, I need him. I need Lucas. It's over, Custis. It will never work. Leave and never, never come back."

Custis stood motionless. He wondered if this was part of the plan, to defuse the situation and save his life. "Now is the time, Sarah. It can all be over, and we can finally be together."

"I love Lucas. He is the father of my children, and I'm staying here on the ranch with him and my girls. It's over, Custis, it's over."

Custis slowly nodded and surrendered. "All right, Sarah. All right." He removed the newspaper from his jacket, dropped it on the ground, and walked away. Custis pulled himself up onto his horse. He watched as Sarah ran back to her house while Lucas stood and straightened his clothing.

x x x

The ride back to town seemed to take hours. Custis felt empty. His history had vanished, and he had been robbed of any future with Sarah. Years of work and discovery had been stolen. But most hurtful of all was Sarah. She was gone forever. This is what she wanted. That is what she said, but it couldn't be true. Lucas had manipulated her thoughts. She was scared. She was afraid it would all come out. That's what Lucas probably told her. There would be publicity and ugly accusations. But in the end, she had made her choice. She had chosen Lucas. It was over.

As Custis rode through town to the livery yard, he watched two young boys playing kickball in the street. One was a little bigger than the other, and both had thick, blond hair with cowlicks. He had flashes of the circus poster, three hate-filled delinquents, and running away as fast as he could. He stopped his horse near the two boys. They looked up at him, one squinting from the sun.

"You must be brothers."

"Yes, sir," the smaller one answered.

Sir. Odd for this town. Maybe it won't be generational.

"You go to school?"

"No, sir, not today—it's Saturday."

Custis dismounted and pulled the reins down to his side. "Here," he said, handing the reins to the older brother. "He's all yours."

The boys quickly looked at one another and grinned. The younger one reached out for the reins, but his brother pulled his arm back. "Daddy said we are not to take things that ain't ours."

"That's a good rule." Custis removed a piece of paper from his pocket. "Here is a bill of sale. He's yours now." He handed over the reins and walked toward the livery. "I don't know what his name is, so you will have to come up with something on your own."

The boys beamed.

Custis walked into the livery and to the corner to retrieve his bags. The liveryman was standing close by. "See, I told ya they'd still be here."

Custis examined the bags. It was obvious the buckles and straps had been opened and the contents riffled. Custis immediately stood back up. He shook his head, tightened his lips, and punched the liveryman square in the mouth.

The man fell backward into the straw and clutched his jaw. "What was that for?"

"Going through my stuff!"

Custis grabbed his bags and left.

PART V

43

1902
OHIO

Walking back into a schoolroom offered nothing except a distant sense of academic function. Old worn desks with scattered, stained chairs sat empty on a single-level floor. Chalk-dusty blackboards in want of new slate rested on questionable legs at the front of the classroom. A faucet dripped slowly into a rust-stained sink, all overlooked by a bank of paint-sealed windows, their hazy glass stingy with light.

Custis set a large box of supplies on the front desk. It rattled with glass beakers and flasks, a sound that offered him a sense of familiarity. He looked around the room. The paint-cracked walls were bare, the cabinets empty, most having lost their doors. He tried opening the windows but had to settle with propping the door. A dusty rag lay on the chalk rail, useless in the fight to clean the blackboard. He scavenged for a small piece of chalk and wrote his name up high. *Professor Custis*. He stepped back and looked at his handwriting. Muscle memory, habit, or maybe denial. He wiped away half of the chalked name with his bare hand and stood facing what was left. *Custis*. A mere moment in time had been given the power to sweep away years of his life and most of his dreams. He reached back up with the tiny piece of chalk and added *Mr.*

Custis took a chair from the corner, placed it behind the desk at the front of the room, and waited. He rubbed his jaw with his hand and remembered his clean-shaven face. It felt odd not to have a mustache. Eleven years of pretending had finally ended. His brief taste of freedom was now overshadowed by loss. No longer was he a beneficiary of complete liberties or benefits. His friendships at Centennial had been deceptive and contrived, and his dream of having a life with Sarah was no longer viable. Her words had been sharp, absolute, and devastating. Two weeks had passed, each day ending with Custis writing letters to Sarah. He'd carefully address and seal each letter, but they were never mailed.

Custis felt the grittiness of the chalk dust on his fingers. He rubbed his hands together and brushed off his pant leg. His clothing was neat and fresh, a red necktie topping off his bright white shirt. He pulled down on his vest and straightened his tie. *Maybe I should take it off. Perhaps it's too formal.* He was accustomed to wearing laboratory coats or leather aprons, and without their security, he felt open and vulnerable.

For the first time in years, Custis sensed his six-foot-three-inch frame in the small room. He felt too prominent for such a claustrophobic space. Even the windows seemed as if they had been lowered by design. The unmatched desks and tabletops reminded him of a storeroom for discarded furniture. There were no rising theatre seats or laboratory workstations. It lacked sound amplification design, soapstone countertops, and Bunsen burners. No gas—*that explains the missing Bunsen burners*. Custis looked around the four walls. *Not even a stupid clock.*

Custis inhaled deeply. How could students learn in such unconducive surroundings? He pulled the pocket watch from his vest and put it on his desk. It was still early, and he had plenty of time to straighten the room. But maybe he shouldn't. He was the stranger coming in midyear. This was their classroom. As threadbare as it was, it belonged to them.

Custis heard muffled voices and footsteps. Laughter and hollering came closer and closer. One by one, the students began to filter in. Some carried tattered books, some loose papers, others nothing. They stared at Custis. Maybe it was his eyes. Some stopped abruptly and were pushed from behind, stacking up one after another. Male and female, all eventually took their seats.

Custis tried to mask his fear, his hands in and out of his pants pockets. He should have taken off his necktie. His insides shook. He couldn't let them know. It was merely a protective mechanism in the brain, simply a temporary emotion—one he wanted to disappear at once.

Custis had never taught such young children. Some must be six years old, others maybe eleven or twelve. It had been a mistake. Custis had craved something different, a distraction from colleges and universities, an escape from any reminders of his failures and limitations. He had turned down the professorship at Wilson Place College, although it would have been a simpler choice. Custis needed something else. Going back to Wilson Place felt exactly like that—going back. But now, rather than bringing forth complex and radical disciplines ready to bust open the world, Custis could safely muddle through rudimentary topics while figuring out what to do with the rest of his life.

392   M. DAY HAMPTON

Custis didn't know what to say. He'd had it all planned out, but now he couldn't remember the lesson plan. He tried to say good morning, but nothing came out. Custis smiled politely and nodded his head as if greeting a stranger on the street.

Custis looked into the eyes inspecting him. *They're all so undeveloped. They look so tiny.* They all stared up at him, except for one boy in the back. Custis felt even taller now. He sat down in his chair at the front of the class, his knees rising higher than the seat. He continued to study the students as stragglers wandered in. *What might their stories be? Were their lives like that of his own? The one in the back, the one avoiding eye contact—had he been told to do so?* Custis wanted to look closer at the boy. Was he just shy, or was he hurt? Or this one, down in front. What was his version of life? And the girl, where would her childhood path lead?

Custis looked at their shoes. Most were worn and scuffed; some were rubbed dark with oil, while others were too small or too large. Custis looked down at his own, polished and thick-soled.

Each student sat quietly. Custis thought of Professor Alger and silently tried to weed out the potential failures. But now, Custis saw no failure. He saw gumption in their eyes, in the way they sat, in the way they held themselves, in the way they watched his every move. *Gumption is the catalyst of all success.* He looked at their faces and imagined all of them sitting in large theatre classrooms filled with equipment, wearing white laboratory coats and surrounded by too many books. He saw them all working with apparatuses, using microscopes, incubators, and scales, measuring liquid in beakers, flasks, and test tubes.

The girl in front removed her scarf, but Custis saw her emerging from a fume hood. A boy toward the back opened his notepad, but Custis envisioned a large, thick chemistry book. Another student tapped a girl's shoulder with his pencil. Custis imagined laboratory partners dressed in white coats and protective gloves. A girl wearing thick glasses evolved into a mature young lady wearing dark protective goggles. The boy in the back, hiding his face, was now deep in thought, concentrating, holding a thick medical journal out in front of him.

Custis stood to his feet and cleared his throat. All eyes were upon him, except for the student in the back of the room. "My name is Mr. Custis. I understand this is the third, fourth, fifth, and sixth grade, and I have been told I have some outstanding students this year."

A hand went up in front.

Custis immediately stopped. *Here we go.* "Yes?"

"You have pretty eyes."

The students giggled.

"So do you. Who knows what the colored part of the eye is called?"

"Gunnar doesn't have an eye. A dog bit him."

Two students immediately turned and looked at the boy in the back of the room.

"You must be Gunnar. I am pleased you are in my class, Gunnar, and it is such an honor to meet my very first student by name. I have waited a long time for this."

Gunnar nodded slowly, then began to turn his head toward Custis but stopped. It was more than just shyness that kept Gunnar from looking forward. Custis felt his tentativeness. *He must be terribly scarred.*

"What about everyone else? I would love to hear about each of you."

Some students squirmed in their seats. Others raised their hands enthusiastically. Custis called on all of them, listening intently. All had stories to tell, except for Gunnar—he kept his to himself.

x x x

Another week passed. Gunnar was habitually the last student to come into the classroom and the last to leave. He sat quietly in the back of the class and stayed away from the other kids unless approached first. Most recesses, he stayed inside, and during lunch, he kept to himself on the side porch. He never looked directly at Custis, always trying to shield the right side of his face.

Custis sat at his undersized desk and collected papers as the students filed out of the room. He corralled the papers with his hands into one neatly stacked pile on the corner of his desk. Gunnar, the last student in the room, placed his paper on the top of the stack.

"They call you the teacher with the glass eyes. But they're not glass. Melanin. Eye color is determined by melanin. The sclera is the white part of the eye. The iris is the color." Gunnar briefly glanced at Custis as he spoke.

Custis was filled with excitement, but he couldn't let it show. He had been waiting for just the right moment to make the first move, giving Gunnar time to feel comfortable.

"My eyes are green, while yours are brown. And it is a handsome brown. I wish mine were like yours. The bright sun seems to bother mine terribly, and they tire so easily under lamplight."

"That's because they're light sensitive. The density of pigment is less than darker eyes. When light hits my dark iris, the higher density in pigment blocks the light rays."

"You are correct, Gunnar. Tell me, how do you know this?"

"I just know. I used to read a lot. But it's hard now. The words all go together."

Custis was surprised at Gunnar's insight. He wanted to smile with delight, but Gunnar might have misinterpreted the gesture as mocking.

"How long has it been like that?"

"Since the dog. Summertime. I don't read anymore. My dad said no more school next year since I can't see the words anyhow. I have to work in the fields. He said God didn't want me to see—that was my punishment for not helping him. But my momma said to him that I could finish this year."

Custis's heart dropped. Gunnar's innocence was interrupted by the circumstance. Custis wanted to help but didn't know how without interfering. He riffled through some papers and pulled one from the pile.

"Gunnar, this is your arithmetic homework. The math problems, can you see them?"

"Yes, but they don't line up like they used to."

Custis pulled out a file from the desk drawer and removed several papers. "These are your spelling sheets. This first word is rhinoceros, but I can't read your writing. Can you spell it?"

Gunnar spelled without hesitation. "R-h-i-n-o-c-e-r-o-s, rhinoceros."

"And the word important, out loud."

"I-m-p-o-r-t-a-n-t o-u-t l-o-u-d."

Custis smiled. "And what is 103 times 77?"

"It depends."

"On what?"

"It depends if you mean one hundred three or one hundred and three. And means a decimal point. 100.3 times 77 is 7,723.1, while 103 times 77 is 7,931."

"And the square root of 24.5 times 2?"

"Seven."

Custis laid the papers on the desk but did not look away from Gunnar. "Has anyone talked with you about depth perception?"

"No."

"Your doctor, when he worked on your face?"

Gunnar took a step back from the desk, turning his body's right side even farther away. "No. He said I won't see anymore and to be glad for one eye, that's all."

"I might be able to help you figure out some things if you'd let me."

"Like what?"

"Well, like depth perception, focusing, and concentrating."

"Am I in trouble?"

"Of course not. I think you are very smart, and together we might be able to make some things easier for you. We just need to make some adjustments. Maybe some explanation of some things a little better, so you understand them as being normal, not wrong."

"I need to go home now."

"All right. I will see you on Monday." Custis offered a handshake.

Gunnar looked at Custis, then at his own hand. Gunnar reached out, fumbled a bit, but eventually offered a firm shake.

"I'm curious, Gunnar. Tell me, why you are always the last to come into class and the last to leave?"

Gunnar stopped and looked down to the threshold. "I trip up the stairs and they laugh, so I wait until everybody's in class. Then I wait until everybody's gone before I go."

Custis heard distant voices in his head. *Go for the eyes. Then we'll see how good he can read.* The memory was still fresh. Custis began to perspire. His face was warm. He needed air. Custis wanted to shake his head, free it from the sounds of the past, but Gunnar was watching.

Custis nodded slowly. "All right," he said softly. "I will see you on Monday, Gunnar. Maybe come in early if you can before everyone else gets here. We can start working on some things together."

The innocence of children felt refreshing. They had no secret plot or greed for notoriety, and never was there a need to wonder or question their motives. They were the lucky ones, supported by their parents, freed from the fields and washhouses and placed into his hands. He had been given seventeen souls to unfold and minds to influence, to make strong enough to navigate a world that seemed to be against them in the first place.

44

Monday morning, Custis was in class by six. He had worked most of the weekend at the school. He had installed a new wooden handrail. It was sanded smooth and painted bright yellow. A sharp line of yellow paint was on the edge of each wooden step leading up to the schoolhouse. Custis's left hand was wrapped with a white gauze bandage, while his right hand was splotched with bright yellow paint. He straightened the tables, tidied up the supplies, and corrected some papers. Custis looked out the window from his desk, moving his head back and forth to give him a better look down the road. He checked his pocket watch. Gunnar should be arriving soon. Custis paced from his desk to the open door and back. He saw a small figure walking toward the schoolhouse.

Custis peeked out the window. Gunnar stopped at the front steps, hesitantly reached out, and fingered the railing. Step by step, slow but precise, Gunnar reached the porch.

Custis quickly moved to his desk and pretended to be correcting papers. As Gunnar entered through the classroom's open door, he looked down at the brightly painted yellow threshold. His step through the door was without pause.

Custis looked up from his work and smiled. "Good morning, Gunnar."

Gunner grinned. He looked back at the threshold. "It's so easy."

"Yes, it can be, but some things will always be difficult. Think of it as a challenge."

Custis extended his right arm. "Concentrate on my hand. Look only at it. Don't look anywhere else. Now slowly reach out and take it. Feel with your fingers, grasp, hold firmly, maintain the grip."

Gunnar slowly reached out, took Custis's hand with agility, and smiled. "I did it."

"Yes, you did, and you did it well."

Gunnar turned to the door and pointed outside.

"Did you do this just for me?"

"Me?"

"I see the paint on your fingers, Mr. Custis."

"Oh, it was still wet when I got here this morning. It surprised me too. Come, sit down. I'd like to talk with you about your eyesight."

Gunnar looked directly at Custis. A scar reached from his right ear to the bridge of his nose. The skin had been sutured closed over the socket where his right eye should have been. Puncture mark scars were on his right jaw and the corner of his lips.

"What happened to your hand?"

Custis pulled up his left hand and remembered the gauze bandage. "Oh, just a cut."

"You're not much of a carpenter, are you?"

"No. Never was, I'm afraid. But that doesn't keep me from trying." Custis smiled. "Tell me more about when you were hurt last summer. What did the doctor say?"

"Some of it I don't remember. It wasn't a real doctor; it was a woman who helped with babies. She said the dog pulled out my eye. That's all I remember."

"I am so sorry you had to go through something like that. You must have been so strong."

"It's all right. It's all over now. It doesn't hurt anymore, mostly."

Gunnar looked directly at Custis. Half of his face was disfigured. The marks were thick and raised. "Will the scars ever go away?"

"Scars are actually a good sign. The body repairs itself by forming scabs and new skin. It means your wound is completely healed."

Gunnar nodded his head. "They said I might die of infection."

"See, scars are a reminder that you lived. You won, Gunnar."

Gunnar smiled. "My daddy has scars." Gunnar held out the palms of his hands. "Right across here on both. From work. The reins from the mules."

Custis watched Gunnar looking at his own bare hands. Gunnar closed his fingers, making fists, then held them down by his side.

"Do you know why you trip and fall, why you spill things?"

"Because I'm a clumsy Cyclops. That's what they call me."

Custis felt reinfected with memory. Sometimes, the injury caused by words far outlived the physical trauma. Custis wanted to grab the boy, pull him in close, and take away all that was bad. He wanted to defend him from others, protect him from callousness, liberate him from what may come. Custis now realized what Martin Tennison must have felt on that dry prairie so long ago.

"No. You are not clumsy. It's because normally, two eyes team up and put things together as one. That's called binocular vision. When one eye is closed or taken away, it's called monocular vision. It makes it difficult to judge the distance of things. Depth perception is the ability to judge how far away or close something is. To throw and catch a ball, pour milk into a cup, reach out to shake someone's hand, and step up or down stairs. With time, all this will become easier. Without two eyes working together, everything is kind of flat. No more dimension, so to speak."

"It makes me dizzy."

"Yes. It affects your balance. Eventually, that may go away after your eye becomes stronger on its own. And you are right-handed, so you're probably right-eye dominant. Now that your left eye is the boss, it's harder to adjust, but not impossible. Your single peripheral vision will play tricks on you. It's supposed to detect only motion, not detail. That's what your mind wants—detail it can't have."

Custis walked over to a box and picked up a handful of dishes. He placed them down on the table. Gunnar looked at the plate, knife and fork, a glass, and a pitcher of water.

"You need to trust what you see. Eating is tricky, as your fork and your glass will be slightly different from where you think it is. Take things slowly and remind yourself that you will very soon get used to where everything is placed. Sometimes you will have to use your touch to see how far away something really is. You're probably already pretty good at that. Just go slow. Casually touch the knife and fork with your opened hand before trying to pick them up. No one will ever notice. Before you pour milk, first put your fingers on the edge, the rim of the cup. Like this. You try it."

Gunnar placed his fingers on the rim.

"Now concentrate on the pitcher. Slowly reach out and get a strong, sure hold on it before lifting. There you go."

Gunnar poured from the pitcher without spilling a drop.

"That's only halfway now. You must concentrate on placing the pitcher back down on the table. You'll get tired, fatigued, as your brain tries to adjust and make the best use of your remaining vision. When you are tired, rest."

Custis removed the dishes and gave Gunnar a pencil and paper. "When you begin to write, feel the pencil tip on the paper. Press the point down on the paper before you start writing. Make sure it's in the correct place, exactly where you want it to be. If it's not, adjust it. All you have to do, Gunnar, is practice, think it through."

Gunnar nodded, smiled, and took his seat in the back of the class.

Throughout the day, Custis noticed a change in Gunnar. He sat up a little straighter, concentrated on his writing, and went outside during the breaks. It was a beginning, a small, tiny step. Custis did not want the day to end.

The rest of the week proved to be even more productive. Each morning Gunnar was the first to arrive, the first to go up the stairs, and the first to go back down, making sure everyone had the opportunity to notice. Custis wanted to keep working with Gunnar, offering advice and providing support, but now the weekend would cause an inconvenient delay.

"Gunnar, can you give me a minute? I'd like to talk with you."

The other children had just about emptied the room. Some were already halfway down the road. Custis waved at the last student, then turned toward Gunnar.

"I just want to check on you, see how you're doing. Have you been practicing at home?"

"Yes, but my daddy gets so angry with me."

"Why do you think he gets mad?"

"I try and work, help him in the fields, but my head gets to hurting so bad, and then I can't help him."

"Such as bad headaches?"

"I guess so."

"Maybe it's the harsh sunlight. Let me see if I can get you a pair of special glasses to protect your eye. Maybe that's all you need. You're doing very well with your studies. I just wanted you to know that I'm proud of you, and I admire how hard you work."

Custis closed the schoolhouse and began his walk home. He watched his footsteps and moved from the dusty rut to the side of the road where the grass was thick but in need of rain. The faces of the children passed back and forth in Custis's head. All of them were smart, some mischievous. Their minds soaked in everything, good and bad. It was a stage in life Custis had not experienced. He had never attended school at such an age. Maybe it was this environment that Custis needed.

He found himself smiling, contemplating not chemical reactions or mathematical theories, not even energy or force. His thoughts were on Gunnar. Ideas bounced in his head, ricocheting from one thing to another. It felt good. He felt needed and challenged again.

Custis opened the door to his boardinghouse room. It was small, confining, and suddenly quite depressing. Room and board had been part of the employment arrangements, along with a modest open account at the corner market, local laundry service, and one Sunday evening meal at the church each week. The Black community could not afford much of a stipend but managed to offer what they could.

On the walk to Sunday dinner, Custis noticed a small, dilapidated house. It was down a lane some distance from the main road. The dwelling was primarily covered in ivy and climbing vines. A rock chimney partially dotted with pink roses stuck up from the north end of the house. Pasture grass had reclaimed the lane bordered by an indication of what remained of a wooden fence. It was near the church and within walking distance of the school.

Custis thought of his room, small and cramped. He stared at the house from a distance. In his mind he envisioned a beautiful country home, fresh white fencing, a sheep, and a big, dumb dog sleeping on a wraparound porch. It was enough. Maybe two rooms, hopefully three. He could have an office, do his cooking, and come in as late as he wished.

Custis shook his head. He couldn't believe where his thoughts had led him. His savings were small. His life's plan had been stolen away, turned upside down, and stomped into the ground. And now, because of one small boy walking up some stairs, Custis was ready to start again. Yes, it all made sense. Centennial had shut hard and locked the door, but now Gunnar was showing him an open window. Centennial could not take away his intelligence, his convictions, or his ambition. He could construct a home, build a small laboratory and workshop for his projects. It would be modest, but it would meet his needs—all except for taking back the past and mending his broken heart.

x x x

Custis arrived at the church. Sunday supper was held out back under the pin oaks and portly maples. Custis had prayed throughout his life. He had prayed for himself and for others, for help and for guidance. Custis was, in fact, still alive, and he had been guided down several paths as he had requested. He had also prayed for patience but only received more things to be patient about. Custis did not attend the church service. God might need a bit of respite from him. However, turning down Sunday's picnic bounty would be foolish.

People were scattered about, some at makeshift tables while others sat comfortably on the ground. The shade from the tree canopy gave a deep, rich hue to Sunday clothes and patchwork quilts. He saw children running barefoot in the thick green grass. *It must feel so soft and cool.* Custis grazed through the potluck dishes, filled his plate, and found an empty table nearby. He had second thoughts about skipping the service and tried to avoid eye contact. He was there for the food, and it was delectable. He lowered his head and savored the food in his mouth. *What did I just eat? It tastes so delicious.* He took another bite. Feeling like a glutton, he'd go back for more just as soon as people stopped looking.

"We didn't see you inside, Mr. Custis, but we're glad you're here amongst us."

"Pastor Griffin." Custis immediately stood as the pastor sat down.

"Please sit, eat; enjoy the meal."

"I haven't tasted food like this for years."

Custis hovered over his plate and took another bite. He suddenly stopped chewing as he sheepishly reached up, removed his hat, and placed it in his lap under the table.

"Have all you want. Looks like you could use it. It'd be rude not to eat what was brought for you."

"No, sir. I appreciate what people are doing for me."

"The children seem to enjoy going to school again. At least that's what their folks tell me. We sure hope you can stay on with us."

Custis nodded his head. He wanted to ask a question but caught himself and stopped. He felt foolish, but oddly he couldn't get the thought of the little dilapidated shack out of his head. "There's a little white house down the street. Looks abandoned. Do you know who owns it?"

"The one right down there, with a long lane leading up to it? Covered with growth? It seems that the earth has reclaimed it, doesn't it?"

Custis nodded his head.

"Used to belong to Old Lady Hill. She died way back. Left it to the church. The preacher before me used it as his house, but after that, it was just abandoned. It was in real bad condition then. I can't imagine what it looks like inside now. We never had the funds to fix it or take care of it."

"Might you sell it?"

"Nope. That was one of the conditions. She never wanted us to sell it. Someday, when we can, we'll burn it down and use the land for growing."

Custis continued to eat.

"You interested in it or something?"

"I need a new place to live. Somewhere where I can stretch out. But I don't have much money."

"We never really had a plan for you other than the boardinghouse. I don't see a problem with you staying there for as long as you like. But it needs a lot of fixing. I don't think any of us can really help much. Money is kind of tight as it is. Some folks are already leaving for the cities. Factory work is steadier than farming."

"I'd like to take a look at it, if you don't mind. It might give me something to do when I'm not at school. It might take my mind off things."

Pastor Griffin looked out over the group of people in the distance. "I'll let the others know what you're doing. Maybe we'll see you *inside* next Sunday?"

Custis tried to smile. He didn't want to make a promise that he didn't plan to keep. He stood and shook hands with the pastor and went back to the potluck for seconds.

✗ ✗ ✗

The house had apparently been painted white at one time, but once Custis looked closer, he realized that was debatable. Until the ivy and roses could be removed, it was hard for him to evaluate. The roofline was sagging, but that could be fixed with a few properly placed trusses. He found the front door, cut an opening in the ivy, and went inside. The house proved to contain two large rooms, a fireplace and a stove, and a covered porch. Critters, most likely raccoons, had ransacked it. It would require new roofing. A third room attached to what was left of the kitchen looked perfect for an office. Custis would need a desk, solid and sturdy. Maybe crafted out of loblolly pine.

Custis felt a spark of energy, a lightness in his movements. After the weekend, he was excited to get to school. Gunnar would be full of joy and share stories of his hard work. Custis waited on the school porch and greeted each student. He expected Gunnar to be early, the first one there. Custis looked down the road and waited as long as he could before starting class.

The day passed slowly. Custis was distracted—it was difficult to conceal. He looked out the window and stayed outside during lunch. It wasn't harvest season, but maybe it was different in Ohio. Gunnar might be sick and could be back tomorrow. Custis thumbed through his journal and confirmed that no one else had been recently ill. Maybe it was his headaches again.

45

Each morning came without Gunnar, and each day left Custis feeling more concerned. He filled his afternoons with work around the Hill house—pulling and cutting away ivy, clearing varmint nests, and cleaning floors. Late in the evenings, he fashioned a pair of sunglasses. Two lenses made of thin glass stained dark with heated dye. A slight coating of metallic oxides—cobalt would have to do—to absorb and reflect the incoming light. He fitted the lenses into a pair of old eyeglass frames he had solicited from the church members. But with all of this, he couldn't tear his thoughts away from Gunnar. It was easy to rationalize a sickness for one or two days, but now it was nearing five.

Custis stood in front of the class. "Does anyone know where Gunnar Lowry lives?"

A girl in front raised her hand. "I do, Mr. Custis. Close to my house but farther down."

"Thank you, Kat. Maybe you can show me. May I accompany you this afternoon?"

Kat nodded enthusiastically as the other students snickered something about being a teacher's pet. But Kat kept her smile.

The afternoon finally came. Custis closed the school and walked down the dirt road next to Kat. "May I carry your books, Kat?"

Kat smiled as if nothing else in the world had ever mattered to her. She was small for her age, bright, and did not stop talking the entire way.

Custis left Kat in front of her home and followed her directions to the Lowry farm. He pulled the sunglasses from his pocket and cleaned them one more time with his shirt. He walked down a long dirt driveway bordered by wood fence rails on either side. One area of the fields had been recently tilled. The earthy perfume smelled like beets freshly pulled from soft, dark garden soil. Custis closed his eyes and breathed it in. He remembered Mary walking from the garden holding a basket of greens. He thought he heard her laughing.

"Hey! You! What are you doing on my property?"

The voice was loud and angry, but distant. Custis popped open his eyes and rapidly looked around. He saw a man stomping from the field. The man strode with purpose toward a broken-down house, never once looking away from Custis.

"You on my property."

Custis waved. He felt the need to clarify that he was indeed a friend and not a foe. Custis sensed a lack of humor in Mr. Lowry's confrontation and kept the thought to himself.

"You must be Mr. Lowry. I'm Mr. Custis, Gunnar's teacher. I only wanted to check on Gunnar. He's been absent all week."

"Get off my property. You got no business here."

Mr. Lowry approached the front step of the house. Custis could see Gunnar standing in the doorway. A woman stepped out the door and guided Gunnar back into the house. Custis was twenty feet away now. There was no need to keep yelling.

Mr. Lowry stood firm. His shirt was wet with sweat and stained deeply by hard work.

"Mr. and Mrs. Lowry, I'm Gunnar's teacher. I was worried about him. He's been gone for a week. I've brought him a pair of sunglasses to help with his eye." Custis proudly held the glasses outward.

Mr. Lowry took off his hat and wiped his forehead with his arm. He placed the sweat-stained hat back on his head, but now it sat a little crooked. "He's fine. He's not gonna go back to school now. So you can leave."

Custis could not imagine a father keeping a son from going to school. But he did not have children, and Gunnar wasn't his. "I'm really sorry to hear that. He's such a smart boy."

"He *was* smart. But now he's all cattywampus."

"He's still smart, Mr. Lowry."

Custis looked over at Mrs. Lowry, who was standing in front of her son.

"Mrs. Lowry, he's the smartest student in the classroom. Smarter than children two grades ahead of him." Custis slowly walked closer.

Mr. Lowry began striding toward Custis. He looked mad. His voice was still brash. "The boy can't see. He can't even get up the stairs to the house without tripping or drink without spilling it all over himself. Half his brain went with his eye. He can't even play ball without getting hit in the face."

"I understand that, Mr. Lowry. But all of that can improve with a little guidance and a lot of practice."

"He's not even good for farming, tilling the land, or working horse straps no more. He turned lazy, can't near get him out of bed, and he can't near remember what he been told. He's as stupid as a rock. So don't go putting ideas in his head, because long after you gone, we still got him."

"I believe it also has something to do with the bright sunlight. It's causing headaches and discomfort. The more he's exposed, the more it looks as if he's tired, exhausted. I'd like him to try these sunglasses."

Lowry had closed the distance between himself and Custis. He was a large man. Not as tall as Custis, but strong-looking, muscular, and weathered by the outdoors.

"He just as well be left alone. All this school is a waste of time now." Lowry looked as if he were about to throw a punch. "He might as well just accept his lot in this life. He ain't nothing now except another mouth to feed."

Custis's insides brewed with anger. He felt his chest rising with each breath. He needed to calm down, but his emotions passed the point of rescue. He had just witnessed a man throwing away the future of his own child. *"Another mouth" is what life comes down to?* Custis felt as if Gunnar had been beaten, then buried alive in a creek. Custis felt his fingers tighten, slowly forming into fists.

"Don't go putting foolishness in his head."

Custis felt the weight of rocks being piled on top of him, the cold water robbing him of air.

Lowry stepped directly in front of Custis. "He can't see the face in front of him."

Custis could smell Lowry's hot breath. It stunk of staleness.

"He'll never be nothing but a half-wit. Do you hear me? He's a half-wit! He can't see nothing coming at him."

Custis's mind exploded. No other thoughts were processed through his brain except for Lowry's words. Custis clenched his teeth, doubling his fists. The glasses dropped to the ground. Custis punched Lowry in the face as hard as he could.

Lowry fell backward to the ground.

Custis towered over Lowry, his fists still clenched. "Bet you didn't see that coming, did you? And you got two eyes." Custis wiped the spit from his mouth, then yelled, "He just needs practice and support, and you're not man enough to even give him that. How much does support cost? Tell me!" Custis picked up the sunglasses and tossed them on Mr. Lowry's chest before turning and briskly walking away. "He's the smartest boy I know!"

In a flash of clarity, Custis realized what he had done. His job would be taken away, and probably his house, so why stop now? He had nothing else to lose. Custis stopped, turned back at Lowry, and screamed, "You're the half-wit!"

Custis hurriedly walked down the lane to his house, his fists still clenched, his feet kicking at rocks. By the time he returned, he had conceded to forfeiting yet another phase of his life. By morning, he would be terminated. He might be arrested. If he survived jail time, he would never be allowed to teach again.

Something was different near the front of his house. Fresh-cut lumber was stacked next to where the porch had been. The old rotten boards had been removed. Three new posts were temporarily holding up the roof. An old claw hammer, a handsaw, and a bucket of used nails were next to the lumber. Custis slowly walked around the supplies. His fists softened and his arms hung gently at his sides. Probably the congregation. Donations from families, giving up their own supplies, leaving it all there in selfless anonymity. Others graciously gave their labor—a gift of appreciation to a man who had just attacked a young boy's father. Custis felt no better than a thief sneaking around under cover of darkness.

Custis gritted his teeth. He didn't know whether to scream or cry, whatever came first. He pulled himself up and lifted his legs to get in the front door. He began tossing clothing into his luggage case. He would leave before being run out of town. Custis stopped. He looked at the clothes in his hands. He had no place to go. The bank was closed, the trains weren't running. He'd finish packing tonight but leave first thing in the morning.

He remained awake for most of the night, running various scenarios through his head: going to jail, being physically thrown out of town, but mostly worried about Gunnar being punished.

Custis woke up in the chair. The late morning was bright, and the air was warm. He jumped to his feet. It was Saturday. There was no school, but the sheriff would be arriving soon, maybe flanked by community members. Custis grabbed his hat and luggage, flung open the front door, and instantly fell to the ground. A drop of two feet that felt like ten from the missing porch. He landed hard and with surprise. Now he really hated his life.

Custis gathered himself and began walking down the lane, toward a new journey, a new chapter of his life. He replayed the events in his head. Maybe the fight hadn't happened. Perhaps it all had been a dream. Custis looked at his right hand. He opened and closed his fist. It was sore, and his knuckles were swollen.

Custis got to the end of the lane and stopped. He set his luggage on the ground and looked down the street both ways. Nothing. He needed to turn himself in. He no longer wanted to run away. The townspeople would probably be at the school. All would be inside, taking a vote on what to do next. They had not taken advantage of him but instead showed him nothing but kindness. Custis removed his hat and combed his hair with his fingers. He rubbed his stubbled face and debated going back to shave. He straightened his clothing, his spine, brushed off his pants, and put his hat back on. He walked toward town, leaving his luggage sitting at the end of the lane.

As Custis approached the front of the school, he saw three figures: two people standing on the porch and one sitting down. This would be the sheriff. He looked up and down the street. There were no others. Custis continued walking forward.

It was Gunnar and his parents.

Gunnar stood next to his father. He was wearing the dark sunglasses. His mother sat on the yellow-striped steps. Custis stopped in front of the stairs and removed his hat. Lowry's face was swollen, and his left eye had turned puffy.

"Mr. Lowry, I need to apologize to you. I should not have lost my temper. I have no idea what took hold of me."

Lowry said nothing.

"Mrs. Lowry, you too. I am very regretful."

Lowry stepped down off the porch, leaving his wife and son behind him. He stared directly at Custis. He took off his hat and rubbed the brim with his fingers. Today he was clean-shaven and wore a fresh white shirt and jacket. "It'd be all right. The missus here, she knocked some sense into me too. It's me needing to apologize to you. Apologize to my son too. You just trying to help." Lowry cleared his throat. "You really think my boy is smart?"

Custis could see his eyes starting to tear. Injury or not, Custis knew he was the cause. "Yes, I do. I know that he is. His intelligence far exceeds anyone I've known of his age."

"I don't want him to end up like me." Lowry held out his hands, exposing deep, thick scars. "God gave me these scars to remind me every day that no boy of mine should ever have to do the same."

Mrs. Lowry stepped from behind her husband. "He's the only one we got. Can't have no more. I told God to take my eyes instead. I prayed hard, too. But God has other plans."

Lowry looked at his wife, then back at Custis.

"It was me that brought home that ol' dog. I never knew a dog could get so mean. I just wanted my boy to have a dog. It's all my fault. I caused all this pain. When he come home crying, it's like me, my own heart is crying inside too." Lowry removed a handkerchief from his pants pocket and wiped his nose. "He *is* smart. More smart than any-one else I know." Lowry placed his hand on Gunnar's shoulder, looked at his face, and smiled. Lowry turned back to Custis. "Would you help me with my boy? Maybe he'd be a teacher like you. Or a fancy lawyer who helps other people like us."

Custis smiled. He wanted to cry out, *I'm a fool.* He was barely able to speak. "Of course, yes, I will. It is not going to be an easy road. He will be a young Black man fighting for his right to an education."

Mrs. Lowry placed her arm around her son, then looked back at Custis.

"It's not fair. We can't magically change other people or snap our fingers and replace the laws. We can only hold true to our own char-acter's mettle. Never allow Gunnar to believe he is less of a man. He's got intelligence, and he's got gumption. And he's got both of you to support him. *Never* underestimate the power of family."

Custis took Lowry's extended hand. He felt the hard callouses and scars as they shook.

Lowry reached out, grabbed Custis's shoulders, and hugged the fool right out of him.

x x x

Each morning for the next two weeks, Custis rushed to the school-house to be with the children. He watched Gunnar's interactions and compared behaviors day to day. At times Gunnar appeared confused, lost his concentration, and looked very tired. He'd rub his eye and sometimes shake his head. Custis kept him after class.

"There is something going on, Gunnar. Can you tell me how you are feeling?"

"I'm good. The glasses help."

"Does your eye hurt sometimes?"

"Just a little bit. I see a black circle, a big dot, and I shake my head to make it go away."

"What else is going on? Do you still have headaches?"

"Sometimes. In the middle of the night even. Then I get sick to my stomach."

"I've noticed you've missed a couple math problems on your papers."

"Sometimes I can't remember, but then the next day I do."

"May I look at your eye and touch your head?"

Gunnar stepped closer and stood still. Custis looked into his eye and felt his head with his fingertips. He softly felt his face and manipulated the scarred skin over the missing eye. His skin felt warm and clammy.

"All right, Gunnar. Thank you. Do you have plans for this evening?"

"I have homework to do, unless you want to change that for me."

Custis smiled. "Mind if I walked home with you today? Talk to your parents?"

"Oh, yes, that would be fun. Then I have someone to talk to all the way home."

"Fine. Maybe we can collect a bouquet of wildflowers along the way for your momma."

"I can't smell flowers anymore, but they're still pretty."

"Can you smell anything?"

"Not anymore. It all went away."

It was more than the sun. Something was terribly wrong.

46

M r. and Mrs. Lowry insisted Custis stay for dinner. Mrs. Lowry placed her wildflower bouquet in the center of the table surrounded by a grateful family. After supper Custis asked if he could speak privately with Gunnar's parents.

"It be all right, Mr. Custis," Mr. Lowry said. "Gunnar can hear what you got to say."

"I've noticed at school that Gunnar is still having issues with his eye. He is still having headaches."

"You said them glasses would most likely fix that."

"I thought they would too. I'm sure they have helped, but I believe something else is wrong now."

Mrs. Lowry sat forward in her chair. "What is wrong?"

"I am not a medical doctor, Mrs. Lowry, but I have been around many sick and hurt people. I have studied medicine—a hobby, I might say—nearly all my life. I think, based on what is happening to Gunnar, his signs and symptomology, he may have some type of interruption near or behind his eye."

"What do you mean? Interruption?" Mr. Lowry looked at his wife, then at his son.

"I'm not a doctor, nor do I have the necessary tools to examine his eye properly. But I think he might have some type of small mass, a tumor that is interfering with his eyesight. The first step is getting him to a real doctor that can take a look."

"Our doctor don't come through here but two times a year, and he's not due 'til harvest."

Mrs. Lowry held Gunnar's arm.

"I'd like to take him to see a doctor friend of mine. He's from Wilson Place College. It's a half day's train ride away."

Mrs. Lowry started to cry.

"It's all right, Momma."

She clasped her hands together and said, "We ain't got the money, not even for the train fare, but we'll sell off all we got."

Mr. Lowry nodded in agreement.

"We don't have to do that just yet, Mrs. Lowry. I've got another plan."

"I've never been on a train before," Gunnar said.

"Wilson Place has a small teaching hospital in general medicine. My friend runs the school and teaches surgery. I want to take Gunnar there for an examination."

"Surgery? Like before? He almost died."

"Gunnar told me about it. I'm not saying he needs surgery for sure, but that type of treatment, performed in a hospital, is different than what was done earlier with Gunnar."

Mr. Lowry abruptly stood, walked over to a tall cabinet, and riffled through the top shelf. He pulled a metal tin down and placed it on the kitchen table. He sat down, opened the lid, and emptied the contents on the tabletop. It was mostly change—lots of coins, a few bills, and three buttons.

"This what we got right now. I been fixin' to sell off one of my old plows. I can get near four dollar, and the crop coming in real good this year." His fingers worked feverishly separating and stacking the coins.

"Mr. Lowry, the train fare—please, let me cover that, and let's just wait and see what a real doctor says."

x x x

The train ride took less than five hours. Custis and Gunnar met with Doctor Lane Carr in his office.

"Professor Custis, so good to see you. I knew you'd be back."

"I could use some help with my friend here, Gunnar Lowry."

"Yes, your telegram said something about a fine young man. Good to meet you, Gunnar."

"Pleased to meet you, sir. Can you fix my eye?"

"I don't know yet, but I certainly hope so. Can my doctors take a look at you? It can sometimes be intimidating, but they're all pretty good fellows."

"Yes, please."

"You are so brave, just like Professor Custis said you were."

An examination took place later in the day. Custis met Doctor Carr back in his office.

"There is a tumor, Custis. We don't know exactly where it is. It appears to be pressing on the optic nerve, maybe. It will start affecting other portions of his brain, speech, and movement. His sense of smell is already disturbed. His temp is up, and there's swelling on his face."

"And can you operate?"

"Not safely. It would all be exploratory once we open the skull."

"Will he still have sight?"

"It would be nice to say he will still be alive. I do not know. If there is a tumor and he does not have the surgery, he will lose sight and maybe his functions before he dies."

"How long before he dies?"

"I don't know. Maybe a year."

"Listen, it's a long story, but I developed a machine using sound radiation. It can map the human body, the interior of the human body, without breaching the skin."

"What are you talking about?"

"I designed and fabricated it at Centennial University in New York. It took over eleven years. It works. It maps out in points. Those are translated into numbers and then converted into graphs, then rendered into a picture. It happens on a living and breathing human body."

"You lost me at 'Centennial.'"

"I told you it's a long story."

"Go on."

"The machine works. It uses sound waves. A transducer sends out high-frequency sounds that humans can't hear and records the echoes, and the waves bounce back to determine the size, shape, and consistency of soft tissues. It would show us where exactly the tumor could be. I can make another. Right here, at this campus. I now know all its working components. It's costly."

"Transducer?"

"Transduction, really. Converting energy from one form to another."

"You need financing."

"Yes."

"That was a statement, not a question. How long will it take you?"

"If I had a team, financing, and all the stars lined up for me, maybe two months."

Doctor Carr leaned back into his chair. "If Gunnar has a tumor on his optic nerve, he may be blind by then. Once that damage has occurred, there is no going back for repair. He could even be in paralysis by then. You don't have months to play with. You may only have weeks, maybe days."

"The exploratory surgery. What will that be like?"

Dr. Carr removed a skull and stand from a display cabinet and placed it on the desk. "Surgery is invasive. I've seen it done before, but never here at Wilson, though. It's brutal. Horrible. Painful. Risky. Anytime you open a man's skull, well, after that, it all depends on God. We worry about infection the most. We haven't the knowledge or technology needed in this field yet."

"His elevated temperature already indicates an infection. What if we don't open up the skull?"

"And just pray over him? I've done that before. We can remove his eye, then eliminate the tumor." He fingered the parietal bone on the specimen. "He'd have no sight, be dependent. What kind of life would that be? Actually, work is being done in Chicago to access the pituitary gland through the nasal passages. Transsphenoidal surgery. We still have to break through bone. They have had no survivors."

"No. Don't go through the skull. Gunnar lost his right eye to a dog attack."

"It must have been horrible. The scarring is massive."

"What I'm saying is, if we go through the empty right orbit, we may be able to take a lateral approach?"

"No, it won't work. We'd have to break the lachrymal and ethmoid bone. Just too hard, and not enough room to see."

Dr. Carr rotated the skull. He intently leaned in close and stared at the temporal bones. It was as if he were in a private conversation with whomever it used to be. The quiet moment lingered effortlessly until Dr. Carr abruptly leaned back in his chair. "You have schematics?"

"Yes, right here in my case."

Dr. Carr scanned the drawings. He tapped the end of a pencil on his lips. He was silent and stared at Custis. Seconds passed, which felt like minutes. Dr. Carr tossed his pencil to his desk. "Make the machine." He jumped to his feet and hurried out his office door.

Custis stood and watched Carr stop in front of another open office. Gunnar stood up from a bench in the hallway.

"Get everyone on the senior team back in here now. And Doctors Nelson, Landry, and Thompson as well. Now, I said." He returned to his desk. "Three weeks—you have three weeks. I'll do all I can for you."

"I'll have to send a telegram to my school, tell them of my absence. And Gunnar's parents."

"You and Gunnar can stay in our dormitory. We need to watch him closely. I'll send two first-year students back to your home. One will temporarily take over your teaching responsibilities, and one can escort Gunnar's parents back here."

Custis stood in astonishment. Custis had always been so guarded with his work and introverted in decision-making. Other than Martin and Sarah, he had depended only upon himself. This must be true fellowship.

"You better get started."

Custis sent a telegram to Pastor Griffin briefly unfolding the events. Custis requested that he contact Mr. and Mrs. Lowry and advise them. *"Medical student coming to escort to Wilson Place by train. Gunnar fine. Temporary teaching replacement for me arriving at school tomorrow. Advise students to cause no harm."*

x x x

The study of general medicine at Wilson Place College was small compared to its better-recognized curriculums in law, teaching, arts and philosophy, and industry. Advanced medical research and science were usually offered only at White universities.

The small laboratory was closed to all but Custis and his assistants. Three students were assigned to obtain supplies: one to Springfield, the other two to Chicago. For days, Custis worked with little sleep. He napped in the laboratory when he could, but mostly he worked straight through the nights. Dr. Carr had given him the brightest medical students and a full complement of pupils from industrial arts. All were committed to the project and worked tirelessly.

Soon, the entire school was active with excitement and anticipation. Law students observed and crafted new patents while architectural students designed fresh graphs and schematics.

Custis knew all their names, always being careful to add honorifics—doctor, specialist, counselor, draftsman, and intern.

"Professor Custis, I never thought we could ever participate in such research," Specialist Hartman said. "Everyone here, sir, well, they believe."

Custis waited for more. *Believe in what?* But that was it. Self-explanatory and it was enough.

Fourteen days passed. Trials began. More students volunteered to be patients. The team discussed modifications, made corrections, and tested and scrapped ideas. On the twenty-second day, a little past midnight, a fourth-year drafting student developed a graph of the brain of a second-year metallurgist.

"Congratulations, Specialist Bentley," Custis yelled. "No sign of cobwebs."

It was time for Gunnar. It took another two days to render the graphs into a rudimentary picture of a living human brain.

Custis sent for Dr. Carr and gathered all his assistants in the laboratory.

Dr. Carr called his third- and fourth-year medical students in for observation. The theatre was at capacity. Quiet . . . all was so quiet.

"Professor Custis, tell us what we are looking at."

"Four graphs, four pictures. Anteroposterior and posteroanterior here, and lateral here. This mark, this mass, represents the left eye. This is bone, here, here, and here."

"Fascinating, mind-boggling. But does it show a tumor?"

"No, I don't think it does. But there is some type of anomaly in the right orbit. I don't know what it is. The patient has had a reoccurring nasal discharge. It could be an abscess."

"That would explain the fever. Maybe so infected it affects the olfaction?"

Custis nodded his head. "Maybe. But it doesn't explain the vision issues in the left eye. Maybe it was the bright sun exposure after all, and this abscess is concurrent, combining both symptomologies."

Custis forced himself back into the mind of a resolute scientist. He could not let his heart overrule his mind. The heart is not smart. The graphs were no longer those of a ten-year-old boy with distraught parents wrapped in fear just down the hallway who had placed all credence in a schoolteacher. He tricked his mind in believing it was an unknown and anonymous male patient requiring intervention. "I think it would be operable. The worst case is the patient dies of infection. We could easily go through the right orbit and extract the abscess if there is one. We don't know the extent of the original trauma, but something is in there. Exploratory surgery, this way, will involve no bone. At the least, we can examine the surrounding real estate and evaluate for another plan if necessary."

Dr. Carr nodded his head. "There's so much scar tissue present, so it won't be easy to plan a safe incision route that'd be best for recovery. We have a young doctor who is magnificent with this type of reconstruction work, far better than anyone I've seen. Doctor Dixon." He looked directly at Custis. "She was trained by a reconstruction surgeon from the war. She has the hands of a miracle worker."

Custis smiled. A female surgeon! "That's exactly what we need."

Dr. Carr stood and put his hands on his hips. "We can do this."

The entire audience began clapping. Custis felt euphoric. He examined the picture again as he sat down on a nearby stool. Eleven years of work now condensed down to twenty-two days. He felt a soft pat on his back. He turned to see who it was, but no one was there. He knew it was his mother. She had been with him all along.

x *x* *x*

Custis met with Gunnar and his parents in a small office. He explained what the doctors believed and told them about the subsequent plan. "They want to operate tomorrow."

Mr. Lowry stood, walked over to the window, and stared outward while Mrs. Lowry stayed seated at the table. She nodded as she looked at Gunnar.

Gunnar stared downward.

"I'm not scared, Mr. Custis."

Custis remembered the exact words he had told Martin the day the town mob arrived at the ranch. In truth, Custis was scared then, and he was scared now.

"I know, Gunnar. You are a brave young man, and Dr. Carr will do everything he can to keep you safe."

"Are you going to be operating too?"

"No. Dr. Carr and his assistants are far more capable. I will be sitting right here next to your momma and daddy."

"I don't want to die. I need to take care of them."

The words penetrated nearly twenty-eight years of memory like a flash of lightning.

Mr. Lowry walked back over to Gunnar. "That's why we doin' this, son, cause we want you to live 'til you old enough to die. If Mr. Custis say this is right, then that's all we need."

✗ ✗ ✗

Dr. Carr removed an abscess the size of a walnut from Gunnar's right orbit. The prognosis was excellent except for the looming threat of infection. Custis was there when Gunnar woke.

"Gunnar, your parents are right here next to the bed. We're all here."

"I can't see. Am I blind? Did they take my eye?"

"No, son. They got your head all wrapped up. Your momma is right here too."

Custis smiled. "Your head is bandaged to protect your eye from unnecessary movement. I think Dr. Carr was afraid you'd be moving and jumping all over the place. Dr. Carr said everything went fine. It was just an infection."

Custis stepped back from the bed and watched Gunnar's parents dote on their son. It was not *just an infection.* It was a transformation for the entire world. A Black college of different disciplines had melded as one community and revolutionized a method of treating and saving lives.

Custis left the room and walked into the hallway. The corridor was crammed with students. Young men and women, wearing what must have been their most worthy attire, silently stood waiting. Down the hall, around the corner, through the hospital's main doors, and onto the quad. Their eyes lingering, anxious but still. Custis tried to smile. He felt his lips tighten, his chin quiver. He nodded and blinked away his pending tears. He stepped back and opened the door. "Mr. Lowry, gently pick up your son and bring him here. Go on, get him."

Mr. Lowry carefully picked up Gunnar and held him in his arms. His mother fussed with a blanket. Custis remembered a dark night, long ago. In the nursery of a hospital, he had picked up Emma and held her dead body in his arms. *We saved one, Emma. We saved one.*

Mr. Lowry carried his son into the hallway. He suddenly stopped and looked down the corridor lined with students.

"What is it, Daddy?"

"Everybody here, son. Everybody, as far as you can see. Just as far as you can see."

Mr. Lowry gently walked forward. He tried to look at each student as they slowly parted way. Each smiled, some nodded, and many touched Gunnar's arm. The only sound was the soft shuffling of shoe soles on the tile floor.

x x x

Custis met with Dr. Carr back in his office. Congratulations, relief, and excitement filled each man.

"I want you to stay here at the college. Make your machines, continue this research."

"I appreciate that, Lane."

Dr. Carr paused and cleared his throat. He sounded solemn. "Without your sound radiation apparatus, I would have killed him, Custis. I would have opened the skull. I was so sure it was a tumor behind his eye."

"You are a fantastic doctor and a great leader. I have no doubt you and this college can proceed on your own. I can't stay. You have all my schematics, research papers, theories—everything you need to go forward. Most importantly, you have experienced student doctors with firsthand crafting, building, and operating knowledge. You'll have to compete with Centennial now. They will have the patent. I've made a few changes and improvements that may help you avoid litigation. It may be a long haul, but they will not want the publicity."

"You'd give up all your work, your life's passion? Just walk away? After everything you must have gone through?"

"I've written to the Royal Swedish Academy of Sciences and

explained how Centennial stole the machine from me. I've sent them proof, and I will continue to fight. Gunnar's records will offer even more evidence. I want Wilson Place to be the vanguard in sound radiation.

"This road I've chosen has cost me more than you could imagine. I chose to deny who I was just so I could be accepted. I changed my identity, who I was on the outside. It changed me on the inside as well. At first, I was ashamed. After a while, it was impowering. Then it became rather ironic. There I was, amongst some of the brightest men in the world, who had no idea they were consorting with a Black man. It was all a big deception. Most of my little students believe it as well. And the girls. They seem the most oppressed. I'm not walking away from anything. I'm walking toward something else I need to do. I'm going back to my kids. I need them and have so much to do. The work and possibilities are boundless. They make me happy."

Saying the words out loud was invigorating. Custis was not leaving something behind, but rather, he believed his machine had opened another door.

47

The school had multiplied in size several times over. Most of the funding came from alumni, local Black churches, and small premiums from the government for various patents that Custis had filed.

The classrooms had been divided into fewer grades, giving the students more individualized attention. Small classroom buildings were constructed behind the main schoolhouse as funds became available. Custis was one of eleven teachers now. Some said it was because of Custis's leadership and determination that the school had turned into a model institute around the Midwest. The publicity did not come without struggles and complications.

Threats of violence stirred fear among the school faculty. Intimidation flowed rampant into the homes and families of the pupils. The passing of each school year brought more hostility. Desks, chairs, files, and books were seized in the dark of night, then burned in front of the school. The students returned to class bringing chairs, stools, and tables from their own homes. Drunken bigots could neither seize nor destroy their love for learning, nor their courage and resilience.

Groups of White men became more brazen. Now, in the light of day, the attackers were armed and setting fires around the school. Outwardly, Custis always remained calm. Teachers fled with their students as Custis directed them to safety.

"Go there, that way, and run as fast as you can." He pointed in the direction, sometimes turning the child physically. "Hold hands. Help each other and run."

The attackers descended upon a single classroom building and blocked the exit. Fire from their thrown torches lapped up the exterior wall as smoke rose over the roofline. Custis heard the screams from the children inside. He rushed to the back side of the building. Children emerged from a high transom window and dropped to the ground. He grabbed their legs, lowered them down, and felt the children's fear as they clutched his arms. Some were crying, but most were wordless, and all were terrified. "It'll be all right. Just run to the others." One after another came through the window.

He heard the teacher's voice, "That's all of them."

"Go back and check one more time. Quickly! Check in the lower cabinets and under the desks."

Custis looked at the children running away. They would be safe now. He could hear the hate-fueled mob screaming, chanting, and laughing from around the front of the building. Smoke was coming out of the transom window. Another child appeared in the window frame. Custis reached up, grabbed his arms, and brought him down.

"You're all right now." The boy would not let go of Custis. "Can you run for me?"

The child shook his head and gripped even tighter.

Custis heard the teacher inside. "I can't get out—I can't get through."

Custis screamed at the other teachers in the distance. "I need help! Help!"

Miss Baker came running. Right behind her was Mr. Cullum. Miss Baker pried the boy's hands away and held him in her arms.

Custis yelled up at the window. "Are you on a chair, a stool?"

The voice replied from inside, "Yes, but I can't pull myself up."

Custis motioned for Mr. Cullum. "Help lift me."

Mr. Cullum braced himself under the window, interlocked his fingers, and hoisted Custis upward. Custis grasped the window frame and pulled himself halfway through. His belly rested on the pane. He saw the teacher reaching upward to the window. Flames were inside the front wall and burning the ceiling.

"Jennah, grab my hands, and I'll pull you through."

"I can't do it. I tried."

"Give me your hands now and hold on to me."

Custis pulled Jennah upward. He lost grip, and she fell back to the floor. Custis slid through the window and landed awkwardly on the floor. Smoke was filling the room. He coughed and tried to cover his face with his jacket. Jennah was struggling to breathe. He pulled a table closer and then placed a stool on the tabletop. Jennah reached for the window as Custis lifted and pushed her through. Custis heard a whimper from behind. Someone was crying. He scanned the smoke-filled room. All the cupboard doors were open. It was clear under the desks. There was no one else. He heard the cry again. Custis crawled beneath the layer of smoke to the opposite side of the classroom. He looked in the back of the opened broom closet. A small girl huddled in the back, behind the buckets and brooms. She looked petrified. Her eyes were wide open, unblinking.

"I'm going to carry you out now. It's time we leave here and return with the others."

The girl shook her head and pushed back tighter into the corner.

"Come on, honey, let's go find your momma."

Custis lifted the girl from the cabinet, held her tightly, and raised her to the window. He heard several voices from outside screaming at him to get out. "One more, here she comes." Custis loosened his grip and allowed the girl to fall into the hands of those below. He pulled himself up and through the window. Custis dropped toward the ground and into the arms of teachers and parents. They pulled at him and wanted him to run away.

"No!" Custis stood firm.

Custis felt rage inside, seething to explode. It was as if he had the strength of one hundred men fighting without tangled webs of deceit, dark nights, or trickery. It was no longer about himself or making a machine. It was about the ramifications of senseless and horrifying acts of intimidation, terror, and murder. It was about children and their right to have an education. It was about humanity.

Custis looked at his colleagues. Fear must have consumed their minds, but their eyes revealed something else. He felt his fury transforming into a different command of those hundred men inside of him.

Custis turned. He walked instinctively toward the mob and didn't stop until he stood between them and the front of the burning school-room. Rising torches, brandished guns, and wielded clubs had lost their power over him. Custis was no longer afraid. He thought he may have gone insane, but he didn't care. He unclenched his fists and looked at the face of each man before him. The attackers stood firm, their eyes alive with blaze.

Ugly voices came from within the mob.

"Get out of our town!"

"You have no business teachin' here!"

Custis yelled loud and clear. "I will not! No matter what you burn, these children will continue to learn. You can take my life! But soon, it will be you outnumbered by those who do not believe in hatred or murder, and *you* will be held to account."

An empty liquor bottle landed at his feet. Custis didn't flinch but gently raised his arms as if stopping a runaway horse. The heat from the flames stung his back. He slowly closed his eyes. He was a little boy again and was standing next to the chicken coop. The three delinquents appeared out of the darkness. They might burn his house down, but this time he would protect and save his mother. He saw himself run inside, wake his momma, and escape through a loose wall board at the back of the house. He held her hand and led her away. Custis heard her voice—*Stand tall, son; we always be together.*

Custis felt someone at his side. It was Cullum, shadowed by Jennah and Miss Baker. Others followed. Parents joined in along with older students. Men, women, and children of the community stood silently together. They locked arms and formed a human barrier to protect the rest of the school. Some onlookers and nearby neighbors walked around the befuddled mob and joined Custis, standing three and four deep. One by one, the attackers dropped their torches and turned away.

χ χ χ

The rebuilding had taken over a year, and replacing equipment and supplies took several more. New buildings and rooms were designed with surreptitious exits, low windows, and vaulted ceilings that would act as a natural vent. At times, the hypervigilance that Custis's role demanded took its toll. Lack of sleep and fifteen-hour days were common. Classroom work stretched into administration duties, which evolved into government correspondence requesting more support. Sometimes, he wondered how much longer he could go on. But with each successful graduation, seeing some students go on to higher education, he was more determined than ever to continue his work.

After the war, Custis established programs through the church for families orphaned and widowed from the war itself, and then from the Spanish flu that had followed. The school was closed for over a year. Custis worked in clinics throughout the area in the meantime. It reiterated his purpose and direction, a reaffirmation of humanity.

Over the years, Custis had managed to rebuild his entire home. His garden was large and helped feed families in need. He taught students about ground and crop rotation, fertilizer, compost, and the difference between good and harmful insects. One room of his home was a dedicated library where he tutored adults on the weekends. They were, for the most part, parents of students or members of the congregation— his community.

On Sunday afternoons, after the church supper, Custis diverted himself to the river. He had a favorite place, one he did not share and that not many seemed to know about, less than a half mile from his home. There, the world could be deafened by the powerful sound of crashing water. He scouted its rocky edges and fly-fished its ceaseless whirlpools.

Each cast would take him away, deeper into thought, reminiscing about a different time. Muscle memory worked the line back and forth, casting away bitterness and leaving sweetness in its place. He thought of running through grass-covered prairies, the renewing smell of fresh-cut alfalfa, the enchantment of reading by candlelight, sweat-lathered horses at the end of a hard day's work, the reward of twinkling night skies . . . and Sarah. She'd be fifty-nine years old. Her children would be grown. She could even have grandchildren by now.

The sound of thrashing through the brush came from behind.

Custis instantly turned. He lowered his rod and reel to the ground and stepped away from the river's edge. It sounded like someone walking, someone coming closer. Custis was alone and outside of his community. Responding to sporadic threats had been part of his life, but now he was without help, without witnesses. Dangly tree limbs and brambles lined the edge of the woods. He wanted to run, but the water flow made it difficult to determine the intruder's direction.

Then nothing.

Custis held his breath and waited. He felt vulnerable, an easy target. Memories from long ago burst back into his head. He was ten years old again, cloaked in moon shadows and twisted trees. But now, the bright sunlight would offer no favor. He lowered himself to his haunches and listened. He thought he heard a click of a gun. He could spring to the left and roll behind the boulders, or go to the right, dive into the water, and be swept away downstream to safety. He removed his fishing creel—the weight of the fish might slow him down.

The sound of footsteps busting through dry leaves and twigs got closer. A movement came from the edge of the tree line. Custis stared silently at a figure of a man. A white shirt, dark pants, and hat. He carried a coat over his arm, and it looked as if he struggled to keep his balance on the uneven ground. He appeared to be older, maybe seventy. Gray hair protruded from beneath the brim of his hat.

48

The old man looked at Custis and stopped. "Ah, Professor Custis."

He looked familiar. He even sounded familiar.

"I've been looking for you most of the day. The pastor from the church said I might find you here. I saw a car parked up on the roadway at the bridge. Thought it might be yours."

Custis was bewildered. *Who is this old White man stumbling and thrashing through the woods?* Custis stood up fully and took a step toward the man. Obviously, not a foe. Custis began to smile, then grinned as big as possible. "Professor Alger? Professor Alger!"

"Yes. I'm afraid I'm not as young as I used to be. I might have overdone it, exerted myself."

"What on earth are you doing here?"

Both men hugged, patted one another on the back, and hugged again.

"You look wonderful, Professor Alger. I can't believe you found me way out here!"

"I waited at your house for as long as I could. I decided I needed the exercise and came looking for you. Actually, I became famished," he admitted a bit sheepishly.

"I just can't believe it. Let me get my rod, and we'll head back home." Custis gathered his gear and held up his creel. "Fresh trout for dinner!"

Custis helped Professor Alger back up the embankment, through the woods, and back to his car. "It's just a short drive back. Why are you here?"

"Plenty of time for that. I've left my bag at your home. I hope you don't mind."

"Of course not. How long can you stay? I've got the room."

Custis wanted to hear everything about Professor Alger's life. He listened intently and couldn't stop smiling. He was with an old friend again.

"Shortly after you left Centennial, I left as well. I moved my family to Stanford University, where we still reside. Both my children attended. Such a beautiful place, California is. Some days, when I feel I have nothing to do, I lecture at the university. It seems to keep me on my toes.

"I lost my Gladisen in 1919 to influenza after the war ended. I miss her every hour of my life. Ellis has children of his own. He is an architect, like his great-grandmother in Greece. He lives in Chicago."

"And my sweet Caroline?"

Professor Alger smiled as they pulled into the driveway. "She is still your princess. She has only fond memories of you. She lives in Sweden with her husband but will move out West to California next year. She claims I'm 'getting on' and wants to be nearby. She writes for newspapers and magazines. Her husband is a businessman. In shipping."

Custis got the professor settled in the spare bedroom, fixed him a drink, and prepared the fish and fresh vegetables over an open fire pit behind the house.

"I try to cook outside, especially fish. Smells up my books inside."

"You have a beautiful home, *Renauldos*. I hope you don't mind me still calling you Renauldos. You will always be Renauldos to me. It's so peaceful here. I have read about your work in lower education. Quite astounding. It's being implemented in California."

"I had submitted my studies and my methodologies to the State of Ohio, hoping to procure additional funding. At first, they wanted nothing to do with it. They said it would cause too much controversy because of its panoptic scope of Black children. But it was not about Black children. It was about children and their abilities to learn. I resubmitted it several times, and finally it reached the right person. They saw the value, the potential, and asked my permission for publication. The children gave me a reason to go on. I was doubtful at first, giving up a professorship. But the children. . . . There was a boy named Gunnar who made the difference. After he graduated, he went on to college. I lost contact with him and his family after the war. Gunnar Lowry. Wonder where he is now."

"I have something for you, Renauldos. It's inside."

"Let's go inside then. The bugs will be out in force soon."

Custis and the professor shared more stories. The professor retrieved his satchel, removed an envelope, and handed it to Custis.

"What is this?" Custis removed a small photograph. He stared at it as he leaned back into his chair. The envelope fell to the floor. The photograph was old and faded, worn at the edges, and creased nearly in half. He turned it over—Sarah's handwriting: *To Cus*. A million memories flooded his mind. In an instant, the pain of leaving her years ago was fresh again. He stared at the photograph. He tried to blink away the tears.

"I don't . . . I don't understand." Custis cleared his throat. "Where did you get this?"

"The day you left, I went to your laboratory. I gathered what I could without being obvious. I found that in your desk. I knew they would destroy anything they could. I know what happened, Renauldos. I know what they did to you."

Custis could not muster words through his emotions.

"I went before the university board shortly after you left. I fought but lost the battle. Sometimes that is what happens when standing up to bullies, so it never really is a failure, is it? The university destroyed any record of you attending or working there. I should have contacted you then, but I couldn't bear to give you more bad news. Preston Langmuir IV was given credit for everything. That is why I moved my family as far away as I could. It was a good change, and I have you to thank. My Gladisen's only wish was that her children could choose their own lives."

Custis sat silently. He wanted to know everything. His body trembled. He had locked away that part of his life long ago.

"Your friend, Mr. Andoe, gave me your letter. I still have it, back home. After he and his wife moved to the Oregon Coast, we kept in contact. He had a good life there with his wife for many years."

"He must have died by now."

"Yes. But he was happy. He wrote about being friends with a dolphin named Dolly and something about being with happy fish amongst the redwoods."

Custis smiled. "Happy salmon."

"Yes, I believe that is correct. He once wrote to me that during those beautiful sunsets over the ocean, he toasted good wishes to you.

He wished you could see the Pacific Ocean. It is so distinct from the Atlantic."

Both smiled. Custis wanted to laugh, but he couldn't get through the sadness.

"Each year, I wrote to the Royal Swedish Academy of Sciences and presented your case. Your friends McKay and Marshall did as well. They *are* your friends. I even submitted the papers I took from your laboratory as proof. Three years ago, Caroline and I traveled to Sweden. Caroline appeared in front of the committee. She went over all the evidence again. We thought that a fresh voice might be heard. I don't think they were used to hearing from a woman. It brought quite the attention. She is brilliant, you know. That is where she met her husband. We are not sure if it was her presentation or her position and access to major newspaper outlets that affected change."

"What are you talking about, Professor?"

"Renauldos, the committee rescinded all association with Preston Langmuir and has reinstated you. You, Renauldos, are a nominee for a Nobel Prize. Mr. Langmuir never actually won the prize. The original nomination will hold, and you are the rightful entrant. History will show Ronald Custis the First as the official nominee for the Nobel Prize in the mechanics of sound radiation in 1901. You stand as one of the first of the Nobel Prize nominees, honored for the greatest benefit to humankind. Your machine, Custis, has opened up a whole new study. Its mechanical application was even used during the war, as a passive sonar system. The possibilities will be endless."

"I stopped writing the Nobel Committee about six years ago. I finally gave up. I followed what was happening in medicine but had no idea about the sonar."

"Yes. Its foundation has bifurcated and diverged into several fields."

Custis slowly shook his head in disbelief. "So, for twenty-four years, you fought for me?"

"Twenty-two, actually. It took me just short of two years after that to find you. We assumed we could find you at Wilson Place. Through correspondence, we finally learned you had turned down a professorship years ago. I learned about your colleague, Doctor Lane Carr. He was the catalyst behind Wilson Place Medical School."

"Yes, I gave the school everything I had on sound radiation. Even built another prototype with new modifications."

"The university expanded into a medical research center. Dr. Carr passed several years ago, and the school eventually lost track of you. During the war, it was nearly impossible to travel. We actually thought you might have enlisted. We checked with all branches of the military. That took longer than the war itself. Then, my Gladisen. It took all I had just to stay alive myself. After the war, McKay traveled to Ohio looking for you. Then several years later, one of his Ohio contacts sent him an article regarding your school and its successes. Many people championed you, Renauldos. We had quite the delegation. All the letters are on file. They will be kept forever. Even a letter from Mr. Andoe."

"I'm amazed. It's not real."

"It *is* real. There is more. Centennial University has agreed to host a ceremony of sorts. They requested no publicity."

"I'm trying to absorb all this, but my first inclination is not positive."

"I would think not. Chancellor Adams is long gone. In fact, the entire board has been replaced through attrition. Caroline took the liberty to advise the new board that publicity would come one way or the other, and it would be up to them to decide what kind."

"Caroline?"

"Yes. She's quite the litigator, it turns out. They also agreed, at the persistence of Marshall, to open their campus to more diversification."

"Marshall?"

"Yes. Marshall located numerous commentaries on the success rate of the students and the subsequent paragon schools. Your students,

Renauldos. I'm afraid the articles were not all positive. Others did not like your influence on the school systems that followed. You must have fought so many uphill battles."

"Yes. We still are. We had anonymous donations to rebuild. The burning of the school took place in broad daylight. It was an act by few, stopped by many. No one was killed, thank the Lord."

"Cowards will continue to be cowards. Seems like there is no shortage of ignorance."

Custis looked at Professor Alger. He was now an old man—frail but still bursting with poise.

"The university and Nobel committee hope to make a presentation in the campus theatre as early as next month. Caroline and Ellis have already made arrangements."

"I'm still in disbelief. It will be so strange being on the campus again. Marshall and McKay—I never really knew if they had been part of Preston's scheme. They were my friends all along."

"Yes, they are. Think of it, Renauldos. Think of what Centennial has been forced to concede. Maybe my granddaughter will someday graduate from there. It is because of you. The Nobel committee, they are finally righting a wrong. If you have doubts, and rightfully so, just know what you have already accomplished for our collective humanity. And you showed grace and humility while doing so. Not many others in this world could have done the same."

Custis tried to grasp the information and keep it in logical formation. "Professor, so many people believed in me. All these years. I need to go back."

49

1925
MANHATTAN, NEW YORK

Professor Alger waited for Custis outside the entrance of Centennial University. The same ornamental black wrought iron gates stood closed between two sentinel stone columns. Custis stopped and touched the cold black iron with his fingertips.

The two men, dressed in tails and top hats, looked up at the towering gates. Professor Alger cleared his throat. "The university now allows a nominal admittance of Black students. Still very segregated, but it is change." He smiled, took a step back, and nodded to his friend.

Custis cautiously pushed open the left gate, then the right.

"Ferrous metal," Professor Alger said. "Once called holy metal from its use in the crusades for its inflexible and unyielding strength. Now, with but a finger it has been harnessed."

The two men stepped through the threshold. Custis paused, looked back at the opened gates, and said, "Let's leave them that way."

Together, they walked familiar sidewalks until reaching a side door of the main auditorium. Dimly lit hallways wound around to the backstage.

"I'd like you to meet the chancellor, Renauldos."

Custis followed the professor through cramped spaces, passing the stage crew along the way. The backstage was softly illuminated by floor lighting. Tuxedo-dressed men gathered in small huddles and sipped from long-stemmed glasses while holding fresh cigars. The long-drawn velvet curtain muffled the chatter and commotion from the audience. Custis brushed up against the drapery. He felt its softness. A single piece of material now separated Custis from what he had struggled and fought to achieve for most of his life.

Professor Alger approached a group of men. "Renauldos, this is the new chancellor." The man turned and faced Custis. Professor Alger continued, "Chancellor Marshall."

Professor Alger chuckled as Custis's mouth dropped open.

Custis smiled as big as possible. "Eugene Marshall, the same Eugene Marshall who tried to drunk-ski off the roof of the laboratory?"

"The same! My God, look at you, old man."

They shook hands and embraced with a strong hug and hard pats on the back.

"When did you become the chancellor?"

"Came back here after you left. It took me seven years to work my way up to chancellor. Someone had to tidy things up for you." Marshall laughed. "Really, I got tired of traveling all over the world. It's bigger than I thought. Family first, you know. I came back and settled down and helped raise my own children rather than hire nannies. Loved every minute of it, too. Maybe I can retire now that we've got you straightened out. I'm proud of you, brother."

"Where's McKay?"

"McKay couldn't make it, but he sends his regards. Works for the State Department in Washington. He's in the Netherlands. Had something to do with the peace treaty with Turkey."

"Guess stealing that stove from Simpson University didn't come up in his background."

"I think it's why the government wanted him, actually."

"It's good to see you."

"The same, my friend. See you afterward."

Professor Alger retook Custis's arm. "There's someone else I want you to meet."

He turned Custis around. A Black man stood in the back, dressed in a black tuxedo and white tie. He stepped from the darkened hall. He was tall and fit, and wearing a black patch across his right eye. His smile was broad and confident.

"Mr. Custis," the man said as he extended his hand. "Do you remember me, Mr. Custis?"

The sight of Gunnar Lowry went straight to Custis's heart. A man stood where Custis's mind still saw a little boy, too scared to speak. "Of course I remember you. I think of you often. I'm just in shock. Your parents?"

"They are doing well. We live in Indianapolis. I was able to move them off the farm, take care of them, and do a bit of traveling. Can you imagine that? My parents, who never planned to leave a small parcel of land in Ohio, have seen places they only dreamed of. They're in the audience. My father can't wait to see you at the reception."

Professor Alger stepped in. "Mr. Lowry earned his juris doctor degree from Harvard Law."

Custis could not speak. If he did, he would surely burst into tears. He grabbed Gunnar and hugged him intensely. "Gunnar, the impact you and your parents had on me! They made me feel as if I could make a difference in this world. You gave me the strength I needed at a time when I thought I had no more strength to give."

Professor Alger patted Custis on his back. "Oh, dear, it's about to start. I'll be sitting up on the stage with you. Caroline and Ellis are in the second row. She'll be the one wearing a tiara, just for you. Said she wanted you to know she was out there."

Custis peeked out the side of the stage. The room was packed. The balcony looked crowded as well. "Suddenly I'm not feeling well. This is more than I anticipated."

Professor Alger walked onto the stage with Custis. Marshall was at the podium. The room erupted in applause. The sound of clicking cameras burst through the darkened auditorium. Custis sat down next to the professor within a group of men he did not know. The stage lights blinded him. He squinted and blinked, trying to adjust. Marshall was speaking. His words echoed through the hall. The audience laughed and clapped. The room fell silent, but people were still clapping, still laughing. Hundreds of memories flickered in his head. A small boy with a wish, a young man with an impossible dream, and now a man being named as a nominee for the world-renowned Nobel Prize. He looked down at his hands clasped together on his lap. Another set of hands in his. A girl. Sarah's hands.

Chancellor Marshall introduced Professor Alger. Professor Alger bumped his shoulder into Custis, waking him from his reverie. Custis clapped his hands as the sound returned to the room. Professor Alger leaned down and whispered to Custis. "Remember, Renauldos, it is a very rare blessing for a man to be able to see what he has done."

Professor Alger thanked the university and committees. He spoke kindly of Custis, the project, the work, and the tenacity of others. He introduced Custis as Professor Ronald Custis the First.

Cameras were raised. People clapped. The audience stood. Custis found himself standing behind the podium. His eyes adjusted. There was Caroline, and beside her must've been Ellis. He focused on Caroline, on the glinting of her tiara. Behind her, a man. In the fourth row. Gunnar, and his parents on either side. All standing and clapping. He saw former students and professors. Above in the balcony, flashes of people looking down at the stage below.

Custis trembled. He hoped his voice would hold steady, and he turned and looked back toward Professor Alger. He glimpsed a woman down the darkened hallway. His mother. He heard her voice. *I brought you another book from Mrs. Cramer.* Custis smiled. *You did nothing wrong that night, son. I'm so proud of you.* He blinked his eyes, and the image was gone. Custis felt a warmth come over his entire body. He felt his shoulders lift, his legs strengthen, his mind clear. His mother had been with him all along just like Emma had said.

The applause began to wane, and people took their seats. Custis had to speak now. He held on to the podium with both hands. He shifted his weight back and forth and kept reminding himself to keep his knees unlocked. The room was silent. They were waiting.

Custis cleared his throat. "I started this project because I wanted to make a difference in someone else's life, but I'm afraid that's not what happened. In fact, the difference was made in mine."

A single methodical clap came from above. *Clap. Clap. Clap.*

"Well done, Professor, well done." A man's voice, satirical and brash, came from the side of the balcony.

Custis shaded his eyes with his hands. He looked up into the glare. The audience shifted and murmured. They must have been looking as well.

"The great and fabulous Renauldos Custis the First, from Greece, is it?"

Custis could see the figure of the man. He leaned over the balcony railing, looking below. Professor Alger stood up and walked to the podium. He motioned for the house lights.

"Ah, Professor Alger," the voice said. "I see all your tireless struggles have finally paid off."

The house lights came on in a burst of five switches, with the last illuminating the man above. Preston Langmuir.

"You know, I had to sneak in. Professor Alger, you must have overlooked my invitation. I was all dressed up and had nowhere to go."

The sight of Preston was sickening. His voice sharply reverberated inside Custis's head. For a moment, Custis believed it was his imagination again. But this time, other people were reacting to Preston as well. The vision was real.

Preston put on his black top hat and pulled himself up onto the railing. He was wearing a long dinner coat, black trousers, and tie. He sat on the cap rail and dangled his legs over the edge of the balcony. The patent leather finish on his shoes shone in the light. He drank from a champagne glass, tilted his head back, and lost his hat. Preston giggled, regained his balance, and kicked off his shoes. "I don't like these, either." The shoes fell below and landed with sharp thuds below, one hitting a man on his arm.

Custis stepped from behind the podium and stood at the edge of the stage. *You bastard.* He hated this man. He hated him for what he had done, and he hated him for what he was doing.

"Preston, please get down. It's over; it's all over."

A man approached Preston from the side. Preston held up his hand. "Please don't. I will have no qualms about pushing you over the edge." The man backed away.

"Please, Preston. Just come down and talk with me."

"Oh, now, Renauldos. What would you like to say? Sorry that you took everything away from me? Sorry that Father told me how disappointed he was? Or sorry that his son is a drunkard? Which is it, Custis?"

Custis heard something different in his voice. This time, it was more than Preston's need for attention and success, more than his own need to fill his narcissistic mind. The game was over. Preston had failed. His world had dissolved, personally and publicly.

Marshall ran offstage and bolted up the staircase leading to the balcony. The top railing could not have been more than four inches wide. The fall would be over twenty feet. Preston leaned back and forth. The audience below became restless. Some panicked and pushed people out of the way. Caroline and Ellis reached out and guided others to the side. The front and side doors of the auditorium opened, and people rushed to get out. The reporters with their all-consuming cameras added to the chaos.

Preston raised his voice over the sound of the crowd. "Funny how life turns out. All the work I did for you, Custis. Being your guinea pig in the experiments. Or did you forget?"

"Come down and talk with me. I owe so much to you, Preston. Please step down. You're going to get hurt or injure someone else. You don't want to hurt anyone else, do you?"

"Dear, dear Renauldos. Please do not pacify me. You won, Custis!"

Marshall reached the back of the balcony. He eased toward the railing as Preston focused on Custis below. Carefully and quietly, each step deliberate, closer and closer.

"Every time I thought it was over, you just kept coming back for more. There was no stopping you."

"It doesn't matter anymore, Preston. It's all over; it happened so long ago."

"You were my father's special project, a favor for a favor. And I was charged with making it happen. And I did for many years. Until this, this circus of old men trying to make amends for their racist, bigoted behaviors. But now, everything has been taken away. I was going to be the next railroad ambassador for Nova Scotia trade. Father promised. Then, who knows where that would have led. Maybe a senate seat?"

Custis pulled a piece of paper from his jacket pocket. He held it up in the air. "Look, Preston. I have acknowledged you here in my speech. It was because of you, your help with the experiments, all your support. Come down, and I will show you my speech."

"No. It appears it is entirely too late. My father—" Preston paused. "He doesn't even know what father means. He raised me with casual disinterest. I told him about Emma, by the way. You know what he said?"

"It doesn't matter what he said. It all so irrelevant now. You got to see your daughter, Preston, your daughter. In the end, you took care of her the best you could at the time. Come down for her—come down for Emma."

"I told him she died. 'One less urchin to suck off the tit of society.' Funny thing is, I could have been a real father, but he even took that away from me."

Custis jumped down from the stage into the audience section. He tried to keep his eyes on Preston as he motioned for the audience beneath the balcony to move more quickly. "Preston, I never told you that she is an angel. Emma. She is with my mother. I went back to her. She spoke to me and told me not to be afraid. Come down for her."

Preston released the champagne glass, shattering on the floor below. Preston stood up on the rail. "I will tell you what I will do for you, dear boy." He held his arms out horizontally, tilted his head back, and closed his eyes. "I hereby, being of sound mind and body, donate said body to the furtherance of science."

Preston leaned forward.

Marshall rushed toward the railing.

As Preston fell headfirst, Marshall lurched with open arms but only managed to grab Preston's lower leg. Marshall fell over the railing. With one arm, Marshall grabbed on to the top rail and hung over the balcony as Preston slipped through his grip. Screams filled the room. Preston landed on a row of fixed chairs near Custis. His back was broken, his head nearly decapitated.

50

C ustis had not been in the chancellor's office in almost thirty years. The clock had been replaced by a functioning window that looked out over the campus. Photographs on the bureau opposite the desk showed Marshall's wife and children. Custis looked out the window to the stairs below. The sun was beginning to rise as Marshall shook the police inspector's hand. Custis walked back to the sofa and sat down carefully, hoping not to wake Professor Alger on the other end.

Custis had removed his tie and jacket and scrubbed his face. He had been able to wash himself, and the dark spots of dried blood on the front of his white shirt were the only evidence that something horrible had happened.

Marshall stepped through the door and sat at his desk. He looked exhausted. The professor stirred awake and sat up straight. "The inspector assured me that everything is in order. He said the press has agreed not to print any photographs of the body. Preston's father has been notified, of course. I will be meeting with the board this evening."

Marshall took a deep breath. "I'm just thankful no one else was injured. I'm so sorry this happened, Custis. It was supposed to be such a glorious time for you."

"It only bothers me because everyone came from so far away. I'm sure it was a hardship for some."

"I think we all could use some rest now. How long will you be in town?"

"I have another night at the hotel. Then, I'm not sure."

"Professor? What about you?" Marshall asked.

"Caroline and Ellis are already on their way home. I'm scheduled to leave tomorrow afternoon."

Marshall sat back in his chair. "Let's all go and get some rest. Regroup tomorrow. Meet in the cafeteria for breakfast."

Custis shook his head. "Last night's ceremony was an exception to the rule. Today, your Black students are still segregated in your cafeteria. I cannot have breakfast with you."

"You will tomorrow. Let them fire me. It's about time I retire anyway."

x x x

Long tables with tins full of food stretched across the cafeteria. The room was loud with chatter rising above the sound of clanking plates, glasses, and silverware. Marshall, Custis, and the professor walked in and stood in line. Each picked up a plate, choosing their food without much thought or enthusiasm. By the time they found a seat, the room had become quiet with all eyes upon the Black man sitting among the Whites.

Marshall stood back up and addressed the room. His voice was firm and direct. "This is Professor Ronald Custis. He has just been reinstated as a Nobel Prize nominee for his work in 1901 that involved the mechanics of sound radiation. More importantly, he is my friend. Anyone with a problem with that, I suggest you leave. Anyone?" He looked around the room. In a calmer voice, he added, "And Professor Alger, from Stanford University."

The students slowly turned back to their respective tables, and the clanking and chatter commenced again.

Marshall jabbed at the food with his fork. "I can't remember last eating in the cafeteria."

"That must be the reason it got quiet then." A smile flickered at the corners of Custis's mouth.

"This food is terrible," Marshall said.

"I disagree." Custis stuffed his mouth.

A hand appeared in front of Custis. He heard a voice. "I just wanted to meet you, sir," a student said.

Custis tried to smile, but his mouth was bulging with food. He shook the student's hand and returned to his plate. Another hand appeared in front of Custis. "It is an honor, Professor Custis. One of the very first Nobel nominees in history. Your discovery helped win the war."

Custis took the hand and looked up. A line of students wrapped around the room. Custis stood to his feet and greeted each student. Professor Alger gave up counting at twenty-nine and finished his breakfast.

"It seems as if he has quite the fan club now. You look like a proud papa, Marshall."

"I am, Professor. I am."

"Though judging by the gender disparity, it appears you still have more work to do."

Marshall's smile did not waver, and his eyes did not leave Custis. "My daughter is seven years old. She wants to fly aeroplanes. Can you imagine that? She'll need a degree. Engineering, physics. Figure I have ten, eleven years to get this place straightened out and ready for her."

"Those are some soaring ambitions for both of you."

"I suppose this is what keeps us going." Marshall glanced at the professor. "You know, the tiny bit of good that comes with all the bad."

"It does seem tiny now, but in the end, it could change the course of history for many others. I like to think of it as a ten to one ratio— for every ten things gone wrong, if one goes right, then you are making progress."

"I'll keep that in mind, Professor."

A man approached Marshall, bent down, and whispered in his ear. Marshall nodded, and the man left. "Let's collect Custis. Someone outside is insisting on meeting him."

Marshall and Professor Alger approached Custis, who was still talking with some students. "Professor Custis, excuse me. I have someone in my office wanting to see you."

Custis gave his regards to the remaining students and left the cafeteria. On the walk to the administration building, the campus was alive with activity. Students bustled along the walkways, some giving way, tipping their hats, and saying, "Good day, sir."

"I don't recall anyone doing that to old man Adams," Custis said.

Marshall snickered. "Well, they're not doing that to me. It's you, Custis. They're acknowledging you."

Custis stopped. A burst of memories swirled in his head. A young boy selling eggs, stepping from the sidewalks, diverting his eyes, yielding to others as they passed by. "For me?"

The professor touched Custis's arm. "They are not stepping away because society expects it of them. They are stepping away out of respect for you."

Custis tried to process these new behaviors and reactions toward him. He was no longer pretending to be someone he was not. He was Ronald Custis the First, a Black man in a predominantly White institution. In this moment, a better world seemed possible for the people for whom he might have paved the way. The adrenaline made him queasy. Custis slowed and held his stomach.

"Are you all right, Renauldos?"

"I think it must be the sausage."

As they entered the administration lobby, three people stood to their feet: Gunnar Lowry and his parents. Custis reached out and hugged Gunnar. "I am so sorry you had to witness something so horrific."

"That's not why we are here, Mr. Custis. My father and mother insisted."

"Mr. and Mrs. Lowry. It's so good to see you, and I am so terribly sorry for what happened."

"My wife and I wanted to meet with you. I, well, *we* wanted to thank you. We wanted you to know, well, the other night, your speech. You said you wanted to make a difference for others, and you made a difference for us. You saved my little boy. You saved me. My eyes have seen things that my heart once said were impossible."

"We have three beautiful grandbabies." Mrs. Lowry wiped away her tears. "You opened the door for Gunnar, and he has opened the world to us, and for all of the other people he has worked with."

"It's because of you two, your support and love," Custis managed to say.

Gunnar handed Custis a book. It looked new. "I wanted you to have this. It's a book I wrote. A textbook that is now used in law schools."

Custis gently opened the cover. *Business Law*, by Gunnar Lowry, Esq.

"It's probably a bit boring for you, but I wanted you to have it."

"I will keep it forever."

"We have to get off to our train," Gunnar said.

Custis walked the three to the gate and returned to Marshall's office. Custis closed the door and found the closest chair. "I have to sit down for a while."

Professor Alger laughed. "You know, a man sometimes never knows what he has truly accomplished until he gets to heaven. Again, you are one of the fortunate."

Custis was spent. He held his head in his hands. His eyes were tired and dry. It felt as if his cognizant thoughts had nowhere to go.

Marshall said, "There's something else, Custis."

"I'm not sure I can process anything else."

"No, this is good. I would . . . I mean . . . the entire board would like to offer you a professorship here. You are welcome to work as you like."

Other than having Sarah, it was all that Custis had dreamt about since being a small boy. The university was finally opening its doors, and Custis could lead the way for others. He thought of Wilson Place and could not help but compare its impetuses and foundations with those of Centennial. Here at Centennial, his work could continue. The possibilities would be endless.

"I appreciate that more than you know. It would be an honor to work for you, my friend. But if I return to teaching, it will be with elementary children, where I can make a real difference. And besides, I've decided to go back home . . . to my real home."

Custis had spent thirty-five years away from the ranch. He had followed the course he had been given and had made a difference in the world. Those changes would go on and some he would never know. But there was one profound regret he had carried for twenty-five years.

"I've got some unfinished life I need to square away, figure out why things happened the way they did. I am sure I have some apologies to offer, amends to make. I have witnessed death and have felt death. Life is so brief, after all. It's just too damn short."

1925

NORTH CAROLINA

Custis stopped his automobile under the ranch entrance. He turned off the engine and listened: not a sound. The motor's constant roar and the nonstop wind of riding in an open car had temporarily desensitized his hearing. He took off his cap and wiped his forehead, then shook his head and pulled at his ears. Nothing. He opened and closed his mouth and wiggled his jaw.

Custis felt raw. His mind was exhausted. Driving for days, he had relived his life. He wanted to erase the bad, leaving only the good. It was over—the tireless pursuits, the struggles and pain. No more punishing himself for things he could not change. Sometimes gratefulness does not rise to the top until you understand that letting go is not as hard as holding on to something you could never really have. Now, there was certainty in his life. He was grateful to God for being alive, the world did not play fair, and he would love Sarah for the rest of his life.

Sarah had been married for thirty-four years. At times in his life, Custis had wanted to kill Lucas. He had even imagined the means. But now, hatred no longer governed his thoughts. He felt nothing for Lucas, not even fear.

Custis looked at the house in the distance, just past the roofline of the barn. He could now hear a midday lilting whistle from a red-breasted thrush, a breeze from the south, and a squeak from the rusty hooks holding the Tennison Ranch signboard overhead. Custis looked up at the arch. It was worn and in need of paint. He looked at the sign, gently swaying back and forth.

Is that a yes or no, Lord? Looks the same to me. He started the engine and drove slowly toward the closure of twenty-four years.

The ranch looked lonely. The fields were overgrown with grasses. Cattle were scattered leisurely about, while the absence of thorough-breds made the ranch seem quiet. Custis parked in front of the barn. He stepped from the vehicle and looked about. There was no one around. The main house looked a bit rundown. Only one rocking chair still sat on the front porch. The doors and windows were closed. It should have been opened to let in the breeze. It wasn't quite right, not the way it used to be.

Custis walked up to Sarah's house. Two automobiles were in the drive. Through the screen door, he could see that the front door was open. Chairs and a table were on the porch. Fresh flowers in a vase sat on the railing—Sarah's routine. Custis's heart raced with determination to continue forward with each step up onto the porch. He tried to remember what he had planned to say. It depended on who he would greet first. He hadn't heard himself talk for over five days. He rubbed his throat and wondered how three years must have felt for little Sarah. Maybe he had no more voice. He needed to turn around.

A figure inside the house moved, just behind the screen door. "Can I help you?" came a man's voice.

It must be Lucas. "Lucas?" Custis's throat was rough and dry.

"No. Owen."

The screen door opened. "Owen?"

"Yes. Owen Brannon. How can I help you?"

"It's Custis."

Owen looked surprised. A smile came to his face. "Oh, dear Lord. Custis!" Owen reached out and hugged Custis. He took him by the shoulders and brought him in for another embrace. "I can't believe it's you. Come in. Please come in. You look good."

"I came to see Sarah. Lucas, really. He said he'd kill me if I ever came back. Well, I'm back."

"Come in, please. Don't worry about Lucas. He's gone."

Gone. Gone for right now? Or dead? Is that why the ranch looks so different? But where's Sarah?

Custis followed Owen inside the house. He passed through a foyer, down a short hallway, and into a living room. The home was decorated and nicely arranged. Photographs were beautifully framed and positioned all around the room. Some sat on tables while others were arranged on walls. Custis stared at a painting of Sarah and her father which hung over the mantle.

"She's so beautiful. How is Martin? His house looked closed up."

"He's still with us. Lives at the house. We had to hire a full-time nurse for him. He's starting to decline."

"Lucas? You said he's been gone? Sarah, is she home? In town, or probably out working in the fields?"

"Sit down, Custis, please."

Custis sat down on the sofa across from the fireplace. He looked at the painting and smiled. "She has the best little glint in her eyes. Always did."

"Custis." Owen's face washed pale. His eyes drooped and filled with tears. He cleared his throat. "We lost Sarah. She died in the first part of this year."

Custis heard the words. He felt his body going limp. He looked up at the painting. He felt the emptiness, his insides imploding, colliding together, and turning to negative air. He stopped breathing. "What did you say?"

"Cancer. Last year. We did all we could."

Custis fell back into the sofa. His eyes opened wide. "It's not true. Please tell me it's not true." He felt adrenaline rushing from his stomach to his head. A sickness filled his insides; his muscles tightened and pulled him forward.

Owen said nothing. He sat across from Custis and lowered his head.

"Lucas divorced her shortly after you left last time, and he moved away. He rarely saw his girls again. I'm sorry, Custis."

"But why didn't she let me know? Why didn't she write?" Custis wiped the tears from his face. He could not stop crying. He could barely speak. "Why didn't she tell me?"

"She wanted to, Custis, but she couldn't. And the cancer, she didn't want you to watch her die like she watched her mother wither away to nothing."

Custis couldn't breathe. He had to stand up. He turned in a stiff circle and collapsed back on the couch. He shook his head. Sarah was dead. That wasn't supposed to have happened. It couldn't really be true.

Owen looked over at Custis. "I married Sarah. We took care of the girls. We had a child ourselves, a girl. We raised all four girls together." Owen wiped away his tears again.

Custis wanted to curl up and disappear. He felt a horrific scream trapped inside, unable to get out. He should have stayed. He should have fought to keep Sarah. He should have done a lot of things differently.

Time seemed to have stopped.

Owen poured two drinks and handed one to Custis.

"Where'd you get this?"

"Martin stored kegs of it away, down in the basement, right before Prohibition started. He always had an uncanny ability to predict things. And he was right on this one for sure."

Owen looked up at the painting over the mantle. "I still weep. On this side of heaven, it's all right if we do. Pretty sure we're supposed to, anyway. But Sarah looked just like this painting before she got so sick. She's smiling up there, not crying like us. She has no more pain. No more tears. She's waiting for us."

They sat in the house for more than an hour, neither saying more than a few words. "Stay right here for as long as you like, Custis. I know this is a shock for you."

"Where are the girls?"

"Jillian is living in Charlotte, married with two of her own. Audrey lives nearby. She and her husband have taken up the work at the university. They teach agriculture sciences together. Audrey runs the lab. And Jessy, she's in veterinary school in Chicago. The only female in her class. She wants to come back home, here, and practice."

"And your daughter, the fourth?"

"She's a mathematician. She's brilliant."

Custis felt as if he had regained a portion of his mind. He had finally stopped crying. Maybe it was the whiskey. "And Martin? How is he doing without Sarah?"

"A part of Martin died with her. He was so brokenhearted. The girls all stayed around as long as they could. They come when they can, spend time with him. It's so hard now. His mind is going. Dementia. Mornings seem to be the best, when he is fresh."

"I'd like to go see him."

"I can take you over there. He may not remember you. Come morning, it will be different. He's nearly eighty-one now. He loved you, Custis. Loved you like his own son."

"He is a good man. Far better than anyone I have ever met."

"I'm sorry for all that you have gone through. I have grown to hate the power other people have over all of us.

"Come, let's get some fresh air, walk over to the house."

Custis stood up and followed Owen. He stopped, reached down, and picked up a framed photograph from a side table.

"That's Jessy."

"That's what I guessed. The three dogs, lamb, and cat gave it away."

"Here is Jillian and her family." Owen handed him another frame.

"She's beautiful. Looks like her mother, doesn't she?"

They walked into the hallway. Custis looked at the framed pictures hanging on the wall as he passed by. "This must be Audrey."

Owen smiled. "Yes. And her husband."

Custis looked at another photograph hanging next to Audrey's. The girl in the photograph had dark hair, unlike her sisters. Owen's daughter. Custis focused on the girl's eyes. They were brilliant and crystal clear. "She's quite beautiful." Custis tilted his head. He felt mesmerized, sensed by something he could not label. "The contrast and brilliance make her eyes translucent. Maybe the exposure. Are they blue like her mother's? What is her name?"

He felt Owen stepping back.

Custis turned and looked at Owen, then back at the photograph. He took a step closer and touched the photograph as if he could feel her smooth skin on his fingertips. He wanted to feel the warmth of her smile, the softness of her hair. But it was only cold, hard glass protecting a young girl from the truth.

"Sarah named her Loraine."

He stared at it, frozen, unable to speak as his mind traveled back in time. He was home from college, the harvest, the rides out to the new property with Sarah. "Loraine. That was my mother's name."

"I know."

She resembled Custis, with the same eyes and high cheekbones.

Owen stood and waited. "She has bright green eyes, just like yours."

Owen lowered his head. He cleared his throat and began to weep. "She's your daughter, Custis, but I'm the only dad she knows. She knows nothing of you being her father. I love her more than life itself. I love all the girls as if they were my very own."

Custis looked at Owen. He felt his own broken heart collapsing. His legs would crumble at any moment. In Owen's eyes, he saw a father's love consumed by a father's fear.

"How can I meet her? Will I be able to meet my daughter?"

Owen trembled as he looked at Custis. His voice quivered.

"I can't lose her now, Custis. It will be so hard on her. I can't lose any of the girls. We deceived them. Every adult they trusted lied to them. They'll feel duped and irrelevant, maybe rightfully so. This is horrible. Just by learning that their grandpa knew all along, they'll be crushed. They could even be angry with their mother and live with unresolved questions for the rest of their lives. I can't let that happen."

"Is there no way to introduce me as a family friend? The older girls must still remember me coming to the ranch and working the harvest. Why can't I just be me? The boy that Martin raised, and we won't tell her anything different?"

"It would just be more a devastating tangle of web. We lied in the first place to protect the girls, and Sarah. Adding on more lies after the fact would be inexcusable."

Custis lowered his head and closed his eyes. He pressed his lips together and breathed in deeply. He cleared his throat and nodded.

Custis looked back up at the photograph. "What about Lucas? Is that why he left her, because of Loraine, abandoned her?"

Owen nodded. "He knew Sarah was in love with you. He stayed

until Loraine was born." Owen stopped, waited, and took a deep breath. "After he saw that baby, he left the next day. He told Sarah that she had embarrassed him beyond repair. He didn't want a colored child or a wife that slept with a colored man. I didn't want her or the other girls growing up without a father. I convinced Sarah to marry me. Martin agreed that it would be best for the girls. I loved her so much. But it was always you she thought about, her whole life. You were her soul mate. You were her true love. Oh, she loved me enough, I suppose. I told her that it didn't matter that I wasn't her first choice. We were such good friends. I loved her, and we pretended the baby was mine."

"Why didn't Sarah let me know? Why didn't Martin send for me?"

Owen paused and looked directly at Custis. His face was blank, his eyes still. Custis wondered if the conversation was over.

"It was Lucas." Owen's voice went limp. "He threatened to go to court, take the girls away from her if she ever tried to get you back. Martin contacted just about every attorney on the East Coast. No one would take the case. All of them said the same thing. Lucas would be awarded the children without a doubt. They said that a White man with a Black woman was not unheard of. But a Black man with a White woman was seen as rape, or even proof beyond doubt that the woman was duly insane and unable to care for children. Lucas was evil."

Custis reached for a nearby chair as Owen sat down on the lower steps of the staircase. Custis rested his head in his hands, then wiped away his tears with his fingertips.

"The day you left, the last time, to go back to Ohio, after the harvest, when Lucas came home early, I knew something was wrong. I could feel it. All the girls were with Martin, up at the main house. They said their daddy told them to stay with Martin for a while. I went to check on Sarah. I started to go up on the porch, then I heard Lucas. He called her awful names, just awful. I heard him say he would have her committed. I didn't completely understand what was going on. I didn't confront Lucas. He would have fired me. I needed to be here on the ranch so I could protect her and the girls. After a while, I figured it out.

"Then when you came back a couple days later, I heard the commotion in the barn. You and Lucas fighting. Then I heard Sarah. Screaming, screaming at you to leave and never come back. By the time I got through the stalls you had already gotten to your horse.

"I can still see Sarah's face when she told me the whole story later on. She was so scared. Sarah couldn't take the chance of losing her girls. Then when Lucas found out Sarah was pregnant, he knew the baby wasn't his. Sarah said that Lucas threatened to take the child, put it in an orphanage in another state, never to be seen again. And he could have, too. She thought about going public, ruining Lucas, his political reputation, but in the end, she'd still lose the children.

"It nearly killed her, Custis. Lucas was a vile man. I could have killed him myself, with my bare hands. Maybe I should have. Sarah lived in fear every day, worrying that she'd lose her daughters. The stress finally caught up to her. They don't know what causes cancer, but I think it was living with the stress and worry every day. Lucas slowly killed her, day by day."

Custis wept. So many emotions, too strong to manage. He was full of regret, filled with anger about things he could not control. In a way, he was even mad at Sarah. She hadn't married Custis because he wasn't the father of her first child. But then, to have to allow another man to raise a daughter who was not his own—it must have shattered her.

"By the time Loraine turned of age, it was too late. So much time had passed. Sarah wrote you letters, Custis. She just couldn't mail them. It was about Loraine then. She only knew me as her father. Even after the girls were grown and gone, Sarah was afraid Lucas would tell them the truth just to hurt everyone out of spite and turn the girls against their mother. Sarah couldn't imagine what it would do to Loraine.

Jillian had gotten married and had a son. So then another little heart would be involved."

Custis held his head and rubbed his temples. It must have been torturous for Sarah to make such impossible decisions, to go against her own beliefs. She had been so strong to keep her children together, to be able to raise them into beautiful souls.

"Sarah loved her grandson, David Martin. When he was born, Sarah teased and said she had no idea what to do with a little boy. But she really did. They were best friends. She taught him how to ride and fly-fish. They were both so beautiful together. Two peas in a pod."

Custis thought of his mother's death. He had used that pain as a template to gauge all other. No pain could ever be worse. But he was wrong. The thought of Sarah being put in the position of losing her children, the choice she was forced to make, taking the secret to her grave, hurt more than all other grief combined.

"There's more, Custis. Lucas finagled his way into the railroad business and, with other politicians, worked to get a railway line right through the middle of the ranch. He blackmailed Martin to sign over the ranch to him with the promise of stopping the proposal in Congress."

Custis slowly closed his eyes and shook his head.

"I was hoping that wouldn't be true."

"Martin signed it over, and Lucas and his assembly cronies magically stopped the eminent domain process."

"Sarah lost her ranch to that miserable beast."

"No." Owen grinned. "Martin signed his name, but he signed 'Martin Luther' and dated it eighteen-oh-three rather than nineteen-oh-three. I guess Lucas was so full of himself he didn't notice it until after the state voted to commence the line construction thirty miles east of here. So, no, Lucas does not own the ranch and never will."

Custis smiled. "Martin, not one to mess with. *Sola gratia, sola fide,* and *sola scriptura.*"

Owen paused, looked bluntly at Custis, and said, "Sometimes I have no idea what you're talking about."

"Martin Luther."

Owen rubbed his face and eyes with both hands. "You know, through all of this, Sarah never uttered a bad word to those girls about their father. Martin and I wanted to kill him. We talked about hiring to have it done, but Martin didn't want to take a chance with another person involved. We knew since Lucas was a public figure, there'd be an investigation. We had it all planned out, how to make it look like an accident. Martin even traveled to Raleigh. He came back and said he just couldn't do it, to kill another human being, no matter how evil he was.

"I'm so sorry." Owen took a deep breath. "Let's go see Martin."

Owen walked toward the house, stopped, and turned around. His voice quavered. "Over the years, she fell in love with me. She died in my arms. Her life was the best part of mine."

"Right now, I'd like to shout out loud just how thankful I am for you. I should have been able to be here for her. Sometimes I hated her for being White and hated myself for being Black. I've seen both sides now. Color is only the excuse for something so much deeper."

Custis reached out, shook Owen's hand, and hugged him. "I have no doubt how much you loved her. You gave Sarah the possibility to go on. You raised wonderful children together, and you were, and are, an amazing father. The girls must love you immensely."

Custis's final heartbreak was over.

52

Custis and Owen walked up the stairs to Martin's house, past the one rocking chair on the porch. Custis stopped and touched the arm.

"What happened to the second rocking chair?"

"I took it up to the cemetery for Martin."

The screen door screeched open, revealing a nurse. "Mr. Tennison is about ready to go down for a rest," she said.

"Thank you," Owen said. "This is Dr. Ronald Custis. He's come a long way. He'll be staying with us, hopefully for a few days."

"Nice meeting you, Doctor. Are you here to treat Mr. Tennison?"

"No, I'm not that kind of a doctor. It's a common mistake. I'm a friend of the family."

"No, you *are* family," Owen said.

Custis found Martin in his library. He wasn't reading or working, just sitting on the sofa. His face was ashen and listless, and his eyes were fixed on something across the room. His left hand trembled against an open book that rested in his lap.

"Martin? It's Custis. I came to see you."

Martin turned his head. His face was wrinkled with eight decades of hard work, sunshine, and loss. His clothes hung on a smaller frame, his shoulders a little less broad. His cloudy eyes stared at Custis. "Hello." His voice was unemotional.

"What are you reading? The book in your lap?" Custis sat down next to Martin.

"Martin, this is Custis. Remember, you raised him and Sarah together," Owen said.

Martin's eyes opened wider, and he smiled as he looked directly at Custis. "You know my Sarah?"

"Of course. I loved her, Martin. She was my best friend."

"She'll be back pretty soon. We need to get the horses changed out to the number three. No, that's not right. The number four."

"I can do that for you, Martin," Owen said as he looked at Custis, then back at Martin. "You sit and visit with Custis."

Martin turned and looked at the book in his lap. He closed the cover and slowly handed it to Custis. An uncombed lock of his once-black hair hung down across his forehead. "It's not mine. I don't know where it came from."

"I can put it back for you. Ah, it's such a good story, too."

Martin turned his face toward the window. The late afternoon sun offered its long rays of warm tint. The light illuminated his cloudy eyes, but his stare was without sensation.

The nurse came into the room. "I better get him upstairs while I can.

He seems overly tired today. Time to go, Mr. Tennison." She walked to his side and waited for him to stand.

Martin turned and looked at Owen. "Sarah will be home soon. The girls and I can wait upstairs for her."

Custis watched Martin walk out of the room. The man who had pulled a dying boy out of a creek, carried him across the prairie in his arms, and given him the strength to live no longer remembered how to change out of his own clothing.

"It's worse this time of day." Owen took the book from Custis's hands. "He is still able to read and comprehend, but as the day goes on, he reverts back to this. After we lost Sarah, he became so depressed. He never seemed to fully come out of it. I was afraid he might kill himself. I think the girls are the only reason he goes on. Then this awful whittling away of his mind came on. We have twenty-four-hour care for him because of it."

Custis walked around the room and looked at the books, the paintings, and the photographs. He picked up a framed certificate, walked to an oversized leather chair, and sat down. His eyes read the certificate, side to side, top to bottom. Custis fell into a surreal spiral of memories. The library and certificate were the same; only the people sitting there now had somehow been thrust forward into the future.

"Do you mind . . . may I keep this?"

"Of course, you can have anything you wish," Owen said.

"Tell me about Sarah. Was she ever happy in her life?"

"She was. At first, after Lucas left, she focused on the girls, the baby. We were married in the barn. Audrey and Jillian were the maids of honor, and Jessy acted as my best woman, so to speak. It was several months after Loraine was born, I was in the nursery, holding her in the middle of the night, watching her sleep in my arms, when I looked up and saw Sarah watching me. It was the first time she told me she loved me. I used to do that a lot, let Loraine sleep in my arms. I wanted to remember each second because I knew she would be our last."

Custis was empty. He had wept all the tears he had. "Thank you for taking care of her and the children, for all you have done."

"All the girls love me. Audrey was the last to start calling me Father. All of them call me Daddy now. Grown women, mind you, still calling me Daddy."

"Girls are allowed to do that forever. It's one of their rules." Custis wiped his nose with his handkerchief.

Strange, he knew what it felt like being a fatherless child, but now he felt like a childless father.

"I'm so happy Sarah had you. You must have gone through so much. You had several hearts to protect, including your own. I can't imagine your strength."

Owen nodded his head slightly. "I'll stay here with you tonight for as long as you need the company."

"Thank you, I'll be all right."

"I made sure your room upstairs was ready for you. We have two housekeepers now, the nurses, and one full-time cook. Try to get some sleep, and I'll meet you back here in the morning. Let's hope Martin has a good morning."

Custis slept restlessly. At 4:00 a.m., he gave up and walked downstairs. A light was on in the library. Martin sat in the big leather chair, drinking coffee and reading a book. His white hair was neatly parted. His clothing looked fresh and sharp.

"Martin?"

"Custis? Oh, my God. Is it you?" Martin stood from his chair, tossed the book away, and started toward Custis. "I can't believe it. I dreamt about you. Is it really you?"

Both men hugged.

"We lost our girl, Custis. We lost our Sarah."

"Owen told me last night. I'm so sorry, Martin. It was never supposed to end this way."

"You were here last night?"

"Got here late afternoon. You were tired, feeling poorly."

"I don't remember too well anymore. Come, I have the coffee on."

Both men walked into the darkened kitchen, poured coffee, and returned to the library. Martin motioned for Custis to sit and took the chair behind the desk.

"Did Owen tell you everything?"

"He told me you were sick and about Sarah and the children."

"But did he tell you everything . . . about the girls, I mean?"

"He told me he helped raise all the girls as his own. That Loraine only knows of Owen being her father."

"All the girls, all so beautifully kind. They can fly-fish the pants off anyone. I love them so very much."

Martin rubbed his forehead with his fingers. "I can't remember when Loraine will graduate. Wait. She already has, with honors, too. How long will you stay?"

"I'm not sure, Martin. Things are not what I hoped they would be. I never knew about Sarah until last night. I'm still trying to process it."

"It was hard on all of us. It was like watching Heather die all over again. But this time, four granddaughters were involved. The grief and longing I feel for her are more than any human should ever have to experience. My mind is going. It's difficult to comprehend sometimes. I think it's God's way of not wanting me to drown in my own sorrow."

After breakfast, Custis and Martin sat on the front porch and reminisced. As the day progressed, Martin's mind grew tired. He repeated his stories, had difficulty finding the right words, and became angry. Late in the afternoon, he required help from the nurses to get him upstairs to bathe and go to bed.

That night brought more restless sleep. Custis lay awake in bed and listened to Martin's muffled cries from down the hall. He heard the nurse's voice as she tried to calm and console a displaced man. The darkness still had its magical power of conjuring and distorting reality.

Custis tried to separate his thoughts. The ranch was valid: houses, barn, livestock, and land so beautiful your eyes would never tire of it. But its blood, oxygen, and heartbeat were almost gone, leaving it nearly lifeless. It would never be the same. Life never is.

It wasn't the ranch that Custis loved, after all. Sarah had been its soul all along.

Just before sunrise, Custis found Martin in the library. He was smoking a cigar and sipping whiskey from a glass. "Come in, Custis. Let me fix you a whiskey. It's hard to get these days, you know."

"I would love to have a whiskey with you."

"They call it delirium. An irreversible, chronic disorder. The first stages of losing my mind. Things come back in spurts. So, I get up early, come to my library, and read my books while I can. I get letters off to the girls while my thoughts are somewhat clear. There will come a time—soon, I think—when I won't be able to."

"I'm sorry, Martin."

"I'd like to go for a ride today before it's too late—one last ride. I can't go by myself. I get confused and lose my way. Owen had to come and find me last time. I remember being so scared, not knowing which direction to go. I have spent my life on this place, and I didn't know which way was home. It's a bastard, Custis. Heather and Sarah, the cancer. It was so painful for them. But they died with grace; they fought hard to the very end. Me? There is no grace about this."

Custis walked over to the desk, found paper and a pen, wrote a note, and left it on the desk. "Come on, let's go saddle up."

Custis and Martin walked to the barn just as the sun rose over the ridge. The barn smelled the same, a reassuring memory for Custis. Several horses nickered, stuck their heads out the top of the stall doors, and impatiently waited for their breakfast.

"They'll need their alfalfa and oats. They get a bit feisty if they're not fed first thing," Martin said.

"By all means then, we can wait until they eat."

Martin pointed out two mares, which Custis brushed down and saddled. Martin mounted his horse with the skill of a young man while Custis was still in negotiations with his. They rode past the house and two other barns.

"Martin, do you want to go up to the cemetery?"

"I'd like that."

As they approached the top of the hill, Custis stopped his horse. He saw the top of the rocking chair protruding above the grasses. "I don't think I can bear to see the headstone right now, her name carved in something so permanent."

"It's all right. You stay right here. I'll be back."

Martin tipped his hat and rode ahead. Custis watched him tie his horse on the wrought iron fence and stand within the perimeter. He stood for as long as he could before sitting in the chair. It had been nearly an hour before Martin touched each marker, got back on his horse, and met up with Custis again.

"Thank you, Custis. I touch the engraved letters on each one every time I'm here. It's to remind me that, yes, there *are* some things written in stone." Martin turned and looked out over the ranch. "I'm not long for this world, Custis. There's no beating this thing. My alienists—I've gone to the best—say there is no hope. I will only get worse. Even Shakespeare wrote about it, symbolically, through King Lear. I want to tell you some things while I can. Please don't think I'm crazy. I have no more stocks or bonds. I sold it all off. I took everything out in cash and gold. Owen knows, and the girls all know. The ranch is free and clear. These Roaring Twenties will not last. Nothing will last, even this Prohibition. People won't stand for it much longer. They'll rebel.

"The banks, now they've created a brand-new type of long-term investing designed to lure the common man. They will overlever-age and borrow to buy more stock. The demand from middle-class

Americans to the very poor and new immigrants from Europe will exceed anything our country has ever seen."

"You think our country will go broke?"

"Something is bound to happen. I don't know exactly what it will be. My head isn't as good as it used to be. We're on the verge of an agricultural recession. Small farmers will inevitably be driven out of business. Better technology and machinery have increased the supply, but the demand has remained the same. The country is overfarmed and overgrazed. Awhile back, a research study by our students went to the state level, then federal. Nothing, nothing became of it. My family, Owen too, will be financially stable for a long time. But the others around us? I'm not so sure."

Martin stopped his horse and looked around. "I miss this place already. Can't take it with you, as they say." He looked directly at Custis. "I can't even take my memories with me."

Martin nudged his horse forward. "I'd like to do something for you, Custis. I named you in my will. The girls grew up believing you were a child I raised, so there'll be no question on their part."

"I'm doing fine. I have a small bank account and a pension from the school. I've been stowing away my savings from various patents and copyrights."

"Take it all out of the banks. Buy gold and keep gold."

"I had a friend who immigrated from Ireland. No food there. Nothing left. So many people died."

"You need to go to California. The land is fertile there, black with richness."

Custis remembered the plan. He and Sarah would go to California, start a new life, and send for her father. It seemed like it was still so fresh. But Sarah was gone now. A lifetime had passed by.

"Years ago, when I ran the roundhouse build in central California, they told me about another valley closer to the sea. I've read about it since then, the valley. It's not yet overfarmed. And the weather there, too, will allow you to grow different crops year-round. There's a thirty-degree drop overnight. It's perfect for certain crops. Ohio gets rather cold in the wintertime, and nothing will grow there."

Martin paused his horse. He turned around and looked one way, then the other. "Where are we going?"

"Home, Martin. We're going home."

53

Custis led Martin home to the front of the house. Owen sat in the rocking chair.

"Morning. How was the ride?"

"Unplanned. Martin said he'd like to go for a look around the ranch. He got a little confused after a while, and we came back."

Owen stepped from the porch and helped Martin from his horse. "Come on, Martin. We've got breakfast inside."

"We can't lollygag for long," Martin said. "We've rounded up most of the heifers and need to finish up the branding." Martin dismounted with Owen's help and began to wander away.

"This way, Martin. Custis will take care of the horses. Let's go inside."

Custis grimaced at the change in the man. "He was so fluid earlier, maybe just a bit forgetful, searching for words sometimes."

"Every morning if we're lucky. But by noon, he's confused. By evening, completely lost. The most important thing is to make him feel safe and protected."

Safe and protected. Custis dissected the words. *Make him feel safe and protected.* Martin was at the end of his life. Making others feel safe and protected was precisely his life's accomplishment.

Owen placed his hand on Martin's back as they went up the porch stairs. Martin pulled his shoulder away and brusquely said, "Get your hands off me. I'm not a damned child."

Owen did not hesitate. He smiled kindly. "You'll feel better after some lunch. Pancakes and ham today, leftover from breakfast. And blackberry jam for our biscuits."

Throughout the day, Custis watched Martin drift further away. He became angry, scared, sometimes combative—behaviors Martin had never displayed before. By nightfall, he was lost in his own private world.

Custis thought of his machine. He worked the levers and dials in his head. Broken bones could easily be repaired, an infected appendix removed, even a gangrenous limb detached to save the body. Anomalies could be corrected, tumors treated or removed from the organ. But the mind was different, the spirit, that ephemeral definition of who someone is. How could that be mended? *The mind, the enduring unsolved mystery of the human body.*

x x x

Custis waited downstairs for Martin. The morning was still dark, the coffee hot. Martin seemed clear and happy and full of energy.

"Do you remember our ride yesterday?"

"Of course I do. We went to the cemetery, rode around a little, and watched the cattle. I must say, my butt is a little sore."

"Do you remember what we talked about?"

"You mean about getting your money out of the banks? The direction of our country? The fertile land in California?"

"Yes, that about covers it."

"Listen, I know I've not got too much time left. I only have so many clear moments, and I don't want to waste them. We need to talk."

"We can right after you eat something. I got a tongue-lashing yesterday from your nurse for taking you out without food in your stomach."

"Grab some biscuits, and let's go out to the barn. The aroma of alfalfa feeds my brain."

Custis and Martin walked to the barn.

"I don't want to linger, Custis. I don't want to be a burden to the girls. They all have their own lives to worry about. I'm an old man. Sarah's gone. I have no one to take care of me except strangers. I don't want Owen to have to watch me wither away. I know how that feels. I'm ready to be with my Heather again. I've waited so long."

Custis was silent. Martin's words were horrifically agonizing to hear. Custis understood Martin's desire to be done with the world. But Custis still hated how the end of life was so irrevocable.

"Owen has taken away all my guns. He's afraid I'll do something. Delirium disorder. It's such an undignified death. Cognitive function disintegrates into nothing. I watched my mother die of it. Five years it took her to die. The last year she was in an asylum for the mentally deranged. Sometimes I can still smell it. I know what will happen to me. Please, Custis, I don't want to go through that. I can't even remember where my mind takes me anymore. I wake up in my own piss. They have to restrain me at night. They don't hang out the laundry until after I go to bed. They don't want me to see it and feel ashamed."

Custis looked in Martin's eyes. He saw not a man but a fellow human pleading for help. He saw a husband still in love with his wife.

"I don't want to live anymore, Custis. Please, I need your help. I've never asked you for anything. I'm begging you. Please kill me. I'm ready to go home."

Custis listened to the resolve in Martin's voice. If the sound had been visible, it would have wrapped around Martin's shoulders like a warm blanket on a winter's day. It was a father's guiding hand on the shoulder of a timid child. "I can't kill you, Martin. I'll stay and take care of you. Like you did all those years for me. No strangers, just me."

"I need to brush down a horse. They're magical you know. They understand."

Custis smiled. "Yes, they are magical, indeed."

x x x

Later in the morning, Custis found Martin in the library. "Martin, are you all right?"

"No, I'm not. Please sit with me. I was looking for a book, but I can't remember now. I feel a little lightheaded. Why do you look so sad?"

"Do you remember what you asked me to do this morning?"

"What did I ask you to do?"

Custis breathed in deeply. He wiped his eyes with the heel of his hands and pulled his shoulders back. "To fix us some lunch."

At night, when all the light was gone, the sounds seemed bolder and more intrusive. The mind contorted and amplified common noise into disturbing clamor. Custis listened to footsteps up and down the staircase, muffled voices, and whimpering cries leading to shouts calling for help. He pulled the blankets back and walked barefoot into Martin's bedroom. He saw the nurse trying to calm a dying man. He was lying in bed struggling to free himself. A twisted sheet was across his chest and tied in simple knots to either side of the bed frame. Custis felt claustrophobic. He remembered being in hard splints. He couldn't move his arms. His legs, bound and bandaged from toe to hip. He was in a small room again, screaming out for his mother.

The nurse tried to hold Martin's hand, reassuring him everything was fine. Martin was no longer shouting but was now crying himself to sleep.

Custis remained awake for the rest of the night. At 4:00 a.m., he heard Martin walk down the stairs. He met him in the kitchen.

"Morning." Martin handed Custis a cup of coffee. Both sat down at the kitchen table.

"Do you remember yesterday?"

"Yes. I remember what we talked about. I can't remember the rest of the day. It must be just awful, me at night. I know it's bad. I know they tie me down so I won't fall out of bed or make a run for it. But they remove the bindings before I wake. I know they do."

"What did we talk about yesterday, Martin? I want to know exactly what you remember."

"I asked you to kill me. I know it's an impossible situation. I'd ask no other person for this kind of help."

"I don't have access to medication. I can take it from the nurse's supply, but she likely does not have enough to cause death."

"No. I've tried. Sometimes they give me knock-out drops, but I can't get to their supply."

"Phenobarbital. They probably administer it to you late at night. It's a sedative, a hypnotic."

"I've even tried to get to the horse meds." Martin set his cup on the table. "I want you to shoot me, Custis."

"I can't shoot you. I can't murder you."

"I want to die. It's the only way. You'd put down a horse or an old dog if they were in such pain. They tie me down. I don't want to hurt anyone. I don't want my girls to see me this way. I don't want this to be the last memory of their grandpa. Please. Please help me. If you cannot do it, then let me do it. Get me a gun, Custis, just get me a gun."

Custis knew Martin's heart must be filled with anguish. The words were clear and ensured with resolve.

"I will help you, somehow. I just need some time. Let's talk about it tomorrow morning. Let's get through today."

Custis thought about his own mortality, how close to death he once had been. He thought of Heather's death and the heartbreaking memories Sarah and Martin had carried the rest of their lives. What dictates the disparity of life or death? Hope—when hope is no longer present, it's time to let go. Martin's mind was deteriorating; his body would soon follow and pass into an agonizing and irrevocable death.

X X X

Custis spent the rest of the day with Owen. They rode the back property, counted cattle, and repaired some fencing.

"What will you do after Martin passes?"

"Not sure. The girls are spread out pretty much. Jessy wants to come back and have a veterinary practice here. Who knows, maybe she'll start her own veterinary school right here someday. I'll stay, most likely. I don't know how to do anything else but work the farm. People gotta eat, so the cattle business should stay good. Martin has everything in writing. His wishes and such. He's pretty much sold all his stocks. He's holding everything liquid, as he says. There's enough money to keep everything going. But we'd rather keep him."

"Yes, he's told me what he believes is going to happen. He wants to make sure his family comes out safe."

"All the girls will be taken care of financially."

"Does anyone else know about Loraine?"

"No. They're all just sisters, joined at the hip. Martin does, or did. It didn't matter to him. As sad as I am losing Sarah, and now, soon, Martin, I feel like I've been the luckiest man alive. I'm sorry the world is how it is. Maybe someday. Things always seem to change, don't they?"

The night passed slowly. Custis was restless. He waited in the library.

Martin walked in and sat at his desk. He looked at Custis and said, "You don't have to ask. I remember. Time is running out for me. I will soon stop remembering, I will stop being able to act." Martin breathed in deeply. "There's no hope for me."

The words hit Custis hard in the chest. He wanted to burst out sobbing with teeming emotion. He had to remain strong for this one last time. Custis felt his legs buckling. He fought to hide the emotive force reverberating inside. His quivery voice would inevitably act on its own. He straightened his shoulders.

"I know."

Custis removed a small revolver from his pocket. He opened the empty cylinder and placed the gun on the desk in front of Martin. He put one round next to it.

Martin stared at the gun. Tears filled his eyes. "Thank you, Custis."

"Listen to me, Martin. I will keep this for you today." He placed the gun and bullet back in his pocket. "Tonight, after you go to sleep, I will leave it here in the library." He stood, glanced around, and pulled a book from its place on the shelf. "Here, behind this book. *Call of the Wild*. In the morning, when you wake, I will be gone. If you remember this conversation, you will find this gun and one round behind that book." Custis's voice broke.

Martin nodded.

Custis began to cry. "Thank you for giving me my life. You made such a difference. Thank you for letting me know and love Sarah."

"I should be thanking you. You are my son, and I love you."

"It has been my honor. I love you as well."

Custis leaned over and gently kissed Martin on the top of his head. Without making eye contact, Martin reached up and clasped Custis's hand.

By 3:00 a.m. the next day, Custis was dressed and packed. He left a letter addressed to Owen on the bureau. He picked up his luggage and quietly walked downstairs to the library. In the darkness he fumbled for the desk lamp, turned it on, and looked around. The books, paintings, railway schematics, and photographs were just as interesting as they had been years ago. With each movement of his eyes, years turned into seconds. He was a little boy again. An entire life, down to a mere millisecond. He felt as if beings walked among themselves, around the room . . . ghosts, or demons, or even angels. As memories flashed through his mind, he felt their ethereal reactions, ever-changing but never quite vanishing.

He wandered around the perimeter, and the weightiness of the gun in his coat pocket brought him back. He pulled the book from its place. Custis removed the gun from his pocket. He opened the cylinder, removed the round, and placed the gun on the shelf. He felt the bullet between his thumb and finger. A small piece of lead would be Martin's conclusion. He set it on its end, next to the gun, and closed his eyes. *Give me the strength to walk away now.* He replaced the book to its space.

Custis picked up his bag, turned off the light, and left the room. He pushed open the screen door. The familiar sound of the screech, the unruffled morning air, and the aroma of dry grasses all seemed exceptionally intense. He turned and guided the screen door to a soft close and looked down at the rocking chair. He picked it up by the arm, walked to his car, and placed it and his bag in the back seat.

The early morning sky was still dark as midnight. Custis sat quietly in the seat, holding on to the steering wheel with both hands as if to brace himself for something unknown. Beneath the still, smudged stars of the heavens, he wiped his eyes and focused on the moon. All was quiet and calm.

The sound of the car engine cranking over split through the darkness. Custis looked up at the house. Martin's bedroom light came on. A silhouetted figure approached the window, opened the curtain, and stood motionless.

Custis turned the car away from the house. As he drove down the lane, he flipped on the headlights. The beams illuminated the grassy fields on either side in colors of silver, gray, and black beneath the white board fences in need of a fresh coat of paint.

EPILOGUE

After Custis left the ranch, he had no itinerary, no plans or strategies in mind other than to see California—a place he and Sarah should have gone. He simply drove westward and followed the sun each day until it disappeared behind the horizons of mountains or deserts or prairies. At night he forced thoughts of Martin from his head and hid the visions behind the mountains with the sun. He'd feel something in his hand, a gun and his finger pulling the trigger, and each time he'd burst awake, never hearing the blast. But sometimes, deep in the night, Custis would dream of the ranch.

New calves, playful fillies, and never-ending hillocks of unblemished grassland filled his mind. Martin's last wish had been granted and with it, a lifetime of choices was released from Custis and freed back into the atmosphere. Custis would allow himself to make one more crucial decision in his life: upon reaching the Pacific Ocean, he'd have to turn right or left.

He camped along the way, broke down seven times, and learned to carry spare tires, extra gasoline, more water, and food that would not spoil. It took five weeks. His eyes saw places he had only read about. Custis journaled each sight as if to confirm their actual existence. Each evening, he'd pull the rocking chair from his car, sit, watch the sunlight unwind from the trees, and wait for the stars to erase his darkness. The rocking chair that Martin had made for Heather all those years ago now had arms worn bare of paint, smoothed down by hands from those in love, those in conversation, those in need of rest, and children.

He found the fertile land that Martin had spoken about and with it a slower pace of life. There, on the thirty-eighth parallel, the Napa Valley gave him the rest of his life. He bought land he never used, a new car he rarely drove, and a quaint farmhouse he never quite furnished. He raised a steer for meat, but come time to render, Custis couldn't bring himself to have it butchered. Lucky eventually died of old age. There wasn't much real purpose for an old steer, except for keeping the grasses down. Lucky died fat and content.

His home was small, set back from the road and surrounded by large, overgrown maple trees. Custis didn't need much, and he liked to think of it as voluntary simplicity free from the minutiae of everyday life. He kept one place setting in the kitchen, one chair, and a small wooden table. At first, he planned on solitude to bring healing and resolve. He rarely went into town, but when he did, it was usually the hardware store. He finally discovered the secret to inner peace—a short attention span. After all, he never knew an unhappy dog. He kept mind and body busy with projects inside what appeared to be an old, dilapidated barn.

The roofline was bowed. The old redwood siding was on the faded side of blue, and the large front doors hopelessly sagged, seemingly stuck in purgatory. Defiant climbing roses devoured the back side and half of the front. It rested in a secluded section of the acreage among a wayward vineyard of errant cabernets. No one ever bothered it. It had no value. But the outside was just pretending, a shell disguising the inside—a small research laboratory. For years Custis tinkered with machinery, subsequent patents, and wine making. He put wines into storage, catalogued patents, and memorialized new theories and ideas in journals.

Custis grew tomatoes, cucumbers, and strawberries. He grew mounds of lavender just to watch the butterflies and bees. He grew fields of alfalfa for the deer, and he grew old quietly. His days became long. He learned to never consolidate enjoyable things but rather concentrate on each separately. It helped to pass the time.

x x x

An old Ford coupe was in the carport, covered in a layer of dust. By 1952, the house needed repair but could still be considered livable. The house faced west, and most afternoons, Custis sat on the front porch in the paint-bare rocking chair. He'd slowly rock back and forth and watch the color of the sky turn from fire into hues of lavender and heather.

His eyes had grown old and his body tired.

"Hello."

Custis was startled. He stopped rocking. It was the sound of a boy's voice coming from somewhere nearby. "Salutations! Who goes there?"

"I'm Red Johnson. I live down the road."

Custis focused his eyes and saw the boy more clearly. "How do you do, Mr. Johnson? Come on up here and let me get you a glass of iced tea."

The boy stepped up to the porch. "My friends call me Red."

"Does that mean I'm your friend?" Although the boy didn't answer, a spark of delight lit inside Custis. The young stranger's voice was disarming. He looked to be the size of a young teenager. Custis stepped into the kitchen, poured two mason jars of iced sweet tea, and returned to the porch. *Where are my glasses?*

"I don't see too well anymore, but do they call you Red because of your hair?"

"Yes, my brother started it."

That was all it took for Red to start talking about George, his big brother. Once he got going, Red didn't stop. It wasn't until several visits later that Red finally asked Custis for his name.

"My friends call me Custis."

"Does that mean we're friends?"

"Why, it certainly does."

Over the next few weeks, the two met just about every day after school. Custis would ask Red about his homework and encouraged him to complete it there on the front porch where he could offer help. Math was Custis's specialty, of course. They would trade stories, laugh, and sometimes just pass the time together, saying nothing at all.

"How old are you, Custis?"

"I'm old enough, I suppose. I've been waking up on this side of the grass for a long, long time. My nose and ears don't fit my head anymore. Seems that they're the only things that keep on growing. I used to think maybe my head was shrinking, but no, it's the other way around."

Some days Red would bring letters written by his brother, mailed from the thirty-eighth parallel in Korea. Sometimes he'd read through them twice. Custis always listened with intensity. Custis could hear the loneliness and worry in Red's voice.

"You know what, Red? They say when you have mastered being alone, only then are you ready for the company of others. He'll be back soon. I just know it."

When they weren't talking about George, Red listened quietly to Custis's stories. Custis spoke of his younger years. "After you die, your soul returns to where it was the happiest. When I die, I'm going to Carolina." He paused and wiped his nose. "1901."

Custis closed his eyes and leaned his head back into the rocking chair.

"I was thirty-six years old and in love with the prettiest girl in the world, and she was in love with me. She taught me to fly-fish, of all things. And I'm gonna get her back. That's the only thing that was ever worth a damn, 1901."

Some days, Custis would fall asleep in the rocking chair only to wake and find Red still sitting next to him.

"I'm not much longer for this world. There's a strange thing about dying, now that I'm getting close to it. No matter what you have or how important you are, how fancy your education is, or how much money you have, we're all gonna die. Makes us all equal, so to speak. And nobody can talk their way or buy their way out of it. That's the one thing we all have in common. In the end, no one is more important than the man next to him. Oh, I suppose I made a difference. That's why I left in the first place, to make a difference in someone else's life. But I'm afraid the difference was made in mine."

Custis told Red all about the town and his girl. He remembered every detail, the sights, sounds, and smells.

The days became colder. Custis still sat on the porch, covered with a quilt, having morning coffee. He still loved autumn the best.

One day, a large automobile came up the drive and stopped in front of the porch. A woman stepped out, closed the door, and looked around.

"Hello, out there," Custis said.

"Hello. Are you Ronald Custis?"

"No." Custis grinned. "I'm just Custis. That's what my friends call me."

Custis could see that the woman was nicely dressed. Her car was clean. It shone in the late morning sunlight. She stepped closer to the porch stairs. She looked down at the steps. Each edge was painted bright yellow.

"Helps me not trip."

"That's near genius."

Custis stopped rocking. The woman was beautiful. She had dark hair and striking eyes. She looked familiar. "Whom do I have the pleasure of talking to?"

"My name is Loraine Brannon."

Never had Custis felt as if his heart completely stopped beating. Tunnel vision nearly squeezed out everything except for the sunlight on her face. She said something else, but sounds became contorted and sluggish. Repressed memories and figments merged as one. Custis wasn't sure his brain was actually operating. Or maybe he was dying right in this moment. After twenty-seven years, his mind finally heard the shot from Martin's gun.

Custis stood. The porch floor had become soft and shaky. The quilt fell from his lap. He took a step forward and held on to the railing. His legs betrayed him, shaking uncontrollably.

The woman raced up the stairs and grabbed onto Custis.

"Everything is OK. Please, Mr. Custis, sit back down."

"You are Loraine?"

"Yes, Loraine."

Custis wept. He tried hard to stop. He felt so old, helpless, and out of control. He touched her hand. She held on to his. He replayed her words. *'Everything is OK,' but what does that mean? What is OK?*

"I'm so sorry, Loraine. I'm so very sorry." Custis wanted to see her face, but his vision was blurry. He wiped his tears away and stared at her again.

Loraine looked into his eyes. A pair of spectacles sat next to a closed book, on the table next to the chair. She reached over and carefully placed them on Custis's face. He could finally see her—see her eyes, soft, green eyes.

"There, you might be able to see a little better now."

Custis held his breath as he stared into Loraine's face. "Sarah? My sweet, sweet Sarah?"

"No, Sarah was my mother. I'm Loraine."

"You look just like her. You are my daughter?"

"Yes, I am. Mother loved you. I always suspected it from the way she spoke about you. My father, Owen, wanted us to meet."

Custis had so many words to say. He had dreamt of this day coming. He felt strangely at peace. He couldn't find the words. He tried over and over.

"I'm sorry this is happening so fast for you."

"I wanted to see you and the other girls so badly. But I couldn't, I was told no . . ."

"I know, Daddy told me. Owen. Owen told me everything. Even about Lucas. How he threatened to take my sisters away, what he did to you. I am the one that is sorry. I had to find you. I just had to . . . for my mother."

"Did she tell you?"

"No. Owen told me several years later, after she died. At first it was shocking. Then after it set in, I could only imagine the pain she must have been in. The torment she chose to endure to keep her family together, to protect me. I felt so guilty knowing she was so broken inside. I know she loved my dad, but I know she loved you as well."

"We couldn't be together and still be safe."

"I know. And the world is slow to change."

"I was so afraid for her, and for our children, if we were ever to try and marry. It was illegal."

"Well, in half the country it's still illegal, and besides, I'm here to tell you that I am just fine. I am proud of who I am, and no one will ever take that away from me. I think my dad must be the best man on this earth. He carried such a heavy load. I love him even more than I ever have."

Custis reached out and hugged Loraine. "You are so beautiful. Inside and out, just like your mother."

Both cried. Loraine tried to stop. She wiped her tears away and attempted to laugh. "So, I hear you like to ride horses?"

Custis giggled. "Do I ever! I wish I could do that all over again. I have an old donkey, out at the barn. Sassy is the closest thing to a horse that I dare get near."

"I'd like to meet him."

"Let me get my shoes on. Grab my cane and help me down the stairs. I'll introduce you two."

They carefully strolled side by side down a narrow dirt path wide enough for one, bordered by overgrown grass and lavender mounds. Loraine paused and reached down and touched the spikes. "My mother always loved lavender. She had a lavender garden behind Papa's house."

"*Lavandula angustifolia*—the queen of medicinal plants. It is said Cleopatra used lavender to seduce Julius Caesar and Mark Antony. Tutankhamun's tomb contained traces of it, still fragrant. The first time I saw your mother, she was wearing a lavender blouse. It was the only color I could see at the time. I never could appreciate another color as much as I do lavender."

Custis stopped and looked down at the last of the spent tubular blooms against his pant leg. "I planted it here, along the trail. Each time I walk past and brush against it, the stems are bruised, and it becomes more potent. It calms my soul and takes me back to her."

"It's so beautiful here. Everything feels as if it knows its purpose. What are all these trees? I saw similar groves throughout the roads getting here."

"Prune orchards. This is the last of the prunes on my property. I've been working with grapes for several years."

"My grandfather had orchards at one time."

"Your grandfather, Martin, was a good man. I loved him very much."

"Yes. He told me all about you as a young boy he helped raise. I miss him every day."

Custis had carried the responsibility of Martin's death for twenty-seven years. Custis stumbled. He felt Loraine's hand around his arm. Her grasp never altered. His feet were still moving, taking steps forward. *Oh, my God, the aftermath. Who had to find him?*

He remembered Preston, his suicide, and felt the wetness on his face again. He wiped his face and looked at his hands expecting to see blood. He imagined Martin's hands, trembling as he held the gun to his head. Custis had prayed, that morning, to have cold, indifferent logic but had broken with empathic reasoning and left the gun. Martin had helped Custis fight for life, and Custis helped Martin fight to let his go.

"I was twenty-three when he died. Funny, sometimes you just don't realize how much a person means to you until they're gone."

"I'm so sorry, Loraine. It must have been so horrible. It has weighed on my soul. I thought I would go insane with everything that had happened."

"He was in the first stages of what they now call Alzheimer's. We expected to have him a couple more years or so. I thought there was going to be more time. The stroke left him almost lifeless."

Stroke? That's what they must have told her. She was away at school. They didn't want her to know the horrendous truth. Poor Owen, having to deal with it.

"What did you say? He had a stroke?"

"A stroke, yes. His nurse found him in his bedroom, next to the window, early one morning. She called for Daddy. He ran upstairs and found him on the floor, lifted him up, and placed him back in his bed.

I was able to get back home just before he died. He thought I was Momma."

Custis collapsed inside. For years he had never second-guessed his decision to leave the gun. But taking responsibility for Martin's heart-rendering death had taken its toll. He wanted to cry and laugh out loud, to breathe in deeply over and over again, to feel the liberation. He dug deep inside for the strength to mask his emotions, keeping them from needless exposure.

The lifted burden should have made Custis light enough to soar away. He felt surprised at the lumber of his body. There was no place to sit. He held on to the fence and pretended his legs were strong and sure. Loraine wasn't looking—he could take a moment to recover. He leaned over the top rail like cowboys do when admiring their stock.

"Well, this must be Sassy. Hello, boy. Aren't you so handsome?" Sassy brayed into the air as Loraine scratched the long, soft ears.

"Actually, Sassy is a girl. She belongs to the ranch down the road. She's always over here. Her owner finally gave up trying to keep her home. She's lived here ever since. She goes home for dinner but is always back by morning. I finally built her a shed. Drove me crazy at first, but now she's my morning rooster. She wants to be here, obviously, but she doesn't seem to like me. Be careful. She's bit at me several times. I think she's a reincarnation of an old horse I used to have to ride. Ol' Firecracker."

"She's so cute. Just full of love." Loraine petted her head, scratched behind her ears, and kissed her muzzle.

Custis shook his head. "Story of my life."

"This place is wonderful. I've never felt air so light and fresh. It's effortless. The sky is so blue, almost neon. And the hills look like giant lush pillows. I can see why you're here. It's like living inside a poem."

"Your grandfather told me about this valley years ago. I've managed with some old patents and some new ones along the way to pay for things. I took his advice. He had some financial premonitions. I only call them premonitions because no one could have predicted what would happen to our country, but he did. Prohibition put just about everyone out of the wine business. This area had it hard. Some of us managed to get special permits for communion wine." He paused. "Thank God.

"I managed to buy up a little property, not that I needed it, but others needed out worse. I haven't got much use for things, and other families had little mouths to feed. There were many that came here needing work, so full of want and despair. I had most of the land worked and replanted in vineyards. I even have Zinfandel rootstock from the old country, the Piedmont area of Italy. My prize, though, is a rootstock of a Nebbiolo from Barolo.

"I still work on theories and concepts and fabricate some minor equipment. I worked a long time on the topography here, soil diversities, climate studies and effects, and I always planned to have a little winery. Now I just lease out my land and crops, except for the Nebbiolo. Age seems to have caught up with me rather quickly. I thought getting old would take longer. Sometimes it felt as if it moved so slowly, but in the end, it passed so quickly I didn't even live it. What about you, Loraine? I'm afraid you know more about me than I do of you."

"I live in Florida."

"Ah, no wonder you think the air is light and effortless here."

"I work as a mathematician for the government."

Custis beamed. "A mathematician? But isn't that still such a man's world? You must be fabulous at it. Stellar."

Loraine grinned. "It is, and I work hard. I'm the only female on the team."

Custis cackled. "I bet you work circles around all of them."

"It's difficult, but I have a few supporters."

Custis laughed as he shook his head.

"Married for nineteen years."

"And children?"

"No. But my sisters do, and now Audrey has grandchildren."

"And what about little Jessy?"

"She runs a veterinary hospital on the ranch. It's now affiliated with the university. Daddy still lives there too. Jillian became a teacher after her children got older. She and her husband live in Savannah. Their oldest is fighting in Korea. It's supposed to be a conflict, so I guess he is *conflicting* in Korea."

Custis hated not being as strong as he used to be, not thinking as fast as he should and not being able to do the things he wanted to do. He looked at Loraine's hand wrapped around his arm. His skin was old, thin, and bruised. He had missed out on sharing extraordinary lives.

"Are you all right, Custis? We better get you back to the house."

"Of course."

Custis and his daughter turned and walked arm in arm as Sassy brayed until she was out of breath or had depleted her attention span. The sun hung in the western sky. The long beams of sunrays jutting out over the mountaintop turned the flying gnats into tiny fireflies dancing on center stage.

"Do Jessy and Jillian and Audrey know about me?"

"Yes, of course. Even though we are all separated by miles, we seem to always pick up right where we left off. When I told Jessy I was coming out here to see you, she asked me to find out if you ever learned to ride."

"No—not well, at least." Custis smiled and thought of a long time ago. *Probably why I'm so crippled up.*

"Daddy said you came to the ranch in 1925 and learned about Momma."

"I left a letter for Owen before I left the ranch. Once I got out here, I wrote to him again, gave him my address. He wrote back a couple of times. He told me he was trying to find a way to tell you and your sisters about me. About me and Sarah. He said he and your mother never wanted you to be hurt; she couldn't bear to tell you the truth. He said she died while still trying to protect you. He wanted to do the same. He protected all of you. I couldn't destroy that, Loraine. I just couldn't.

"I knew Sarah had her reasons, and I wanted to honor her wishes as well. I wanted to meet you so badly. It took all I had to stay away. It's why I ran away to California. I didn't trust myself. It was the farthest I could get without leaving the country. I thought about that too."

"It was hard on Daddy. He was so afraid I'd disown him. And for me, after the shock wore off, it was painful. At first, I thought my sisters would abandon me. But not a chance. They've been so supportive. They encouraged me to contact you, but I just couldn't. I was scared, just plain scared. Daddy told me the truth about ten years ago. It took me longer to come out here than it should have. It's taken me this long to get myself together.

"We had your address, but we weren't sure it was current. I remembered Daddy once told me you had several inventions. One being the reason you received your Nobel Prize nomination. I contacted the U.S. Patent Office and learned that you had applied for patents and listed your home address in California. It was the same.

"After ten years of knowing, I guess what really changed was me. The catalyst is that my husband no longer wanted to be married to me. I felt used and thrown away at first. I suddenly felt as if I had no foundation, that life was about to leave me behind. But then something came over me, something lifted me, and I felt so free. Maybe it was an angel, I don't know. I wanted to find you."

"Did Owen tell you about Lucas, Phillip Lucas?"

"Yes, my sisters' father. We know all about him, what he did to Mother, to Papa, and to you. We never much saw him as we were growing up, but I found out later he kept that noose around my mother's neck. I am so sorry he caused you so much pain and sorrow."

"And regret, but I suppose I did that to myself. I loved your mother so deeply. But there were no solutions at the time."

"A brilliant mathematician once said, 'When an unsolvable problem cannot be solved within the current framework of mathematical knowledge or by existing methods, the limitations and barriers prevent the solution. Our job as mathematicians is the possibility of solving related or more concurrent problems instead or, rather, first.'"

Custis paused over her words, then smiled. "Where were you sixty years ago?"

"Those same problems still have not been resolved. Those were your words, Custis. I read them in one of your patent applications. You alone could not have changed the miscegenation laws or intolerance.

"I hope you don't mind, but I read some of my mother's letters you wrote to her years ago. Most of them were still sealed. I guess she figured if she didn't open them, we would all remain safe with her. Some mentioned going to California."

"That was when I was in New York, just starting out. We had planned to go to California after my work at Centennial.

"Living these last years in solitude gave me the mettle to finally look my demons straight in the eyes. My anger and regret turned into fewer visits, softer in duration—a quiet grace. Finding a new joy in the magnificence of nature eased my loneliness and sorrow. Mother Nature found me, I suppose. She has a way of lifting my soul. My little dose of nepenthes, as Homer would say. But there is always a void inside of me, an absence. I've let it become the best part of me. I've quit punishing myself for the past."

They returned to the porch. The air was already cooling. "The temperature drops near thirty degrees at night. The diurnal range means warm air during the day ripens the fruit, concentrating the flavors and tannins. Then the cooler air at night helps preserve acidity and their aromas. It's perfect here for growing grapes."

"I never knew that made a difference. Here, let me help you up the stairs."

"I seem to be a little out of breath. I think I'm doing pretty good for being eighty-seven."

"You're doing amazing."

"Can you stay? There is so much more."

"I was hoping you would ask. I have a hotel room in town. Here, sit and take a rest. I'll go get us some water, if that's all right?"

"Of course. Just inside, there's some sweet tea in the icebox. You know, your grandfather made this rocking chair." Custis rubbed the arms and slowly rocked.

"Let me go get you some cool tea. Be right back." Loraine stepped into the house.

"The only thing I ever stole," he hollered.

Loraine returned with two glasses. She pulled up a wooden crate and sat next to Custis. "Here you go. This should hit the spot."

Custis took a long drink. "There was a time in my life when I hated this world. I was so angry. It had taken my mother and deprived me of something that I should have been free to have. But *should haves* never much solve anything. I've got a feeling, Loraine, you know exactly what I'm talking about. You, a woman, a mathematician, working in a man's turf. It must be complicated."

Loraine slowly nodded her head. She looked at Custis and smiled.

"I hope you show them exactly who you are. Kick them in the balls if need be."

They both laughed.

Custis leaned back in his chair. "I've had a simple life here. Each morning I'm restored by the birdsong and the fluttering of light between the tree leaves. I watch it until it transforms into starlight.

Then I close my eyes and dream I'm with her again. Oh, I've been in every attitude of pain and grief. But after all these years, I've learned that grief is just another form of love, stuck someplace where it can't get out. It becomes smoother as time passes. The bleeding stops, but still it has no logic, no predictable path. Memories that made me cry on Tuesday can make me laugh on Friday." Custis finished his tea. The ice cubes clanked against the empty glass as he set it down on the side table.

Loraine reached over and squeezed Custis's hand. "I'm here now."

Custis leaned his head back on the chair and glanced out into the distance. "When I saw Owen the last time, he told me that your mother's life had been the best part of his. I'll always remember that. Powerful words. Her life was the best part of mine as well." Custis closed his eyes and breathed. He turned and looked at Loraine. "Please know that today is the very best day of my entire life."

Loraine nodded her head and smiled. "Thank you." She kissed him on the cheek. "I am so blessed to have found you. Let me go get more tea for us. I can't wait for more stories. I'd love to hear about my grandmother. I have her name, after all."

Custis whispered, "After all." He turned his head forward and looked just beyond the porch. He breathed in and smiled. "You know, my momma is watching over the both of us. She loves you immensely."

Loraine stepped into the house and returned with a pitcher of tea. She stopped just before reaching Custis. The rocking chair was still. She slowly set the pitcher on the table, reached down, and placed her hand on Custis's heart. Just for a moment, she remained completely still. She removed his glasses and closed his eyes. Custis was still smiling.

x x x

Loraine made arrangements for her father. She met the undertaker back in town, signed documents, and returned to the house. A pickup truck was parked in the driveway. A workman had arrived and was boarding up the windows. As she pulled in, she saw a boy walking from the house and stopped her car next to him. He had red hair and looked forlorn.

"Hi there, you OK?"

"Hi. Yeah. I'm Red. I live down the road some." Red looked back at the house, then back at Loraine. "I don't know what happened."

"Just a minute; let me park my car."

"Did he die or something?"

"Yes, Red. I'm sorry. He was my father." Loraine parked the car in front of the house. She looked up at the workman on the ladder boarding up the upstairs windows.

"Almost done, ma'am."

She nodded her head and turned to Red. "He was my father. I'll take him home to Carolina. Bury him next to my mother, which is where he belongs."

"Was she his girl, the prettiest girl in the whole world?"

"Yes. She was."

"He told me he was still in love with her."

"Yes. I saw the pictures on the walls inside."

"There're more under the mattress."

"Thank you. I just made preparations for him. I came back to gather up his belongings."

"I can help if you like. He was my friend."

"Of course, I would be honored."

Loraine removed some empty boxes from her car, handing some to Red. Both went inside. Red lifted the mattress and exposed several photo albums and envelopes. Loraine picked up a small photograph of her mother. It was nearly torn in half. The back was inscribed, *To Cus*.

"This was my mother."

"She *is* pretty. She looks like you."

Loraine gathered the items from the mattress and removed photos and newspaper clippings from the walls. She opened a closet door and found several sealed boxes. Red used his pocketknife to open the lid and held it back for Loraine. She pulled a framed certificate from the box. It was signed *Martin Tennison, Heather Sarah Tennison II, XXX, Dr. Xander Lyman, and Ronald Custis I.*

Red looked at the signatures. "Why is there an XXX?"

"That must be Mary's signature. People of color were not allowed to read or write at that time. That's how Mary made her mark, three XXXs. She lived on my grandfather's ranch and helped raise my mother and Custis."

Loraine reached back into the box and pulled out the next item. A book published in 1922 by Gunnar Lowry, Esq. *Business Law.* The rest of the box contained personal journals and a large envelope. It was Custis's last will and testament. He left everything to the four girls from North Carolina, naming them individually. "Look. Here's a letter addressed to Red Johnson."

"Hey, that's me."

Loraine handed him the letter.

"Do you think I should open it?"

Loraine smiled. "Of course. You're Red Johnson."

My dear Red. Here is enough money for you and your mother to buy your very own home. Up north from here, I've read about a place in the Sierra Nevada foothills, a town called Paradise. It is a small lumber community surrounded by pine, fir, and cedar trees. Railroad tracks run right through the middle of it and will lead to the best fishing and hunting country you could ever imagine. There are apple orchards scattered about, snow in the wintertime, and the sweetest dogwood blooms in the spring you'll ever see. They say things are gentler there. It is a place where time passes differently. Tell your mother there will be no more reasons to rush away. It sounds like a place where you will both be safe, a place where both of you can finally call home.

As for me, I am exactly where I want to be. I'm in Carolina now, with the prettiest girl in the world. She is right here next to me, hold-ing my hand.

·   *Your friend always, Custis.*

x x x

The conductor stood on the platform directly in front of the opened car. His mustache was long and thick, his sideburns a bushy gray. As he welcomed the passengers, he tipped his hat at the ladies.

"Good morning."

"Welcome aboard."

"Fine morning."

"Mind the step."

A porter reached down, taking bags from oncoming passengers. Custis waited in the crowd. He set his bag on the ground and cupped his bandaged hands together. He stretched his fingers out and lifted the gauze. The blisters had completely healed, no scar, not even a red mark. Custis felt young again. The wrinkles were gone. His hair was dark and without any gray. He lifted his bag again, strapped it around his shoulder, and followed the flow of the crowd.

Custis felt as if he were a lost sheep following the movement of the herd. He walked up to the car, reached for the metal handrail, and stepped up with one foot. It felt oddly familiar. The step made him a head higher. He turned and looked out over the crowd. *Please just let me see her. Give me a miracle, Lord.*

The conductor looked at Custis and stopped his movement with his hand. "Let me get that for you, Professor Custis. Welcome aboard, sir."

"What?" *How did he know my name?*

The conductor smiled and nodded. Custis looked back at the mass of people. There was no more segregation or order of class, no more rushing of persons or pushing through. Men and women, all together, hugging one another, all laughing and smiling. He saw Sarah in the back of the crowd, standing next to her father. Martin's arm was around another woman. She waved at Custis. She looked so happy.

Custis knew it was Sarah's mother. Next to her, side by side, hand in hand, stood Custis's mother. She smiled and waved her arm. He had never seen her look more beautiful. She and Heather hugged. Both cried out in happiness. Sarah stepped toward Custis and waited.

Custis dropped his bag, jumped from the train steps, and began to weave his way to Sarah. People patted him on the back, offered their congratulations, and welcomed him home. Sarah wrapped her arms around him and wouldn't let go. He kissed her deeply. Martin hugged them both. Custis was home again, 1901, with the prettiest girl in the world.

The End

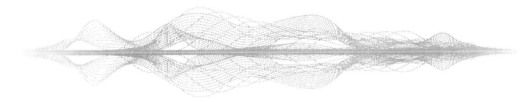

AUTHOR'S NOTE

I wasn't planning on writing another book. Four years ago, after I released *Behind Picketwire,* a dear friend said she didn't want the story to end. She encouraged me to keep writing, maybe a sequel. In that first novel, Custis is a minor character (he appears in just one chapter), an older man who befriends the young protagonist. The entire scene takes place when Custis is sitting on his porch. *When Sounds Collide* is his prequel.

When we meet someone new, we can't see their accomplishments, struggles, or background; everyone has a life's worth of unspoken narratives. I've been fascinated by this thought since I was young. Working with elderly residents in a nursing home was my first after-school job. I befriended the residents though I knew nothing of life, the elderly, or of death. I'd look at their framed photographs and taped-up newspaper articles across their rooms. My fifteen-year-old mind would wonder who they "used" to be and make up their stories by surveying their treasured objects. Years later, when I thought of creating Custis, I recalled my eighth-grade science teacher. He was short, fit, balding, allocentric, and wore a white lab coat. Not far into my adult life, I ran across his obituary, which allowed me to glimpse the unspoken details of his life. He fought in WWII and was honored as a jet fighter pilot, among many other noble accomplishments. He was an American hero, and his myriad of students had never known. That lesson will stay with me for the rest of my life.

After publishing *Behind Picketwire*, I gathered thoughts, plans, ideas, and words, all on torn pieces of paper, napkins, cardboard, or anything else I could spontaneously write on, hundreds of thoughts taped to the wall behind my desk. Custis came to life.

My research led me across the country to the Carolinas, New York, Washington, DC, and the Midwest, through museums, historical sites, universities, and churches. Historical books, correspondences, and interviews were invaluable in building the foundation for this book. Although my story is set in the late 1800s, it not historical fact but rather, a possible love story between two individuals.

Custis and Sarah have been a part of my life for the last four years, and I'll miss them as I ease back into the real world. Maybe I'll write another book, or maybe I'll repaint over the tape marks on the wall behind me.

M. DAY HAMPTON is the award-winning author of the novel *Behind Picketwire*, to which *When Sounds Collide* is a prequel.

Made in United States
Orlando, FL
22 February 2025

58782904R00298